ALLISON PEARSON

I Don't Know
How She Does It

A Comedy about Failure,
a Tragedy about Success

VINTAGE BOOKS

London

Published by Vintage 2011

28 30 29

First published in Great Britain in 2002 by Chatto & Windus

First published by Vintage in 2003

Vintage
Random House, 20 Vauxhall Bridge Road,
London SW1V 2SA

www.vintage-books.co.uk

Addresses for companies within The Random House Group Limited
can be found at: www.randomhouse.co.uk/offices.htm

The Random House Group Limited Reg. No. 954009

A CIP catalogue record for this book
is available from the British Library

ISBN 9781784708580

Penguin Random House is committed to a sustainable future for
our business, our readers and our planet. This book is made from
Forest Stewardship Council® certified paper.

Printed and bound in Great Britain by Clays Ltd, St Ives plc

BUT.

I DON'T KNOW HOW SHE DOES IT

Allison Pearson, an award-winning journalist and author, is a columnist and chief interviewer for the *Daily Telegraph*. Her first novel *I Don't Know How She Does It*, became an international bestseller and was translated into thirty-two languages. It is now a major motion picture, adapted by Aline Brosh McKenna and starring Sarah Jessica Parker. Her most recent novel, *I Think I Love You*, is set to become a stage musical. Allison has given inspirational speeches around the world on women's issues and she can be contacted via her website www.allisonpearson.co.uk. She is a patron of Camfed, a charity that supports the education of more than a million African girls (www.camfed.org). Allison lives in Cambridge with her husband and their two children.

FOR EVIE,
WITH LOVE

Juggle: v. & n. v. **1** intr. *perform feats of dexterity, esp by tossing objects in the air and catching them, keeping several in the air at the same time.* **2** tr. *continue to deal with (several activities) at once, esp with ingenuity.* **3** intr. & tr. *(foll by with)* **a** *deceive or cheat.* **b** *misrepresent (facts).* **c** *rearrange adroitly.* n. **1** *a piece of juggling.* **2** *a fraud.*

Concise Oxford Dictionary

The wheels on the bus go round and round,
Round and round, round and round,
The wheels on the bus go round and round,
All day long.

The babies on the bus go Waah Waah Waah,
Waah Waah Waah, Waah Waah Waah,
The babies on the bus go Waah Waah Waah,
All day long.

The mummies on the bus go Shh Shh Shh,
Shh Shh Shh, Shh Shh Shh,
The mummies on the bus go Shh Shh Shh,
All day long.

Trad.

Part One

1

Home

1.37 am: How did I get here? Can someone please tell me that? Not in this kitchen, I mean in this life. It is the morning of the school carol concert and I am hitting mince pies. No, let us be quite clear about this, I am *distressing* mince pies, an altogether more demanding and subtle process.

Discarding the Sainsbury luxury packaging, I winkle the pies out of their foil cups, place them on a chopping board and bring down a rolling pin on their blameless, floury faces. This is not as easy as it sounds, believe me. Hit the pies too hard and they drop a kind of fat-lady curtsy, skirts of pastry bulging out at the sides and the fruit starts to ooze. But with a firm, downward motion – imagine enough pressure to crush a small beetle – you can start a crumbly little landslide, giving the pastry a pleasing home-made appearance. And home-made is what I'm after here. Home is where the heart is. Home is where the good mother is, baking for her children.

All this trouble because of a letter Emily brought back from school ten days ago, now stuck on the fridge with a Tinky Winky magnet, asking if 'parents could please make a voluntary contribution of appropriate festive refreshments' for the Christmas party they always put on after the carols. The note is printed in berry red and at the bottom, next to Miss Empson's signature, there is a snowman wearing a mortar board and a shy grin. But do not be deceived by the strenuous tone of informality or the outbreak of chummy exclamation marks!!! Oh, no. Notes from school are written in code, a code buried so cunningly in the text that it could only be deciphered at Bletchley Park or by guilty women in the advanced stages of sleep deprivation.

Take that word parents, for example. When they write 'parents' what they really mean, what they still mean, is mothers. (Has a father who has a wife on the premises ever read a note from school? Technically, it's not impossible, I suppose, but the note will have been a party invitation and, furthermore, it will have been an invitation to a party that has taken place at least ten days earlier.) And 'voluntary'? Voluntary is teacher-speak for 'On pain of death and/or your child failing to gain a place at the senior school of your choice'. As for 'appropriate festive refreshments', these are definitely not something bought by a lazy cheat in a supermarket.

How do I know that? Because I still recall the look my own mother exchanged with Mrs Frieda Davies in 1974, when a small boy in a dusty green parka approached the altar at Harvest Festival with two tins of Libby's cling peaches in a shoe box. The look was unforgettable. It said, what kind of sorry slattern has popped down to the Spar on the corner to celebrate God's bounty when what the good Lord clearly requires is a fruit medley in a basket with cellophane wrap? Or a plaited bread. Frieda Davies's bread, manoeuvred the length of the church by her twins, was plaited as thickly as the tresses of a Rhinemaiden.

'You see, Katharine,' Mrs Davies explained later, doing that disapproving upsneeze thing with her sinuses over teacakes, 'there are mothers who make an effort like your mum and me. And then you get the type of person who' – prolonged sniff – 'doesn't make the effort.'

Of course, I knew who they were. Women Who Cut Corners. Even back in 1974, the dirty word had started to spread about mothers who went out to work. Females who wore trouser suits and even, it was alleged, allowed their children to watch television while it was still light. Rumours of neglect clung to these creatures like dust to their pelmets.

So, you see, before I was really old enough to understand what being a woman meant, I already understood that the world of women was divided in two: there were proper mothers, self-sacrificing bakers of apple pies and well-scrubbed invigilators of the twin-tub, and there were the other sort. At the age of thirty-five, I know precisely which kind I am, and I suppose that's what I'm doing here in the small hours of 13th December, hitting mince pies with a rolling pin till they look like something mother made. Women used to have time to make mince pies and had to fake orgasms. Now we can manage the orgasms, but we have to fake the mince pies. And they call this progress.

'Damn. Damn. Where has Paula hidden the sieve?'

'Kate, what do you think you're doing? It's two o'clock in the morning.'

Richard is standing in the kitchen doorway wincing at the light. Rich with his Jermyn Street pyjamas, washed and tumbled to Babygro bobbliness. Rich with his acres of English reasonableness and his fraying kindness. Slow Richard, my American colleague Candy calls him, because work at his ethical architecture firm has slowed almost to a standstill and it takes him half an hour to take the bin out and he's always telling me to slow down.

'Slow down, Katie, you're like that funfair ride. What's it called? The one where the screaming people stick to the side so long as the damn thing keeps spinning?'

'Centrifugal force.'

'I know that. I meant what's the ride called?'

'No idea. Wall of Death?'

'Exactly.'

I can see his point. I'm not so far gone that I can't grasp there has to be more to life than forging pastries at midnight. And tiredness. Deep-sea diver tiredness, voyage to the bottom of fatigue tiredness; I've never really come up from it since Emily was born, to be honest. Five years of walking round in a lead suit of sleeplessness. But what's the alternative? Go into school this afternoon and brazen it out, slam a box of Sainsbury's finest down on the table of festive offerings? Then, to the Mummy Who's Never There and the Mummy Who Shouts, Emily can add the Mummy Who Didn't Make an Effort. Twenty years from now, when my daughter is arrested in the grounds of Buckingham Palace for attempting to kidnap the King, a criminal psychologist will appear on the news and say: 'Friends trace the start of Emily Shattock's mental problems to a school carol concert where her mother, a shadowy presence in her life, humiliated her in front of her classmates.'

'Kate? Hello?'

'I need the sieve, Richard.'

'What for?'

'So I can cover the mince pies with icing sugar.'

'Why?'

'Because they are too evenly coloured and everyone at school will know that I haven't made them myself, that's why.'

Richard blinks slowly like Stan Laurel taking in another fine mess. 'Not why icing sugar. Why *cooking*, Katie, are you mad? You only got back from the States three hours ago. No one expects you to produce anything for the carol concert.'

'Well, *I* expect me to.' The anger in my voice takes me by surprise and I notice Richard flinch. 'So, where has Paula hidden the sodding sieve?'

Rich looks older suddenly. The frown line, once an amused exclamation mark between my husband's eyebrows, has deepened and widened without my noticing into a five-bar gate. My lovely, funny Richard, who once looked at me as Dennis Quaid looked at Ellen Barkin in *The Big Easy* and now, thirteen years into an equal, mutually supportive partnership, looks at me the way a smoking beagle looks at a medical researcher: aware that such experiments may need to be conducted for the sake of human progress, but still somehow pleading for release.

'Don't shout,' he sighs, 'you'll wake them.' One candy-striped arm gestures upstairs where our children are asleep. 'Anyway, Paula hasn't hidden it. You've got to stop blaming her for everything, Kate. The sieve lives in the drawer next to the microwave.'

'No, it lives right here in this cupboard.'

'Not since 1997 it doesn't. Darling, please come to bed. You have to be up in five hours.'

Seeing Richard go upstairs, I long to follow him, but I can't leave the kitchen in this state. I just can't. The room bears signs of heavy fighting; there is Lego shrapnel over a wide area and a couple of mutilated Barbies – one legless, one headless – are having some kind of picnic on our tartan travel rug, which is still matted with grass from its last outing on Primrose Hill in August. Over by the vegetable rack, on the floor, there is a heap of raisins which I'm sure was there the morning I left for the airport. Some things have altered in my absence: half a dozen apples have been added to the big glass bowl on the pine table that sits next to the doors leading out to the garden, but no one has thought to discard the old fruit beneath and the pears at the bottom have started weeping a sticky amber resin. As I throw each pear in the bin, I shudder a little at the touch of rotten flesh. After washing and drying the bowl, I carefully wipe any stray amber goo off the apples and put them back. The whole operation takes maybe seven minutes. Next, I start to swab the drifts of icing sugar off the stainless steel worktop, but the act of scouring releases an evil odour. I sniff the dishcloth. Slimy with bacteria, it has the sweet sickening stench of dead-flower water. Exactly how rancid would a dishcloth have to be before someone else in this house thought to throw it away?

I ram the dishcloth in the overflowing bin and look under the sink for a new one. There is no new one. Of course, there is no new one, Kate, you haven't been here to buy a new one. Retrieve old dishcloth from the bin and soak it in hot water with a dot of Dettol. All I need to do now is put Emily's wings and halo out for the morning.

I have just turned off the lights and am starting up the stairs when I have a bad thought. If Paula sees the Sainsbury's cartons in the bin, she will spread news of my Great Mince Pie forgery on the nanny grapevine. Oh, hell. Retrieving the cartons from the bin, I wrap them inside yesterday's paper, and carry the bundle at arm's length out through the front door. Looking right and left to make sure I am unobserved, I slip them into the big black sack at the front of the house. Finally, with the evidence of my guilt disposed of, I follow my husband up to bed.

Through the landing window and the December fog, a crescent moon is reclining in its deckchair over London. Even the moon gets to put its feet up once a month. Man in the Moon, of course. If it was a Woman in the Moon, she'd never sit down. Well, would she?

*

I TAKE MY TIME brushing my teeth. A count of twenty for each molar. If I stay in the bathroom long enough Richard will fall asleep and will not try to have sex with me. If we don't have sex, I can skip a bath in the morning. If I skip the bath, I will have time to start on the e-mails that have built up while I've been away and maybe even get some presents bought on the way to work. Only ten shopping days to Christmas, and I am in possession of precisely nine gifts, which leaves twelve to get plus stocking fillers for the children. And still no delivery from KwikToy, the rapid online present service.

'Kate, are you coming to bed?' Rich calls from the bedroom. His voice sounds slurry with sleep. Good.

'I have something I need to talk to you about. Kate?'

'In a minute,' I say. 'Just going up to make sure they're OK.'

I climb the flight of stairs to the next landing. The carpet is so badly frayed up here that the lip of each step looks like the dead grass you find under a marquee five days after a wedding. Someone's going to have an accident one of these days. At the top, I get my breath back and silently curse these tall, thin London houses. Standing in the stillness outside the children's doors, I can hear their different styles of sleeping – his piglet snufflings, her princess sighs.

When I can't sleep and, believe me, I would dream of sleep if my mind weren't too full of other stuff for dreams, I like to creep into Ben's room and sit on the blue chair and just watch him. My baby looks as though he has hurled himself at unconsciousness, like a very small man trying to leap aboard an accelerating bus. Tonight, he's sprawled the length of the cot on his front, arms extended, tiny fingers curled round an invisible pole. Nestled to his cheek is the disgusting kangaroo that he worships; a shelf full of the finest stuffed animals an anxious parent can buy and what does he choose to love? A cross-eyed marsupial from the Woolies remainder bin. Ben can't tell us when he's tired yet, so he simply says Roo instead. He can't sleep without Roo because Roo to him means sleep.

It's the first time I've seen my son in four days. Four days, three nights. First there was the trip to Stockholm to spend some face time with a jumpy new client, then Rod Task called from the office and told me to get my ass over to New York and hold the hand of an old client who needed reassuring that the new client wasn't taking up too much of my time.

Benjamin never holds my absences against me. Too little still. He always greets me with helpless delight like a fan windmilling arms at a Hollywood première. Not his sister, though. Emily is five years old and full of jealous wisdom. Mummy's return is always the cue for an intricate sequence of snubs and punishments.

'Actually, Paula reads me that story.'

'But I want Dadda to give me a bath.'

Wallis Simpson got a warmer welcome from the Queen Mother than I get from Emily after a business trip. But I bear it. My heart sort of pleats inside and somehow I bear it. Maybe I think I deserve it.

I leave Ben snoring softly, and gently push the door of the other room. Bathed in the candied glow of her Cinderella light, my daughter is, as is her preference, naked as a newborn. (Clothes, unless you count bridal or princess wear, are a constant irritation to her.) When I pull the duvet up, her legs twitch in protest like a laboratory frog. Even when she was a baby Emily couldn't stand being covered. I bought her one of those zip-up sleep bags, but she thrashed around in it and blew out her cheeks like the God of Wind in the corner of old maps, till I had to admit defeat and gave it away. Even in sleep, when my girl's face has the furzy bloom of an apricot, you can see the determined jut to her chin. Her last school report said: 'Emily is a very competitive little girl and will need to learn to lose more gracefully.'

'Remind you of anyone, Kate?' said Richard and let out that trodden-puppy yelp he has developed lately.

There have been times over the past year when I have tried to explain to my daughter – I felt she was old enough to hear this – why Mummy has to go to work. Because Mum and Dad both need to earn money to pay for our house and for all the things she enjoys doing like ballet lessons and going on holiday. Because Mummy has a job she is good at and it's really important for women to work as well as men. Each time the speech builds to a stirring climax – trumpets, choirs, the tearful sisterhood waving flags – in which I assure Emily that she will understand all this when she is a big girl and wants to do interesting things herself.

Unfortunately, the case for equal opportunities, long established in liberal Western society, cuts no ice in the fundamentalist regime of the five-year-old. There is no God but Mummy, and Daddy is her prophet.

In the morning, when I'm getting ready to leave the house, Emily asks the same question over and over until I want to hit her and then, all the way to work, I want to cry for having wanted to hit her.

'Are you putting me to bed tonight? Is Mummy putting me to bed tonight? Are you? Who is putting me to bed tonight? Are you, Mum, are you?'

Do you know how many ways there are of saying the word no without actually using the word no? I do.

Must Remember

Angel wings. Quote for new stair carpet. Take lasagne out of freezer for Saturday lunch. Buy kitchen roll, stainless steel special polish thingy, present and card for Harry's party. How old is Harry? Five? Six? Must get organised with well-stocked present drawer like proper mother. Buy Christmas tree and stylish lights recommended in Telegraph *(Selfridges or Habitat? Can't remember. Damn). Nanny's Christmas bribe/present (Eurostar ticket? Cash? DKNY?). Emily wants Baby Wee-Wee doll (over my d. body). Present for Richard (Wine-tasting? Arsenal? Pyjamas?), in-laws book –* The Lost Gardens of *Somewhere? Ask Richard to collect dry-cleaning. Office party what to wear? black velvet too small. Stop eating NOW. Fishnets lilac. Leg wax no time, shave instead. Book stress-busting massage. Highlights must book soonest (starting to look like mid-period George Michael). Pelvic floor squeeeeze! Supplies of Pill!!! Ice cake (Royal icing? – chk Delia). Cranberries. Mini party sausages. Stamps for cards Second class x 40. Present for E's teacher? And, whatever you do, wean Ben off dummy before Xmas with in-laws. Chase KwikToy, useless mail order present company. Smear test NB. Wine, Gin. Vin santo. Ring Mum. Where did I put Simon Hopkinson 'dry with hairdryer' goose recipe? Stuffing? Hamster???*

2

Work

6.37 am: 'O, come let us a door him. O, come let us a door him. O, come let us a door hi-mmm!' I am stroked, tugged and, when that doesn't work, finally Christmas-carolled awake by Emily. She is standing by my side of the bed and she wants to know where her present is. 'You can't buy their love,' says my mother-in-law, who obviously never threw enough cash at the problem.

I did once try to come home empty-handed from a business trip, but on the way back from Heathrow I lost my nerve and got the cab to stop at Hounslow where I dived into a Toys'Я'Us, adding a toxic shimmer to my jet lag. Emily's global Barbie collection is now so sensationally slutty, it can only be a matter of time before it becomes a Tracey Emin exhibit. Flamenco Barbie, AC Milan Barbie (soccer strip, dinky boots), Thai Barbie – a flexible little minx who can bend over backwards and suck her own toes – and the one that Richard calls Klaus Barbie, a terrifying über-blonde with sightless blue eyes in jodhpurs and black boots.

'Mummy,' says Emily, weighing up her latest gift with a connoisseur's eye, 'this fairy Barbie could wave a wand and make the Little Baby Jesus not be cross.'

'Barbie isn't in the Baby Jesus story, Emily.'

She shoots me her best Hillary Clinton look, full of noble, this-pains-me-more-than-you condescension. 'Not *that* Baby Jesus,' she sighs, 'Another one, silly.'

You see, what you can buy from a five-year-old when you get back from a client visit is, if not love or even forgiveness, then an amnesty of sorts. Entire minutes when the need to blame is briefly overcome by the need to rip open a package in a tantrum of glee. (Any working mother who says she doesn't bribe her kids can add Liar to her CV.) Emily now has a gift to mark each occasion of her mother's infidelity – playing away with her career – just as my mum got a new charm for her bracelet every time my father played away with other women. By the time Dad walked out when I was thirteen, Mum could barely lift the golden handcuff on her wrist.

I'm lying here thinking things could be a lot worse (at least my husband is not an alcoholic serial adulterer) when Ben totters into the bedroom and I can hardly believe what I'm seeing.

'Oh God, Richard, what's happened to his hair?'

Rich peers over the top of the duvet, as though noticing his son, who will be one in January, for the first time. 'Ah. Paula took him to that place by the garage. Said it was getting in his eyes.'

'He looks like something out of the Hitler Youth.'

'Well, it will grow back, obviously. And Paula thought, and I thought too, obviously, that the whole Fauntleroy ringlet thing – well, it's not how kids look these days, is it?'

'He's not *a kid*. He's my baby. And it's how I want him to look. Like a baby.'

Lately, I notice Rich has adopted a standard procedure for dealing with my rages. A sort of bowed-head, in-the-event-of-nuclear-attack submissive posture, but this morning he can't suppress a mutinous murmur.

'Don't think we could arrange an international conference call with the hairdresser at short notice.'

'And what's that supposed to mean?'

'It just means you've got to learn to let go, Kate.' And with one practised movement, he scoops up the baby, swipes the gangrenous snot from his tiny nose and heads downstairs for breakfast.

7.15 am: The change of gear between work and home is so abrupt sometimes that I swear I can hear the crunch of mesh in my brain. It takes a while to get back on to the children's

13

wavelength. Brimming with good intentions, I start off in Julie Andrews mode, all tennis-club enthusiasm and mad, sing-song emphases.

'*Now*, children, what would you *like* for *break*-fast to-*day*?'

Emily and Ben humour this kindly stranger for a while until Ben can take no more of it and stands up in his high-chair, reaches out and pinches my arm as though to make sure it's me. Their relief is plain as, over the next frazzled half-hour, the ratty bag they know as Mummy comes back. 'You're having Shreddies and that's it! No, we haven't got Fruitibix. I don't care what Daddy let you have.'

Richard has to leave early. A site visit with a client in Battersea. Can I do the handover with Paula? Yes, but only if I can leave at 7.45 on the dot.

7.57 am: And here she comes, flourishing the multiple excuses of the truly unapologetic. The traffic, the rain, the alignment of the stars. You know how it is, Kate. Indeed, I do. I cluck and sigh in the designated sympathy pauses while my nanny makes herself a cup of coffee and flicks without interest through my paper. To point out that in the twenty-six months Paula has been our children's carer she has managed to be late every fourth morning would be to risk a row, and a row would contaminate the air that my children breathe. So no, there won't be a row. Not today. Three minutes to get to the bus, eight minutes' walk away.

8.27 am: I am going to be late for work. Indecently, intrepidly late. Bus lane is full of buses. Abandon bus. Make lung-scorching sprint down City Road and then cut across Finsbury Square where my heels skewer into the forbidden grass and I attract the customary loud *Oy!* from the old guy whose job it is to shout at you for running across the grass.

'Oy, Miss! Cancha go round the outside like everyone else?'

Being shouted at is embarrassing, but I am beginning to worry that a small, shameful part of me really likes being called Miss in a public place. At the age of thirty-five, with gravity and two small children dragging you down, you have to take your compliments where you can. Besides, I reckon the short cut saves me two and a half minutes.

8.47 am: One of the City's oldest and most distinguished institutions, Edwin Morgan Forster stands at the corner of Broadgate and St Anthony's Lane; a nineteenth-century fortress with a great jutting prow of twentieth-century glass, it looks as though a liner has crashed into a department store and come out the other side. Approaching the main entrance, I slow to a trot and run through my kit inspection.

Shoes, matching, two of? Check.

No baby sick on jacket? Check.

Skirt not tucked into knickers? Check.

Bra not visible? Check.

OK, I'm going in. Stride briskly across the marble atrium and flash my pass at Gerald in security. Since the revamp eighteen months ago, the lobby of Edwin Morgan Forster, which used to look like a bank, now resembles one of those zoo enclosures designed by Russian constructivists to house penguins. Every surface is an eyeball-piercing Arctic white except the back wall, which is painted the exact turquoise of the Yardley gift soap favoured by my Great Aunt Phyllis thirty years ago, but which was described by the lobby's designer as an 'oceangoing colour of vision and futurity'. For this piece of wisdom, a firm which is paid to manage other people's money handed over an unconfirmed $750,000.

Can you believe this building? Seventeen floors served by four lifts. Divide by 430 employees, factor in six button-pushing ditherers, two mean bastards who won't hold the door and Rosa Klebb with a sandwich trolley and you either have a possible four-minute wait or take the stairs. I take the stairs.

Arrive on Floor 13 with fuschia face and walk straight into Robin Cooper-Clark, our pinstriped Director of Investment. The clash of odours is as immediate as it is pungent. Me: Eau de Sweat. Him: Floris Elite with under-notes of Winchester and walnut dashboard.

15

Robin is exceptionally tall and it is one of his gifts that he manages to look down at you without actually looking down on you, without making you feel in any way small. It came as no surprise to learn in an obituary last year that his father was a bishop with a Military Cross. Robin has something both saintly and indestructible about him: there have been times at EMF when I have thought I would die if it weren't for his kindness and lightly mocking respect.

'Remarkable colour, Kate, been skiing?' Robin's mouth is twitching up at the corners and on its way to a smile, but one bushy grey eyebrow arches towards the clock above the dealing desk.

Can I risk pretending that I've been in since seven and just slipped out for a cappuccino? A glance across the office tells me that my assistant Guy is already smirking purposefully by the water cooler. Damn. Guy must have spotted me at exactly the same moment because, across the bowed heads of the traders, phones cradled under their chins, over the secretaries and the European desk and the Global Equities team in their identical purple Lewin's shirts, comes the Calling-All-Superiors voice of my assistant. 'I've put the document from Bengt Bergman on your desk, Katharine,' he announces. 'Sorry to see you've had problems getting in again.'

Notice that use of the word 'again' – the drop of poison on the tip of the dagger. Little creep. When we funded Guy Chase through the European Business School three years ago, he was a Balliol brainache with a four-piece suit and a personal hygiene deficit. He came back wearing charcoal Armani and the expression of someone with a Master's in Blind Ambition. I think I can honestly say that Guy is the only man at Edwin Morgan Forster who likes the fact that I have kids. Chickenpox, summer holidays, carol concerts – all are opportunities for Guy to shine in my absence. I can see Robin Cooper-Clark looking at me expectantly now. Think, Kate, think.

It is possible to get away with being late in the City. The key thing is to offer what my lawyer friend Debra calls a Man's Excuse. Senior managers who would be frankly appalled by the story of a vomiting nocturnal baby or an AWOL nanny (mysteriously, childcare, though paid for by both parents, is always deemed to be the female's responsibility) are happy to accept anything to do with the internal combustion engine. '*The car broke down/was broken into.*' '*You should have seen the – fill in scene of mayhem – at the – fill in street.*' Either of these will do very well. Car alarms have been a valuable recent addition to the repertoire of male excuses because, although displaying female symptoms – hair-trigger unpredictability, high-pitched shrieking – they are attached to a Man's Excuse and can be taken to a garage to be fixed.

'You should have seen the mess at Dalston Junction,' I tell Robin, composing my features into a mask of stoic urban resignation and, with outstretched arms, indicating a whole vista of car carnage. 'Some maniac in a white van. Traffic lights out of sync. Unbelievable. Must have been stuck there, oh, twenty minutes.'

He nods: 'London driving almost makes one grateful for Network Southeast.'

There is a heartbeat of a pause. A pause in which I try to ask about the health of Jill Cooper-Clark, who was diagnosed with breast cancer in the summer. But Robin is one of those Englishmen equipped from birth with an early-warning system which helps them to intercept and deflect any incoming questions of a personal nature. So, even as my lips are forming his wife's name, he says, 'I'll get Christine to fix a lunch for us, Kate. You know they've converted some cellar by the Old Bailey – serving up lightly grilled witness, no doubt. Sounds amusing, don't you think?'

'Yes, I was just wondering how—'

'Splendid. Talk later.'

By the time I reach the haven of my desk, I've regained my composure. Here's the thing: I love my job. It may not always sound like it, but I do. I love the blood-rush when the stocks I took a punt on deliver the goods. I get a kick out of being one of the handful of women in the Club Lounge at the airport, and, when I get back, I love sharing my travel horror stories with friends. I love the hotels with room service that appears like a genie and the prairies of white cotton that give me the sleep I crave. (When I was younger I wanted to go to bed with other people; now I have two children my fiercest desire is to go to bed with myself, preferably for twelve hours straight.) Most of all I love the work: the synapse-snapping satisfaction of being good at it, of being in control when the rest of life seems such an awful mess. I love the fact that the numbers do what I say and never ask why.

9.03 am: Switch on my computer and wait for it to connect. The network is so slow this morning it would be quicker to fly to Hong Kong and pick up the Hang bloody Seng in person. Type in my password – Ben Pampers – and go straight into Bloomberg to see what the markets have been up to overnight. The Nikkei is steady, Brazil's Bovespa is doing its usual crazy samba while the Dow Jones looks like the printout on a do-not-resuscitate patient in intensive care. Baby, it's cold outside, and not just on account of the fog nuzzling the office blocks beyond my window.

Next, I check currencies for any dramatic movements, then type in TOP to call up all the big corporate news stories. The main one is about Gayle Fender, a bond trader, or rather an ex-trader. She's suing her firm, Lawrence Herbert, for sex discrimination because male colleagues got far bigger bonuses than she did for less good results. The headline reads: 'Ice Maiden Cools Towards Men'. As far as the media is concerned, City women are all either Elizabeth I or a resting lapdancer. That old virgin and whore thing wrapped up in the *Wall Street Journal*.

Personally, I've always fancied the idea of becoming an Ice Maiden – maybe you can buy the outfit? Trimmed in white fur, stalactite heels with matching pickaxe. Anyway, Gayle Fender's story will end the way those stories always end: with a No Comment as, eyes lowered, she leaves a courtroom by a side door. This City smothers dissent: we have ways of making you not talk. Stuffing people's mouths with £50 notes tends to do the trick.

Click on e-mails. Forty-nine arrivals in my Inbox since I was last in the office. Skim down them, sorting out the junk first.

Free trial of a new investment magazine? Trash.

You are invited to a conference on globalisation on the shores of Lake Geneva catered by the world-famous chef Jean-Louis—. Trash.

Human Resources want to know if I will appear in the new EMF corporate video. Only if I get my own trailer with John Cusack tied to the bed.

Will I sign a card for some poor bugger in Treasury who's been made redundant? (Jeff Brooks is going voluntarily, they say, but the compulsories will start soon.) Yes.

The message at the very top of the Inbox is from Celia Harmsworth, Head of Human Resources. It says that my boss Rod Task has had to pull out of the induction talk for EMF's trainees this lunchtime and could I please step in? 'We would be very glad to see you in the thirteenth-floor conference room from 1 pm!'

No, no, no. I have nine fund reports to write by Friday. Plus I have a very important nativity play to attend at 2.30 this afternoon.

With work memos out of the way, I can get to the real e-mails, the ones that matter: messages from friends, jokes and stories handed around the world like sweets. If it's really true what they say, that mine is the time-famished generation, then e-mail is our guilty snack, our comfort food. It would be hard to explain how much sustenance I get from my regular correspondents. There's Debra, my best friend from college, now mother of two and a lawyer with Addison Pope, just across the way from the Bank of England and about ten minutes' walk from Edwin Morgan Forster. Not that I ever get down there to see her. Might as well work on Pluto. And then there's Candy. Foul-mouthed fellow fund manager, World Wide Web whiz and proud export of Rockaway, New Jersey, Candace Marlene Stratton. My sister-in-arms and a woman in the vanguard of the latest developments in world corsetry. My favourite character in literature is Rosalind in *As You Like It*; Candy's favourite character in literature is the guy in Elmore Leonard who wears a T-shirt that says, 'You've Obviously Mistaken Me For Someone Who Gives A Shit.'

Candy sits right over there, next to the pillar, fifteen feet away from me, and yet we scarcely exchange more than a few words out loud during an average day. On screen, though, we're in and out of each other's minds like old-fashioned neighbours.

From: Candy Stratton, EMF
To: Kate Reddy, EMF
K8,
Q: Why are married women heavier than single women?
A: Single women come home, see what's in the fridge and go to bed. Married women come home, see what's in bed and go to the fridge.
How U? Me: Cystitis. Too much SX
xxxx

From: Debra Richardson, Addison Pope
To: Kate Reddy, EMF
Morning,
How was Swdn & NYC? Poor you. Felix fell off table and broke his arm in 4 places (didn't think there were 4 places to break). Nightmare. Spent six hours in Casualty. Good old NHS! Ruby announced ystdy that she loves her nanny, her daddy, her rabbit, her brother, all the Teletubbies and her mummy in that order. Nice to know it's all worthwhile, no?
Rmbr LUNCH on Friday? Tell me yr not cancelling.
Deb xxxx

From: Kate Reddy
To: Candy Stratton
Another relaxing few days. Stockholm, New York, Hackney. Up till dawn forging mince pies for Emily's carol concert – don't even ask.

Plus Pol Pot has given Ben a hideous Nazi haircut and I daren't complain because I was away and being away means you surrender all rights to maternal authority. Plus, I have to remind Rod 'Task' Master that I need to leave early today for the concert.

Any suggestions how to do this without mentioning the words
a/ child or
b/ leave?

Love K8 xxxx

PS: What is SX? Rings vague bell.

From: Candy Stratton
To: Kate Reddy
hon, U gotta cut domstic goddss crap. look other moms in the eye & say, I'm Busy & I'm Proud or U will be ded.
tell rod task U have major mens2ruashn si2ashn. Ozzies even more freakd by womens trouble than Brits.

CUL8R xxxxx

I glance across the office and see Candy swigging from a can which she hoists aloft in a cheery toast to me. Until recently, Candy's diet was confined to coke – the Diet kind and the other kind – which left her pencil-thin with prominent breasts: this got her plenty of lovers, but not a lot of love. A year older than me, at thirty-six Candy is congenitally single and sometimes I envy her ability to do the most fantastic things, like going to have a drink after work or visiting the bathroom at weekends unaccompanied by a curious five-year-old or coming into work hollow-eyed after being up all night having sex instead of coming into work hollow-eyed after being up all night with the wailing product of sex. Candy did get engaged a couple of years back to a consultant from Andersen. Unfortunately, she was so busy working on a final for a German pension fund that she stood him up three dates in a row. The third time, Bill was waiting for her in a restaurant at Smithfield and he got talking to a nurse from Bart's at the next table. They were married in August.

Candy says she's not going to worry about her fertility, though, until Cartier start making a biological clock.

From: Kate Reddy, EMF
To: Debra Richardson, Addison Pope
Dear D
So late in this a.m can't write much now. no way am i cancelling lunch.
Why is truthful Woman's Excuse always less acceptable than false Man's Excuse?
Puzzled, K8.

From: Debra Richardson
To: Kate Reddy
Because they don't want to be reminded that you have a life, stupid.
C U friday.
D xx

I decided not to approach Rod Task in person over the question of leaving work early to get to Emily's nativity play. Better to tag it on casually as a PS to some work e-mail. Make it look like a fact of life, not a favour. Just got a reply.

From: Rod Task
To: Kate Reddy
Jesus, Katie, only seems like yesterday you had your own nativity.
Sure, take the time you need, but we should talk c. 5.30. And I need you to go to Stockholm to hold Sven's hand again. Is Friday good for you, Beaut?
Cheers Rod

No, Friday is not good for me. I can't believe he expects me to do another trip before Christmas. Means I will miss the office party, have to cancel lunch with Debra again and lose the shopping time I was counting on.

Our office is open plan, but the Director of Marketing has one of two rooms with walls; the other belongs to Robin Cooper-Clark. When I march in to Rod to make my protest, the office is empty, but I stay a few moments anyway to take in the view through the floor-to-ceiling window. Directly below is the Broadgate rink, a dinner plate of ice set in the middle of the staggered towers of concrete and steel. At this hour, it's empty save for a lone skater, a tall, dark guy in a green sweatshirt, carving out what at first I think are figures of eight but, as he makes the long downward stroke, resolve themselves into a large dollar sign. With the fog unfurling, the City looks as it did during the Blitz, when smoke from the fires dispersed, magically revealing the dome of St Paul's. Turn in the opposite direction and you see the Canary Wharf tower winking like a randy Cyclops.

Coming out of Rod's room, I run smack into Celia Harmsworth, though no injury is done to either party because I simply bounce off Celia's stupendous bust. When English-women of a certain background reach the age of fifty, they no longer have breasts, they have a bosom or even, depending on acreage of land and antiquity of lineage, a bust. Breasts come in twos, but a bust is always singular. The bust denies the possibility of cleavage or any kind of jiggling. Where breasts say, *Come and play!*, the bust, like the snub-nose of a bumper car, says, *Out of my way!* The Queen has a bust and so does Celia Harmsworth.

'Katharine Reddy, always in such a hurry,' she scolds. As Head of Human Resources, Celia is effortlessly one of the least human people in the building; childless, charmless, chilly as Chablis, she has this knack of making you feel both useless and used. When I went back to work after Emily was born, I found out that Chris Bunce, hedge fund manager and EMF's biggest earner for the past two years, had put a shot of vodka in the expressed breast milk I was storing in the office fridge next to the lifts. I approached Celia and asked her, woman to woman, what course of action she suggested taking against a jerk who, when confronted by me in Davy's Bar, claimed that putting

23

alcohol into the food intended for a twelve-week-old baby was ''Avin a bit of a larf.'

I can still remember the moue of distaste on Celia's face and it wasn't for that bastard Bunce. 'Use your feminine wiles, dear,' she said.

Celia tells me she is delighted that I can talk to the trainees at lunchtime. 'Rod said that you could do the presentation in your sleep. Just slides and a few sandwiches, you know the drill, Kate. And don't forget the Mission Statement, will you?'

I make a quick calculation. If the induction lasts an hour including drinks, say, that will leave me thirty minutes to find a cab and get across the City to Emily's school for the start of the nativity play. Should be enough time. Think I can make it so long as they don't ask any damn questions.

*

1.01 pm: 'Good afternoon, ladies and gentlemen, my name is Kate Reddy and I'd like to welcome you all to the thirteenth floor. Thirteen is unlucky for some, but not here at Edwin Morgan Forster, which ranks in the top ten money managers in the UK, in the top fifty globally in terms of assets and which, for five years running, has been voted money manager of the year. Last year, we generated revenue in excess of £300 million which explains why absolutely no expense has been spared on the fabulous tuna sandwiches you see spread out before you today.'

Rod's right. I can do this sort of stuff in my sleep; in fact, I pretty much *am* doing it in my sleep, as the jet lag takes hold and the crown of my skull starts to tighten and my legs feel as though someone is filling them with iced water.

'You will, I'm sure, already be familiar with the term "fund manager". Put at its simplest, a fund manager is a high-class gambler. My job is to study the form of companies round the world, assess the going in the markets for their products, check out the track record of jockeys, stick a big chunk of money on the best bet and then hope to hell that they don't fall at the first fence.'

There is laughter around the room, the over-grateful laughter of twentysomethings caught between arrogance at securing one of only six EMF traineeships and wetting themselves at the thought of being found out.

'If the horses I've backed do fall, I have to decide whether we shoot them right away or whether it's worth nursing that broken leg back to health. Remember, ladies and gentlemen, compassion can be expensive, but it's not necessarily a waste of your money.'

I was a trainee myself twelve years ago. Sitting in a room just like this one, crossing and uncrossing my legs, unsure whether it was worse to look like the Duchess of Kent or Sharon Stone. The only woman recruit in my year, I was surrounded by guys, big animal guys at ease in their pinstriped pelts. Not like me: the black crêpe Whistles suit I had spent my last forty quid on made me look like a Wolverhampton schools inspector.

This year's bunch of novices is pretty typical. Four guys, two girls. The guys always slouch at the back; the girls sit upright in the front row, pens poised to take notes they will never need. You get to know the types after a while. Look at Mr Anarchist over there with the Velcro sideburns and the Liam Gallagher scowl. In a suit today, but mentally still wearing a leather jacket, Dave was probably some kind of student activist at college. He read economics the better to arm himself for the workers' struggle while morally blackmailing all the kids on his corridor into buying that undrinkable Rwandan coffee.

Right now, he's sitting there telling himself he's just going to do this City shit for two years, five tops. Get some serious dough behind him, then launch his humanitarian crusade. I almost feel sorry for him. Seven years down the line, living in some modernist mausoleum in Notting Hill, school fees for two kids, wife with a ruinous Jimmy Choo habit, Dave will be nodding off in front of *Cold Feet* like the rest of us, with a copy of the *New Statesman* unopened in his lap.

The three other guys are pink-gilled landed types with prep-school partings. The one called Julian has an Adam's apple so overactive it's practically making cider. As usual, the girls are unmistakably women, whereas the men are barely more than boys. Between them, EMF's two female trainees cover the spectrum of womanhood – one is a doughy Shires girl with a kindly bun face and a velvet headband, the daytime tiara of her class. Clarissa somebody. Glance down the list of potted biographies and see that Clarissa is a graduate in 'Modern Studies' from the University of Peterborough. Pure back-office material. Must be a niece of one of the directors; you don't get into EMF with a degree like that unless you're a blood relation of money.

The girl next to her looks more interesting. Born and brought up in Sri Lanka, but educated at Cheltenham Ladies and the LSE, one of those granddaughters of Empire who end up more English than the English – the sweetness of their courtesy, the decorum of their grammar. With remarkable leaf-shaped eyes that gaze steadily out through tortoiseshell specs and a cat-like composure, Momo Gumeratne is so pretty she should only enter the Square Mile with an armed guard.

The trainees return my appraising stare. I wonder what they see. Blondish hair, decent legs, in good enough shape not to be pinned for a mother. They wouldn't guess I was Northern either (accent ironed out when I came to study down South). They may even be a little scared of me. The other day Rich said that I frightened him sometimes.

'Now, I'm sure that everyone here will have seen that line they put in tiny, bottom-row-of-the-optician's-chart print on your bank and building society accounts? "Remember that the value of your investment can go down as well as up!" Yes? Well, that's me. If I pick 'em wrong, the value goes down, so at EMF we do our very best to ensure that doesn't happen and most of the time we succeed. I find it useful to bear in mind when I'm selling three million dollars of airline stock, as I did this morning, that ours is the only flutter in the world which can leave a little old lady in Dumbarton without a pension. But don't worry, Julian, trainees are limited in the size of the deal they can make. We'll give you fifty grand for starters, just to get some practice.'

Julian's cheeks flush from smoked trout to strawberry and the doughy girl's hand shoots up: 'Can you tell me why you sold that particular stock today?'

'That's a very good question, Clarissa. Well, I had a four million dollar holding and the price was up and was continuing to rise, but we'd made a lot of money already and I knew from reading the trade papers that there was bad news coming about airlines. So the job of fund manager is to get our clients' money out *before* the price is weakened. All the time, I'm trying to balance the good things that might happen against the Act of An Almighty Pissed-Off God that may be lurking just around the corner.'

In my experience, the biggest test for any Edwin Morgan Forster trainee is not their ability to grasp the essentials of investment or to secure a pass for the car park. No, the thing that shows what you're really made of is if you can keep a straight face the first time you hear the firm's Mission Statement. Known internally as the five pillars of wisdom, the Mission Statement is the primest corporate baloney. (By what freak of logic did hardcore capitalists of the late twentieth century end up parroting slogans first chanted by Maoist peasants, who were not even permitted to own their own bicycle?)

'And our Five Pillars are:

1 / Pulling together!

2 / Mutual honesty!

3 / Best results!

4 / Client care!

5 / Committed to success!'

I can see Dave struggling manfully to suppress a smirk. Good boy. Glance up at the clock. Shit. Time to go. 'Now, if there are no more questions –'

Damn. That other girl has her hand up now. At least you can rely on the men not to ask a question. Even when they don't know anything, like this lot, but especially not at my level, when asking a question means admitting that there are still things in the world that are beyond you.

'I'm so sorry,' the young Sri Lankan begins, as though

apologising for some error she has yet to commit. 'I know that EMF has, well, as a woman, Ms Reddy, can you tell me honestly how do you find working in this job?'

'Well, Ms –?'

'Momo Gumeratne.'

'Well, Momo, there are sixty fund managers here and only three of us are women. EMF does have an equal opportunities policy and as long as trainees like you keep coming through we're going to make that happen in practice.

'Secondly, I understand that the Japanese are working on a tank where you can grow babies outside the womb. They should have perfected that by the time you're ready to have children, Ms Gumeratne, so we really will be able to have the first lunch-hour baby. Believe me, that would make everyone at Edwin Morgan Forster very happy.'

I assume that will stop the questions dead, but Momo is not as mousy as I thought. Her coffee skin suffused with a blush, she puts up her hand again. As I turn to pick up my bag, indicating that the session is over, she starts to speak:

'I'm really sorry, Ms Reddy. But may I ask if you have children of your own?'

No, she can't. 'Yes, the last time I looked there were two of them. And may I suggest, Ms Gumeratne, that you don't start your sentences with I'm sorry. There are a lot of words you'll find useful in this building, but sorry isn't one of them. Now, if that's all I really must go and check the markets – winners to pick, money to manage! Thank you for your attention, ladies and gentlemen, and please do come up if you see me round the building and I'll test you on our Five Pillars of Wisdom. If you're really lucky, I'll give you my personal Pillar Number Six.'

They look at me dumbly.

'Pillar Number Six: if money responds to your touch, then there's no limit to what a woman can achieve in this City. Money doesn't know what sex you are.'

*

2.17 pm: You can always pick up a cab from the rank outside Warburg's. Any day except today. Today the cabbies are all at some dedicated Make Kate Late rally. After seven minutes of not being hysterical at the kerbside, I hurl myself in front of a taxi with its light off. The driver swerves to avoid me. I tell him I'll double the fare on the clock if he takes me to Emily's school without using his brakes. Lurching around in the back as we weave through the narrow, choked streets, I can feel the pulse points in my neck and wrist jumping like crickets.

2.49 pm: The woodblock floor in Emily's school hall was obviously installed with the express purpose of exposing late-arriving working mothers in heels. I tick-tock in at the moment when the Angel Gabriel is breaking the big news to the Virgin Mary, who starts pulling the wool off the donkey sitting next to her. Mary is played by Genevieve Law, daughter of Alexandra Law, form representative and Mother Superior – in other words, defiantly non-working. There is serious competition among the Mothers Superior to secure leading roles in the production for their young. Trust me, they didn't give up that seat on the board or major TV series for little Joshua to play the innkeeper's brother in a Gap poloneck.

'A sheep was *perfect* for him last year,' they cry, 'but this Christmas we really feel he could tackle something a little more challenging.'

As the three wise men – a wispy red-haired boy propelled by two little girls – walk across the stage with their presents for the Baby Jesus, the hall door opens behind us with a treacherous squeal. A hundred pairs of eyes swivel round to see a red-faced woman with a Tesco's carrier bag and a briefcase. Looks like Amy Redman's mum. As she edges, cringing and apologetic, into the back row of seats, Alexandra Law shushes her noisily. My instinctive sympathy for this fellow creature is outweighed almost immediately by an ugly swelling of gratitude that, thanks to her, I am no longer the last to arrive. (I don't want other working mothers to suffer unduly. Truly I don't. I just need to know that we're all screwing up about the same amount.)

Up on stage, a wobbly wail of recorders heralds the final carol. My angel is third from the left in the back row. On this big occasion, Emily has the same inky-eyed concentration, the same quizzical pucker of the brow she had coming out of the womb. I remember she looked round the delivery room for a couple of minutes, as if to say, 'No, don't tell me, I'll get it in a minute.' This afternoon, flanked by fidgety boys, one of whom plainly needs the loo, my girl sings the carol without faltering over any of the words, and I feel a knock of pride in my ribcage.

Why are infants performing 'Away in a Manger' in a headlong rush so much more affecting than the entire in-tune King's College Choir? Dig down into a bosky corner of my coat pocket and find a hankie.

3.41 pm: At the festive refreshments, there are a handful of fathers hiding behind video cameras, but the hall is aswarm with mothers, moths fluttering round the little lights of their lives. At school functions, other women always look like real mothers to me; I never feel I'm old enough for that title, or sufficiently well qualified. I can feel my body adopting exaggerated maternal gestures like a mime artist. The evidence that I am a mother, though, is holding tightly on to my left hand and insisting that I wear her halo in my hair. Emily is clearly relieved and grateful that Mummy made it: last year, I had to drop out at the last minute when deal negotiations hit a critical phase and I had to jump on a plane to the States. I brought her a musical snow-shaker of New York, snatched up in Saks Fifth Avenue, as a consolation present, but it was no consolation. The times you don't make it are the ones children remember, not the times you do.

I am anxious to slip away and call the office, but there is no avoiding Alexandra Law, who is accepting rave notices for Genevieve's Virgin Mary and for her own Bavarian Lebkuchen. Alexandra picks up one of my mince pies, jabs a dubious fingernail into the hill of icing sugar on top before pushing the whole lot into her mouth and announcing her verdict through a shower of crumbs: 'Sen-say-sh'nul mince pies, Kate. Did you soak the fruit in brandy or grappa?'

'Oh, a dash of this and that, Alex, you know how it is.'

She nods. 'I was thinking of asking everyone to make stollen for next year. What d'you think? Do you have a good recipe?'

'No, but I know a supermarket that does.'

'Ha-ha-ha-ha! Very good. Ha! Ha! Ha!'

Alexandra is the only woman I know who laughs as though it was written down. Mirthless, heaving, Ted Heath shoulders. Any second now she will ask me if I've gone part-time yet.

'So, are you working part-time now? No. Still full-time. *Good heavens*! I don't know how you do it, honestly. I say, Claire, I was just saying to Kate, I don't know how she does it. Do you?'

★

7.27 pm: The strain of being an angel has taken its toll on Emily. She is so exhausted that I calculate I can turn over three pages of the bedtime story without her noticing. Must get on with that e-mail backlog. But just as I am skipping the pages, a suspicious eye snaps open.

'Mummy, you made a mistake.'

'Did I?'

'You left out the bit where Piglet jumps in Kanga's pocket!'

'Oh dear, did I?'

'Never mind, Mummy. We can just start at the beginning again.'

8.11 pm: The answerphone that sits on the table next to the TV is full. Play messages. A West Country burr informs me that KwikToy is returning my call about undelivered Christmas presents. 'Unfortunately, owing to unprecedented demand, the items will not now be with you until the New Year.'

Christ. What's wrong with these people?

A message from my mother comes next and takes up most of the tape. Nervous of the technology, Mum still leaves pauses for the person at the other end to reply. She rang to say not to worry, she will manage fine without us over Christmas: somehow her reassurance is more piercing than any complaint could be. It's that knockout one-two mothers have perfected down the centuries: first they make you feel guilty and then you feel resentful at being made to feel guilty, which makes you feel even worse.

'I've put some books for Emily and Ben in the post and a little something for you and Richard. I hope they'll be the right sort of thing.' She is afraid of not pleasing in this as in so much else.

After my mother's wan reproachfulness, it's a relief to hear the voice of Jill Cooper-Clark wishing me a happy Christmas. Sorry she hasn't got organised with cards this year, been a bit dicky – laughter – although at least her new specialist looks like Dirk Bogarde. Sends her love and asks me to give a call some time.

Finally, I hear a voice so drained of warmth I barely recognise it: Janine, a former broker friend. Janine gave up work last year when her husband's firm floated on the stock market and Graham came into the kind of wealth that buys you a yacht called *Tabitha*, once owned by a cousin of Aristotle Onassis. When Janine was still working, we used to enjoy the battle-weary camaraderie of running a home while trying to make it across Man's Land avoiding sniper fire. These days, Janine does afternoon classes at the Chelsea Physic Garden on how to get the most out of your seasonal windowbox. She has winter and summer covers for her sofas, which get changed at the correct time of year, and lately she has arranged all the family photographs in padded albums, which sit on the coffee table in her drawing room exuding the mellow smells of leather and contentment. Last time I asked Janine what she was up to, she said, 'Oh, you know, just pottering.' No, I don't know. Pottering and me, I don't think we've been introduced.

Janine is ringing to check if we're coming to their New Year's Eve dinner. She's sorry to bother us. She doesn't sound sorry. She sounds spitty with the indignation of a hostess scorned.

What New Year's dinner? A few minutes of excavating the heap on the hall table – tandoori leaflets, dead leaves, a single brown mitten – turns up an unopened pile of Christmas post. I riffle through the envelopes till I get to the one addressed in Janine's careful copperplate. Inside, is a card photo-montage of Graham, Janine and their perfectly untroubled children plus an invitation to dinner. RSVP by the 10th December.

I now do what I always do on such occasions: I blame Richard. (It doesn't have to be his fault, but someone has to be landed with the blame, or how is life to be tolerated?) Kneeling on the kitchen floor, Rich is making Ben a reindeer out of cardboard and what looks like the missing brown mitten. I tell him we are no longer even capable of turning down the events we will be unable to attend: our social ostracism is nearly complete. I am suddenly overcome with longing to be one of those women who reply promptly to invitations on thick creamy notepaper with a William Morris border. And in fountain pen, not in some drought-stricken jade felt tip I have raided from Emily's pencil case.

Rich shrugs. 'Come off it, Kate. You'd go mad.'

Perhaps, but it would be nice to have the choice.

11.57 pm: The bath. My favourite place on earth. Leaning over the empty tub, I clear out the ducks and the wrecked galleon, unstick the alphabet letters which, ever since the vowels got flushed down the loo, have formed angry, Croat injunctions around the rim (*scrtzchk!*). I peel off the crusty, half-dry Barbie flannel that has begun to smell of something I vaguely remember as tadpole; and then, starting at one corner, I lift up the non-slip mat whose suction cups cling on for a second before yielding with an indignant burp.

Next, I ransack the cabinet, looking for a relaxing bath oil – lavender, sea cucumber, bergamot – but I am always out of de-stressors and have to settle for something with bubbles called Vitality in nuclear lime. Then I run the water hotter than you can bear; so hot that when I climb in my body momentarily mistakes it for cold. Lie back, nostrils flaring over the surface like an alligator. I look at the woman rapidly vanishing in the steamy mirror by my side and I think this is *her* time, her time alone, save for the odd, overlooked Barney the dinosaur bobbing up suddenly between her knees with its serial-killer grin.

The bath is ancient, its porcelain riddled with grey-blue veins. We ran out of money after doing the kitchen so the house is in ascending order of crud: the higher up you go the lower the standards. Kitchen by Terence Conran, sitting room by Ikea, bathroom by Fungus the Bogeyman. But with my contact lenses out and in candlelight, the bathroom's leprous peeling speaks to me of some vestal Roman temple rather than five grand's worth of absent damp course.

As the bubbles evaporate on my hands, scaly pink islets are revealed along the knuckles. It's already got behind my right ear. Stress eczema, the nurse at work called it. 'Can you think of any way to relieve some of the pressures in your life, Kate?' Oh, let's see now: a brain transplant, a Lottery win, my husband being reprogrammed to figure out that things left at the bottom of the stairs usually need to be carried to the top of the stairs.

Can't see how I can go on like this. Can't see how to stop either. Can't help wondering if I was too hard on that Sri Lankan girl at the induction today. Momo Somebody? Seemed sweet enough. She asked me to be honest. Should I have been? Told her that the only way to get on at EMF is to act like one of the boys; and when you act like one of the boys they call you abrasive and difficult, so you act like a woman, and then they say you're emotional and difficult. Difficult being their word for everything that's not them. Well, she'll learn.

If I'd known at her age what I know now, would I ever have had children? I close my eyes and try to imagine a world without Emily and Ben: like a world without music or lightning.

I sink back under the water and urge my thoughts to float free, but they feel stuck to my brain like barnacles.

Must Remember
Talk with Paula outlining firm new approach to children's haircuts/time-keeping etc. Talk with Rod Task outlining firm new approach to

role with clients, ie *I AM NOT THEIR EMERGENCY GEISHA*. Pay rise: repeat after me, *I Will Not Accept Extra Work For No Extra Money!* Get quote for new stair carpet. Buy Christmas tree and stylish lights (John Lewis or Ikea?) Present for Richard (*How to be a Domestic Goddess?*), in-laws (cheese barrel or alpine plants advertised in S. Times colour supplement: where did I put the cutting?) Stocking fillers for E&B. Fruit jellies Uncle Alf. Travel sick sweets? Ask Paula collect dry cleaning. Personal shopper how much? Pelvic floor squeeeeze. Make icing for Christmas cake: too late, buy roll-on stuff. Cards stamps first class x 30. Wean Ben off dummy! Remember Roo!! Ring KwikToy useless bloody present co. and threaten legal action. Nappies, bottles, Sleeping Beauty video. Smear test!!! Highlights. Hamster?

3

Happy Holidays

I CAN GET MYSELF and two children washed and dressed and out of the house in half an hour, I can juggle nine different currencies in five different time zones, I can make myself come with quiet efficiency, I can prepare and eat a stand-up supper while on the phone to the West Coast, I can read *Guess How Much I Love You?* to Ben while scanning the prices on Teletext, but can I get a minicab to take me to the airport?

As part of an ongoing programme of cutbacks, Edwin Morgan Forster will no longer send a car to deliver me to Heathrow. I must order my own. Last night I booked a local minicab, which this morning failed to show. When I rang to protest, the guy at the other end said he was very sorry but the soonest they can get a car to me is half an hour.

'It's a busy time of day, love.'

I *know* it's a busy time of day. That's why I pre-booked the cab last night.

He says he thinks he may be able to get me something in twenty minutes. I hotly reject this insulting offer and slam phone down. And immediately regret it as all the other companies I call either don't have a car available or suggest an even more disastrous waiting time.

Am frantic, when I spot a dirty bronze card sticking out from under the doormat. It's for a taxi company I've never heard of: 'Pegasus – Your Winged Driver.' When I dial the number, the guy at the other end says he's coming right over. Relief is shortlived. This being Hackney, what turns up at the door is Pegasus – Your Stoned Driver. Parked at almost forty-five degrees to the kerb, Pegasus's chariot is a Nissan Sunny of impenetrable gloom hung about with veils of nicotine and

36

hash. I climb in, but it's technically impossible to breathe in the cab, so I try to roll down the window and stick my head outside like a dog.

'Window not working,' volunteers the driver, factually and without regret.

'And the seatbelt?'

'Not working.'

'You do realise that's illegal.'

In the rear-view mirror, Pegasus shoots me a pitying look that instructs me to get a life.

The cab not turning up made me so tense I had this stupid, stupid row with Richard. He found Paula's Xmas bonus cheque which I'd hidden in Emily's lunchbox. He said he simply couldn't understand why I spent more on the nanny's Christmas present than on the rest of the family put together.

I tried to explain. 'Because if I don't keep Paula happy she will leave.'

'Would that really be so bad, Katie?'

'Frankly, it would be easier if you left.'

'Ah. I see.'

I shouldn't have put it like that. Damned tiredness. Always makes you say what you don't mean to say, even if you feel it at the time. After that, Rich sat at the kitchen table pretending to have found something fascinating to read in *Architectural Digest* while managing to look like Trevor Howard at the end of *Brief Encounter* – all chin-up decency and glittery eyes.

He wouldn't even look at me when I said goodbye. Then Ben stood up in his high-chair and started yodelling for a hug. No. Sorry. Not in a clean suit: the state of him! Smeared with jam and apricot fromage frais, like his own personal sunrise.

The cab stops and starts and stops again along the Euston Road. If this is one of London's main arteries, then London needs a coronary bypass. Its citizens sit in their cars, hearts furring up with fury.

Once we're past King's Cross, I open my post. There's a card from Mum enclosing a magazine's Yuletide supplement: '26 Recipes for a Magical, Stress-Free Christmas!' Flick through the pages in mounting disbelief. How can anything stress-free involve caramelising a shallot?

We continue to crawl westwards, over the flyover and past the brick-pink semis, like mile upon mile of gaping dentures. When I used to live in a house like that, Christmas was still a pretty simple affair. It was a tree, a pimply turkey, satsumas trapped in an orange net, maybe some dates clinging gummily together in a palm-tree canoe and a bumper tin of Quality Street eaten by the whole family in front of *Morecambe and Wise*. Your big present was always waiting for you downstairs next to the tree – a doll's house, roller skates, maybe a bike with stabilisers or a bell – and there was a stocking whose thrilling misshapen weight your feet discovered at the end of the bed. But Christmas, like everything else, has moved up a gear. Now it's productions of *The Nutcracker* you have to book tickets for in August, and Kelly Bronze. When I first heard the name, I assumed Kelly was one of those inflatable Baywatch babes, but she turns out to be the only kind of turkey that's worth eating any more. And once you've spent an hour on the phone being held in a queue in order to beg the supermarket to put you on the waiting list for Kelly, you have to get the bird home and stuff her. According to my Yuletide supplement, stuffing, which was once stale breadcrumbs with diced onion and a spoonful of fusty sage, has evolved into 'porcini butter with red rice and cranberry to revive jaded palates'.

I don't believe we had palates in the Seventies: we had sweet teeth and heartburn that you eased by sucking lozenges the colour and texture of gravestones. It's a good joke when you think about it, isn't it? Just as women were fleeing the role of homemaker in their millions, there was suddenly food that was worth cooking. Think of all the great stuff you could be making, Kate, if you were ever in your kitchen to make it.

8.43 am: Pegasus has chosen a 'quick' back route to Heathrow. So, with one hour twenty-two minutes to take-off, we are sitting outside a row of halal butchers in Southall. Feel my heart revving; foot jammed on an invisible accelerator.

'Look, can't you go any faster? I absolutely *have* to make up time.'

A young guy in white cotton pyjamas steps out into the road in front of us, a lamb the size of a child slung over his shoulder. My driver brakes suddenly and from the front of the car comes a laconic drawl: 'Last time I looked, lady, running people over still against the law.'

Close eyes and concentrate on calming down. Things will feel much more under control if I make efficient use of the time: call KwikToy ('Round the Clock Fun!') on mobile to complain about no-show of vital Christmas presents.

'Thank you for choosing KwikToy. We are sorry, you are held in a queue. Your call will be answered shortly.' Typical.

Start to work my way through torn-out Yellow Pages list of north London pet shops. It comes as no surprise to learn there is a national shortage of baby hamsters, though there might be one left in Walthamstow. Am I interested? Yes.

When I finally get through to KwikToy, a clueless operative seems reluctant to admit they have any record of my order. Tell him that I am a major shareholder in his company and that we are about to review our investment.

'Aright,' he concedes, 'there has been some delivery difficulties owing to unprecedented demand.'

I point out that the demand can hardly be described as unprecedented.

'The birth of the little baby Jesus. Been celebrating that one for 2,000 years. Toys and Christmas. Christmas and toys. Ring any bells?'

'Would you be asking for a voucher, Miss?'

'No, I would not be asking for a voucher. I am asking for my toys to be delivered *immediately* so my children will have something to open on Christmas Day.'

There is a pause, a beep and an echoey shout: 'Oy, Jeff, some posh tart's doing her nut on the phone about the Goldilocks porridge set and the pushalong sheepdog. Whatmygonnatella?'

9.17 am: Arrive at Heathrow with time to spare. Decide to try to make it up to the driver for yelling. Ask his name.

'Winston,' he offers suspiciously.

'Thanks, Winston. That was a really good route. I'm Kate, by the way. Such a great name, Winston. As in Churchill?'

He savours the moment before replying: 'As in Silcott.'

9.26 am: Barging through a choked departure lounge, I remember something else I have forgotten. Need to call home. Mobile not in service. Why not? Try a payphone, which eats three pound coins and fails to connect me while repeating the message: 'Thank you for choosing British Telecom.'

Finally get through on credit-card phone next to the boarding desk, watched by three members of staff in navy uniforms.

'Richard, hello? Whatever you do, don't forget the stockings.'

'Lingerie?'

'What?'

'Stockings. Is there a lingerie angle here, Katie? Suspenders, black lace, three inches of creamy thigh, or are we talking boring old Santa gift receptacle?'

'Richard, have you been drinking?'

'It's an idea, certainly.' As he puts the phone down, I swear I can hear Paula offering Emily a Hubba Bubba.

MY DAUGHTER IS NOT ALLOWED BUBBLE GUM.

From: Kate Reddy, Stockholm
To: Candy Stratton
Client threatening to drop us on account of worrying dip in fund performance. Spun them a line about Edwin Morgan Forster asset managers being like Björn Borg – brilliant base-line stayers playing percentage shots and aiming for consistent victories over the long term, not flashy burnout artists going for quick profits and then double-faulting. Seemed to buy it. God knows why.

Kept popping out of Bengt Bergman boardroom to Executive Washroom, locking self in cubicle and using mobile to call pet shops in Walthamstow. Up until three days ago, Emily's letters to Santa made no mention of hamster. But suddenly upgraded to Number One item.

Swedish clients all have names like a bad hand of Scrabble. Sven Sjostrom kept spearing rollmops off my plate at lunch and saying he was a passionate believer in 'closer European union'.

Trust me to get only non-PC man in Scandinavia.

Yeurk, K8 xxxxx

From: Candy Stratton
To: Kate Reddy
Sven Will I See U Again?
Sven Will We Share Precious Moments?
go for it, hon, it will relax you!
luv Cystitis xxx

From: Kate Reddy
To: Candy Stratton
That is NOT FUNNY. Remember, I am a happily married woman. Well, I'm married anyway.

From: Debra Richardson
To: Kate Reddy
Have just had unspeakable humiliation at hands – or rather mouth – of hateful school secretary at Piper Place (i know, i know, should stop this education madness). Yes, Ruby could be assessed for a place for 2002, 'But I must warn you Mrs Richardson that there are over a hundred little girls on our list and we have a strong siblings policy.'
Do you have any Semtex? These smug cows have got to be stopped.
What's new??

From: Kate Reddy
To: Debra Richardson
Have not put Em down for school yet. By the time I get round

to it, will probably have to have sex with the headmaster to have any chance of getting her in . . . More pressing problem: two days to wean Ben off dummy cos mother-in-law thinks dummy is tool of the devil, only used by gypsies or chain-smoking lowlifes who 'park children in front of the video'. What else supposed to do with children in Yorkshire?

Have found hamster for Emily. Apparently female hamsters v. bad-tempered and sometimes bite or eat their young. Now why would that be?

2.17 am: Blizzard. Flight home delayed. Precious seconds set aside for last-minute shopping in London being eaten up. Scour Stockholm airport shop for Christmas presents. Which would Rich prefer? Wind-dried reindeer or seasonal video entitled: *Swedish Teen Honeys in the Snow?* Still refusing to buy Emily vulgar, messy Baby Wee-Wee as seen on breakfast TV. Compromise on the local Swedish Barbie-type doll – wholesome individual, probably a Social Democrat, wearing peacekeeper khaki.

*

Christmas Eve, Offices of Edwin Morgan Forster
I should have known where my pay negotiations were going when Rod Task came round the back of my chair, air-patted my shoulder three times like a vet preparing a cat for a jab and described me as 'a highly valued member of the team'. It was mid-afternoon, the dregs of the day, and the sky over Broadgate was the colour of tea.

Rod explained that there would be no bonus this year: the bonus I have been counting on to finish the building work on the house and for so much else. Times were tough for everybody, he said, but the really great news was they were giving me a major new challenge.

'We think you're the person to do client-servicing, Katie, 'cos you do it so damn well. Anyway, you got the best legs.'

A short, burly Aussie, with a voice other guys use to get the attention of a bartender, Rod first heaved his bulk over from

Sydney to join EMF as Director of Marketing three and a half years ago. Brought in to put some lead in the English firm's propelling pencil. I really thought that I'd have to leave. There was his inability to look me in the eye – and not just because I'm two inches taller than him – the way he would comment on parts of my body as though they were on special offer, his habit of ending every meeting with an injunction to 'Get out there and kick the fucking tyres!' After a few weeks, when Candy sweetly asked Rod for an English translation of this phrase, he looked perplexed for a few seconds, then gave a broad grin: 'Screw the client for every penny you can!'

So I was going to have to leave. But then Emily hit the Terrible Twos and I bought a book called *Toddler Taming*. It was a revelation. The advice on how to deal with small, angry immature people who have no idea of limits and were constantly testing their mother applied perfectly to my boss. Instead of treating him as a superior, I began handling him as though he were a tricky small boy. Whenever he was about to be naughty, I would do my best to distract him; if I wanted him to do something, I always made it look like it was his idea.

Anyway, Rod says that from today I assume responsibility for the Salinger Foundation. Based in New York. Chief Executive by the name of Jack Abelhammer. Two hundred million dollar business, needs someone of my calibre. I'll be able to familiarise myself with the portfolio over the holidays, of course, plus I will continue to babysit all my old clients while Rod finds the right person to take over a few of them.

I ask Rod what Abelhammer is like.

'Good swing.'

'I beg your pardon?'

'Short game needs work.'

'Oh, golf.'

'Whatcha think I'm talking about, Katie, sex?'

The holiday doesn't strictly begin till close of play today, but the office is practically deserted: unofficially, we are now in the limbo between boozy lunch and alcoholic tea. When I get back to my desk, Candy is perched on the heater under the window with her legs stretched out and resting on top of my chair. She is wearing an amazing cantilevered scarlet blouse, purple fishnets and there is gold tinsel in her hair.

'OK, let me guess,' she says. 'He took a crap on you and you offered to wipe his ass?'

'Excuse me.' I grab her ankles and spin her feet off the chair. 'Actually, things went very well. Rod thinks my client-handling skills are a major asset so, as a vote of confidence, they are giving me this big foundation all to myself.'

'Right.' When Candy laughs you get a glimpse of a mouthful of enviable American teeth.

'Don't look at me like that.'

'Kate, a major vote of confidence round here always comes with at least four zeros on the end of it, you know that. What else'd he say?'

I don't have time to reply because Candy puts a finger to her lips as Chris Bunce, bastard in residence, sways past us on his way to the Gents with a long lunch under his belt. A major cokehead, Bunce manages to look both skinny and bloated. Since I made it clear to him, quite politely, that I wasn't interested in the contents of his boxers, the sexual tension between us has given way to teasing skirmishes with occasional rounds of live ammunition being fired when I get a deal that he wants. (Guys like Bunce see rejection as an insult that must be repaid with compound interest, like the Third World debt.)

Candy tips her head towards his retreating figure: 'Lot of dirt getting into EMF one way and another. D'you offer to clean the office for them too?'

'What do you take me for? Rod said that no one was getting a bonus.'

'And you believed him?' Candy closes her eyes and sighs a smile. 'That's what I love about you, Kate. Smartest female economist since Maynard Keynes and you still think when they mug you they're doing you a favour.'

'Candy, Maynard Keynes was a man.'

She shakes her head and the tinsel sends out prickles of light.

'He was not. He was a fruit. Way I see it, women have to claim all the guys in history with a strong feminine side as ours.'

6.09 pm: Packing the car for the journey up North to my parents-in-law takes at least two hours. There is the first hour during which Richard pieces together a pleasing jigsaw of baby belongings in the boot. (Louis XIV travelled lighter than Ben.) Then comes the moment when he has to find the key that unlocks the luggage box that sits like an upturned boat on our roof. 'Where did we put it, Kate?' After ten minutes of swearing and emptying every drawer in the house, Richard finds the key in the pocket of his jacket.

After Rich has told me to get the kids in the car 'right now', there follows twenty minutes of frantic unloading as he 'just makes sure' he has packed the steriliser which he 'knows for a fact' he wedged next to the spare tyre. This is followed by a furious re-packing, punctuated by 'fuck-its!', when items are squidged on top of one another any old how and the remnants are jammed into all available foot space front and back. The Easi-wipe changing mat, the Easi-clip portable high-chair with its companion piece, the vermilion Easi-assemble portacot. Bibs, melamine Thomas the Tank Engine bowls. Sleepsuits. Emily's blankie – a tragic hank of yellow wool that looks as though it has been run over several times. We always travel with an entire bestiary of nocturnal comforters – Ben's beloved Roo, a sheep, a hippopotamus in a tutu, a wombat that is an eerie Roy Hattersley double. Ben's dummies (to be hidden from Richard's parents at all costs). Emily's surprise hamster is stashed in the boot.

Strapped into their seats in the back of the car like cosmonauts awaiting blast-off, Emily and Ben's contented bickering soon gives way to hand-to-hand combat. In a moment of weakness – when do I have a moment of strength? – I have opened the chocolate Santa dispenser meant for Christmas morning, and given them a couple of foil-wrapped pieces each to keep them quiet. As a result, Emily who, fifteen minutes ago was wearing white pyjamas, now looks like a dalmatian with a dark-brown muzzle around her mouth and cocoa smudges everywhere else.

Richard, who has a heroic indifference to the cleanliness and general presentation of his offspring for eleven and a half months of the year, suddenly asks me why Ben and Emily look such a mess. What's his mother going to think?

I swipe at children with moist travel tissues. Three hours on the A1 lie ahead of us. Car is so overloaded it sways like a ship.

'Are we still in England?' demands an incredulous voice from the back.

'Yes.'

'Are we at Grandma's house yet?'

'No.'

'But I *want* to be at Grandma's house.'

By Hatfield, both children are performing a fugue for scream and whimper. I crank up the *Carols from King's* tape and Rich and I sing along gustily. (Rich is the descant specialist while I take the Jessye Norman part.) Near Peterborough, eighty miles out of London, a small nagging thought manages to wriggle its way clear from the compost heap that presently comprises the contents of my head.

'Rich, you did remember to pack Roo?'

'I didn't know I was meant to be remembering Roo. I thought you were remembering Roo.'

*

LIKE ANY OTHER family, the Shattocks have their Christmas traditions. One tradition is that I buy all the presents for my side of the family and I buy all the presents for our children and our two godchildren and I buy Richard's presents and presents for Richard's parents and his brother Peter and Peter's wife Cheryl and their three kids and Richard's Uncle Alf who drives across from Matlock every Boxing Day and is keen on rugby league and can only manage soft centres. If Richard remembers, and depending on late opening hours, he buys a present for me.

'What have we got for Dad, then?' Rich will enquire on the

drive up to Yorkshire. The marital we which means you which means me.

I buy the wrapping paper and the Sellotape and I wrap all the presents. I buy the cards and a large sheet of second-class stamps. By the time I have written all the cards and forged Rich's signature and written something warm yet lighthearted about time flying and how we'll definitely be in touch in the New Year (a lie), it is too late for second-class mail so I join the queue at the post office to buy first-class stamps. Then I fight my way through Selfridges' food hall to buy cheese and those little Florentines that Barbara likes.

And then, when we get to Barbara and Donald's house, we unpack the stuff from the car and we put all the presents under the tree and the food and the drink in the kitchen and they chorus: 'Oh, Richard, thank you for getting the wine. You shouldn't have gone to all that trouble.'

Is it possible to die of ingratitude?

Midnight Mass, St Mary's, Wrothly
The grass on the village green is so full of ice tonight it's almost musical: we clink and chink our way from the Shattocks' old mill house to the tiny Norman church. Inside, the pews are packed, the air dense and dank and flavoured with winey breath. I know that you're meant to disapprove of the drunks who only come to church this one time in the year, but standing here next to Rich, I think how much I like them, envy them even. Their noisy attempts at hush, the sense that they've come in search of heat and light and a little human kindness.

I hold it together, I really do, until we get to that line in 'O Little Town of Bethlehem' when I have to press both gloves to my eyes:

'Above thy deep and dreamless sleep the silent stars go by.'

4

Christmas Day

5.37 am, Wrothly, Yorkshire: It's still dark outside. The four of
us are in bed together in a sprawling, tentacular cuddle. Emily,
half mad with Santa lust, is tearing off wrapping paper. Ben is
playing peepo with the debris. I give Richard a packet of wind-
dried reindeer, two pairs of Swedish socks (oatmeal), a five-day
wine-tasting course in Burgundy and *How To Be a Domestic
Goddess* (joke). Later on, Barbara and Donald will give me a
wipeable Liberty print apron and *How To Be a Domestic Goddess*
(not joke).

Richard gives me:

1. Agent Provocateur underwear – red bra with raised black
   satin spots and demitasse cup over which nipples jut like
   helmeted medieval warriors peeking above parapet. Also
   a suspender/knicker device apparently trimmed with
   trawlerman's netting.
2. Membership of National Trust.

Both fall into the category of what I think of as PC presents:
Please Change. Emily gives me a fantastic travel clock. Instead
of an alarm, it has a message recorded by her: 'Wake up,
Mummy, wake up, sleepy head!'

We give Emily a hamster (female, but to be called Jesus), a
Barbie bike, a Brambly Hedge doll's house, a remote-control
robot dog and a lot of other stuff made out of plastic that she
doesn't need. Emily is thrilled with the Peacekeeper Barbie I
snatched up in Stockholm Duty Free until she opens Paula's
present: Baby Wee-Wee, which I have expressly forbidden.

Risking hysteria, we try to get most of the kids' gifts
unwrapped upstairs so that my parents-in-law will not be
appalled by the reckless metropolitan surfeit ('Throwing your

money about') and the outrageous spoiling of the younger generation ('In my day, you counted yourself lucky to get a doll with a china head and an orange').

Some things are harder to keep quiet. It's difficult to pretend to grandparents, for instance, that your child is just an occasional video watcher when, during breakfast, she gives a word-perfect rendition of every song from *The Little Mermaid*, adding brightly that the DVD version has an extra tune. At the table, I sense another source of conflict when I remind Emily to stop playing with the salt.

'Emily, Grandpa asked you to put that down.'

'No, I didn't,' says Donald mildly. 'I *told* her to put it down. That's the difference between my generation and yours, Kate: we told, you ask.'

A few minutes later, standing by the Aga stirring scrambled egg, I am suddenly aware of Barbara hovering by my side. She finds it hard to conceal her disbelief at the contents of the saucepan. 'Goodness, do the children like their eggs dry?'

'Yes, this is the way I always do them.'

'Oh.'

Barbara is obsessed with the food intake of my family, whether it's the children's lack of vegetables or my own strange unwillingness to plough through three three-course meals a day. 'You need to build your strength up, Katharine.' And no Shattock family gathering would be complete without my mother-in-law pressing me into the African Violet nook next to the pantry and hissing, 'Richard looks thin, Katharine. Isn't Richard looking *thin*?'

When Barbara says thin it immediately becomes a fat word: hefty, breathless, accusing. I shut my eyes and try to summon reserves of patience and understanding I don't have. The woman standing before me equipped my husband with the DNA that gave him the lifelong figure of a biro refill, and thirty-six years later she blames me. Is this fair? I rise above such slights on my wifeliness, what there is of it.

'But Richard *is* thin,' I protest. 'Rich was skinny when we met. That's one of the things I loved about him.'

'He was always slim,' concedes Barbara, 'but now there's nothing left of him. Cheryl said as soon as she saw him get out of the car: "Doesn't Richard look run down, Barbara?"'

Cheryl is my sister-in-law. Before she married Peter, Richard's accountant brother, Cheryl was something in the Halifax building society. Since she had the first of her three boys in 1989, Cheryl has become a member of what my friend Debra calls the Muffia – the powerful, stay-at-home cabal of organised mums. Both Cheryl and Barbara treat men as though they were livestock who need careful husbandry. No Christmas in the Shattock family would be complete without Cheryl asking me if my Joseph cashmere róll-neck is from Bhs, or if it's really all right that Rich should be upstairs bathing the children *by himself.*

Peter is a lot less help with the family than Richard, but over the years I have come to see that Cheryl enjoys and even encourages her husband's uselessness. Peter plays the valuable role in Cheryl's life of The Cross I Have to Bear. Every martyr needs a Peter who, given time, can be trained up not to recognise his own underpants.

Things I take for granted at home in London are viewed up here as egalitarianism gone mad. 'Somme,' says Richard in grim triumph, walking through the kitchen holding aloft a bulging nappy sack whose apricot scent is fighting a losing battle to subdue the stink within. (Rich has evolved a classification system for Ben's nappies: a minor incident is a Tant Pis, an average load is a Croque Manure, while an all-out, seven-wipes job is a Somme. Once, but only once, there was a Krakatoa. Fair enough, but not in a Greek airport.)

'Of course, in our day the fathers didn't pitch in at all,' says Barbara, flinching. 'You wouldn't get Donald going near a nappy. He'd drive a mile to avoid one.'

'Richard's fantastic,' I say carefully. 'I couldn't manage without him.'

Barbara takes a red onion and quarters it fiercely. 'You've got to look after them a bit, men. Delicate flowers,' she muses, pressing the blade down till the onion cries softly to itself. 'Can you give that gravy a stir for me, Katharine?' Cheryl comes in and starts defrosting cheese straws and vol-au-vent cases for tomorrow's drinks party.

I feel so alone when Barbara and Cheryl are twittering together in the kitchen, even though I'm standing right there. I reckon this must be how it was for centuries. Women doing the doing and exchanging conspiratorial glances and indulgent sighs about the men. But I never joined the Muffia; I don't know the code, the passwords, the special handshakes. I expect a man – my man – to do women's work, because if he doesn't I can't do a man's work. And up here in Yorkshire, the pride that I feel in managing, the fact that I can and do make our lives stay on track, if only just, curdles into unease. Suddenly I realise that a family needs a lot of care, a lubricant to keep it running smoothly; whereas my little family is just about bumping along and the brakes are starting to squeal.

Richard walks back into the kitchen, minus nappy, puts his arms round my waist, hoists me up on to the rail of the Aga, rests his head in the crook of my neck and starts to twiddle my hair. Just like Ben does.

'Happy, sweetheart?'

It sounds like a question, but really it's an answer. Rich is happy here, I can tell, with the womanly bustle and the fug of baking and me not on the phone every five minutes. 'He's a real homebody, Richard,' says Barbara proudly.

I tell Rich, and I'm only partly joking, that he would have been better off marrying some nice Sloane with a super line in mince pies.

'Well I didn't, because I would have died of boredom. Anyway,' he says, stroking my cheek and tucking a stray tendril of hair behind my ear, 'if we need mince pies I know this incredible woman who can fake them.'

After Christmas lunch with the Shattocks I just want to cuddle up with Leonardo DiCaprio in *Titanic* on the TV, but instead end up shadowing Ben round the sitting room as he hauls himself up on to spindly occasional tables, chewing on lamp wires or snatching fistfuls of silvered almonds. I weigh up the danger of denying him silvered almonds, thereby risking an embarrassing tantrum ('Can't she even control her own child?'), or allowing him to go ahead and choke, thereby endangering his life and Barbara and Donald's Wilton carpet.

I manage to escape while Ben is having his nap. Lying on the bed with my laptop, I compose an e-mail to another world.

From: Kate Reddy, Wrothly, Yorkshire
To: Debra Richardson
Dearest debs, how was it 4 U?
All the elements of the traditional English Xmas here: sausage rolls, carols, subtle recriminations. Mother-in-law busy preparing emergency food parcel for son neglected by callous City bitch (Me).
You know that I always say I want to be with my children. Well, I really want to be with my children. Some nights, if I get home too late for Emily's bedtime, I go to the laundry basket and I Smell Their Clothes. I miss them so much. Never told anyone that before. And then when I'm with them, like I am now, their need is just so needy. It's like having a whole love affair crammed into a long weekend – passion, kisses, bitter tears, I love you, don't leave me, get me a drink, you like him more than me, take me to bed, you've got lovely hair, cuddle me, I hate you.
Drained & freaked out & need to go back to work soonest for a rest. What kind of mother is afraid of her own children?
Yrs Wrothly,
K8 xxxxxxx

I am about to hit Send, but instead I press Delete. There's only so much you can confess, even to your dearest friend. Even to yourself.

5

Boxing Day

WELL, WE MADE it through the season of goodwill all
right. Except for Boxing Day lunch. I forget the
derivation of Boxing Day, but the feeling of wanting to invite
your loved ones outside one at a time and punch them in the
face, does that come into it somewhere?

Anyway, it was all my fault, Richard said, and he wasn't
wrong exactly, but I plead gross provocation. Whenever we're
at my in-laws' house, I feel as though the children have turned
into hand grenades. Any second the pin may work loose and
they'll explode all over the eau-de-nil chaise longue or take out
an entire cabinet of Royal Worcester egg coddlers. Rich and I
scurry after them, lunging at falling ornaments, fielders in the
dying light of a doomed Test match.

12.03 pm: Today is the Shattocks' annual drinks party.
Barbara has put me on nuts duty – cashews, pistachios, peanuts
for the older kids. Donald's money is new, he owns a chain of
sporting goods shops across the North, but he makes every
effort, as Englishmen will, to make the money look old. Like
growing moss on a freshly laid path. The boys were the first
Shattocks to go to public school, but they went to the best.

As I pour nuts into the family's little crystal finger bowls, I
think how grateful I am to be useful, while a more complicated
feeling brings a pain to my chest. Like heartburn, only I haven't
eaten yet. Christmas at the Shattocks' is hard for me: here I am
in the bosom of a relatively functional family and every Yule
from my childhood reverberates in my bones. I only have to
hear Harry Belafonte singing 'Mary's Boy Child' on Radio 2
and I'm there, with Dad lurching into the kitchen, back from

the pub, bearing some peace offering for my mother – a frothy lace nightie in the wrong size, a gold watch he'd had off a mate on the market. My father always made an entrance like a movie star, sucking up all the available air in the room. Julie and I were left breathing shallowly behind the settee, praying that she'd forgive him again, that she'd have him back so we could have the kind of Christmas that families were meant to have, the kind Richard's family has.

I take some nuts through to the big L-shaped sitting room with the french windows on to the garden. A beaming Donald takes my arm and presents me to one of his golf chums. Somewhere in his sixties, the man is wearing a sports jacket and red shirt with a tie only marginally less busy than the test card.

'Jerry, can I introduce my daughter-in-law Katharine. Katharine's a career woman, you know. Kept her own name. Very modern.'

Jerry perks up: 'Do you travel with your work, then, Katharine?'

'Yes, I go to the States a lot and . . .'

'So who looks after Richard when you're away?'

'Richard. I mean Richard looks after Richard. And the children. And we have a nanny who looks after the children and . . . Well, it all works somehow.'

Jerry nods distractedly as though I'm bringing him news of some Minoan aqueduct. 'Oh, that's marvellous. Do you know Anita Roddick, love?'

'No, I –'

'You've got to hand it to her, haven't you? All that hair. Very striking for her age. And not a spare ounce on her. They often let themselves go at that time of life, don't they?'

'Who?'

'Italians.'

'I didn't know Anita Roddick was Italian –'

'Oh, aye. There's a woman up our road, spit of the young Claudia Cardinale before the macaroni cheese got to her. What line did Donald say you were in?'

'I'm a fund manager, sort of investing money on behalf of

pension funds and companies in—'

'Can't go far wrong with the Bradford and Bingley, I always say. Thirty-day deposit account instant access.'

'That sounds good.'

'I suppose it's your lot want us in the ruddy Euro, is it?'

'No—'

'Before you know it, Katharine, Gordon Brown'll have us going down the Feathers with a pocket of Krautmarks. What did we win the war for? Answer me that.'

There is a point during these conversations when the person you are for the rest of the year, struggling to come up for air through the layers of wrapping paper and saturated fats, finally bursts out like the alien from John Hurt's chest.

'Actually, Jerry,' I say more loudly than I intend, 'entry to the Euro will depend on the level of fiscal imbalances, progress in supply-side reform and the state of the Capital Account. Anyway, the global economy is run by Alan Greenspan and the Federal Reserve, so really our focus should be on the US rather than Europe.'

Jerry rears up and backs into the china cabinet which tinkles like sleighbells. 'Well, it's been lovely talking to you, love. Richard's a lucky lad, isn't he? I say, Barbara, your Richard's done well for himself. Your Katharine could go on *Countdown*, she's got that good a head on her shoulders and a lovely little face with it.'

Clutching a tumbler of medium sherry, I let myself out through the french windows and fall gratefully into the garden's biting air. Lower myself on to the rockery. Come on, Kate, why did you put down that good-hearted old boy in there just now? Showing off. Showing him I wasn't just another blonde in a twinset. He didn't mean any harm. How's poor Jerry supposed to know what manner of woman I am, what strange new species? Back in London, at Edwin Morgan Forster, they think I'm deviant for having a life outside the office. Up here, people think I'm a freak for having a job instead of a life.

Yesterday, I told Barbara that Emily loved broccoli. I've no idea if that's true. At EMF, on the other hand, I pretend I read the *FT*'s Lex column every day before work, although if I actually did I wouldn't sometimes snatch those thirteen minutes on the bus with Emily, testing her spellings, chatting, holding hands. Double agents lie for a living.

3.12 pm: The entire family – Donald, Barbara, the rest of the grown-ups and assorted grandchildren – is crunching across a field, picking its way between Friesians. A heavy frost has turned the cowpats into doilies; the children jump on them, liberating the evil green liquid beneath. Sky like a Brillo pad – scouring clouds suddenly pierced by implausible, am-dram spotlight of sunshine. Am just admiring the warmth it casts on the facing hills when my mobile rings. Cows and Barbara simultaneously open long-lashed eyes wide like Elizabeth Taylor told to play shocked.

'What is that dreadful noise, Katharine?'

'Sorry, Barbara, it's my phone. Hello? Yes, *hello*?'

A man's voice bounces off a satellite into the Dales. It's Jack Abelhammer, the American client Rod gave me as a consolation prize for not getting a pay rise. The voice is full of Waspish scorn (Yanks can't believe the lazy Brit habit of taking an entire week off between Christmas and New Year). I have yet to meet Mr Abelhammer, but he sounds like he's capable of living up to his name and I'm the one about to get nailed.

'For Chrissake, Katharine Reddy, there's no one in your office. I've been trying for two hours. Have you seen what's happened to Toki Rubber Company?'

'I think I must have missed that, Mr Abelhammer. Just remind me.' Play for time, Kate. Play for time.

EMF recently bought a big slug of shares for Abelhammer's fund in Toki Rubber of Japan. Now it turns out that the genius who struck the deal failed to spot that Toki Rubber owns a small US company which manufactures cot mattresses. The same mattresses which have been withdrawn in the States after scientists established a possible link to cot death. Sod. Sod. Sod.

Abelhammer says that when the market opened in Tokyo yesterday, the price collapsed by 15 per cent. Cratered. Can feel my stomach plunge now by equal percentage.

'That stock came highly recommended by you,' snaps Abelhammer. I picture him, a scowling silver tycoon in some New York tower. 'What exactly are you going to do about it? Miss Reddy, can you hear me?'

Spooked from their daydreams, a couple of Friesians have wandered over for an exploratory nuzzle of my borrowed Barbour. Whatever happens, I must not let my most important client know I am being licked by a cow.

'Well, Mr Abelhammer, sir, what we must avoid here at all costs is a knee-jerk reaction. Clearly, I need a few days for further analysis. And obviously, I'll be talking to our Japanese analyst. As you're probably aware, Roy is the best in the business.' (A lie: analyst is Romford cokehead currently on shag'n'vac in Dubai with pole-dancer he picked up in Faringdon Road. Chances of getting appalling little runt out of bed: nil.) 'And I will be calling you with a considered plan of action.'

Across the field, into Abelhammer's chilly transatlantic silence floats my mother-in-law's voice, clear as a cathedral bell: 'Really, these Americans, absolutely no sense of tradition.'

7.35 pm: Back at the house I am swabbing dung off Emily's Mini Boden trousers. Lilac needlecord. (Paula seems to have packed for a week in Florida not Yorkshire. Should have done the suitcase myself.) Cheryl comes into the utility room and pulls a face. Her kids were wearing brown drip-dry polyester. 'I find it terribly practical.'

2.35 am: A figure is stooping over our bed. Sit up, reach blindly for light switch. It's my father-in-law.

'Katharine, there's a Mr Hokusai on the telephone, calling from Tokyo. Seems very anxious to talk to you. Could you kindly take it in the study?'

Donald's voice is frighteningly calm, as if withholding all the things he could possibly say. As I stumble past him in my nightie, he raises a silvery eyebrow. Catch sight of myself in the

57

hall mirror. Realise am not wearing nightie. Am wearing Agent Provocateur bra.

3.57 am: Emily is sick. Excitement, I think: too much Tweenies chocolate plus large and unaccustomed helping of Mummy. I'm just off the phone to the Japanese rubber company and slipping into bed next to a snoring Richard when there is a cry from the neighbouring room, as though an animal were being hunted in a dream. I go in and find Em sitting up in bed, cupping her left ear. There is sick everywhere: over her nightie, her duvet – oh God, *Barbara's* duvet – her blankie, her sheep, her hippopotamus, even her hair. She looks up at me with beseeching horror: Emily hates any loss of dignity.

'I feel sick, Mummy, don't let me be sick again,' she pleads.

I carry her across the landing to the bathroom and hold her over the toilet, arching her clear of the rim as my mother always did for me. I feel my palm cool on her forehead; feel her stomach stiffen suddenly and then relax as what's left in there comes out. Then, when I have undressed us both, we take a silent bath together and I comb the cranberries from her hair.

After finding clean nightwear, changing the bed linen and tucking Em in, I scrape the Russian salad gunk as best I can from Barbara's duvet cover which I leave to soak in the bath, then I lie on the floor next to my child's bed and estimate the losses if Abelhammer is so furious that the Salinger Foundation quits Edwin Morgan Forster. Two hundred million dollar account. Heads will roll. And my head is not even highlighted. No time. Emily presented me with a drawing of myself yesterday.

'Oh, is Mummy wearing a lovely brown hat?' I exclaimed.

'No, silly, the top of your hair is brown and the bottom is yellow.'

I'm surprised to feel big little-girl tears start to roll down my cheeks and drip warmly into my ears.

8.51 am: Surface. Feel like a diver in lead boots. Emily is still asleep. Touch her forehead; much cooler. Downstairs, Barbara is tight-lipped in Windsmoor and shooting charged glances at the kitchen clock.

'Katharine, I hope you don't think I'm speaking out of turn, but you want to put a bit of make-up on before you come downstairs. You don't want Richard thinking we've stopped making an effort, do we? They soon cotton on to that sort of thing, do men.'

I tell her I'm sorry, but that I've been up half the night with Emily and I haven't really slept. I sense her eyes on me: that cool, appraising stare she gave when Rich first brought me home: the way you might look at a heifer in a show-ring.

'Oh, I know you're peaky at the best of times, love,' she owns cheerfully. 'But a spot of rouge can work wonders. Personally, I can't speak too highly of Helena Rubinstein's Autumn Bonfire. Cup of tea?'

I didn't mean to describe myself as the main breadwinner at Boxing Day lunch. It just came out that way. There was a general conversation around the table about New Year's resolutions and Donald – upright but wistful, like Bernard Hepton in *Colditz* – said perhaps Katharine could work a bit less in the coming twelve months. That would have been fine – gallant, sweet, caring even – if my sister-in-law hadn't added with a snort, 'So the kids can pick her out in an identity parade.'

Oooff. Clearly Cheryl had had one glass of red wine too many, and what was required of me was to rise above it. But after three days of enforced wifely humility, I didn't feel able to rise above anything. And that was when I began a sentence with the words, 'As the main breadwinner in our house . . .' A sentence I would never finish as it happens because, when I looked at the startled faces round the table, it seemed safer to let it die away like a bugle call.

Donald pushed his specs up his nose and helped himself to parsnips, which I know he can't stand. Barbara put her hand to her throat as though to cover the puce flush of shock spreading beneath. It couldn't have been worse if I had announced breast implants or lesbianism or not liking Alan Bennett. All upsets in the natural order.

Rich, meanwhile, was making valiant efforts to pretend I had said bread sauce instead of breadwinner and was dispensing lumps of that porridgey glue to his relatives. 'The trouble with you, Kate,' he told me later in our room as he sat on the bed while I packed a bag for my crisis meeting in London, 'is you think that if people have the correct data they will buy your analysis. But they don't want your data. People – parents – they get to an age when new information is frightening, not helpful. They don't want to know that you earn more than me. For my father it's literally unthinkable.'

'And for you?'

He looks down at his shoelaces. 'Well, to be honest, I have a pretty hard time with it myself.'

1.06 pm, 27 December: The heating has bust on the train down to London, the windows of the empty carriage are iced up; it's like travelling inside a giant Fox's glacier mint. I join the queue at the buffet. My fellow Christmas refugees are all eager for alcohol. Either they have no family or are in flight from too much family, both of them lonely and exhilarating conditions.

I purchase four miniatures – whisky, Bailey's, Bailey's, Tia Maria. Back in my seat for just a few seconds when I hear the mobile chirrup in my bag. I can see from the number that it's Rod Task. Before answering, I take the precaution of holding the phone away from my ear.

'OK, can you explain how we bought this shitload of stock in some fucking Jap outfit that makes fucking mattresses that fucking kill kids? Jeezus wept, Katie. Do you hear me?'

I tell Rod that I wish I could hear him, but sadly he's breaking up and the train's about to go into a tunnel. Press Cancel. As I'm mixing the second Bailey's with the whisky, it occurs to me that maybe the reason I got Salinger as a client was because someone knew that Toki Rubber was about to go belly-up and unloaded it on to me. Naïve, Kate, naïve.

A few seconds later, Rod rings back so that he and I can have a conference call with the appalling Abelhammer in New York. Delivering the customary reassurances to a client three and a half thousand miles away, I watch my words rising up in steamy rings of hot air. With a gloved finger, I scratch one word on the frosted glass: RICH.

'Hoping for a Lottery win, are you, love?' the Scouse steward says, pointing at the window when he comes along later to collect my empties.

'What? Oh, Rich isn't money, I say, 'he's a man. Rich is my husband.'

Must Remember: New Year's Resolutions

Adjust work-life balance for healthier, happier existence. Get up an hour earlier to maximise time available. Spend more time with your children. Learn to be self with children. Don't take Richard for granted! Entertain more – Sunday lunch & so on. Relaxing hobby?? Learn Italian. Take advantage of London – theatres, Tate Modern, etc. Stop cancelling stress-busting treatments. Start a present drawer like proper organised mother. Attempt to be size 10. Personal trainer? Call friends, hope they remember you. Ginseng, oily fish, no wheat. Sex? New dishwasher. Helena Rubinstein Autumn Bonfire.

6

The Court of Motherhood

A DENSE, CHURCHY HUSH fills the oak-panelled room. In the dock stands a blonde in her mid-thirties dressed in a white cotton nightie with a red bra clearly visible underneath. The woman looks exhausted yet defiant. As she faces the gentlemen of the court, she tilts her head like a gun dog that has got the scent. Occasionally, though, when she scratches behind her right ear, you could be forgiven for thinking she is close to tears.

'Katharine Reddy,' booms the judge, 'you appear before the Court of Motherhood tonight charged with being a working mother who overcompensates with material things for not being at home with her children. How do you plead?'

'Not guilty,' says the woman.

The prosecuting counsel jumps to his feet. 'Can you please tell the court, Mrs Shattock, I believe that is your correct name, can you tell the court what you gave your children, Emily and Benjamin, for Christmas?'

'Well, I can't remember exactly.'

'She can't remember,' sneers the prosecution. 'But it would be fair to say, would it not, that presents approaching the value of £400 were purchased?'

'I'm not quite sure –'

'For two small children, Mrs Shattock. Four. Hun. Drud. Powwnds. Am I also to understand that, having explained to your daughter Emily that Santa Claus would buy her either a Barbie bicycle or a Brambly Hedge doll's house or a hamster in a cage with a retractable water bottle, you then went ahead and gave her all of the three aforementioned items plus a Beanie Baby she had expressed interest in during a brief stop in a petrol station outside Newark?'

'Yes, but I bought the doll's house first and then she wrote to Santa and said she wanted a hamster . . .'

'Is it also true that when your mother-in-law, Mrs Barbara Shattock, asked you if Emily liked broccoli you said that she absolutely loved it, even though you were at that time unsure of the answer?'

'Yes, but I couldn't possibly tell my husband's mother that I didn't know whether my child liked broccoli.'

'Why not?'

'It's the kind of things mothers know.'

'Speak up!' demands the judge.

'I said mothers know that kind of thing.'

'And you don't?'

The woman can feel her throat constricting and when she swallows she gets no moisture in her mouth, but a thin cardboardy coating. This, she thinks, is what it would taste like if you were forced to eat your words. When she starts to speak again, it is very softly.

'Sometimes I don't know what the children like,' she admits. 'I mean, the things they like change from day to day, hour to hour even, Ben couldn't stand fish and then suddenly . . . You see, I'm not always there when they change. But if I told Barbara that she'd think I wasn't a proper mother.'

The prosecution turns to the jury, his long, pale face twitching with a tight little smirk: 'Will the court please note that the defendant prefers to tell a lie rather than suffer any embarrassment.'

The woman shakes her head fiercely. She appeals to the judge. 'No, no, no. That is so unfair. It's not embarrassment, Your Honour. I can't describe it. It feels like shame, a deep, animal shame, like not being able to pick out your own hands or face. Look, I know there's no way that Richard, he's my husband, well there's no way that Richard would know whether Emily liked broccoli or not, but him not knowing seems normal. A mother not knowing feels unnatural . . .'

'Quite so,' says the judge jotting down the words 'unnatural' and 'mother' and underlining them.

'Obviously,' the woman says quickly, fearing she may already have said too much, 'obviously, I don't want to spoil my children.'

We see her stop speaking. She appears to be thinking. Of course, she wants to spoil her children. *Desperately.* She needs to believe that, in this way at least, they're better off for her not being with them. She wants Emily and Ben to have all the things she never had. But she can't tell the men in the court that. What do they know about turning up on your first day at junior school in the wrong shade of grey jersey, because your mum bought yours at the Oxfam shop and everyone else in the class was in the new gunmetal range purchased from Wyatt & Moore? Nothing. She knows they know nothing about what it is to have nothing.

Clearing her throat, the woman attempts to find the cool, unemotional register that experience has taught her the men will respect: 'Why do I work so hard if not to buy my children things that give them pleasure?'

The judge peers over his half-moon glasses: 'Mrs Shattock, we are not concerned here with the realms of philosophical speculation.'

'Well, maybe you should be,' the woman says, rubbing fiercely behind her right ear. 'There's more to being a good mother than an in-depth knowledge of vegetable preferences.'

'Silence! Silence in court!' says the judge. 'Call Richard Shattock.'

Oh no, please don't let them call Richard. Rich wouldn't testify against me, would he?

Part Two

7

Happy New Year

Monday, 5.57 am: 'Aaaannnd *open* the world. Aaaand *close* the world. *Open* the world aaand *close* the world.'

I am standing in the middle of the living room, legs wide apart and arms above my head. In each of my hands I hold a ball, one of those squidgy ones that feels like a giant octopus head. With the balls, I am required to draw a circle in the air. 'Aaaaaand open the world, aaaaand close the world.'

The person telling me to do this is a loopily cheerful fifty-something woman with a crystal on a chain round her neck; she probably runs a protection league for animals that everybody else would be perfectly happy to see run over – rats, bats, stoats. Fay is a personal trainer hired to help me with my intensive new year relaxation and exercise programme. I got her over the phone from the Juno Academy of Health and Fitness. Not cheap, but I figure it will save me a lot if I can get back into my pre-pregnancy clothes. Plus, it must work out less expensive than joining gyms that I never have time to visit.

'The only exercise you ever get, Kate, is lifting your wallet with all those health club membership cards in it,' says Richard.

Unfair. Unfair and true. According to conservative estimates, my annual swim at the most recent health club, sneaked between lunch at Conundrum and a new business pitch in Blackfriars, worked out at £47.50 a length.

Anyway, there I was expecting Cindy Crawford in pink Lycra and what do I find when I open the door but Isadora Duncan in green Loden. A windblown færy creature, my personal trainer was sporting the kind of double-decker cape previously only worn by Douglas Hurd as Foreign Secretary. 'The name's Fay,' she said and, from one of those carpet bags that Mary Poppins keeps her hatstand in, she produced what she called 'my Chi balls'.

Rotating the Chi balls in slow, patient circles is not exactly what I had in mind. I ask if we could possibly move on and do some work on my stomach. 'You see, I had a Caesarean and there's this overhang of skin which just won't go away.'

Fay shivers at the interruption, fastidious as a greyhound at a sheepdog trial. 'My approach is to the whole person, Katya. I may call you Katya, mayn't I? You see, once we have freed up the mind, we can move on to the body, gradually introducing the various parts to each other until we establish a harmonious conversation.'

'Actually,' I tell Fay with as much harmony as I can muster, 'I'm incredibly busy, so if we could just say, Hello, stomach muscles, remember me? that would be terrific.'

'You don't have to tell me you're busy, Katya. I can see by the weight of your head. You really have a very heavy head. A poor stressed head. And the neck ligaments. *Loose! Looose! Loooose!* Barely supporting your poor head. And this in turn is bringing truly intolerable pressure on to the lower lumbar region.'

And there I was thinking you paid these people to make you feel better. After thirty minutes of Fay, I feel as though my next appointment should be with an embalmer. Now she suggests I lie flat on my back, extend my arms over my head and pretend I'm lying on a rack. My mind flicks to thoughts of traitors having secrets dragged out of them in the Tower of London at 25 quid an hour by ye olde personal torturer. According to Fay, this exercise will realign my spine, the spine that is one of the saddest and most misshapen Fay has ever seen.

'That's it, that's it, Katya, excellent,' she beams. 'Now, bring your arms slowly forward over your head and repeat after me, If we com-pete, we are not com-plete. If we com-pete, we are not com-pleeete.'

7.01 am: Departure of Fay. Truly intolerable pressure lifts immediately. Treat myself to bowl of Honey Nut Loops: I cannot do exercise and self-denial in the same morning. Sitting at the kitchen table am suddenly aware of unaccustomed sound, a dry scratchy wireless hiss. Look round the room for its source. It takes a few seconds to track it down: silence. The sound of nothing is shouting in my ears. I have five minutes to myself, drinking it in, before Emily and Ben come whooping through the door.

After the holidays, I always sense a special edge to the children's neediness. Far from being satisfied by the time we've had together they seem famished, as ravenous for my attention as newborns. It's as though the more they have of me, the more they're reminded how much they want. (Maybe that's true of every human appetite. Sleep begets sleep; eating makes you hungry; fucking stokes desire.) Clearly, my kids have not grasped the principle of Quality Time. Since we got back from Richard's parents, every time I go out the door it's like the Railway Children seeing their father off to jail. Ben's face is a popped red balloon of anguish. And Emily has started doing that hideous coughing thing in the night – she hacks and hacks until she makes herself sick. When I mentioned it to Paula, for reassurance, she said, 'Attention-seeking,' with a quiet note of triumph. (Implying that attention is lacking, obviously.)

Then there are Emily's non-stop requests for me to play with her, always at the most inconvenient times, as if she was testing me and at the same time willing me to fail. Like this morning, when I am desperate to get to a doctor's appointment, she comes up and hangs on my skirt.

'Mummy, I spy with my little eye something beginning with B.'

'Not now, Em.

'Oh, *pleeeze*. Something beginning with B.'

'Breakfast?'

'No.'

'Bunny rabbit?'

'No.'

'Book?'

'No.'

'I don't know, Emily, I give up.'

'Bideo!'

'Video doesn't begin with B.'

'It do.'

'It *does.*'

'It does begin with B.'

'No, it doesn't. It begins with V. V for van. V for volcano. V for violent. If you choose the right letter, Emily, it saves an awful lot of time.'

'Katie, give her a break, she's only five years old,' says Richard, who has ambled downstairs, hair still damp from the shower, and is now carefully cutting out a Cruella De Vil mask from the back of a Frosties packet.

Glare across the table at him. Trust Rich not to back me up. He is so bad at presenting a united front.

'Well, if I don't correct her, who's going to? Not those all-spellings-are-equally-valid mullahs at school.'

'Kate, it's I-Spy, for God's sake, not *Who Wants To Be A Millionaire?*'

Rich, I notice, no longer looks at me as though I am merely mad. A certain sideways flicker to the eyes and corrugating of the brow suggests he is now weighing up how long he should leave it before calling the ambulance.

'Everything's a competition for you, isn't it, Kate?'

'Everything *is* a competition, Rich, in case you hadn't noticed. Someone wanting to smash your conker, someone wanting a prettier special-edition Barbie, someone wanting to take your biggest client away just to prove you couldn't handle it.' As I unload the dishwasher, I think of Fay and her daft mantra. What was it? 'If we compete, we are not complete.' She should try that one in the offices of Edwin Morgan Forster. 'If we do not com-pete, we are out on the str-eet. In the sh-eet.'

'Mummy, can I watch a bideo? *Pleeeeze* can I watch a bideo?' Emily has climbed up on to the granite worktop and is attaching a Barbie slide to my hair.

'How many times have I told you, we don't watch bideo, Jesus, *video*, at breakfast time.'

'Kate, seriously. What you need is to slow down.'

70

'No, Richard, what I need is a helicopter. I've got an appointment at the doctor's for which I am going to be ten minutes late, making me even later for my conference call with Australia. The Pegasus minicab number's on the board, can you ring? And tell them not to send that weirdo in the Nissan Sunny.'

*

RICHARD IS A nicer person than I am, anyone can see that. But in suffering, in bitter experience, I am his superior and I carry that knowledge like a knife. Why am I so much tougher on Emily than he is? Because I guess I'm scared that Rich would bring up our children to live in an England that doesn't exist. A place where people say, 'After you' instead of 'Me first', a better and a kinder place, for sure, but not one that I have ever lived in or worked in.

Rich had a happy childhood and a happy childhood is a terrific preparation, indeed the only known apprenticeship, for being a happy adult. But happy childhoods are no bloody good for drive and success; misery and rejection and standing in the rain at bus stops are the fuel for those. Consider, for instance, Rich's tragic lack of guile, his repeated undercharging of clients he feels sorry for, his insane optimism up to and including the recent purchase of erotic underwear for a wife who, since the birth of her first child, has come to the nuptial bed in a Gap XXXL T-shirt with a dachsund motif.

Children do that to you. He is Daddy and I am Mummy and finding the time to be Kate and Richard – to be You and Me – well, it slipped down the agenda. Sex now comes under Any Other Business, along with parking permits and a new stair carpet. Emily – she can barely have been three then – once found us kissing in the kitchen and turned on her parents like Queen Victoria discovering a footman with his finger in the port.

'Don't do that. It gives me a tummy ache,' she hissed.

So we didn't.

*

71

8.17 am: Despite my specific request, Pegasus Cars has once again sent round the Nissan Sunny. The back seat is so damp you could start a mushroom farm in here. Tensing both thigh muscles and buttocks and hoiking up my Nicole Farhi grey wool skirt, I do my best to squat an inch or two above the mildew.

When I ask the driver if he could possibly find a quicker route to the surgery, he responds by turning the volume on the tape-deck so high my cheekbones start to shiver in gale-force music. (Is this gangsta rap?)

After my attempt to be friendly to Winston before Christmas, I have no plans to talk to him again. But as I am fighting my way out of the car door, he turns round and, on an exhalation of yellow smoke, says: 'I hope they got something strong enough in there to treat you with, lady.'

Bloody cheek. What does he mean by that? Things don't improve when I get in to see the GP and ask for my annual supply of the Pill. Dr Dobson taps his computer and the screen starts to flash a green hazard light as though I am some devious criminal mastermind wanted by the CIA.

'Ah, Mrs Shattock, I see you haven't had a smear test for . . . How long is it now?'

'Well, I did have one in '96 and you broke the slide. I mean, they wrote and said it had broken in transit and could I come in again. But, obviously, I'd already been in and time is very tight, so if I could please just have my pills?'

'And there has been no time in the last four years when you could drop in for another test?' A basset hound in human form, Dr Dobson has that wet-eyed solicitude common to dogs and caring professionals.

'Well, no. I mean you have to ring for an appointment and hang on for ages because they never seem to answer the phone and . . .'

His finger moves to a date halfway down my notes. 'And on one occasion you failed to cancel. The 23rd of March of last year.'

'Taiwan.'

'I beg your pardon?'

'I was in Taiwan. Hard to cancel when it's the middle of the night in another hemisphere and you haven't got an hour to hang on the phone hoping the receptionist in Drayton Lane will pick up out of idle curiosity.'

The doctor tugs anxiously on his tie – it is beige and apparently woven from Shreddies. 'I see, I see,' he says, clearly not seeing at all. 'Well, I don't think it would be sensible for me to prescribe you another year's worth of Microgynon until you've had your smear, Mrs Shattock. The Government, as you may have heard, is taking a very pro-active role in cervical health.'

'The Government thinks it would be better for me to have another baby?'

He shakes his head sadly: 'I wouldn't put it that way. The Government is merely keen to encourage women to avoid a life-threatening illness with a simple test.'

'Well, if I have another baby I really will be dead.' God, I can't believe I just said that. What do you mean by that, Kate?

'There's no need to get upset, Mrs Shattock.'

'I am not upset,' I insist, rather too shrilly. 'I'm just a very busy woman who doesn't need any more children right at the moment if you don't mind. So if you could please let me have my pills.'

The doctor takes a slow, careful note with an ancient biro that has a clump of ink snot on its nose. It gives every word it writes a pre-smudged outline. He asks me if I have any other symptoms.

'But I'm not ill.'

'Are you sleeping properly, how is your sleep?'

For the first time since Loopy Fay arrived at six this morning, my features relax enough to form a smile. 'Well, I have an eleven-month-old son with teeth coming through. Sleep doesn't really go with the territory, does it?'

Dr Dobson returns my look, but with wary creases at the edges – creases that act like inverted commas around the smile. I realise that the expression on his face can properly be

73

described as long-suffering. Who is long in suffering if not a doctor? The amount of pain he must see. Anyway, he tells me to come in any time I feel I need to. Any time at all. Says he will ring down to the nurse right away and see if she can fit me in for a smear now. 'You can surely spare ten minutes?'

I surely can't, but I do.

*

Offices of Edwin Morgan Forster, 9.06 am
Arrive late and dying to go to the loo. Will have to wait. Need to submit seven fund reports having talked to twelve different managers by Wednesday. Also must present in-depth briefing on Japanese Toki Rubber Company fiasco by Wednesday. Then Rod Task pitches up at my desk and tells me I have to go and salvage my career by giving blowjob to Jack Abelhammer in New York on, why, Wednesday. Not sure the term blowjob was actually used, but he definitely said 'on your knees, honey'.

From: Kate Reddy
To: Candy Stratton
Terrific start to the day. Smear test. Like having sex with the Tin Man. Can't they make that damn probe out of rubber, or would they just get sad women like me queuing up to have it done twice a week?
Get in here sixteen minutes late and Guy is at my desk telling everyone he's Almost Certain that Kate will be in At Some Point. Felt like Mummy Bear and wanted to growl, Who's been sitting in my chair? Said nothing. Wouldn't give the little creep the satisfaction.
Plus I have to go to NYC to 'placate' client. Have never met Jack Abelhammer, but I H8 him already.

From: Candy Stratton
To: Kate Reddy
Dear Desdemona, U shd watch Guy 'Iago' Chase. Don't drop that handkerchief, honey. He wants yr job so badly his gums ache.

74

PS: Have fckd brainless Scarecrow and Cowardly Lion (Sat night, Nobu), but never tried Tin Man. Able Hammer sounds prmsng tho.

From: Kate Reddy
To: Debra Richardson
Glad to hear you're still alive after Xmas. Not sure I am. (How can I tell?) Sorry about Felix's knee and Ruby's ear infection. Can someone pls coin new word for holiday with children that doesn't imply
a/ holiday
b/ rest
c/ pleasure.
helliday?
K xxxxx

2.35 pm: Just as I am going into European Group meeting, Paula calls. Says she thinks she may have caught the sick bug Emily had over Christmas. Is it all right if she leaves early today? Think: No, that is Absolutely Out Of The Question, this is your first day back at work after two whole weeks off. Say: Yes, of course, you poor thing, you sound terrible.

I ring Richard at the office. He is in a meeting about designing some Peace Pagoda for British Nuclear Fuels. Leave urgent message asking if he can get home and hold the fort soonest.

8.12 pm: Squeak home in time for Emily's bed. Bump into Richard in the hall. Says no, he hasn't sorted out the new parking permit yet. Yes, they both had their hair washed. Run upstairs. Am desperate to make it up to her after this morning's harsh words over I-Spy. All milky warmth, my daughter curls my hair round her finger. 'Who is your favourite Tweenie, Mama?'
   'I don't know, sweetheart.'
   'Milo is the biggest.'
   'Ah. What did you do at school today, love?'
   'Nothing.'

'Oh, I'm sure you did. What did you do, Em?'
'I spy with my little eye something beginning with W.'
'Window?'
'No.'
'Wallpaper?'
'No.'
'Well, what could it be, I wonder. Wecorder?'
'Yesssss! You are clever, Mummy.'
'I try, darling. Really I do.'

Must Remember

Thank You letters. Dismember Christmas tree and hide in rubbish bags from binmen who won't take trees away (Not part of our job, love). Cheque for Bouncy Babies class (94 quid a term – cheaper to enrol in astronaut training). Emily new ballet leotard (blue not pink). Find osteopath to check out 'heavy head'. Ring Mum, return call from sister or she will be confirmed in view am posh cow who has lost touch with her roots. HIGHLIGHTS! Passport expiry please God no. Ask cool friend what is gangsta rap. No cool friends. Make cool friend. Downstairs ballcock Richard? Babysitter Sat/Weds. Pay newspaper bill/read back issues of newspapers, call nanny temp agency if Paula still ill. See amazing new kung-fu film – Sitting Tiger? Sleepy Dragon? Trim Ben's nails. Name-tags, dentist appointment, ring Juno Academy of Fitness and book personal trainer who will contract stomach instead of trying to expand soul. Ben birthday Teletubbies cake where? Pelvic floor squeeeze. Return Snow White video to library! Emily school applications GET ORGANISED. Be nicer, more patient person with Emily so doesn't grow up to be needy psychopath. QUOTE FOR NEW STAIR CARPET. Call Jill Cooper-Clark. Social life: invite people Sunday lunch – Simon and Kirsty? Alison and Jon? Think about half-term plans. What already? Yes, already. Swimming party on Sunday for 'Jedda' – girl or boy find out? Empty bladder more frequently. Prepare to meet Jack Abelhammer.

8

Teething Troubles

Tuesday, 4.48 am: There is a scream from Ben's room. A Hammer Horror scream. Third time tonight, or is it fourth? Teething again. And we're already over the legal Calpol limit. I'll probably be exposed in the *News of the World* as Monster Mum Who Doped Tot For Kip. They're right to call it a broken night – cracked and unmendable. You crawl back to bed and you lie there trying to do the jigsaw of sleep with half the pieces missing. Perhaps he'll go back by himself. Please let him go back. It's always around now, when the dark is silvery with the first inkling of light, that you start cutting desperate deals with God. 'Oh God, if You'll just let him go back to sleep, I'll . . .'

I'll what? I'll be a better mother, I'll never complain again, I'll savour every grain of sleep I get from now until my dying day.

No, he won't go back. Benjamin's experimental *are-you-there?* yelps have given way to full-throated Pavarotti aria. (*Nessun Dorma* means None Shall Sleep, doesn't it?) The book tells you to leave baby to cry, but Ben hasn't read the book. He doesn't understand that after forty minutes or so of continuous crying, baby will settle. The book says that Ben may have attachment issues: I think he's just figured out that the Mummy who isn't here in the day is available for nocturnal cuddles.

Brain is willing to get out of bed, but my body lags behind like a morose teenager. Next to me, Richard lies on his back, hands folded across his chest, exhaling king-size sighs. Sleeping like a baby. (Where the hell did that expression come from?)

Climbing the stairs, my legs feel encased in callipers.

Through the landing window I can make out the terrace of houses at the bottom of our garden with their spooky sightless eyes. An early riser turns on a kitchen light and the room ignites with a saffron flare like a match. The windows offer a pretty good view of the wealth of the people inside: our area lies to the north-east of the City, so plenty of astute financial types like me have moved in here and ruined ourselves doing up damp and peeling Victorian wrecks. Our houses are the ones with no covering at the window, their owners preferring to rely on expensively restored shutters while our poorer neighbours still comfort themselves with proper curtains or hide their business behind nets like veils. In the Seventies, couples like us tore out all the old Victorian fittings – fireplaces, cornices, baths with a beast's gnarled claw at each corner – in the name of modernity and now we, in the name of a newer kind of modernity, have paid a fortune to have them put back again. (Is it coincidence that we spend far more than our parents ever did on the restyling and improvement of our homes – homes in which we spend less and less time because we are out earning the money to pay for French chrome mixer taps and stripped oak floors? It's as though home had become some kind of stage set for a play in which we one day hope to star.)

Upstairs, I find Ben rattling the bars of his cot. He grins and extrudes a thread of spittle that bungee jumps off the end of his chin right down to the crotch of his sleepsuit and shimmers there, twirling in the dark.

'Hello, you. What time do you call this, eh?'

I hoist him out and, overcome by the joy of our reunion, he tries a brand-new incisor on my neck. *Ow.*

I never wanted a boy. After Emily, I suspected my body could only make her kind and, anyway, I was more than happy to have another girl – beautiful, self-contained, intricate as a watch. 'Boys are like *so over*,' Candy announced to a lunch for female colleagues this time last year. My bump was so big the wine-bar manager had to fetch a chair, because I couldn't slip inside the booth with everyone else. We all laughed. Nervous,

78

insubordinate laughter, but tinged with triumph: the laugh of the Celts when they knew the Romans' time was nearly up. But then, three days later, they handed him to me in the delivery room. *Him!* Something so small, faced with the vast and implausible task of becoming a man, and I loved him. Loved him like a shot. And he couldn't get enough of me. Still can't. A mother of a one-year-old boy is a movie star in a world without critics.

He's so heavy suddenly, my baby: that lithe body is filling out with boyness. Thighs as dense and plump as a boxer's glove. I carry him to the blue chair, hold his hand and begin to croon our favourite song.

'Lavender's blue dilly dilly, lavender's green,

When I am King dilly dilly, You shall be Queen.'

Mothers have been singing it for centuries and still no one has the faintest clue what it means. The singing of lullabies is a bit like motherhood itself: something to be done instinctively in the dark, although its purpose feels magically clear.

I sense every part of Ben relax, his weight shifting inside the Babygro like sand until he is evenly distributed across my chest. You have to judge the moment just right, you have to guess when doze has deepened into dream. I stand up and move stealthily towards the cot, not letting him drop down until the very last second. *There.* Hallelujah! Then, just when I'm thinking I've got away with it, his eyes snap open. His bottom lip trembles for a few seconds like Rick glimpsing his lost Ilsa in *Casablanca*, then the whole mouth forms a tremulous O and the lungs fill for a reprise of the scream.

(Babies never extend any credit. They have a tyrant's disdain for fairness. They grant no time off for cuddles received, no parole for long hours spent nursing in the dark. You can answer that cry a hundred times and on the 101st they'll still have you court-martialled for desertion.)

'All right, all right. Mummy's here. It's OK, I'm still here.'

We go back to the blue chair, I hold Ben's hand and begin the sleep ritual over again.

5.16 am: Ben finally flat out.

5.36 am: Emily asks me to read a book called *Little Miss Busy*. No.

7.45 am: Paula back today and feeling much better, thank God. Ask her to remember Teletubbies cake for Ben's birthday on Friday, oh, and candles. And go easy on the biscuits in case the other mums are crazy Sugar Ayatollahs. (Last year, Angela Brunt issued a fatwa on *raisins*.) Paula asks me for a large amount of cash, sufficient to cater Buckingham Palace garden party, but don't dare query.

8.27 am: So out of it by the time I get to Broadgate that I pick up two double espressos at Starbucks and down them like vodka shots. I read somewhere that people suffering from sleep deprivation are in what's called a hypnagogic state, a sort of purgatory between sleeping and waking, where surreal images drift across the brain. Like being permanently stuck in a David Lynch movie. This could account for the fact that Rod Task is ceasing to come across as a merely annoying Aussie bully and is starting to resemble unblinking Dennis Hopper with madman's laugh. I sit at my desk wearing the old pair of glasses I keep in the drawer to give an impression of intense cerebral activity, then I select the most mindless task available, one where making mistakes will matter least. So long as I don't buy or sell anything I should be OK. I have twenty-nine e-mails. Can hardly believe the first one.

> From: Jack Abelhammer, Salinger Foundation
> To: Kate Reddy, EMF
> Katharine,
> I can't tell you how relieved I am to have worked the problem
> we ran into over the holidays. Clearly it was a bad time for you
> too.
> It's great news about Toki Rubber and the patenting of the
> unbreakable prophylactic. Amazing recovery of stock. I admire
> your coolness under pressure. Maybe we can celebrate when

you get here on Thursday? Terrific new lobster joint down the street.
Best, Jack

From: Candy Stratton
To: Kate Reddy
What say we hit Corny & Barrw for bottle or 2 so we can get arrestd for disordly cnduct & miss fckg stratgy mtng?
U look wreckd.
C xxxxx

From: Kate Reddy
To: Jack Abelhammer
I don't have to be drunk to be disorderly. Need to go to bed for a week.
love and kisses K8 xxxxxx

From: Kate Reddy
To: Candy Stratton
URGENT! Tell me you just got that msg.

From: Candy Stratton
To: Kate Reddy
Wot msg?

From: Kate Reddy
To: Candy Stratton
About being drunk and disorderly. Quick. HURRY!

From: Candy Stratton
To: Kate Reddy
Srry, hon. U mst have sent to some other lucky gal.

From: Kate Reddy
To: Candy Stratton
To client in New York actually. Am dead woman. No flowers please.

From: Candy Stratton
To: Kate Reddy

Holy shit. Snd anothr Right This Minute.

Dear Sir, my evil, depraved twin, also calling herself Kate Reddy, has just sent U a crazy and offensive e-mail, please ignore.

Anyway, don't worry. Abelhammer's American, right? Remember we have No Sense of Humour.

3.23 pm: Team leaders start to file in for strategy meeting in Rod Task's office. My eyelids are closing like a doll's. Only thing keeping me awake is the thought that Jack Abelhammer will sue for sexual harassment. Yanks are obsessed with 'inappropriate behaviour'. Still no e-mail back from him. Hopes that he will put mine down to charming British eccentricity are fading as fast as the daylight. Lost in a nightmare reverie, I fail to notice the approach of Celia Harmsworth. Extending one bony finger, the Head of Human Resources prods the place where Ben sank his teeth in this morning. Feels at least three lifetimes ago.

'Something on your neck, Katharine?'

'Oh, that. The baby bit me.'

A couple of guys seated at the table start to snigger into their Perrier. Celia gives the wintry smirk you see on the face of the Wicked Queen when she's handing the apple to Snow White. Make my excuses and shoot to ladies' room pursued by Candy. Lighting is terrible in here, but the mirror reveals what appears to be a love bite left by a teenage vampire halfway down my neck. Try foundation. No use. Try face powder. Damn. Bite looks angry and foaming, like an aerial view of Mount Etna.

Candy comes in waving Touche Eclat concealer and starts to dab it on my neck.

'Hey, did Slow Richard give you a hickey? That's terrific, honey.'

'No, the teething baby did. My darling husband slept through it all. But I nearly bit him to wake him up.'

Back in Task's office, my male colleagues are doing what they like doing best: they are having a meeting. If this meeting goes really well, if they drag it out long enough, then they can reward themselves with another meeting tomorrow. With luck, the lack of progress in Meeting One can be reviewed in Meetings Three, Four and Five. When I first arrived as a trainee in the City, I assumed that meetings were for making decisions; it took a few weeks to figure out that they were arenas of display, the Square Mile equivalent of those gorilla grooming sessions you see on wildlife programmes. Some days, watching the guys manoeuvre for position, I reckon I can actually hear the bedside whisper of David Attenborough commentating on the beating of chests and the picking of nits:

'And here, in the very heart of the urban jungle, we see Charlie Baines, a young ape from the US Desk, as he approaches the battle-scarred head of the group, Rod Task. Observe Charlie's posture, the way he indicates his subservience while desperately seeking the senior male's approval . . .'

Most women I know around here have a very low tolerance for this kind of politicking. For obvious reasons, we miss out on the willy-waving that goes on at the corporate urinals, and seeking out some dandruffed drone to flatter him in a wine bar after work does not appeal. Frankly, who has the energy? Like the good, diligent girls we were at school, we still think that if we do our very best and get our work done on time, then

a/ merit will have its own reward and

b/ we can be home by seven.

Well, it doesn't. And we can't.

A light vibration from the phone in my jacket pocket tells me a text message has landed. I press View. It's from Candy.

Q: Hw many men
   ds it tk
   to scrw in
   a lightbulb?
A: One.

He just holds it
& waits for the
world to
revolve arnd him.

My snort of laughter attracts hostile stares from everyone around the table except Candy, who is pretending to take furious notes on Charlie Baines's suggestions for something he calls organisational amelioration.

The review of monthly reports goes on and on. I'm losing my battle with unconsciousness again when I suddenly notice that Rod's computer is still displaying his Christmas screensaver. It shows a snowman gradually disappearing in a blizzard. I think how restful it would be to be buried in snow, how delicious to slip into its cold, accepting nothingness. Think of Captain Oates at the South Pole: 'I am just going outside and may be some time.'

'You've only just come back in, Katie,' snaps Rod, aiming his Mont Blanc pen at me like a dart.

Realise that I must have spoken thoughts aloud like crazy woman who wanders streets dressed in bin bags, giving running commentary on her paranoid inner world.

'Sorry, Rod, it's Captain Oates. I was just quoting him.'

A roomful of fund managers swivel eyes in unison. At the far end of the table, within licking distance of Rod, my assistant Guy's thoroughbred nostrils flare appreciatively at the first whiff of humiliation.

'You remember Captain Oates,' I prompt my boss, 'the one who walked out of a tent to certain death on the Scott expedition to the South Pole.'

'Typical bloody Pom,' snorts Rod. 'Meaningless self-sacrifice. What do they call that, Katie, honour?'

They're all looking at me now; wondering how I'm going to get out of this one. *Come on!* Kate to brain, Kate to brain, are you receiving me?

'Actually, Rod, the South Pole expedition is not a bad management model. How about we apply it to our worst-performing fund? The one that's sapping our resources? Maybe the worst fund needs to take a walk in the snow.'

At the suggestion of cost-cutting, Rod's eyes take on a viscous piggy gleam. 'Huh. Not bad, Katie, not bad. Look into it, Guy.'

Eyes swivel away. That was a close one.

7.23 pm: Crawl home only to find Paula in a huff. A nanny huff can descend as suddenly as sea mist and be twice as treacherous. I can tell this is a bad one because she is actually clearing up the kitchen. What I really want to do is collapse on the sofa with a glass of wine and figure out if any characters I recognise are still alive in *EastEnders*, which I haven't seen since June, enough time for entire dynasties to have fallen in Albert Square and for Phil Mitchell to have spawned at least two more love children with his late brother's ex-wives. Instead, I have to navigate with extreme care around the events of the day. I praise the nutritious contents of Emily's lunchbox, I promise to pick up some name-tags tomorrow, saying it's really no trouble (as if); then I try a blatant cultural suck-up by mentioning a soap star who has just given birth and is featured across seven whole pages in Paula's new copy of *Hello!*

Two pregnancies have wrecked my short-term memory, but left me with freakish, instantaneous recall of the names of all celebrity babies. Knowing the offspring of, say, Demi Moore and Bruce Willis (Rumer, Scout, Tallulah) or Pierce Brosnan (Dylan, also the name of the Zeta-Jones/Michael Douglas first sprog and of Pamela Anderson's second) may not be of any immediate professional use, but it has lifted my stock with Paula on several critical occasions.

'Dylan's getting to be a very popular name now,' observes Paula.

'Yes,' I say, 'but think of Woody Allen and Mia Farrow's little girl. She was called Dylan and ended up wanting to change her name.'

Paula nods: 'And they called the other one something stupid too, didn't they?'

'Satchel!'

'Yeah, that's it.' Paula laughs and I join her: the limitless folly of stars being one of the great democratic pleasures. Can see the huff is starting to lift when I stupidly push my luck and ask Paula if she managed to find a Teletubbies cake.

'I Can't Remember Everything,' she says and sweeps out with a swish of her invisible black cape. While the front door is still reverberating, I discover the cause of the huff lying open on the worktop. The *Evening Standard* has a story about how much London nannies are paid and their incredible perks – top-of-the-range car, private healthcare, gym membership, use of jet, use of horse.

Horse? Thought we were doing OK by letting Paula use my car while I take the bus. Whatever happens, I am *not* going to be blackmailed into paying out more money. We are at our absolute limit already.

8.17 pm: Tell Richard we will have to give Paula a pay rise. Plus possible riding lessons. A terrible row follows in which Rich points out that, after we have paid her tax and National Insurance, Paula actually gets more than he does.

'Whose fault is that?' I say.

'What do you mean by that?'

'Nothing.'

'I know your nothings, Kate.'

Over supper, we sit within a few centimetres of each other at the kitchen table, simmering quietly. Richard has cooked spaghetti and put together an avocado and tomato salad. We start a cautious conversation about the children – Ben's huge appetite, Emily's new fixation with *Mary Poppins* – and I am starting to like him again when, twiddling some spaghetti on to his fork, he casually mentions that he made the pesto himself this afternoon. This is simultaneously admirable and horribly demoralising. I can't bear it.

'How did you find time to make pesto? And the plates? I suppose you'll be taking up pottery next. Why the hell can't you do something that needs doing? How about replacing the parking permit for instance?'

'The new parking permit is in the car,' he says, 'if madam would take a few seconds out of her schedule to look.'

'Oh, we are the ideal husband, aren't we?'

There is a screech of metal on wood as Rich scrapes his chair away from the table: 'I give up, Kate. You ask me to do things to help out and then when I do them you despise me for it.'

Somehow I can't formulate a reply to this. It seems both an incredibly brutal thing to say and impossible to argue with. Women often joke that they need a wife to take care of them, and they mean it: we all need a wife. But don't expect us to thank the men who assume the role of homemaker for taking it away from us.

'Kate, we have to talk.'

'Not now, Rich, I need a bath.'

*

STILL OUT OF bath oils. I find an old packet of lavender salts at the bottom of the airing cupboard. It promises to 'soothe and motivate': I add some of Ben's Pirate Pete bubbles, which turn the water school-uniform navy.

I climb into the scalding blue lagoon and lie back with my favourite reading matter – in recent years, let's be honest, my only reading matter. Better than any fiction, Jameson's *Country Property Guide* is a glossy brochure crammed with photographs of desirable properties for sale around the British Isles. We could exchange the Hackney Heap for, say, a converted mill in the Cotswolds or a pocket-size castle in Peeblesshire. (Where is Peeblesshire? Sounds a bit far.) The pictures are fabulous, but what I really like are the specifications. On page 18, there is a house in Berkshire boasting an annexe study with a barrelled ceiling and gardens full of mature fruit trees. What is a barrelled ceiling? I'm not quite sure, but I want one. And mature fruit trees! I picture myself wafting through a wood-panelled library where there would be freshly cut blossom in tall vases on the way to the country kitchen boasting a blend of traditional

87

cupboards and up-to-the-minute appliances. Standing next to the Aga – not for cooking in, I would be using the Neff double-oven for that – I would write dates on the labels of the jelly made from apples picked from mature fruit trees in extensive gardens while my children played contentedly in the recessed nook upholstered in tasteful fabrics.

'Kate's porn.' That's what Richard calls the Jameson's brochure when he comes across a copy stashed guiltily under my side of the bed. He's got a point. All the mouth-watering pictures, laid out for my viewing pleasure, allow you to take possession of those lives without having to go to the trouble of actually leading them. The more depressed I get in my own house, the more consuming my property lust.

Thinking of Rich reminds me of our pesto fight and I wince at my part in it. His very kindness and sanity are enough to inspire the opposite in me. Why? Richard thinks that I indulge Paula, that I let her get away with things no employee you reward with generous pay and conditions should be allowed to get away with. He thinks she's a reasonably bright twenty-five-year-old girl from Kent who, while being pretty nice to our kids, tries to take us for every penny she can. He thinks she deliberately shrinks his socks if he asks her to do anything outside her job description. He thinks she has too much power in our house. He's right. But Rich doesn't worry about childcare the way I worry: men think about childcare with their wallets, women feel it in their wombs. Phones may have become cordless, but mothers never will.

Me, I look at Paula and I see the person who is with my children all the hours I'm not: a person I have to rely on to love and to cherish and to watch out for the first symptoms of meningitis. If she leaves the place in a mess, if she makes a petty point of not putting the dishwasher on because it contains adult as well as junior crockery, if she doesn't give me the correct change from the supermarket and 'loses' the receipts, then I'm not going to make a fuss.

People say the trouble with professional women of my generation is that we don't know how to behave with servants.

Wrong. The trouble with professional women of my generation is that we *are* the servants – forelock-tuggingly grateful to any domestic help, for which we pay through the nose, while struggling to hold down the master's job ourselves.

When I first went back to work, I put my daughter into daycare. There's a nursery about ten minutes' walk from us, and I liked the sunny, resilient Scotswoman who ran it. But, gradually, things started to get to me. The Baby Room was small and lined with twelve cots: I'd persuaded myself it was cosy when we first went to look round, but every day I dropped Emily off it looked more like a Romanian orphanage styled by Habitat. When I asked Moira how the little ones could take a nap with all the noise from the big kids next door, she shrugged and said, 'Och, they get used to it in the end.' And then there were the fines. If you picked up your child any later than 6.30 from Children's Corner, they charged you 10 quid for the first ten minutes, £50 for any longer. I was always later than 6.30. Shame sloshed around like bile in my stomach on the sprint from the Tube to collect her.

Surrounded by thirty other kids, Emily picked up every infection going. Her first winter cold ran from October through March and her baby nose was encrusted with verdigris. Having provided the bacteria for the infection, the nursery was always extremely keen that you keep your sick child at home, with no reduction in fees. I can remember hours on the phone in work talking to temp agencies, pretending to be calling clients, or begging help from friends. (And I hate asking for favours: hate the feeling of being indebted.) Then, one bitter morning, I had to drop a feverish Em off at the house of someone who knew someone in my post-natal mother and baby group who lived in Crouch End. At the end of the day, the woman reported that Emily had cried constantly, save for an hour, when they had watched a video of *Sleeping Beauty* that seemed to comfort her. That day my daughter formed her first sentence: 'Want go home.' But I was not there to hear it, nor was I at the home where she so badly wanted to go.

So, no, Paula may not be ideal. But what is ideal? Mummy

staying at home and laying down her life for small feet to walk over. Would you do that? Could I do that? You don't know me very well if you think I could do that.

I get out of the bath, apply some aqueous cream to scaly pink patches on hands, back of knees and ears, wrap myself in robe and go into the study to check messages before bed.

From: Jack Abelhammer
To: Kate Reddy
Katharine, I don't remember mentioning drink, but disorderly sounds great. Bed for a week could be a problem: may need to reschedule the diary. Perhaps we should make it an oyster bar? love Jack

Love? From a major client? Oh God, Kate. Now see what you've gone and done.

Must Remember

Cut Ben's nails, Xmas Thank You letters? Also letter bollocking council about failure to remove Christmas tree. Humiliate ghastly Guy in front of Rod to show who's boss. Learn to send txt messages. Ben birthday – find Teletubbies cake. Ballet leotard (pink not blue!). Present – dancing Tinky Winky or improving wooden toy? Dancing Tinky Winky AND improving wooden toy. Emily shoes/schools/ teach her to read. Call Mum, call Jill Cooper-Clark, MUST return sister's call – why Julie sounding so pissed off with me? Only person in London not seen brill new film – Magic Tiger, Puffing Dragon? Half-term when/what? Invite friends for Sunday lunch. Buy pine nuts and basil to make own pesto, cookery crash course (Leith's or similar). Summer holiday brochures. Get Jesus an exercise ball. Quote for stair carpet? Lightbulbs, tulips, lip salve, Botox?

9

The First Time I Saw Jack

7.03 am: I am hiding in the downstairs loo with my suitcase to avoid Ben. He is next door in the kitchen, where Richard is giving him breakfast. I am desperate to go in, but tell myself it's not fair to snatch a few selfish minutes of his company and then leave an inconsolable baby. (The book says children get over Separation Anxiety by two years, but no age limit given for mothers.) Better he doesn't see me at all. Squatting in here on the laundry basket, I have time to study the room and notice swags of grey fluff drifting down the window, like witch's curtains. (Our cleaner, Juanita, suffers from vertigo and, quite understandably, cannot clean above waist height.) Also the mermaid mosaic splashback was left half-tiled by our builder when we refused to give him any more cash, so is all tits and no tail.

Through the closed door, I can make out muffled brum-brums followed by Ben's gluey, Sid James cackle. Rich must be pretending that spoonfuls of Shreddies are advancing cars to get him to open his mouth. A honk from outside announces the arrival of Pegasus.

I'm slipping out of my own house like a thief when there is an accusatory 'Woo-hoo' from the Volvo parked across the street. Angela Brunt, ringleader of the local Muffia. Face like a Ford Anglia. With protuberant headlamp peepers set in a tri-angular skull, Angela is heroically plain. It's barely seven o'clock, what's she doing out? Probably just back from taking Davina to Pre-Dawn Japanese. Give Angela thirty seconds and she'll ask me if I've got Emily into a school yet.

'Hello, Kate, long time no see. Have you got Emily into a school yet?'

Five seconds! Yes, and Angela has beaten her own world record for educational paranoia. Tempted to tell her we're considering the local state primary. With any luck will induce massive on-the-spot coronary. 'I think St Stephen's is still a possibility, Angela.'

'Really?' The headlamps do a startled circuit of their sockets. 'But how are you going to get her in anywhere decent at eleven? Did you read St Stephen's latest Ofsted report?'

'No, I—'

'And you do realise state school pupils are two point four years behind the independent sector after eighteen months, rising to three point two by age nine?'

'Gosh, that does sound bad. Well, Richard and I are going to look round Piper Place, but it sounds a bit pressurised. What I really want is for Emily to, you know, be happy while she's still so little.'

Angela shies at the word happy like a horse at a rattlesnake. 'Well, I know they've all got anorexia in the sixth form at Piper Place,' she says brightly, 'but they do offer a terrific, well-rounded education.'

Great. My daughter will become the world's first well-rounded anorexic. Admitted to Oxford weighing five and a half stone, she will rise from her hospital bed and take a dazzling first in PPE. She will then do a job for six years, become a mother, give up work because it's all too much and spend her mornings in Coffee Republic decoding the entrance requirements for St Paul's over skinny lattes with the fluent Japanese-speaking housewife, Davina Brunt. Jesus, what is the matter with these women?

'Sorry, Angela, gotta run. Plane to catch.'

I'm still struggling to pull the minicab door to on its gouty hinges when Angela fires her parting shot. 'Look, Kate, if you're serious about getting Emily into Piper Place I can give you this psychologist's number. Everyone's using him. He'll coach her to give the right answers, draw the right sort of picture at the interview.'

I take a deep, grateful breath of the sweet ganja-rich air in the back of Winston's cab. It takes me back to mellower days, a time before children when being irresponsible was almost a duty.

'And what does the right sort of picture look like, Angela?'

The Brunt woman laughs: 'Oh, you know, imaginative, but not *too* imaginative.'

*

GOD, HOW I DESPISE myself after conversations with Angela Brunt. I can feel Angela's maternal ambition getting into me like a flu bug. You try to fight it, you try to stick with your hunch that your child will do perfectly OK without being force-fed facts like some poor little *foie gras* gosling. But one day your immune system's a bit low and, *Bam!*, Angela's in there with her league tables and her average reading scores and her psychologist's phone number. You know what's really pathetic? In the end, I'll probably put Emily down for Anorexia High: fear of what insanely competitive schooling will do to my child is outweighed only by fear of holding her back, of her somehow falling behind and its being my fault. And the race starts earlier every year: there's actually a kindergarten in our borough with a wall devoted to the Impressionists. The mothers have reluctantly come round to the idea that money can't buy you love, but they think that money can buy you Monet, and that's good enough for them.

Exhausted working mothers enrolling their girls in academies of stress. Maybe it's the only way we understand any more. Stress. Success. They even rhyme.

*

9.28 am: 'What's that lady's problem?'

'What?'

Winston is studying me in the rear-view mirror. His eyes, so brown they're almost black, are flecked with laughter.

'Angela? Oh, I don't know. Urban angst, frustrated woman living vicariously through her kids, insufficient oral sex. The usual.'

93

Winston's laugh fills the cab. Deep and grainy, it reverberates in my solar plexus and, just for a moment, calms me.

Traffic on the way to the airport is so heavy I have plenty of time to dwell on the forthcoming ordeal of meeting Abelhammer. When I talked to Rod Task last night he said: 'Jack seems pretty excited about meeting you, Katie.'

'That'll be because of Greenspan's half per cent interest-rate cut,' I improvised. I could hardly tell my boss that I have sent my client an e-mail promising disorderly conduct and a week in bed, not to mention love and kisses.

I can't seem to stop scratching. I washed my hair last night with a new shampoo: allergic reaction maybe? Or perhaps I've picked up some lower life-form in the back of Pegasus: like a swamp, the prehistoric cab could easily be a breeding ground for any number of invertebrates.

On the other hand, the music swirling round it hails from the opposite end of human development. The hot blare of trumpets and the syncopated snap of the percussion remind me of *Rhapsody in Blue*.

'Is that Gershwin, Winston?'

He shakes his head. 'Ravel.' My cab driver listens to Ravel?

We are passing the Hoover factory when the slow movement starts. It's the saddest thing I've ever heard. Halfway through, a flute comes in and just sort of breathes over the piano; when I close my eyes I see a bird hovering over the sea.

New York Office of Salinger Foundation
3.00 pm, East Coast Time: Arrive with a spinning head at the office of the Appalling Abelhammer just round the corner from the Wall Street Center. Accompanied by my assistant Guy, who shows no sign of jet lag. On the contrary, Guy is hideously up to speed and knows the Nasdaq fluctuations better than his own pulse.

I've picked out suitably offputting outfit for the presentation to Abelhammer. Chaste, charcoal, below the knee; Sicilian widow's shoes: the look is Maria von Trapp before she cut up those bedroom curtains.

My resolve to keep the tone of meeting a couple of degrees below zero melts when Jack Abelhammer walks in. Instead of the grey-haired Brooks Brothers patrician I had imagined, here is a languid, close-cut jock, around the same age as me with a slow-release George Clooney smile that reaches his eyes before the mouth is fully engaged. Damn. Damn.

'Well, Kate Reddy,' says the Appalling Abelhammer, 'it's a real pleasure to put a face to all those figures you've been sending me.'

Huh. I update Salinger on the performance of the fund over the past six months. Everything easy-peasy until one of Jack's junior consultants – a scowling Agent Scully redhead – pushes her wire specs up bridge of nose and says: 'Can I ask, if your forecast returns for Japan are so low, why are you overweight in Japan?'

'Ah, now that's a very perceptive question. One for you, Guy, I think.'

Graciously deferring to my assistant, I take a seat and sit back to watch the little creep try to wriggle his way out of that one. Casually check mobile.

Text Message from Paula Potts to Kate Reddy
Emly snt hme
frm skool with
NITS. hole famly
mst be treatd.
U 2!
cheers paula

I can hardly believe what I'm reading. I've travelled across the Atlantic importing lice like Colorado beetles. Excusing myself from meeting, I hurtle to the loo. In the seasick green light of the Executive Washroom, I try to examine my hair, pulling strands away from head. What do nits look like? Can see a cluster of eggs near parting, but possibly dandruff. Frantically comb hair.

It is impossible to get out of pre-arranged dinner with

Abelhammer. Can hardly use emergency pest control as excuse.

Brody's Seafood Restaurant
7.30 pm: Over dinner, I sit very upright like Queen Mary and some distance away from the table. I have a vision of busy nits abseiling into the client's clam chowder.

'Can I offer you a lift back to the hotel, Kate?' asks Jack.

'Um, fine, but can we stop at a drugstore. I need to get something.'

His eyebrows raise in expectation.

'I mean shampoo. I have to wash my hair.'

'Now? You want to wash your hair right now?'

'Yes. Get London out of my hair.'

Attagirl. Imaginative, but not too imaginative.

Reasons Not to Have Affair with Abelhammer
1 / Have not had legs waxed since Hallowe'en.
2 / Nits could parascend on to immaculate Harvard Business School buzz-cut.
3 / Major client, ergo unprofessional.
4 / Am married.

Shouldn't these points be in a different order?

10

Birthday

Friday, 6.02 am: Today is my son's first birthday and I am sitting in the sky over Heathrow. The plane is much delayed: poor visibility, crowded airways. We have been doing this for fifty-three minutes now, the altitude equivalent of treading water, and it's making me nervous. Can feel my shoeless feet flexing under the blanket to try and keep us aloft. I think of all those jumbos whispering past each other in the fog.

Over the PA comes the voice of the pilot. One of those chummy, Call-me-Pete types. Heart sinks. At moments like this do not want pilot to be called Pete. Urgently want pilot to be chap named Roger Carter from Weybridge, Wing Commander, ex Battle of Britain, mistress in Agadir, good friend of Raymond Baxter from *Tomorrow's World*. Sort of cove who could bring us in to land with one hand tied to his handlebar moustache if necessary. You see, I have to stay alive. I am a mother.

Pilot tells us we will have to head for Stansted. We are running low on fuel. No cause for concern. No, none at all. Today is Ben's birthday. I need to land safely to collect a Teletubbies cake from the bakery, also to dress my son for his first party in burgundy cords and soft cream shirt before Paula can put him in the Desert Storm khaki grunge she favours. My dying is totally out of the question. For a start, Richard could never bring himself to tell Emily about periods; he would delegate to his mother and Barbara would give Em a brief talk about 'personal freshness' before producing something called a sanitary napkin. And she would refer to sex as 'that department'. As in 'there's nothing amiss between Donald and me in

That Department, thank you'. (In the great universal stores of life, I believe That Department is to be found on the floor between Ladies Separates and Domestic Appliances.) No, no, no. I have to live. I am a mother. Death wasn't really an issue before; I mean, obviously you wanted to avoid it for as long as possible, but ever since having children I see the Unsmiling Man with the Scythe everywhere and I jump higher and higher to avoid his swishing blade.

'Everything all right for you, madam?' In this, the dimmest possible cabin light, the stewardess has become a letterbox of lipstick around an ice-white smile.

I address myself to the teeth: 'Actually, it's my baby's first birthday today and I was hoping to be home by breakfast.'

'Well, I promise you we're doing all we can. Can I get you some water?'

'With Scotch. Thanks.'

Stansted Airport
8.58 am: Refuelled plane still sitting on the tarmac. 'Pontius' pilot says it's not his fault, we have to go back to Heathrow. Oh, this is just marvellous. As we gain height, two empty whisky miniatures skitter off my tray nearly landing in the lap of the woman across the aisle. She bestows a languorous smile on me, adjusts her mint-green pashmina, opens a Gucci travel bag. Then she takes out an aromatherapy bottle and dots lavender on to her pulse points, and applies face spritz before taking thoughtful sips from a large bottle of Evian. Then lets her lustrous nit-free head sink back on to a dinky grey cashmere pillow. I want to reach over, tap her on the arm and ask if I can buy her life.

Once I'm sure the goddess is safely asleep, I furtively open my own bag. Contents:

Two emergency sachets of Calpol
Unwashed white medicine spoon with jammy rim
Spare knickers for Emily (swimming)
Nit comb purchased for self in NYC

Lone grubby Tampax

Hideous puce Pokémon toy from last weekend's 'crisis'
  McDonald's visit

Orange felt-tip minus top

Pongy Percy the Puppy book

Wad of Kleenex all dyed orange by felt tip

Pack of Banoffee-flavour, limited edition Munchies (disgusting, but
  only three left)

Coco Chanel miniature Eau de Toilette (atomiser broken)

Little Miss Busy book which Emily pressed on me for the journey

Between my wallet and a wad of dried-out Pampers wipes, I find Jack Abelhammer's card with his home number and a message scrawled on the back, 'Any time!'

At the sight of his handwriting, I get a sensation of claws scuttling across the floor of my belly. The sensation of far-off teenage crushes, of sex when it was still as much a puzzle as a thrill. Over dinner in New York, Jack and I talked about everything – music, movies, Tom Hanks (the new Jimmy Stewart?), the poetry of Emily Dickinson, Cate Blanchett's Elizabeth I, *Apollo 13*, jelly beans, Art Tatum, Rome versus Venice, the mysterious allure of Alan Greenspan, even about the stocks I am buying for him. Everything except children. Why didn't you mention your children, Kate?

2.07 pm: Back from Heathrow, dash into office to show my face. Create impression of intense activity by piling books and financial journals on my desk, then call my landline from my mobile and keep it ringing. Pick it up and have animated, can-do conversation with myself about hot new stock before hanging up. Tell Guy I have to pop out and collect some vital research. Hail cab and get driver to take me to Highbury Corner and wait outside bakery while I leap out to pick up Teletubbies cake. Not bad: Po a little po-faced, perhaps, and Laa-Laa more mustard than yellow. Ten minutes later, pulling into our street, can see a blue balloon tied to the front door. As I walk into the house, Ben waddles into the hall, gives a yowl of recognition and starts to cry. Fall to my knees, gather him in and hug him tight.

This time last year, he was minutes old, naked except for a buttery coat of vernix. Today, dressed by Paula, he is in an Arsenal strip with Adams emblazoned on the back. I do not let on how much this upsets me. Instead, when she leaves the kitchen, I calmly hand Ben a carton of Toothkind Ribena and watch as he upends it, drizzling purple flood from neck to navel.

'Oh, dear,' I say loudly. 'Not juice all over your lovely football kit. Better go upstairs and get changed.'

Yesss!

4 pm: Ben's party is full of Paula's nanny friends with their charges, many of whom I don't recognise. They are part of his life without me. When these unfamiliar girls say his name and my son lights up with pleasure I feel a twinge of – what? If I didn't know better, I'd call it remorse.

In the sitting room, a handful of non-working mums are in animated conversation about a local nursery school. They hardly seem to notice their kids whom they handle with an enviable invisible touch, like advanced kite-flyers, while the Mothers Inferior like me over-attend to our clamorous offspring.

There is an uneasy stand-off between the two kinds of mother which sometimes makes it hard for us to talk to each other. I suspect that the non-working mother looks at the working mother with envy and fear because she thinks that the working mum has got away with it, and the working mum looks back with fear and envy because she knows that she has not. In order to keep going in either role, you have to convince yourself that the alternative is bad. The working mother says, because I am more fulfilled as a person I can be a better mother to my children. And sometimes she may even believe it. The mother who stays home knows that she is giving her kids an advantage, which is something to cling on to when your toddler has emptied his beaker of juice over your last clean T-shirt.

Here in the kitchen, though, I find solace in the company of a handful of familiar women, the tattered remnant of my original post-natal mother and baby group. Amazing to think we've known each other for more than five years now. Judith, the plump brunette over by the microwave, used to be a patent agent. Went back to work for a couple of years, but then one day she discovered dog hairs in the back of the family Peugeot. Trouble was they didn't have a dog. Told herself it was nothing to worry about, until the gnawing sensation in her stomach drove her to slip out of work. She parked outside her own house and trailed the nanny to a flat off the Holloway Road. Inside the unlocked door, she found Joshua fenced in a corner behind a fireguard, watched over by an Alsatian, while the nanny, Tara, amused herself in the next room with a boyfriend who had a Metallica tattoo on one of his pumping buttocks.

We all told Judith it was just incredibly bad luck. A single rotten apple in the wholesome nanny barrel. 'But, what if he *saw* something, Kate?' she sobbed down the phone.

'Josh didn't see anything, Judy, he's not even three. And they don't remember a thing before they're five.'

But Judith never risked childcare again. We knew that she tortured herself with the thought of the dog's jaw so close to her baby's face because, back in those early days, we lacerated our consciences every time we got home and found a new bump or graze on our own infants. These things happened; it was the fact they happened off your watch that seemed to hurt. And then there was the secret, never-to-be-spoken conviction that you would have got there sooner. Got to the table corner before her forehead struck, to the tarmac before his tiny knee. Awacs, isn't that what the Air Force calls it? Nature gives Mother an advance-warning system and Mother is convinced that no minder or man can match her for speed or anticipation.

Judith didn't object when her husband Nigel said that, as he was under such pressure at the bank, he would need to take a skiing holiday while Judith got on with the relaxing business of being at home with three children under four. (The twins arrived soon after the nanny left.) The Judith I first knew would have told hubby where to get off, but that Judith had long disappeared.

The rest of us held firm for a while to the conviction that we had been educated for something better than the gentle warming of Barbie pasta. But then, one by one, we gave up. 'Giving up', isn't that what they call it? Well, I'm not calling it that. Giving up sounds like a surrender, but these were honourable campaigns bravely fought and not without injury. Did my fellow novice mothers give up work? No, work gave them up, or at least made it impossible for them to go on. Karen – she's spooning jelly into Ella's mouth – found herself sidelined at her accountancy firm after it was made crystal clear – by the opaque route of nod and wink – that after having Louis she was no longer considered partnership material. Taking her eyes off the Career Path for a few months, she had found herself on the Mummy Track. (The Mummy Track has the appearance of a through road; you can travel for many hundreds of miles along it before you notice you're going nowhere.) Karen thought she could do her job in four days, one of those days at home; her boss agreed, and that was the problem. If Karen managed, he said, it would create 'an unhelpful precedent'.

Funny thing is, when I was starting out I assumed that babyhood would be the hard part, that if I could just butch my way through those fuzzy first weeks then everything would return to normal. But it gets worse: at least at six months of age they can't tell you it's you that they want.

Five and a half years after the birth of our babies, and only three out of our original group of nine still have jobs: Caroline is a graphic designer who works from home, so she gets to squeeze all her work in round Max's school times. She couldn't make it today because she's putting the finishing touches to a brochure for IBM. Alice – cute face, raven bob, leather gilet, over there by the sink – went back to being a director of documentaries that won awards for rooting out corruption in high places and a particularly plangent kind of sadness in low ones. Every night when she got in late from the editing suite, Alice carried a sleeping Nathaniel into her bed. When else would she get to hold him? It was only for a little while, only while he was little. But Nat didn't grasp that his lease on paradise was short: soon he was lying across the width of the bed, forcing his mother and father into narrow coffins at each side. When Jacob came along, Alice took him into bed too. Soon afterwards her partner, Don, left home, citing a nineteen-year-old researcher and irreconcilable sleeping arrangements.

I look at Alice now, gaunt as an addict. From a distance, she looks as youthful as when we first met, but up close you see how motherhood has stolen her bloom: the boys seem to have literally sucked her blood. She may have a Bafta, but her sons are even needier by night than the talent she corrals by day, and how would she find the time to meet a new man, even if there was one out there willing to take on the bolshy scions of another male? Reading my thoughts, she says with a tight smile, 'My only fix now is the boys, Kate.'

I place my hand on the golden orb of my own boy's head. A clump of chocolate Rice Krispies is nesting in his left ear. Time to sing Happy Birthday. Paula produces a Zippo from her pocket to light the candles (Christ, she's not smoking now, is she?). I carry the cake to the table. Ben's eyes are watery with wonder, mine with regret: is this the last time I'll see a baby of mine turn one? And how much of that first year have I actually seen?

'Oh, Kate, you shouldn't have gone to so much trouble,' says Alice, eyebrow raised and gesturing at the Teletubbies icing.

'Bad mother,' I mouth silently at her across the table.

Laughing, she whispers back: 'Me too.'

Must Remember.
Nits, cheese, Valentine's card.

11

Reason Not the Need

IT'S HARD TO explain how my relationship with Jack began. I really wasn't looking for anyone. I wasn't happy, but I wasn't unhappy either; I was in the grey survival zone where I imagine most of us live most of the time. When a badly injured patient gets admitted to Casualty, the hospital staff do what they call triage. Triage is the assignment of degrees of urgency to decide the order of treatment of wounds. I first heard the term one night when I was watching *ER* – it was that riveting period when we were all wondering how things would work out between Hathaway and Doug – and I thought how much triage sounded like my life. Daily existence was a constant assessment of who needed my attention most: the children, the office or my husband. You'll notice I leave myself out of that list and that's not because I'm a good and selfless person. Far from it. Selfishness just wasn't an option: no time. Most weekends, on the drive home from the supermarket, I would look through the steamed-up windows of a café and see a couple, fingertips touching over cappuccino, or a lone man reading a newspaper and I would long to go in there and order a drink and just sit and sit. But that was impossible. When I wasn't at work, I had to be a mother; when I wasn't being a mother, I owed it to work to be at work. Time off for myself felt like stealing. The fact that no man I knew ever felt that way didn't help. This was just another area in which we were unequal: mothers got the lioness's share of the guilt. So the last thing, the very last thing I needed was someone else to love: and then the e-mails started.

In the weeks that followed our first dinner in New York, Jack e-mailed me, first daily and then hourly. Sometimes we would reply to each other within seconds and it felt like one of those rallies in a tennis match where a great return spurs the other player to an inspired lob. I was cool at first, but he was so playful and persistent that natural competitiveness took over and I was soon running to the back of the court to retrieve the ball and return it with some topspin. So, no, I didn't need him, but he created a Jack-shaped need in me; a need that only he could satisfy. Does the woman in the desert know how thirsty she is till they press the bottle to her lips? I started to look forward to the name Abelhammer dropping into the Inbox more than I have looked forward to anything in my life.

*

From: Jack Abelhammer
To: Kate Reddy, EMF
Nasdaq hit like Pearl Harbor. heavy casualties. client seeks considered professional opinion of respected British fund manager: should I shoot myself now or wait till after lunch?
Jack

From: Kate Reddy
To: Jack Abelhammer
Rest assured respected fund manager has you constantly in mind. Awaiting interest-rate pronouncement from Al Mighty Greenspan.
Professional opinion: long-term recovery inevitable. Don't shoot.
Unprofessional opinion: hide under desk till shelling stops, go out and see if any stock left standing. Eat turkey club sandwich. Then shoot.
Katharine xxxxx

From: Jack Abelhammer
To: Kate Reddy
did you know Alan Greenspan's wife said he was so oblique that when he asked her to marry him she didn't even notice? that guy's harder to read than Thomas Pynchon.

Hey, shouldn't you be in bed? Middle of the night there, right?

From: Kate Reddy
To: Jack Abelhammer
I like the night. More time in it than the day. Why waste it in bed?
K xxxx

From: Jack Abelhammer
To: Kate Reddy
Bed not invariably a waste of time. do you know that speech where the guy tells his lover he wishes that seven years were rolled into one night. must be Shakespeare, right?

From: Kate Reddy
To: Jack Abelhammer
Seven years in one night sounds just about enough hours to pay off my sleep debt. Not Shakespeare. Marlowe, I think. That's the unfair thing about Shakespeare, though – everything beautiful belongs to him whether he wrote it or not. He's the Bill Gates of emotional software.
How come you read Marlowe anyway? Did the Wall St J predict a resurgence in Renaissance playwrights?

From: Jack Abelhammer
To: Kate Reddy
Unfair, milady, unfair. don't judge a man by his portfolio. Was once a poor struggling English major but had to find a way of financing my first-editions habit. Some guys buy boats, I buy a first edition of Ulysses. What's your excuse?

From: Kate Reddy
To: Jack Abelhammer
Was once a poor struggling English minor. Poverty, when it's not being boring, is really quite scary. I didn't want to be scared all my life. In Britain, there are plenty of people who will tell you money doesn't matter: these are the people we call

the middle classes.

Owning first editions such a boy's own thing. respectfully suggest, Sir, you should spend your money on something really important, like SHOES.

K xxxxxxxxxx

From: Jack Abelhammer
To: Kate Reddy
Do you realise you have now sent me exactly 147 kisses and I have not sent you a single one?

From: Kate Reddy
To: Jack Abelhammer
It had crossed my mind.

From: Jack Abelhammer
To: Kate Reddy

xxxxxxxxxxxxxxxxxxxxxxxxxxxxxxxxxxxxxxxxxxxxxxxxxxxxxxxxxxxxxx
xxxxxxxxxxxxxxxxxxxxxxxxxxxxxxxxxxxxxxxxxxxxxxxxxxxxxxxxxxxxxx
xxxxxxxxxxxxxxxxxxxxxxxxxxxxxxxxxxxxxxxxxxxxxxxxxxxxxxxxxxxxxx
xxxxxxxxxxxxxxxxxxxxxxxxxxxxxxxxxxxxxxxxxxxxxxxxxxxxxxxxxxxxxx
xxxxxxxxxxxxxxxxxxxxxxxxxxxxxxxxxxxxxxxxxxxxxxxxxxxxxxxxxxxxxx
xxxxxxxxxxxxxxxxxxxxxxxxxxxxxxxxxxxxxxxxxxxxxxxxxxxxxxxxxxxxxx
xxxxxxxxxxxxxxxxxxxxxxxxxxxxxxxxxxxxxxxxxxxxxxxxxxxxxxxxxxxxxx
xxxxxxxxxxxxxxxxxxxxxxxxxxxxxxxxxxxxxxxxxxxxxxxxxxxxxxxxxxxxxx
xxxxxxxxxxxxxxxxxxxxxxxxxxxxxxxxxxxxxxxxxxxxxxxxxxxxxxxxxxxxxx
xxxxxxxxxxxxxxxxxxxxxxxxxxxxxxxxxxxxxxxxxxxxxxxxxxxxxxxxxxxxxx
xxxxxxxxxxxxxxxxxxxxxxxxxxxxxxxxxxxxxxxxxxxxxxxxxxxxxxxxxxxxxx
xxxxxxxxxxxxxxxxxxxxxxxxxxxxxxxxxxxxxxxxxxxxxxxxxxxxxxxxxxxxxx
xxxxxxxxxxxxxxxxxxxxxxxxxxxxxxxxxxxxxxxxxxxxxxxxxxxxxxxxxxxxxx
xxxxxxxxxxxxxxxxxxxxxxxxxxxxxxxxxxxxxxxxxxxxxxxxxxxxxxxxxxxxxx
xxxxxxxxxxxxxxxxxxxxxxxxxxxxxxxxxxxxxxxxxxxxxxxxxxxxxxxxxxxxxx
xxxxxxxxxxxxxxxxxxxxxxxxxxxxxxxxxxxxxxxxxxxxxxxxxxxxxxxxxxxxxx
xxxxxxxxxxxxxxxxxxxxxxxxxxxxxxxxxxxxxxxxxxxxxxxxxxxxxxxxxxxxxx
xxxxxxxxxxxxxxxxxxxxxxxxxxxxxxxxxxxxxxxxxxxxxxxxxxxxxxxxxxxxxx
xxxxxxxxxxxxxxxxxxxxxxxxxxxxxxxxxxxxxxxxxxxxxxxxxxxxxxxxxxxxxx
xxxxxxxxxxxxxxxxxxxxxxxxxxxxxxxxxxxxxxxxxxxxxxxxxxxxxxxxxxxxxx

7.01 am: Ben has discovered his penis. Lying on the changing mat, he wears the rapt, triumphant expression of a being who has just found the on-off switch for the solar system. Small fingers curled tight around the original joystick, he is absolutely outraged and sheds fat, warm tears when I confiscate his favourite new toy by trapping it in a Midi Pamper and hastily sealing the Velcro flaps on each side.

'No, there's a good boy. We have to put it away now and go downstairs and have our Shreddies.'

What is the correct mother-of-the-world attitude to an infant son's sexuality? Delight that the penis works, of course. Amazement that I could, in my own female body, have grown this caterpillar-sized miracle of plumbing and pleasure. But also strange shyness at evidence of early masculinity with all that it implies – tractors, soccer, other women. One day Ben will have females in his life who are not me and already a splinter of ice in the heart tells me how that will feel.

Downstairs, I pick my way across the debris on the kitchen floor. Over by the bin, there is a hill of raisins: surely can't be the same raisins that were there before Christmas? Must tell Paula to stop kids dropping them. (No use asking cleaning lady: Juanita has problem with cartilage and cannot kneel down.) I find Richard bowed in worshipful attitude before the TV. Unshaven, my husband is at his shaggiest and most primitive, like Ted Hughes left in a tumble-drier. Suspect he has developed a crush on children's TV presenter – Chloe? Zoe? – and when I ask how come he had the kids' show switched on before either of ours was even awake, he murmurs 'very educational' in a gruff, not-now-woman manner. Don't think he has forgiven me since the Great Pesto Row.

I can't help noticing that Chloe-Zoe is dressed for a Geordie hen night rather than a fierce February morning. She wears an orange sleeveless vest with How About It? picked out in pink sequins over small but inquisitive breasts. When did children's presenters start looking like jailbait rather than, say, the estimable Valerie Singleton?

'Richard?'

'Yes.'

'Ben keeps fiddling with himself. I mean, he's only just one. Seems a bit early. Do you think it's normal?'

Rich doesn't even look up. 'Happiest form of entertainment known to man. A lifetime's pleasure ahead of him. Plus it's free,' he says, cocking his head on one side and returning Chloe-Zoe's gruesome chipmunk grin.

A gurgle of pleasure across the room makes me turn round. Ben has crawled over to the fridge, yanked open the door and stands there upending an economy bottle of Toothkind Ribena over a pair of my shoes. Blackcurrant haemmorhaging all over the place. Dive into action, attempting to staunch the slick like exotic yet authoritative Nurse Hathaway. Call for more kitchen roll. There is no more kitchen roll and Ben is now sitting in a puddle of purple glucose. He squeals when I pick him up by the collar of his pyjamas and hold him under the tap.

I ask Richard how he could have failed to get kitchen roll as per my underlined (three times) request on Friday's shopping list. Rich explains he was unable to find the specified Kitten Soft in the supermarket and simply couldn't bring himself to ask for it.

'I don't understand.'

'There are certain words a grown man cannot be expected to say, Katie, and Kitten Soft are two of them.'

'You won't say Kitten Soft Kitchen Roll?'

'Not out loud, no.'

'Why on earth not?'

'I don't know. I just know I'd rather eat a soft kitten than ask for one. Even thinking those words . . .'

With a theatrical shudder, Richard turns to the TV and makes a silent appeal to the melting chocolate-button eyes of Chloe-Zoe.

'But we don't have any kitchen roll, Rich, and, as you may have noticed, we have the Exxon Valdez going on here.'

'I know, but I wasn't sure if Kitten Thingy was the only option or if Absorbent Luxury Three-Ply Cushion stuff would do instead.' He lets out a moose-sized groan. 'It's no good,

Kate . . . Don't make me.'

For future reference, I ask my husband to give me some other words grown men cannot be expected to say. In no particular order they are: Toilet Duck, glade-fresh, rich aroma, deep-dish, filet o' fish, Cheezy Dipper, wash'n'go, Bodyform, Tubby Custard, pantyliner.

8.01 am: Got to dash. Major presentation to EMF directors today. A make or break career opportunity. A chance to impress with cool authority, matchless knowledge of world markets etc. Swipe Ribena glaze off my shoes, leave note for Paula asking her to buy kitchen roll and PLEASE return *Snow White* video to the library. The fine now exceeds production costs on the original Walt Disney movie. Grab my bag and air-kiss sticky Ben who hurls himself at me like Daniel Day-Lewis bidding farewell to Madeleine Stowe in *The Last of the Mohicans*.

'Mum, what's a suffer jet?' Emily is blocking my path to the door.

'Don't know, darling. Have a nice day. Bye now.'

3.26 pm: Presentation is going brilliantly. The Managing Director, Sir Alasdair Cobbold, has just praised my grasp of the problems of European integration. Up here in the boardroom on the seventeenth floor, with London spread out like a Lego village beneath me, for one giddy moment I feel as though I am mistress of all I survey.

I am just moving into the closing sequence when there's a cough at the door. I look across and see Celia Harmsworth hovering in that fluttery, don't-mind-me way people who pretend they're unimportant have of making themselves the centre of attention. 'So sorry to interrupt, Robin,' she simpers, 'but there's a drunk in reception causing a few problems for security.'

Robin Cooper-Clark raises an eyebrow: 'And what has that got to do with us, Celia?'

'The thing is, he says he's Kate's father.'

12

Meet Kate's Dad

THE PATTERN OF meetings with my dad has not altered much in the last twenty years. For months on end I don't hear from him, except for reports passed via my sister of scandalous excesses and a list of ailments you thought had died out with Lord Nelson – lockjaw, scurvy, Vesuvian boils. Then one day, when I've given up on him, when the tug that feels like a bell-pull on the heart has eased, he pitches up and launches into a conversation that draws on a relationship we never had. My dad has always confused sentimentality and intimacy. As far as he's concerned, I'm still his little girl, although when I was a little girl he asked things of me that demanded a woman's strength. Now that I'm grown he wants a child's docility and is quick to anger when he doesn't get it. Sometimes he has been drinking, you can never be quite sure; but always, always, he wants money.

In the chrome and white lobby of Edwin Morgan Forster, Joseph Aloysius Reddy stands out like a creature from a more provisional, primitive age. Visitors in suits can't take their eyes off him. The disbelief he arouses is so strong he might as well be a bad smell. With a third-hand herringbone coat and a skein of grey hair, he's like a tinker come to sell his pots and pans to the crew of the *Starship Enterprise*. Two security guys with crackling walkie-talkies are trying to persuade him to move, but Joe is planted mulishly on one of reception's perforated steel benches, a white plastic bag slumped at his feet. He has the drunk's huffy dignity. Catching sight of me, he uncrosses his arms and points a triumphant finger: 'There. There's our Kathy. What'd I tell you?'

'Thanks, Gerald,' I say quickly to the guard. 'My dad's not

himself today. I'll take over now.' Steer him to the door, making sure to look straight ahead to avoid the pitying smiles that have been the Reddy family's constant companions for almost as long as I can remember.

Once we're safely outside, I mention a Cheapside coffee shop far out of the orbit of my colleagues, but Dad pulls me down the steps towards the King's Arms. A pub that Dickens knew, it has sawdust on the floor and a teenage barmaid with white skin and a studded tongue. We sit at a corner table under the portrait of a red-cheeked earl; my father with a double Scotch and a maxi pack of peanuts, me with a bitter lemon. Bitter lemon was always my mum's drink. First it was a non-alcoholic beverage; only later did it become a state of mind.

''Owse little Emma then?' asks my father. His breath is a powerful mixture of Johnnie Walker and boiled eggs.

'Emily.'

'Aye, Emily. Must be going on seven now.'

'Six. She'll be six in June, Dad.' He nods decisively, as though six is close enough to seven to make no difference.

'And the little lad? Julie says he has a look of me about him.'

Jesus, there really is no parent so bad or so absent that he can't get a kick out of his genetic legacy. I stare furiously into my sour fizz. The mere idea that some ribbon of DNA with Joe Reddy printed on it is unfurling inside my darling son. 'Actually, Ben looks like me, Dad.'

'Well, we were always alike, you and me, Kathy duck. Both lookers, good with figures, both with a bit of a temper on us, eh?' He snatches a swallow of whisky and throws a handful of peanuts into his mouth – everything in immoderation, my father; in that at least we are the same.

'Well, aren't you gonna ask your dad how he's going on, then? Come all this way to see you.'

The accent is Northern, so thick you could cut it like fruit cake, but there is an echo of a lilt from his mother's native Cork. Did I really use to talk like that? Richard says that when he first met me I sounded like something out of Monty Python. That was when I still said baff for bath; before I learnt that class rhymes with arse. Although no one says arse down here: they say bum or bottom. I say bottom to my children now and each time I falter on its plump, prissy contours. My tongue feels like that barmaid's: heavy with foreign objects.

Dad wants me to make it easier for him to ask for what he's come for. But I won't make it easy. I can still remember him standing outside the Abbey National in Holborn when I'd got my first pay cheque and licking his finger to count the tenners I handed him. My own father. If he wants my money let him ask for it.

'Same again?' The barmaid has come over to clear our glasses.

'No.'

'Aye, same for me and get one in for yourself, love.'

Dad smiles and the girl flushes and straightens up in a way I have seen women do before in his presence. He was once a beautiful man, my father – beautiful rather than handsome, and therefore doomed not to ripen but to rot. 'Tyrone Power,' my grandmother used to murmur fondly when she saw him and I, being young and not knowing any old Hollywood stars, assumed that Tyrone Power was the electric effect my father had on people rather than a proper name. An unruly but irresistible force of nature. I look at him now and try to see what others must see: face the shape of a swollen heart, the nose and cheeks stippled with red routes like the delta of some rusty river. Long lashes fringing what my mother claims were the most remarkable blue eyes you ever saw: indigo pools where all that charm and intelligence drowned. A ladies' man, my first boyfriend called him. 'Your dad's a bit of a one for the ladies, Kath. Should have seen him down the club with that Christine on Saturday night.' How I flushed to hear mention of his sex life so close to mine.

'See what you reckon to this.' My father fumbles under the table and out of his carrier bag produces a black box file and from that several well-thumbed sheets of graph paper. There is a drawing of something snouty and padded with squared-off wings at the side. Pigs might fly? I turn it the other way up.

'What is it?'

'The world's first biodegradable nappy.'

'But you don't know anything about nappies.'

'I do now.'

My dad, you should know, has a history in this area. One of the world's great undiscovered inventors, there is very little that he himself has not discovered. When Julie and I were still small he cooked up moon rocks, powdery lumps of resin that were sold as souvenirs from the Apollo 11 landing off a market stall in Chesterfield. 'Just think, madam, your hand is holding the very rock that Neil Armstrong held in his!' They went like a bomb, did the moon rocks, and later, when space travel lost its lustre, they had another incarnation as fancy pumice stones for the hard skin of the ladies of Worksop.

Next came a catflap that prevented pets bringing prey into the house: a good idea, but the cats kept getting garrotted in the springback mechanism. Sometimes Dad's inventions had been invented already, like the blindfold he devised for in-flight passenger naps without ever having been on an aeroplane.

'Joe,' said Mum cautiously, 'I understand that they have eye shades on planes,' but he refused to let such womanly nitpicking get him down. In our house, Dad was the one for the broad sweep; Mum picked up the bits with a dustpan and brush. On his card, my father describes himself as an entrepreneur.

As I skim through his business plan for Reddy's bio-degradable nappy, he says happily: 'I've had a lot of interest, you know. Derek Marshall at the Chamber of Commerce says he's never seen anything quite like it. But I'm a bit stuck for capital, love, and that's your line of work. What do they call it, adventure capital?'

'Venture capital.'

'That's the one.'

Dad says we're not talking big sums this time; seed money, that's all.

'How much?'

'Just enough to get production up and running.'

'How much?'

'Ten grand plus development costs, then there's packaging. Say thirteen and a half. I wouldn't ask, love, only cashflow's that tight at the minute.'

I'm not aware of my expression having altered, but it must have done, because he shifts in his chair in a manner which, in another man, you might take for discomfort. For a moment, I think it must have occurred to him how sick these transactions make me feel. He reaches across the table and places his hand on mine. 'Don't worry, love,' he says. 'If you're pushed I'll take a cheque.'

I leave my father at Moorgate station. From there, he can get the Northern Line directly to King's Cross and take a train home. I give him money for the fare – a crazy amount, it's cheaper to fly to Boston than to go to Doncaster these days – and extra for a cab at the other end. Dad is a bit vague about where he is living at the moment – for which read *who* he is living with – but he promises me that he will go there directly. I stand outside the station, round the corner by the photo booth. When I look back inside a few minutes later he has engaged a young busker in conversation. Casually, magnanimously, he flicks one of the tenners I have just given him into the boy's open guitar case, removes his coat, lays it gently over the busker's sleeping dog and now, oh dear God, he is going to sing.

> *'The water is wide, I cannot get o'er*
> *And neither have I wings to fly.*
> *Bring me a boat that can carry two*
> *And both shall row, my love and I.'*

It's his favourite ballad, a Reddy standard along with 'Down by the Salley Gardens'. The passing suits, scurrying for the escalator, stop and turn their heads, startled by the beauty of the tenor voice, the thwarted yearning Dad does so well. A woman in a camel coat bends to deposit some coins in the case and my father tips an invisible hat to her.

I can hear my mother's voice now, an angry descant piercing

the sad tune. 'He can wrap you round his little finger.'

'No, he can't.'

'Yes he can. Always could. If he's so bloody marvellous, your father, go to him. Go on, go to him.'

'I don't want to go to him, Mum.'

'You always were his. Daddy's girl.'

I plunge back into the noise of the street, buy a copy of the *Standard* to have something to hold in my hands, and head in the direction of the office.

A child's love for a parent is well-nigh indestructible, but down the years the drip, drip of disillusion can corrode it. The first feeling I remember having for my father was pride, a soaring, burst-your-lungs gratitide that he was mine. Better looking than anyone else's dad, he was so clever he could do any sum he liked in his head and recite the football results back as soon as they'd been read out on the telly on Saturday afternoon without a single mistake. Sheffield Wednesday, Partick Thistle, Hamilton Academicals. Saturday mornings, Julie and I would be allowed to accompany him to the bookies, where we would cling on to our hero's legs. I remember the sense of being small down there in the forest of trousers and the smell of felt hats in from the rain. Years later, at university, I watched the middle-class fathers trudging back and forth from their family saloons carrying tea chests and kettles and china mug sets hanging from pine trees, and I longed for their dull embrace.

One winter, it must have been '75 or '76, Dad took us sledging out in the Peak District. Other families had shop-bought sledges: raised off the ground with a lattice of wooden struts to sit on, they had the grandeur of an old-fashioned sleigh ride. Our sledge lay flush with the ground: Dad had hammered it together out of split logs and had added metal runners on the underside which he ripped from the lip of an abandoned car door. 'Give it a bit of go!' he said, rubbing his hands together.

On the first run, Julie fell off right away and the sledge completed the descent by itself. Dad told her not to be such a baby. Now it was my turn, and I clung on, determined to prove that our sledge, the sledge our dad had made, was as good as anyone's. But halfway down the hill, it hit a ridge and veered sharply to the right, slicing towards a steep drop fenced off by a low curtain of barbed wire. The metal strips, added to give a bit of go, made the sledge unstoppable; it slammed under the fencing and the two front prongs dangled over the drop while I lay at the back, two feet from the edge, tangled in wire.

He was panting so hard when he got to me I thought he would die, but he knelt down on the end of the sledge to hold it in place and picked the wire thorns out of my anorak, out of my hands, out of my hair. As the last piece of wire was unsnagged, he pulled me clear and the sledge shot forward. It was a couple of seconds before we heard it crack on the road beneath. I used to think that I remembered that day so well because he had saved my life; now I think it's because it was the only time in our years as father and daughter that he did anything to protect me.

But Dad was my first love and I always took his side even when my mother's hazel eyes disappeared in big racoon circles and she started wearing those brushed-nylon Keep-Out nighties and laughing in the wrong places. One day at the VG stores, a man knocked over the pyramid display of Ideal Milk, the little blue and white cans went tumbling everywhere, and Mum laughed and laughed until Linda behind the counter had to fetch a glass of water from out back. But daughters don't want to pick up the signals of their mother's unhappiness; it might mean their father isn't perfect.

Years after it became clear that Joseph Aloysius Reddy was an unsuitable crush, I still couldn't break it off. How much evidence did I need? There was the day he brought the sheets home from the bed he shared with his new girlfriend for Mum to wash. And the night he carried me downstairs, blinking from sleep, to tell the copper standing in the front room that he, Joseph Reddy, had been at home on a date I had to swear I could remember. And I swore.

'She's got this photographic memory, has our Kathy,' said

Dad to the policeman. 'Haven't you, love? Now where's that lovely smile?'

A father is the template of a man that Nature gives a girl, and if that template is broken or disfigured, well, what then?

Walking through the front door of Edwin Morgan Forster, I am grateful for its cool echoing spaces, for the clip-clop of marble underfoot, for the way the lift welcomes me without protest to its mirrored interior. I prefer not to look at the woman in the reflection: I don't want her seeing me like this. When the door opens on the thirteenth floor, I have my excuses ready, but Robin Cooper-Clark is standing right there.

'Excellent presentation, Kate,' he says, placing a hand awkwardly on my shoulder. 'Absolutely first class. Just need to tie up a couple of loose ends. No hurry. In your own time. No real problems with the family, I trust.'

Hard to imagine what the Director of Investment would say if I told him the truth. The Cooper-Clarks have become friends since Jill and I bonded in horror at a corporate pheasant shoot. Richard and I have been to their place in Sussex several times, but I have never mentioned my father to Robin: I want his respect, not his pity. 'No. Everything's fine.'

'Splendid. Talk later.'

The screen tells me that in the three hours since I last looked, the FTSE is up 50, the Dow is down 100 and the dollar 1 per cent. So steadily, and with great deliberation, I make the calculations I need to make to hold my funds on course.

All I knew was that I wasn't going back there: to the scams, the evasions, the holding your breath in the dark hall.

13

Shopping

JET LAG HAS ITS own micro-climate; grey, sticky, Singaporean. Just back from a lightning hop to Boston, I move through the stinging February rain with almost tropical lethargy. Step out into Long Acre, straight into the path of a courier. Through the visor, I can see eyes full of hatred.

'Yeww stew-pid cow,' he spits. 'Cancha fuckin' look where ya goin'?'

Fourteen minutes to spare before Rod and I have a meeting with consultants in Covent Garden, just off the piazza. Enough time to run into LK Bennett 50% Shoe Sale.

I think I've forgotten how to shop for pleasure. No lingering foreplay for me, no harmless flirtation with chenille and silk before getting off with aloof linen or gorgeous, cuddly alpaca. These days, I shop like a locust: famished, ruinous, hoovering up anything I need and things I definitely won't need but deserve, anyway, because I never have time to go shopping. I grab a pair of fudge pencil heels – good for treading on Guy's toes – and calf-length, Caramac-soft boots. As an afterthought, I pick up some black slingbacks patterned with so many punch-holes it looks like braille for foot fetishists. Funny how two pairs of shoes feels extravagant, but three's a bargain.

Across the shop, I glimpse a glossy brunette, a triumph of Botox over gravity, swaddled in dove grey cashmere. She is considering each shoe like a judge at a flower show. You can tell she has time as well as money on her hands. I see a whole day of browsing stretching ahead of her – a prairie of possibility, dotted with skinny lattes and a delicious light lunch. I notice her eyes land on a pair of zebra mules on the size 6 rack. She must be stopped. Execute *Charlie's Angels* pirouette and get to them just in time.

'Excuse me, I was picking those up.' Her voice is peevish – as aggrieved as someone that languid will allow herself to be.

'Sorry I was here first,' I say, jamming toe into zebra.

'No need to be aggressive,' she smiles and trails away leaving a slipstream of Jo Malone Tuberose. Is she not fragrant? Certainly. Does one not want to strangle her eerily wrinkle-free neck? You bet.

At the till, the assistant pauses when she gets to the zebra mules and turns them over. 'These aren't your size, madam.'

'I know, I'm taking them, anyway.'

The credit-card machine chunters busily and then gags. 'Sorry, madam, your card has been rejected. I'll have to make a call.'

'I don't have *time* for you to make a call.'

The assistant smirks. 'Shall we try another card?'

10.36 am: Six minutes, thirty-five seconds late for meeting. Enter room full of suits, trying to hide gleaming carrier bag behind knees. Rod Task looks up from his notes with a shark's grin. 'Ah, when the going gets tough the ladies go shopping. Good of you to join us, Katie.'

12.19 pm: Four days to go till Emily's half-term, but am way too busy to have booked a relaxing break. And Paula is off to Morocco for the week. When I tentatively enquired this morning if there was any chance of her ever taking a holiday to coincide with ours, she shot me her Joan-of-Arc, put-those-matches-down look. So I offered to pay for her flight. Weak, Kate, very weak.

Pretend to be checking fund valuations while making call to travel agent. How about Florida?

Hyena cackle at the other end of phone. 'Fully booked since October, sorry.'

'Disneyland, Paris?'

Non. Eurostar apparently groaning with loathsome forward-planners. It would be wise to book for Easter now, the agent says: he still has a few spaces left for Easter.

'Have you thought about Centerparcs, Mrs Shattock?' Yes, I have thought about Centerparcs: like going to hell in a Tupperware container.

I try Cornwall, Cotswolds and the Canaries. All full. Eventually get through to some firm called Cymru Cottages. Valda says, miraculously, she has a cancellation outside St David's. 'On the cosy side, mind, but you can't go wrong with an open fire, can you?'

I'm just getting ready to leave for lunch when the postroom lad arrives at my desk looking rather sheepish: he is carrying two bunches of Valentine's Day flowers. One – gardenias, lilies, white roses as big as a hand – looks like Grace Kelly's wedding bouquet; the other consists of garage-forecourt tulips padded out with funeral-director fern. Open the cards. The tulips are from my husband.

From: Debra Richardson
To: Kate Reddy
Meant to tell you, don't be freaked out about nits. Nits are now very middle class. Felix's school just had Nits Day to 'remove the stigma of nits'!
How was your Hammer man in New York?
The only good thing about our situation is that we are Far Too Knackered to Commit Adultery.
Lunch thursday, right?
Deb xxxx

From: Kate Reddy
To: Debra Richardson
Good to know nits have become oppressed minority group with their own EU funding, rather than pest you have to comb out of groaning child's hair every night. (Tried tea tree oil – stank, but no use – now on to chemical stuff brewed by Saddam Hussein. But will it kill the kids before it kills the nits?)
Sorry, can't do lunch: forgot it was half-term.

Think the Hammer man just sent me major Valentine's bouquet.

From: Candy Stratton
To: Kate Reddy
Bad news, hon. Slow Richard rang while U wre out and stoopid secrtry said, 'Oh, your flowers are SO much nicer than those tulips she got.'
pretend U hav florist stalker. Prefrbly GAY florist stalker.
PS: Thnx for crazy zebra shoes. Did you shoot them yourself?

From: Debra Richardson
To: Kate Reddy
Kate, we are too tired for adultery, AREN'T WE? xxxxx

From: Debra Richardson
To: Kate Reddy
Don't do anything disgusting and amoral.
Without telling me EVERYTHING.
D xxxx

1.27 pm: Half an hour for lunchless lightning browse in gleaming electronics emporium near Liverpool Street. The atmosphere in the shop is delirious, malarial. Everyone in here has too much money and not enough time to spend it. I spot a guy from our tech team reverently cupping a digital camera as if it were a chunk of the True Cross.

It only takes a minute to find exactly what I'm looking for. The latest, dinkiest personal organiser. A truly gorgeous thing – implausibly light, but with a pleasing scientific heft and witty too, like a Fifties drinks coaster. The Pocket Memory comes with an impressive raft of promises:

It will simplify your life!
Banish stress!
Pay your bills!
Remember your friends' birthdays!
Have sex with your husband while you finish that great Carol

Shields novel you started some weeks into your first pregnancy!

I say I'll take it. I don't even ask how much. One way and another I've earned it.

2.08 pm: Rod Task approaches my desk like a marine storming a beach. 'Katie, I need your help!' he hollers. Then, ominously, he parts his lips and clenches his teeth to form what he thinks is a smile. (Rod is only really scary when he's trying to be nice.)

Playfully cuffing a daffodil in the vase on my desk, he tells me he wants me to do a final for a $300 million ethical pension fund account. Finals are a sort of beauty contest in which rival investment managers vie to convince a prospective client that they are the most responsible gambler in town. Oh, and Rod forgot to mention the final when he heard about it, so I only have twelve days to prepare, although this is now my fault, because if it wasn't my fault it would mean Rod made a mistake. And Rod is a man, so that can't be right.

I can hear myself starting to protest a long way off – a watery wail of injustice – but Rod bulldozes on. 'They want us to field a team that reflects EMF's commitment to diversity,' he says. 'So I reckon that's gotta be you, Katie, and the Chinky from research.'

'I beg your pardon?'

'Moma, right?'

'Momo is not Chinese. She's Sri Lankan.'

'Whatever,' he shrugs. 'She looks pretty fucking diverse to me.'

'Rod, I simply can't. Momo has absolutely no experience. You just can't –'

My boss has the daffodil by the neck now, and the dejected bloom is weeping yellow ash on to the grey carpet.

'Hey, we don't do can't, sweetie. When did we start doing can't? Can't is for pussies.'

*

WAS I SHOCKED by the way Rod talked to me? Actually, you'd probably be shocked by how unshocked I was.

Chauvinism is the air I breathe – a bracing blend of Gucci Envy and salty gym residue. Like one of those cuboid amber air-fresheners Winston hangs in the cab, the smell stuns you as soon as you enter the City; it lays waste to your septum before curling into your brain. Soon it becomes the only smell in the world. Other odours – milk, apples, soap – seem sickly and feeble by comparison. When I first came to the City I smelt the smell and recognised it immediately as power.

Truth is, I don't mind: let them comment on my legs if those legs help keep me and my children in shoes. Being a woman doesn't get you what you want within Edwin Morgan Forster, but it enables the firm to get what it wants outside – accounts, a reputation for 'diversity' – and they owe you for that. It's the oldest trade of all and it's good enough for me. Sometimes I mind for other women, though. For the older ones, like Clare Mainwaring in Operations, whose grey hair puts them among the firm's Disappeared, and for the kids like Momo who think that having an MBA means that guys won't look up your skirt.

Round here, there are only three kinds of women. As Chris Bunce once explained to me over a drink in Corney and Barrow, back in the days when he was still hoping to get into my knickers: 'You're either a babe, a mumsy or a grandma.' Back then I qualified as a babe.

And the equal-opportunities legislation? Doesn't make it better; just drives the misogyny underground, into the dripping caves of the Internet. We make jokes about men on the Net all the time – wry, helpless, furious jokes – but the stuff some of the guys send: well, a gynaecologist would need to go and lie down. Let them pass as many laws as they like. Can you legislate for the cock to stop crowing?

The way I look at it, women in the City are like first-generation immigrants. You get off the boat, you keep your eyes down, work as hard as you can and do your damnedest to ignore the taunts of ignorant natives who hate you just because you look different and you smell different and because one day you might take their job. And you hope. You know it's probably not going to get that much better in your own lifetime, but just the fact that you occupy the space, the fact they had to put a Tampax dispenser in the toilet; all that makes it easier for the women who come after you. Years ago, when I was still at school, I read this book about a cathedral by William Golding. It took several generations to build a medieval cathedral and the men who drew up the plans knew that not even their sons, but their grandsons or great-grandsons, would be around for the crowning of the spire they had dreamed of. It's the same for women in the City, I think: we are the foundation stones and the females who come after us will scarcely give us a second thought, but they will walk on our bones.

Last year, during the photoshoot for EMF's corporate brochure, they had to 'borrow' workers from the sandwich place in the basement to fill in the blank spaces where the women and ethnic minorities should be. I sat in a fake meeting opposite a Colombian waitress, who was wearing Celia Harmsworth's red Jaeger jacket and was instructed to study a fund report. The photographer had to turn it the right way up.

Later, going downstairs to pick up a bagel, I tried to catch the waitress's eye across the counter, to share a look of girly complicity – Men! What can you do? But she didn't even glance up from her tub of cream cheese.

*

4.53 pm: Got to start work on the pitch for the ethical fund, but distracted by thoughts of Jack's Valentine bouquet, and then there's Emily's birthday. Three and a half months to go and my daughter is already counting the seconds. (The desire to get to a birthday when you're five is as urgent as the desire to miss one when you're thirty-five.) Feeling like a proper organised mother for once, I put in a call to Roger Rainbow, a clown of high repute among the Muffia. Roger's answerphone informs me he is absolutely chocker every weekend, but still has some slots left for Hallowe'en. Bloody hell, it would be easier to book the Three Tenors. Trust me to become a parent in the era when birthdays finally became a competitive sport.

'Oh, I'm sorry. Excuse me, Kate Reddy?'

'Yes.' I look up and standing by my desk is the beautiful young woman who pressed me so hard at the trainees' induction before Christmas. Now, as then, she is blushing but there is nothing frail or floundering in her shyness: her reticence seems to have been cast from some fine but resilient metal.

'Sorry,' she says again, 'but I understand that we're going to be working together on an, um, final. Mr Task said he felt I had an important contribution to make.'

I bet he did. 'Oh, yes, Momo, it is Momo, isn't it? Well, I didn't imagine we'd be working together so soon and it's certainly going to be a real challenge.'

Come on, Kate, give the poor girl a break. It's not her fault she's been dumped on you. 'I've heard so many good things about you, Momo.'

'And vice versa,' she says gratefully, taking a seat. 'We all, well, all the women' – she gestures across the sea of suits – 'we don't know how you do it. Oh, is this yours?'

Disappearing under my desk for a second, she comes back up holding a daffodil.

'Oh, I'm so sorry, it's broken.'

Must Remember
Thank You letters, ring Mum, ring sister. HIGHLIGHTS! Complete IMRO forms. Momo List 'to do'. See amazing new film – Sitting Tiger? Sleepy Dragon? Trim Ben's nails. Ring Juno Academy of Fitness and book new personal trainer, Pelvic floor SQUEEEEZE. Emily school applications GET ORGANISED. Father-in-law's 65th birthday – tickets for Ayckbourn? Call Jill Cooper-Clark. Social life: invite people Sunday lunch – Simon and Kirsty? QUOTE FOR STAIR CARPET! Note for Juanita. Packing for half-term: Roo!!, extra towels, nappies, bottles, Calpol, portacot, wipes, wellies.

14

Half-Term

'KATE, I AM NOT having an argument with you about wellies.'

'Well, I'm having an argument with *you* about wellies. Emily is soaking wet. Just look at the state of her trousers. I have to remember everything. Every single thing. And I swear to God there's no room in my brain for any more information, Richard. I remembered to ask you to check the wellies were in the car.'

'I'm sorry, I forgot. It's not a big deal.'

'No, you're not sorry. If you were sorry you'd have remembered.'

How much do you think the human brain can bear in the way of remembering? I read somewhere that our long-term memory is basically this giant storehouse where all the people and places and jokes and songs we've ever known are laid down like wine, but if you don't visit a memory often enough the route to it is lost, briared over. Like the approach to Sleeping Beauty's castle. Is that why all fairy tales are about trying to find the way back?

Anyway, my memory's not what it was since I had the kids, but I have to try to remember. Someone has to. What's that awful word? Multitasking. Women are meant to be great at that. But Rich, if you ask Rich to hold more than three things in his head at once you can see the smoke start to come out of his ears: the circuits have blown in there. I've heard women on the radio arguing that guys play up how useless they are in order to avoid doing stuff. Unfortunately, extensive scientific trials in the Shattock home have revealed that the inability to remember the dry cleaning and the dishwasher tablets plus the film for the camera is, in fact, a congenital defect, like colour blindness or a dicky heart. It's not laziness, it's biology.

On the endless drive down to Wales on Saturday, I was watching Richard, observing the way he can screen out the kids when he needs to, when there is a destination he has in mind. Life is a road for a man; for women it's a map – we're always thinking about side roads and slip roads and doubling back, while they simply plough on in the fast lane. Their only diversion is an occasional brilliant idea for short cuts, most of which turn out to be longer and more treacherous than the original route.

Is that why men can live in the moment so much better than we can? Posterity is full of men who seized the day, while the women were planning for a fortnight on Tuesday.

So many of the rows Rich and I have nowadays are about remembering, or forgetting. Like the one we had when we got to the beach in Pembrokeshire that first afternoon of the half-term holiday, and it turned out that Rich hadn't packed the children's wellies. I don't know what made me go so berserk. Yes, the kids' feet were soaking, but they were having such a lovely time.

*

SWADDLED IN THREE layers of clothing, Ben and Emily play contentedly by the milk-chocolate channel that emerges from the hillside at the back of Whitesands Bay and foams over stones down to the sea. She has been building a castle with water gardens and a fountain made out of a razor shell, while he picks up a pebble, carries it to the water's edge, drops it in and then goes back to fetch another. They are as happy and intent as I've seen them. But the weather has got worse. Of course the weather has got worse. We are on holiday in Wales, why didn't I remember? Wet Wales. The sun broke through earlier, just long enough to see the freckles begin to swarm over Emily's face, but now the sky is pewter with rain. We decide to cut our losses and take the kids back to the cottage I have rented a few miles inland. Getting them out of the water and into the car takes roughly fifty minutes: requests give way to threats and, when they don't work, we fall back on bribes.

I promise Emily that Mummy will finally get around to reading *Little Miss Busy* to her, so after I've stripped off their wet clothes, given them their tea, bathed them in the tiny freezing bathroom with the wall heater that smells of burnt air, and persuaded Ben to lie in his portacot, my daughter and I settle down next to the open fire – two resentfully smouldering logs.

' "Little Miss Busy loved nothing more than to be hard at work, keeping herself busy. Every day she would get up at three o'clock in the morning. Then, Little Miss Busy would read a chapter from her favourite book. It was called: 'Work Is Good For You'." '

'Can't we read something more fun, Em?'

'No. I want that one.'

'Oh, all right. Where were we? "Miss Busy wasn't happy unless she was busy working." '

'Mummy, you came to Ben's birthday party.'

'Yes, I did.' I can see her thinking. All five-year-olds' thoughts are naked; they haven't learnt to cloak them yet. This one ripples across Emily's brow like a breeze over a dune.

'Did the teacher say you could leave early?' she asks at last.

'No, sweetheart, Mummy doesn't have a teacher. She has, well, she has a boss, this man who's in charge. And she has to ask him if she can leave.'

'Could you ask that man if you could come home early other days?'

'No. Well, yes I could, but I can't do it too often.'

'Why?'

'Because Mummy has to be in the office or . . . otherwise people might get cross with her. Let's finish the story, Em. "Little Miss Busy –" '

'Could you come home early and take me to ballet on Thursdays? Please can you, Mama?'

'Paula takes you to ballet, darling, and she says you're really,

really good at it. And Mummy promises to try and come to your show at the end of term this time.'

'But it's not fair. Ella's mum takes her to ballet.'

'Emily, I really haven't got time to argue with you now. Let's finish the story, shall we?'

' "And Miss Busy didn't rest all day long, not for a minute, not even for a second." '

When they were both asleep upstairs, Rich accused me of not being relaxed and I got incredibly upset. I'd done three solid hours of Lionel Bart's *Oliver!* in the car on the way down, hadn't I?

' "Wh-e-e-e-e-e-ere is love? Does it fall from skies above?" '

Does it hell. And Mark Lester was so desperately beautiful as Oliver and I read the other day that now he's an osteopath in Cheltenham or somewhere. I mean, that can't be right, can it? Like the breaking of a magic spell.

And after *Oliver!*, we sang twenty choruses of 'The Wheels on the Bus', which I did most cheerfully, even though that song drives me absolutely nuts. Then, when Ben threw up in the car outside Swansea, I got him into the service station, washed him in the basin, dried him somehow with the one dry paper towel and changed him before buying all the basics we'd need when we got to the cottage – teabags, milk, sliced bread for toast. I was doing a pretty good impersonation of a mummy on holiday, wasn't I?

But Rich was right. Thoughts of the upcoming final that Rod had sprung on me were keeping me awake at night. I'd left Momo to do the research into the ethical pharmaceutical sector while I was away, but she simply didn't have the experience to hack her way through the material in time. Twice a day, I called her from a phone-box in a high-hedged lane or by some rasping pebbled shore, my mobile signal coming and going like the tide. And, of course, I told Momo what warning signals to look for, how to compare screening criteria, and a dozen other things, but it was like asking a skateboarder to dock a space station. I had specifically instructed Guy to help her out too, but while I was away he would be otherwise engaged, having his bony Machiavellian arse measured for my chair. No way was Guy going to do anything that would put me in a good light.

Plus, as the cottage's phone connection was practically steam-powered, I couldn't pick up my e-mails. Being out of contact with Abelhammer for four days made me realise how much I relied upon him as a safety valve; without his soothing attentions I was ready to explode.

*

Thursday, A car park, St Davids Cathedral
3.47 pm: Am unloading Ben's buggy from the boot of the car when the downpour starts; joke rain, crazy rain, Gene Kelly Singing-in-the-Sodding-Rain rain. Try to wrestle the baby into the buggy straps – his body stiffening as my impatience grows. I feel like an asylum orderly putting a straitjacket on a madman. Richard has fetched the raincover and hands it over; it's a fiendish combination of clingfilm and climbing frame.

Boldly loop big hoop over Ben's head and try to fasten the clips, but I cannot get them round buggy handles so attach to the fabric instead. Seems OK, but I'm left with two elastic loops. What the hell are they for? Drape remainder of cover over the baby's feet, but the rain snatches it and whips it up into my face. Damn. Start again.

'Come on, Kate,' says Richard, 'we're getting soaked here. Surely you know how to put that cover on.'

I surely don't know. How would I know? Only contact with wretched thing was handing over Visa card in John Lewis thirteen months ago and, when the assistant tried to demonstrate the raincover, snapping at her, 'I'll just take it, thanks.' (Can hardly call Paula in Morocco and ask how to use own child's equipment.)

Ben is howling now. Drops of rain join the tributary of snot running over his lips to form a cataract of misery. Have you noticed how all baby equipment comes with the promise of 'easi-assembly'? This is industry shorthand for: only those with NASA training need attempt.

'For Chrissake, Kate,' hisses Richard, who will put up with anything except embarrassment in public.

'I'm trying. I'm *trying*. Emily, don't go near the cars. EMILY, COME HERE THIS MINUTE!'

A coach has pulled up alongside us and disgorged a tour party of seventysomethings. Ladies of the Valleys with freshly baked perms and short padded coats that give their sturdy trunks the appearance of boilers lagged to save on fuel. As one, they dive into their handbags and produce those slithery packets that open out into instant, see-through sou'westers. There they stand, twittering companionably and observing my struggle.

'Aww, poor dab,' says one, gesturing towards my bawling son. 'Getting wet izz 'ee? Nevah mind. Mammy'll 'ave yew right in a minute.'

My fingers are blunt with cold. Can barely hold the bloody clip let alone open it. Under the wrong piece of plastic, an enraged Ben is as puce as packaged beetroot. I turn to the ladies. 'New pram,' I say loudly. And they all nod and smile, eager to be drawn into womanly complicity against the hopeless man-made machine.

'They make stuff so stiff now, don't they?' says one woman in check trews, taking the raincover from me, nimbly flipping it over the buggy and fastening it with practised clicks. 'My daughter's juss the same as yew,' she says, briefly laying a hand on my shoulder. 'Doctor up Bridgend way now, she is. Two little boys. Hard work, mind. Yew don't get no holidays do yew?'

I shake my head and try to smile but my lips are rigid with cold. The woman's hands are red and bony. A mother's hands – one who did the washing-up three times a day, peeled the veg and stirred the Terry nappies in their scummy cauldron. Hands like that will die out in another generation along with waist pinnies and the Sunday roast.

Bowed double against the rain, Richard pushes the buggy along the little road to the cathedral. Emily is so drenched she has made the transformation from child to water sprite. 'Mummy?'

'What is it, Emily?'

'Baby Jesus has got a lot of houses, hasn't he? Is this where he comes on his holidays?'

'I don't know, sweetie. Ask Daddy.'

*

CATHEDRALS ARE BUILT to inspire awe. Sacred fortresses, they always look as though they have been lowered from heaven on to a hill. St Davids is different. It sits on the edge of a small Welsh town – a city in name only – hiding its virtues in a valley so perfectly designed it feels like an engraving. Cattle graze almost up to its walls.

I love this place. The ancient chill that fills your lungs when you push open the door – the trapped breath of saints, I always think. Must have been seven or eight the first time I came here, candyfloss from Tenby on my lips. Licking them now I can still taste its cobwebby sweetness. I have seen grander cathedrals since: Notre Dame, Seville, St Paul's. But the greatness of this church lies in its smallness; it's barely bigger than a barn. You wouldn't be surprised to find an ox and an ass by the font.

St Davids is one of the few places that bids me be still. And here in the nave I realise that, these days, stillness is an unaccustomed, even an uncomfortable sensation. The cathedral is timeless, and my life . . . my life is nothing but time. Rich has taken Emily and Ben to explore the gift shop. Left alone, I find my mouth forming words no one can hear: 'Help me.'

Asking a God I'm not sure I believe in to get me out of a mess I don't understand. Oh, very good, Kate, very good.

On the far wall, there is a slate tablet commemorating a local grandee. In memory of Somebody Thomas and of his relict Angharad. Relict. Same as relic? Will have to ask Rich, he's good at Latin. Had a proper education, not the comprehensive shambles I had to put up with.

Outside, a vertiginous, gingerbread staircase links the cathedral to the tiny city on the hill. I haul the buggy backwards up the steps, feeling each bump in my lower vertebrae. Rich carries a squally Emily on his shoulders. She and Ben need their tea. Guilty bad mother. I always forget children are like cars; without regular injections of fuel they judder and stop.

We walk down a street full of cafés and peer through the windows, inspecting each one for child-friendliness. Is there room for the buggy? Are there older people in there who would rather not share their toasted crumpets with a dribbly Ben? Britain is still no country for young children: venture too far away from Pizza Express and you find the same resentful sighs I remember from when Julie and I were kids.

We settle on a chintzy establishment full of other holiday parents, as jumpy and unrested as us, and make for the farthest corner. Draped over the backs of chairs, our wet coats steam like cows. I read out the menu and Emily announces loudly that she doesn't want anything that's on offer. She wants pasta.

'We can do 'oops from a tin, like,' offers the kindly waitress.

'I don't want hoops,' wails Emily, 'I want pasta.'

Metropolitan brat. All my fault for giving her everything so young. I didn't taste my first pasta till I was nineteen years old. Rome. Spaghetti alle vongole – clammy in both senses, a shaming ordeal of alien shells and unmanageable strands.

Sometimes I worry that I've travelled this far, done this well in life, only for my kids to grow up as jaded and spoilt as the people I was patronised by at college.

As Rich cuts up the children's Welsh rarebit, there is a little twiddly beep from my mobile. It's a text message from Guy.

TurkE crisis.
Rod & R C-C away.
Devaluation?
Turk shares collapsing.
Wot do?

Oh, hell. Jump up, barge past other families, stand on Labrador, run into street. Try mobile, but this time it's making another kind of beep telling me the battery is low. Can't get a signal. Of course I can't get a signal, I'm in Wales. Run back into the café.

134

'Have you got a phone I can use?'

''Scuse me?' The waitress looks blank.

'A payphone?'

'Oh yes, but it's not working like.'

'A fax?'

'Facts?'

'A facsimile machine. I need to send an urgent message.'

'Oh. They might 'ave one over the paper shop.'

Newsagent has no fax, he thinks chemist has fax. Chemist does have fax. Fax needs paper. Back to paper shop. About to close. Bang on door. Beg. Have to buy brick of 500 sheets, of which I need precisely one. Back to chemist. I scrawl a note to Guy using the prescription pen which is tethered to the counter:

> *Guy, MUST weigh up risk of Turkish trade failing and being charged interest rates of 2000 per cent – could cost us shedload of money – versus loss in value of shares if currency devalues.*
> *1 / How much have we got in Turkey?*
> *2 / What's market doing – knock-on effect other regions?*
> *Answers on my desk tomorrow 8.30am. Coming back Right Now, Kate.*

*

9.50 pm: There are huge jams in both directions on the M4. The headlights form a three-mile diamond necklace. From the driving seat, Rich shoots me inquiring, sidelong glances. I am grateful for the dark: it means I don't have to pick up his distress signals until I feel ready.

Finally he says: 'I still think it's a bit odd, Kate. You sending yourself those flowers on Valentine's Day. Why did you do it?'

'As a morale boost. I wanted people in the office to feel I was the kind of person who got flowers on Valentine's Day. And I wasn't sure that you'd remember. Pathetic really.'

Easy to lie when you try. Easier than saying that the flowers came from a client with whom I have recently dined, a client who has since occupied much of my conscious mind as well as rudely gatecrashing my dreams. Time to change the subject.

'Rich, what's a relict? I saw it on a tomb in the cathedral today. "And his relict Angharad."'

'Widow. It means literally what is left behind.'

'So the wife was the remains of the husband?'

'Exactly, Kate.' He laughs. 'Of course, in our marriage, I'd be what was left of you.'

It's said with enough love really to sting. Do I really make him feel that way? That small? Over the miles to come, I embroider any number of plans, strategies to make things better between us. Put things right. But three hours later, as we pass Reading, I start to feel the gravitational pull of London, and the resolve to change my life burns up on re-entry.

Reasons to Give up Work & Go & Live in Country
1/ *Better quality of life.*
2/ *Can buy mansion with en-suite minstrels' gallery for cost of Hackney heap.*
3/ *Chance to be real mother who has time to love husband, learn secret of children's hearts and discover how buggy bloody raincover works.*

Reasons Not to Give up Work & Go & Live in Country
1/ *Would go mad.*
2/ *See above.*
3/ *See above.*

Part Three

15

The Pigeons

WHERE IS A bird of prey when you need one? Since early this morning, two pigeons have been sitting on the ledge outside my office window. On their first date, apparently. For an hour or so, the male seemed to be bowing to the female, making polite little waiterly dips in front of her. Well, I assume that's the male, because the other one is the colour of dishwater and lowers her head in a coy Princess Di way, while he has this magnificent ruff of feathers round his neck, emerald and purple with a petroleum sheen.

It wasn't so bad when the male was whispering sweet nothings, but now he's strutting about with his tail spread out in a fan, hissing and whistling to attract the female's attention. The noise is unbelievable. I give several sharp raps on the window to scare the birds away, but the courting couple only have eyes for each other.

I call over to Guy and tell him to get the Corporation on the phone right away and ask for some guidance on pigeons.

Guy puts on his Jeeves face: 'Do you want me to arrange to have them shot, Kate?'

'No, Guy, they've got a hawk to take them out. Can you ask them when he's making his next visit?'

It's a little-known fact that the City of London employs a falconer who brings his sparrowhawk along every so often to control the pigeon population. Last time he was here, Candy and I were on our way to lunch and my unshockable New York friend was astonished to see a large countryman with a single leather gauntlet, launching a feathered missile into the air above our heads.

'If you've ever wondered why the City has such clean

pavements compared to the rest of London, there's your answer,' I said.

'Oh, I get it,' grinned Candy. 'That way they keep all the shit on the inside.'

From: Debra Richardson
To: Kate Reddy
How ARE YOU? Me so stressed after 3 days of half-term wanted to check into the Priory. Do they do a work-withdrawal programme for sad junkies like us? We went to a 'child-friendly' hotel in Somerset. Felix got us banned after fusing electrics in the breakfast room. Plugged his Thunderbirds fork into the communal toaster and the whole place went dark. Ruby says she hates me.
Are we just causing our children short-term damage, do you think, or will there be major lawsuits later on?
Lunch on wednesday, right?
Yrs in D-nial xxx

From: Jack Abelhammer
To: Kate Reddy
Subject: Japanese Banking Crisis
It is with some concern that your client notes the continuing upheaval in the Far Eastern sector. I understand Origami Bank has folded, Sumo Bank has gone belly up and Bonsai Bank has plans to cut back several smaller branches.
can I get some direction on this, Ma'am? xxxxx

From: Kate Reddy
To: Jack Abelhammer
Subject: Japanese Banking Crisis.
Don't you have a business empire to run, Sir? Jokes about the plight of our Oriental friends are in v. poor taste, although I did hear shares in Kamikaze Bank have nose-dived and 500 back-office staff at Karate Bank got the chop.
Katharine. xx

From: Jack Abelhammer
To: Kate Reddy
Hey, I missed you. I've grown accustomed to your pace. How was the vacation? Hot and relaxing, I hope.
Saw this great movie the other night about a guy who lost his memory, so he has to write all the stuff he needs to remember on his body. I thought of you – you said you always had so much stuff to remember, right?
Jack xx

From: Kate Reddy
To: Jack Abelhammer
Not hot and not relaxing exactly. Still cold here – passed a guy on the ice rink outside the office this morning; he was doing these cool loops and swivels, as though he was writing his name on the ice. Or even someone else's – how romantic is that?
Correct about the movie, though. Most of my body is covered in detailed notes already, but I've kept a spot for you behind my left knee.

From: Jack Abelhammer
To: Kate Reddy
I skate a little – do you? We could try a few moves on thin ice one day.
As for the left knee, be right there. Just feathering my quill.

10.23 am: Now the damned pigeon has started clapping his wings together. As though he's giving himself this big round of applause for being such a great lover. The female, meanwhile, is doing the birdy equivalent of lying on her back and waving her legs in the air. Completely intolerable. I manage to open the window and try to shoo them away. But love, it turns out, is deaf as well as blind.

So much to do I am surprised that my head is not lolling to one side with the weight of activity in there. In two days, I will be attending a final in the US for a $300 million ethical pension fund which I will be presenting with a twentysomething graduate trainee who has all the qualifications for the job – not white, not male – except being able to do the job. Between us, Momo Gumeratne and I will signal EMF's passionate commitment to diversity, a commitment whose finest hour till now has been the inclusion of tacos on the cafeteria menu. Also, I have still not secured the services of an entertainer for Emily's birthday party. Also, I must pick up clothes for the final from the dry cleaners. Also, there was definitely another also.

Damn. That's all I need. A memo on my desk from Robin Cooper-Clark says there's an internal investigation into some stock EMF sold that we didn't actually have. I push the memo across the desk to Momo and tell her to go and put it on Chris Bunce's desk. 'But make sure he doesn't see you, OK?'

The leaf-shaped eyes curl up at the corners as she scans the paper. 'We sold stock we didn't have and now there's a claim against us and Robin wants to know who is responsible?'

'Correct.'

'So, we find out whose fault it is?'

'No, Momo. The aim is to keep passing the buck until you wear the others down. Are you familiar with the game Musical Chairs? Yes, well, this is Musical Memos. The last person left holding the paper is in deep shit. So, if you could just deliver that to Bunce's desk. *Now?*'

I am beginning to recognise the expression on my assistant's face: a sort of tremulous frown where high principle struggles with a fervent desire to please. 'Sorry, Kate, but how do we know Chris Bunce is to blame?'

I swivel my chair away from her to stop me losing my cool. Outside on the ledge, the pigeon family tableau is framed by a crane like a giant set-square. How to account for Chris Bunce, a man who in conversation unconsciously grabs at his crotch as if to check his manhood is still there, or rubs it in excitement when he thinks he's about to get the better of someone? Particularly me.

'Look, Bunce is a seat-of-the-pants artist who never does any of his admin and leaves it to conscientious girlies like you and me to do all the boring stuff that satisfies the authorities. If

IMRO knew what Bunce got up to they'd be in here with a team of alsatians. But Bunce is very good at getting away with it because he plays a mean game of Musical Memos. Am I making myself clear yet?'

'Sorry,' Momo says, as another person would say OK, and walks across the office, holding the memo out in front of her like a sapper with an unexploded mine.

'Are you going to be able to train her up?'

Candy is standing by my desk wearing a skirt so short it's practically a text message. I didn't even hear her come over.

'I don't know. I'm trying to introduce Momo to the idea that not everyone is a nice person.'

'Omigod. We're not talking about a functional childhood, are we?'

''Fraid so.'

Candy shakes her head in wonder and pity. 'Poor kid. She'll never get anywhere.'

11.25 am: Determined to get my new personal organiser up and running. The Pocket Memory will revolutionise my life! The Pocket Memory will banish stress! The Pocket Memory will make my time work harder for me!

After ten minutes reading the Starter Pack leaflet, I discover that the Pocket Memory is not compatible with my computer. I call the helpline. The school-leaver at the other end delivers his prepared script with all the facility of a man translating from the Urdu.

'Have you got a large serial port in the back, madam?'

'Of me or the computer? How the hell should I know?'

'What you need, madam, is a Connect Kit.'

'No, what I need is to make my personal organiser organise.'

'You may order our Connect Kit now, madam. Should you wish to proceed —'

'Excuse me, is this part of your promise to simplify my life? Couldn't I just go to a shop and get the Kit?'

'There aren't that many available, madam. People order them. It will take between five to ten days to arrive.'

'I don't have five to ten days. I am leaving for the States in twenty-four hours.'

'I'm afraid we can't—'

'Can't is for pussies.'

'I beg your pardon, madam?'

'It's an old Australian proverb meaning tell your manager that I have several million shares in his company which are currently under review and that our market research reports are not showing them in a favourable light. Am I making myself clear?'

There is an audible swallow. 'I'll have to have a word with the supervisor.'

Tuesday, 8.11 am: So it's come to this. Richard and I actually lay in bed last night discussing whether we were too tired to have sex. Couldn't quite remember what conclusion we reached until I got up this morning and noticed that my inner thighs were lightly glued together with glacé icing.

Not a good idea before a major presentation. Sportsmen always say they never have sex in the run-up to a big race or match, don't they? You never hear women athletes complain about it, but it must be the same for them, if not worse. There can be little to rival the female orgasm for knocking you out cold. Hours after the earth moved, a deep, tentacular weariness is still trying to drag you under: coming, I mean *really coming*, makes you want to go and lie down till Christmas. I reckon it must be Nature's way of giving the sperm the best possible shot at the egg. (When you think about it, almost everything in female biology is Nature's way of making us want a baby or, when we have one, of making us want to protect it.) Up until last year, I suffered from mild PMT; not nothing, but nowhere near the crampy hell some women go through. Then, as soon as I hit thirty-five, it was war. Every month now, the hormones are out in the streets jumping up and down, waving placards and shouting: 'Save Our Eggs!' My body appears to know that time is short and the passing of each egg is mourned like the loss of a precious stone.

But how can I have another baby, when I don't see the ones I've got? I've hardly been home these past few days. I look up at the office clock and if it's after eight I know that I've missed the kids' bedtimes, and, well, I figure I may as well push on for the night. Momo orders in a pizza or we have something healthy from the canteen in a Styrofoam box, always inedible, and we end up with our usual midnight feast: a bag of tortilla chips and a couple of Crunchies from the machine washed down with Diet Coke.

I picked up the phone when I finally got in last night at 11.55, expecting it to be Momo with some more figures. And who did I get? Barbara, my mother-in-law. I couldn't believe she was ringing that late.

'Tell me not to stick my oar in where it's not wanted, Katharine, but I spoke to Richard earlier and he sounded very tired. I hope everything's all right.'

She thinks *he's* tired?

10.07 am: In a meeting with Rod, Momo and Guy. We are rehearsing the final for the third time, with Rod and Guy taking the parts of the clients, when Rod's secretary, Lorraine, bursts in.

'Sorry to interrupt, Kate, but there's *someone for you* on line 3. He says you said it was urgent.'

'But who is it?'

Lorraine appears reluctant to say. She stands awkwardly in the doorway until finally, in a stage whisper, she volunteers: 'It's a Percy Pineapple.'

Guy rolls his eyes so languidly he's practically looking backwards into his own skull. Momo gazes at her shoes.

'Who the fuck's Percy Pineapple?' asks Rod amiably.

I decide to brazen it out: 'Oh, yes, that'll be Percy Pineapple, the entertainment stock, part of Fruitscape.com, which is coming to the market. Chairman is coming in to see me to discuss the float. Just his little joke.'

Dear God. Still no entertainer for Emily's party. Have worked my way through the trusted favourites – Roger

Rainbow, Zee-Zee the Clown and Katie Cupcake who does the most marvellous things with Smarties and an air-pump. All have prior engagements in Monaco or Las Vegas or dancing attendance on some anal-retentive Mother Superior who had the paper plates and napkins picked out for Jocasta's seventh birthday by the time her waters broke.

I am rapidly sliding down the food chain and have entered the small-ad territory of bearded loons whose mugshots have an uncanny overlap with those printed in the *News of the World* 'Name and Shame' paedophile campaign. There was a flash of hope on Monday when Percy Pineapple of Gravesend said that for 120 quid, no questions asked, love, he could drive up in his van and put on a lovely show for the little girl. But Percy's leaflet came in the post this morning. It shows a chubby homunculus twisting Durex-pink balloons into worryingly priapic dachsunds.

Of course, what Emily really wants is a swimming party, but that is totally out of the question. At the pool you hire for such occasions, the water is tepid, bacteria-rich and, unlike most water, not transparent. Also, would have to take time off for bikini wax: cannot do public nudity with other parents.

11.19 pm: Arrive home to discover the Pocket Memory Connect Kit on the hall table. Richard is shipwrecked on the sofa watching the Arsenal game. He has left me some pasta in the oven: it has the texture and smell of baked toes.

'Would it be totally out of the question for anyone except me to take stuff left at the bottom of the stairs upstairs?'

Rich doesn't look up from the TV: 'Ah, the great She returns. Is it that time of the month already?'

'Are you accusing me of having PMT?'

Rich yelps and drops the remote. 'God, Kate, I look back to your pre-menstrual tension with nostalgia. These days, we have post-menstrual tension, inter-menstrual tension. We have 24–7 tension. Can you switch off when you eventually come to bed or will you be issuing instructions in your sleep?'

I open the dishwasher and notice that the supposedly clean

dishes have a tide-mark of grey sediment. Damn machine must be on the blink. 'It may have escaped your notice, Rich, but I have a major presentation—'

'For it to have escaped my notice, I would have to have been embalmed in Ulan Bator.'

'I do this for us, you know.'

'What us, Kate? The kids haven't seen you since we got back from Wales. Maybe you should become a TV presenter: at least they'd catch you once a day on screen.'

Standing in the doorway, watching my husband's baffled misery from a long, long way off, I think how I know this situation so well and I know the ways out of it: either leave for the airport in the morning with a frost on the ground and hope it has melted by the time I get back, or take my clothes off right now and remind both of us that love is something you can make. I'm so exhausted my body feels like a carcass; no, it feels like a living body carrying a dead one on its back. But I can't bear to leave him like this and some kinds of sex take less time and energy than others.

'Please be on my side, Rich,' I say to him as I get to my feet a few minutes later. 'It's me by myself in the office, against them: I can't be on my own at home as well.'

1.01 am: Have almost finished transferring all the information I need into the Pocket Memory when there is a cry from upstairs.

4.17 am: Emily up three times already. Wrestling with her duvet, damp hair drying in crusty tendrils on her pale cheek. Can't tell me what's wrong. How can she do this to me tonight of all nights? When I have to leave for the airport in three hours. Immediate stab of guilt for even thinking such a thought. Then, just when I've decided this is a pre-emptive punishment for leaving her – like a cat, Emily senses a departure before the suitcase is brought down – she finally moans, 'Mummy, my wee-wee hurts.'

I pour her a large cup of cranberry juice and spend the next twenty minutes on the phone trying to get through to an emergency doctor. He suggests I give her Calpol and take a urine sample into the surgery first thing. Downstairs, I try to find the nearest thing to a specimen bottle – something watertight, but big enough for her to pee into. Only thing I can find is Barbie flask. It will have to do. Back upstairs, kneeling next to the toilet, I have no luck coaxing a wincing Em to perform into the flask.

'Mummy?'

'Yes, love.'

'Can I have a swimming party?'

'Of course, sweetheart.'

The flask is instantly filled to the brim.

Noon, JFK Airport, New York: A hulking Customs inspector bearing a strong resemblance to Sipowicz in *NYPD Blue* rifles through my hand luggage. Totally unconcerned, I look on as he takes out my mobile, spare tights and Pongy Percy the Puppy book. Dips his meaty hand in a side pocket and brings out the Barbie flask. Omigod. Was supposed to leave that on the kitchen table: if flask is here, where is Pocket Memory?

Customs inspector unscrews Barbie container and sniffs: 'Ma'am, how would you describe this liquid?'

'It's my daughter's urine.'

'Ma'am, I think you'd better come with me.'

Must Remember
Absolutely Bloody Everything.

16

The Final

Awake since 4 am, trapped in the revolving door of jet lag.
Room service doesn't start till six so I get a rank metallic coffee
·from machine in the hallway and add a slug from a miniature in
the minibar. Whisky gives a sustained top note to the hellbrew.
Catch sight of an old woman in the bathroom mirror and look
away.

This morning, I dress for battle in full Armani armour. It is
incredibly comforting pulling on a crisp white blouse and a
digestive-biscuit-brown jacket and skirt with seams so sharp
you could take out an appendix with them. I wear the fudge-
coloured LK Bennett pencil heels with white stitching and a
groin-piercing toe. The look I'm aiming for is Katharine
Hepburn Kicks Ass.

Two hours before the final and Momo joins me in the room.
She is wearing a blue silk suit and her dark hair is scraped back
and pinned up. She may be nervous within, but she looks so
mysteriously serene that a religion ought to be founded in her
name.

Today, though, I have to be confident for both of us,
exuding the gale-force bonhomie of a gameshow host who
knows his contract is up for renewal. We've been through the
presentation fifty times already, but there's no harm reprising all
the Don'ts.

'If they offer you a drink don't take it, OK? Don't call them
by their first names whatever you do. This is an ethical fund;
these people like to think of themselves as the kind of people
who like to be Gregged and Hannahed, but if you try it they'll
suddenly realise how much they prefer to be deferred to.

They're thinking about trusting us with an awful lot of money, so it's Sir and Ma'am all round. And remember, we are the suitors.'

Momo looks surprised. 'It's a flirtation?'

'Yes, only we don't flirt. It's like courtly love.'

'The one who was married to Kurt Cobain?'

'Courtly love, Momo. *Courtly*. Did you ever read any Chaucer at school?' She shakes her head. God, what are they teaching them these days?

'No, well, we protest our undying devotion. Desperate to please the beloved, we'd walk a million miles for one of their files, that kind of thing. And the key is to keep reminding them that although we have hundreds of white guys behind us who practically invented banking, we also have an unparalleled commitment to diversity. Ethical funds want decent returns: they want diversity, but they don't want Third World. So we can give them the best of British with a rainbow gloss, which is where you and I come in.'

'Isn't that sort of unethical, Kate?'

Weeks of exposure to my radioactive cynicism and she can still ask that question? What am I going to do with this child? 'If we told the truth, Momo, we'd lose, which would have the virtue of being extremely ethical. But if we bluff our way through and we win, then two women – one of them not white – will have landed a $300 million account for Edwin Morgan Forster, which means that diversity really does pay and that means that one day, instead of being window-dressing, we may get a crack at running the store. Which will be altogether ethical and also mean we can buy ourselves a lot of excellent shoes. Next question.'

'So, lying in a final isn't wrong?'

'Only if you do it badly.'

Momo gives a laugh that is too big for her slight frame; it propels her back on to the bed and one shoe slips off and thumps on to the floor. (Must remember to do something about her shoes: navy flatties, they do nothing for her feet, which are as tiny and articulated as a ballerina's.) Lying there on the swirly orange counterpane, she looks up at me and sighs: 'I don't understand you, Kate. Sometimes I think you think it's all the most terrific bullshit and then it seems as though you really really want to win.'

'Oh, I really, really do. Just watch me. When I was little I used to hide a Monopoly hotel down my sock. If I landed on Park Lane, I'd smuggle the hotel out. My dad caught me one Christmas and hit me with the nutcracker for being a cheating little cow.'

I can see Momo struggling to place this Dickensian episode in the polite, well-ordered childhood that is the birthright of every middle-class girl. She hasn't worked out that I'm travelling on a false passport. Why would she? These days even I'd struggle to spot myself as the impostor in a City line-up.

When she responds, it's as though the sun were in her eyes. 'That's awful,' she says. 'Your father. I'm really sorry.'

'Don't be. Be sorry for the losers. Now let's run through that part where you hand me the list of clients again.'

The phone rings and for a second neither of us recognises its plaintive foreign bleat. It's Rod with a few last-minute suggestions. When I've hung up, I turn to Momo.

'All right, guess what he said.'

She furrows her brow and pretends to be thinking before answering in her best crystal Cheltenham Lady: 'Go out and kick the fucking tyres?'

Suddenly I feel a lot less worried about her. 'OK, you got the job. Rod's not bad, you know, once you learn how to handle him. If you make him think everything you want to do is his idea, he'll be happy as Larry.'

Momo frowns. 'When you talk about the men at work, Kate, it's as though we were their mothers.'

'We *are* their mothers. I have people hanging on to my skirt in the office and then I have them hanging on to my skirt when I go home. You'd better get used to it. Right, let's try the opening one more time.'

The phone rings again. It's Paula, just calling to say she located my personal organiser in the salad drawer. Ben has started hiding things in the fridge. All the information I have needed over the past twelve hours has been with the celery. Meanwhile, Emily is on antibiotics for her urinary infection. Her temperature is still up, but she'd like to talk to me, if that's OK.

Emily comes on the line, at once pipingly eager and breathily shy. Whenever I hear my daughter's voice on the phone, I feel as though I'm hearing it for the first time: it seems implausible that something I grew inside myself so recently should be able to converse with me, let alone bounce off a satellite.

'Mummy, are you at America?'

'Yes, Em.'

'Like Woody and Jessie in *Toy Story 2*?'

'Yes, that's right. And how are you feeling, sweetheart?'

'Fine. Ben got a bump. There was loads and loads of blood.'

At this, I feel my own blood just stop; as if someone took a flash photo of my whole being. 'Em, can I speak to Paula again? Please ask Paula to come to the phone now, there's a good girl.'

I try to keep my voice calm and raise the matter of Ben's bump casually when what I feel like doing is appearing in a ball of fire in my own kitchen with maternal fangs glittering and a headful of hissing snakes.

'Oh that,' Paula says dismissively. 'He just hit his head on the table.'

The metal table with the retina-perforating corners I specifically said must be banished to the cellar in case Ben fell on it? That's the one. Hey, but these things happen, Paula is telling me and, her tone says, anyway, you weren't here so who are you to criticise? Besides, she doesn't think Ben needs stitches.

Stitches? My God. I clear my throat and try to find that sweet, liberal register where an order sounds like a suggestion. Perhaps Paula could take Ben to the surgery? Just in case. A deep sigh and then suddenly she is telling Ben to put something down. At this distance, my children's carer sounds sardonic, detached. Most distressing of all, she sounds like someone who is not me. I can just about hear Ben – he must be over by the window – making those yelps which sound like pain but are just his way

of recording the fierce pleasure of discovery. Paula is saying
there was something else. Alexandra Law called about a Parent
Teachers meeting at school. Will I be attending?

'What?'

'Can you go to the PTA meeting?'

'I really can't think about that now.'

'So I'll tell her no?'

'No. Tell her I'll call her . . . after.'

From: Debra Richardson
To: Kate Reddy
Q: Why is it difficult to find men who are sensitive, caring and
    good-looking?
A: They all have boyfriends already.
How U?

From: Kate Reddy
To: Debra Richardson
Completely mental. Literally. Life of the body a distant
memory. Am now just brain on a stick. About to pitch for
$$$$$$ account with terrified trainee who thinks Geoffrey
Chaucer is rap artist. Plus Emily sick and Ben nearly
decapitated while Pol Pot busy listening to Kiss FM.
Don't want to be grown-up any more. When did we start
having to be the grown-ups?
K xxx

2.57 *pm*: Our prospective client's offices are decorated in a
style I immediately identify as Corporate Cosy. Plaid wing
chairs, a lot of teak and ethnic hangings bought by the mile.
The look says we mean business but, hey, you can do a yogic
headstand in here if the mood takes you.

Momo and I are shown into the meeting room by the largest
female I have ever seen. Carol Dunstan is clearly a major
beneficiary of Workplace Diversity, Fattist Section. The walk
from the lobby has made her breathless; just looking at her is to
wonder what manner of distress it is that requires so much

comfort eating. She makes the introductions, taking us through the eighteen faces round the table. I hear Momo decline a drink. That's my girl. 'And last, but certainly not least, our distinguished colleague from the Salinger Foundation. Mr Abelhammer sits on the state board of trustees, Ms Reddy.'

And truly there he is. In the furthest corner, marked out from the other suits by a posture of almost insolent relaxation and a broad grin. Simultaneously, the person I least want to see and the only person I want to see. Jack.

The presentation goes well. Too well, maybe. Halfway through and I can practically taste the healing sting of gin and tonic on the plane home. I have tried to ignore the fact that my e-mail lover is actually physically here in the room, although I have felt his presence as you feel the sun on your skin.

I talk our prospective clients through the booklet containing mugshots of the guys who manage portfolios back in London. It's a gallery of City types pretty much unchanged for 300 years: well-lunched Hogarth squires, thrusting runts. Men whose last wisps of hair have been blown dry to form a spun-sugar web over a pink saucer of scalp. Heart-attack candidates, their eager prep-school faces buried in the landslide of middle age. Young men with the waxy, stunned look that comes from long, obedient hours in front of a screen. With particular pride, I point out hotshot hedge fund manager Chris Bunce, whose coke habit has given him the eyes of a laboratory rat and the manners to match. At the front, there is a photograph of Robin Cooper-Clark, tall as a birch, quizzical, half-smiling. He looks like God would look, if God had his shirts made at Turnbull & Asser.

Carol Dunstan clears her throat: 'Ms Reddy, New Jersey has recently signed up to the McMahon Principles. Would that be a problem to your asset allocation?'

OK, Kate, let's not panic. Let's think. *Think!* 'No. I'm sure that if we were given a list of stocks that were governed by the, Mc – um – Mahon Principles . . .'

'We don't have a list, Ms Reddy,' says the big woman curtly. 'Naturally, we would expect Edwin Morgan Forster to provide a list that abides by the McMahon Principles. Principles with which you are, of course, familiar.'

Eighteen faces in the room fixed on me. Nineteen, including Momo, who looks up with trusting spaniel eyes. I have never heard of McMahon or his sodding principles. Seconds which normally pass silently, modestly, happy to go unnoticed, are suddenly long, loud and merciless. I can feel the blood surge to my throat and chest: a raspberry flush that can only be triggered by sex or shame. The exhalation of the air-conditioning unit sounds like a woman parted from her lover. *No.* Don't think about lovers. Think about McMahon. Whoever he is. Probably some self-righteous little Celt wanting to take his revenge on the Anglo-Saxon capitalist oppressors. I avoid looking down the far end of the table where Jack is sitting.

Carol Dunstan's prim drawstring mouth is just opening again when a male voice speaks: 'I think we can feel confident, Carol, that with Ms Reddy's wide experience of ethical funds she would be up to speed with the employment practices of companies in Ireland.'

Sudden rush of gratitude as heady as oxygen. Jack has flipped the emergency hatch and given me a way out. I nod in eager agreement. 'As Mr Abelhammer says, we have a team which screens for employment policies. On a personal note, I'd like to add that I am fully behind the McMahon Principles, being Irish myself.'

There is a crash behind me. Momo has dropped a file, but this calamity is lost in the general murmur of appreciation for my ethnic credentials. On a tide of goodwill, I move straight into the close. The close is the bit where you say, Give us the money. But politely. And without mentioning money.

5.11 pm: Momo and I are falling into the cab when there is a squeak of leather behind us.

'I'd like to say what a pleasure it was to witness such a performance, Ms Reddy.'

'Why, thank you, Mr Abelhammer. I was most grateful for your interjection.'

Caught in the static between Jack and me, Momo looks slightly perplexed.

He rests his hand lightly on the rim of the car door. 'I was wondering whether I could interest you both in a drink. Perhaps take in the sights of Shanksville. I see the Sinatra Inn does a cocktail called Come Fly With Me.'

'Actually, Ms Gumeratne and I are very tired.'

He nods his understanding. 'Another time. Take care now.'

On the way back to the hotel, Momo says, 'I'm sorry, Kate, but do you know that guy?'

'No, I don't.' A truthful answer. I don't know Jack Abelhammer, but I may be in love with him. How can you be in love with someone you don't know? It's probably easier, isn't it, all things considered. A blank screen you can type all your longings on.

'He looks like George Clooney,' sighs Momo. 'I think we should have that drink.'

'No. It would be unprofessional before they've made their decision. Anyway, we should have our own drink to celebrate. You were a complete star.'

'I'm sorry, Kate, but you were the brilliant one. I couldn't do what you just did.' Momo permits herself a smile and I suddenly see how tense her face has been. 'I didn't know you were Irish.'

'Just a little. On my father's side.'

'Like McMahon?'

'Yes, only without the principles.'

She giggles. 'What does your father do?'

'Same line of work as me.'

'He's a fund manager?'

'No, but like us he gambles a lot on fancied horses, pretends it's scientific and hopes to God they'll come home, and when they don't, he leaves town.'

'Good heavens,' says Momo, so shocked she forgets to say sorry for the first time since I met her. 'He sounds like a colourful character.'

*

WHENEVER I TALK about my dad to other people I hear myself adopting a different voice: detached, breezy, ironic. A voice you tell funny stories in. Colourful characters are wonderful in Dickens or as bit-parts in movies, when they're played by bloated ex-matinée idols who can be carried all the way to Best Supporting Actor on a wave of public sympathy; you just don't want one in your life if you can possibly help it.

'Pretend we've got plenty of cash, Kathy duck,' Dad once instructed me. We were sitting in a pub garden at the fag-end of a long grey line of Northern towns. Julie and I sat on a bench with half-pint glasses of Dandelion & Burdock, a drink that tastes like Pepsi mixed with creosote, but was believed by us to be the chosen nectar of sophisticated ladies. I was twelve years old, too dizzy from moving town every six months to know what stable behaviour was, and far too much in thrall to my father to protest. Of course there wasn't any money, and when there was, it would be spirited out of my mum's purse by Joe for one of his schemes.

But I pretended we had money. Even then I think I could smell the disappointment settling like damp on my father and I wanted to protect him from it. Disappointment unmans a man so. The women around him have to go on pretending they can't smell it, with him sitting there, hand shaking and using the other one to steady the glass and insisting that there's everything still to play for.

Now here's a funny thing. All the women I know in the City are Daddy's Girls one way or another. (Candy's dad walked out when she was five and I think she's been trying to find him ever since; Debra's ran a motor company in the West Midlands and was occasionally sighted by Deb and her sisters between rounds of golf at the weekend.) Daughters striving to be the son their father never had, daughters excelling at school to win the attention of a man who was always looking the other way, daughters like poor mad Antigone pursuing the elusive ghost of paternal love. So why do all of us Daddy's Girls go and work in a place so hostile to women? Because the only real comfort we get is from male approval. How sad is that? How fucking sad is that?

I close my eyes and try to banish thoughts of my own wayward sire. Since he turned up at the office with that nappy design, he has called most days. The other night, he left a message on the answerphone, saying that the money wasn't enough.

'How much did you give him?' asked Rich, his face draining.

I mentioned a figure that was about a third of the cheque I wrote that day in the pub and Rich hit the roof.

'Christ, when will you learn, woman?'

A good question. There's no statute of limitations on pity, is there?

*

8.18 pm: Must have lain down on the bed and fallen asleep. Woken by the phone. It's Richard. He sounds incredibly pissed off. Says he can't find the detergent ball for the washing machine. Paula called in sick and Ben was running round without a nappy and there was an accident on the duvet. So he's got the cover off and into the machine, but he can't find the ball.

I tell him the ball will probably have got tangled up in the sheets; he should try the ironing basket.

'Where's the ironing basket?'

'The ironing basket is the basket full of clothes next to the ironing board. Rich, aren't you even going to ask me how it went?'

'What?'

'The final.'

'I need you.'

'Oh, come on, Rich, you can manage the washing just this once.'

'Kate, it's nothing to do with the washing, I just need you. Why can't you fly home tonight?'

'I just can't. Look, I'll be on the first plane tomorrow.'

The phone again. I let it ring and ring. Richard asking about hamster food, presumably, or the location of the microwave or his children's ears. Eventually, thinking there might be a genuine problem with the kids, I pick up.

'I was glad to learn that you're Irish. For a moment there I was in danger of confusing you with the Katharine Reddy who runs my fund and told me she was French.'

'I did not say I was French, Jack. I said I had French blood in me.'

He laughs: 'What next? Cherokee? You are a piece of work, Kate.'

Now, I hear a voice, a responsible, sober woman's voice, telling her client quite firmly that under no circumstances does she want to try the Come Fly With Me cocktail in some cheesy roadside diner.

His reply comes straight back over the net: 'No problem. They do a great Bewitched, Bothered and Bewildered.'

A line from that song pops into my head and I sing it: 'Horizontally speaking, he's at his very best.'

Abelhammer lets out a low whistle: 'So, it's true, you do know everything.'

'I don't know the way to the Sinatra Inn.'

17

Night and Day

THE SINATRA INN has the determined gaiety of a fading showgirl. Red velvet booths line the walls; fifty years of elegant dining have rubbed shiny saddle sores in the scarlet plush. The back wall is given over to photographs of the local boy made good (Frank came from Hoboken, just down the road). There is a picture of Sinatra with Lauren Bacall, Sinatra at a rakish angle with the Rat Pack, Sinatra standing at a piano, caught in a cone of light, his skinny tie at half mast, his neck straining for some long-lost note. And Sinatra with Ava Gardner in the Fifties, him looking famished, her insatiable: I can never see those two together without imagining them in bed.

Each booth has its own mini jukebox where you put in your quarter and take your pick of Frank's Greatest Hits. So many titles, so many featuring the word You. Jack Abelhammer and I choose the corner seat under the poster of Frank as Maggio in *From Here to Eternity*. To the waiter, an eager, harassed man with a lot of veal to get rid of, we must appear to be a regular couple having fun over the cocktail list. (Witchcraft looks evil, so I opt for a Night and Day.) In fact, Jack and I are in trouble. Like returning astronauts, we are struggling to make the switch from the weightless world of e-mail, where you can say what you like and mean it or not mean it, to the real world where words, being earthed by gestures, by arms and lips and eyes, have their own specific gravity.

I have never seen Jack out of a suit before. The effect is only slightly less alarming than if he were entirely naked. I laugh and drink and laugh and feel a needle of doubt threading through me. I know Jack Abelhammer the way I know a fictional character. I need him to exist to make reality more bearable, not to complicate it.

'So, what's it to be, signora?' Jack is examining the menu. 'Veal with marsala, veal with mascarpone or veal with our delicious chopped veal? You don't likea da veal? OK, so we have a very gooda *scaloppina a la limone*.'

He slots a quarter into the jukebox, and his finger reaches out to press 'Where or When'.

'No, not that one.'

'But it's beautiful.'

'I'll cry. When I heard Sinatra died I cried.'

'Hey, I love Frank too, but he was real old when he died. Why d'you cry?'

I'm not sure how much I want to tell this most familiar stranger. The version with the colourful character or the true story? My dad had a cache of Sinatra 78s he kept in the sideboard, filed in their brown-paper sleeves in a big toast-rack thing. Julie and I were fascinated by them when we were kids. The brown paper smelt like old people, but the records themselves made everyone seem so young. They had that ebony lustre a cockroach has and a fabulous label in mauve with silver writing like an invitation to a ball. My father always did a great Sinatra impersonation at family get-togethers – standing on a table and spitting out 'Schick-kargo, Schick-cargo, that toddlin' town!' But the songs he liked best were the sad ones. 'All the Way' and 'Where or When'. 'Frank's the Patron Saint of Unrequited Love,' Dad said, 'will you listen to that voice, Katharine?'

'Kate?'

'Frank could make my parents happy,' I say, studying the menu. 'Sinatra was always the truce music in our house. It was safe to come out if my dad put on "Come Fly With Me". I think I'll try another cocktail instead of the veal. What d'you think would happen if you mixed a "Love and Marriage" with a "Strangers in the Night"?'

Jack grabs the tip of the knife I am playing with, so we each have one end. 'Nothing too terrible. Maybe a strange taste in the mouth. I'd say the worst was a bad case of remorse in the morning. What's a bouncy castle?'

'What bouncy castle?'

'A bouncy castle. You have it written on your hand. I haven't seen a girl write on her hand since eighth grade; Kate, you really should look into these great new things called diaries.'

I look down at the spider of biro across my knuckle, a reminder about Emily's birthday. So, here's the rub: to tell him or not to tell him that I am a mother (surely, the only context in which this could be a shameful revelation).

'A bouncy castle is . . . It's a blow-up castle you bounce on. For my daughter's birthday party, I need to remind myself to hire one. I mean, it's not for ages, but by the time I get round to remembering it's usually too late.'

'You have a child?' He seems interested, not appalled.

'Two. Or so they tell me. I don't see as much of them as I'd like. Emily will be six in June, she thinks she's Sleeping Beauty. Ben is one and a bit and you can't get him to stay still he's . . . Well, he's a boy.'

Jack nods solemnly: 'Amazing they're still making us. Strictly, we men should have been phased out with the stego-saurus. But a few of us wanted to stick around and see what the place would be like when you were running it.'

'I'm not terribly good at being laughed at, Mr Abelhammer.'

'That'll be the German in you, Ms Reddy.'

Later, after the veal – a flannel wrapped in a loofah of cheese – there is tiramisu, like shaving foam flecked with almonds. The food is so transcendentally terrible that we are already relishing the shared joke it will become. And then there is dancing. A lot of dancing. I seem to remember singing too, but that can't be right. What kind of a state would I have to be in to sing in public?

'Still a voice within me keeps repeating, You You You.
Night and day, you are the one,
Only you beneath the moon and under the sun.
Whether near to me or far, it's no matter darling where
*   you are*
I think of you. Night and day.'

162

2.34 am: 'Wake up, Mummy, wake up, sleepy head!'

Sit up in blind panic. Cover breasts with hands, then realise it's dark. Emily? Here in New Jersey? Takes a few seconds to find the light switch, a few more to figure out the voice is coming from the alarm clock, the travel one with the recorded message that Emily gave me for Christmas. It must be getting-up time back in London. 'Come on, Mummy, lazy bones, you'll be late.' Emily's voice is tinged with pride in her assignment: when she's bossy she sounds exactly like her mother.

I peer around the room for signs of adultery. My dress is on a hanger; shoes under the chair, underwear in a neat pile on top. Jack has carried me back, undressed me and put me to bed. Like a child. Suddenly, I think how unbearable it would have been if he'd been here when Emily's voice sang out in the darkness, stopping us in our –

Oh, God, my head. Must get water. Into the bathroom, switch on light. Light like a drill. Switch off light. Drink one glass of water, then another. Not enough. Climb into shower with mouth open and let water gush in. On the way back to bed, I see that the top page of the hotel stationery has something on it. Switch on desk lamp:

'Some things that happen for the first time,
Seem to be happening again,
. . . But who knows Where or When?'
Sleep well, love Jack

10.09 am: Newark Airport: The plane is delayed for ever. I am stretched out across a bank of seats in the Club Lounge. The fog outside the window is matched by impenetrable gloom inside my head. I think of last night while trying not to think of last night. Infidelity Reddy-style: all the guilt and none of the sex. Brilliant, Kate, just brilliant.

You get drunk with a client who carries you back to your hotel room, removes all your clothes and then politely takes his leave. Hard to know what to feel: outraged at the sexual invasion or mortified by the lack of it? Perhaps Abelhammer was repelled by the non-matching bra-brief combo, or maybe he fled at the sight of the Reddy stomach which, after two pregnancies and an emergency Caesarean, resembles one of her grandmother's rice puddings – the top-skin puckered over the granular slush beneath. One problem with being unconscious in the presence of a prospective lover is the inability to pull one's belly button to spine as advised by personal trainer.

At the thought of Jack undressing me, my whole being feels like a stocking silkily descending a leg.

'Kate, are you, OK?' Momo is back with black coffee and the British papers.

'No. Terrible. Anything in the news?'

'Just the Tory Party killing each other. And working mothers all cracking up. It says that 78 per cent would give up their job tomorrow if they could.'

'Ha! Can't be accurate. Those of us who are really stressed out don't have time to fill in stupid surveys. What are you thinking, Momo?'

She is doing that cute wrinkly thing with her nose: 'I'm sorry, but I'm not going to have any. Kids. I really don't know how you do it, Kate.'

'Compartments, that's how. They go in one compartment, work goes in another: and you have to stop them leaking into each other. It's tricky, but not impossible. Anyway, you must have children. You're beautiful and intelligent and there are enough gruesome morons reproducing out there.'

Momo shakes her head. 'I like kids, I really do, but I want to go on with my career and you said yourself how the City sees mothers. Anyway,' she says coolly, 'I'm overeducated for looking after small children.'

How to explain to her? So many women of Momo's age look at the likes of me, driven crazy by our double lives, and decide to put off having kids for as long as possible. I've seen it in my friends. They get to their mid-thirties, panic, pick the wrong guy – any sperm donor will do by then – find they can't get pregnant, embark on IVF, painful and ruinous. Sometimes it works; mostly it doesn't. We think we've outwitted Mother

Nature, but Nature isn't called Mother for nothing. She has her way of slapping us down, making us feel small. The world is going to end not with a bang, but with a woman staring through a glass panel at her frozen eggs and wondering if she'll ever have time to defrost them. I try to shut out the noise of the airport and think of what Emily and Ben mean to me, then I gather what remaining strength I have and let Momo have it.

'Children are the proof we've been here, Momo, they're where we go to when we die. They're the best thing and the most impossible thing, but there's nothing else. You have to believe me. Life is a riddle and they are the answer. If there's any answer, it has to be them.'

Momo reaches into her bag and passes me a tissue. Is it the thought of the children that's made me cry or the thought that last night I didn't think of them at all?

Flight from Newark to Heathrow, 8.53 pm: Adrenalin always gets you through a job, but on the way home the fact that I've been away kicks in like a hangover. Home. I feel both vital to it – how will they manage without me? – and painfully peripheral: they manage without me.

When I'm abroad, I sit in my hotel room in front of the laptop and call up my e-mails using Remote Access. You hear it dialling a long way off, somewhere at the far end of the universe. It takes a few seconds of bronchial static, then the bips do a tapdance off a satellite and come bouncing back. Remote access. Isn't that how I communicate with my children? Dialling them up when I need to, but otherwise keeping them at a distance. If I'm ever with Emily and Ben properly, for a few days and nights, I'm always struck by how shockingly alive they are. They're not the shyly smiling girl and boy in the picture I just showed Momo, the one I keep in my wallet. Their need for me is like the need for water or light: it has a devastating simplicity. It doesn't fit any of the theories about what women are supposed to do with their lives: theories written in books by women who never had children, or had children but brought them up as I mostly bring up mine – by Remote Access.

Children change your heart: they never wrote that in the books. Sitting here in the front row of Club, nursing a large gin, I feel that absurd organ inside my chest, swollen and heavy as a gourd.

Momo is right next to me. Since the tears at the airport my assistant has been anxiously attentive; unnerved by this wistful stranger talking about the meaning of life, Momo wants normal Kate service to be resumed as soon as possible and I'm pretty keen to get it back myself.

'Kate, I'll swap you my *Harvard Business Review* for your *Vanity Fair*.' She offers me a supplement with a sober grey typeface.

'Does it have any pictures of Johnny Depp?'

'No, but there's a terribly interesting article on The Dos and Don'ts of Kinesthetic Presentation. Guess what Point One is?'

'Undo two more blouse buttons than is strictly respectable?'

'No, Kate, seriously. "Ensure that your physical moves signal your intentions to the client."'

'Like I said. Two blouse buttons.' (Why do I feel compelled to relieve this lovely, solemn girl of her illusions? Perhaps I feel it's better I get in first, before the men take them away.)

Across the aisle from us, a harassed brunette in a baggy pink sweater is trying to quiet a yelling baby. She stands up and jiggles her. She sits down again and attempts to pull the baby's thrashing head into the cave of her shoulder; finally, she lifts her sweater and tenders a breast. The suit in the neighbouring seat takes one look at the mammary boulder and makes a dash for the toilet.

There is a little-known Universal Law of Infant Crying: the greater the mother's desperation and embarrassment, the louder the volume. Even without looking round, I can gauge the effect the mechanical howling has on my fellow passengers. The cabin crackles with the static of resentment: men who are trying to work, men who are trying to get some rest, women who may be savouring their last few hours of freedom and don't want a reminder of what they can get at home, women away from their own kids and pricked by guilt.

The mother has a look on her face I know all too well. It's two parts manic apology ('Sorry about this, everyone!') to three parts defiance ('We've paid for our seat, just like the rest of you and she's only tiny, what do you expect?'). Baby can't be more than two or three months old; a pre-hair furze, fine as dandelion down, forms a corona around a skull that has the tensile strength and beauty of an egg. When she screams, you can see the pulse jump in the blue hollow at her temples.

'No, Laura, no, sweetie, that hurts,' the mother chides as the infant tugs furiously on her long dark hair. I get a sudden deep pang for my Ben. He does that when he's overtired too: a baby's frustration at not being able to enter sleep is that of an alcoholic locked out of a bar.

Momo looks on with a twentysomething's horrified incomprehension. Under her breath, she asks me why the woman can't shut the kid up.

'Because the baby wants to go to sleep, but the pressure in her ears is probably really hurting. The only way you can equalise the pressure is to get her to drink something, but she won't latch on to the breast because she's too exhausted to suck.'

At the word suck, Momo gives a fastidious little shudder inside her Donna Karan grey wool. Says she finds the whole idea of breastfeeding deeply weird.

I tell her that it's the opposite of weird. 'In fact, it may be the only time in your life when your body makes perfect sense to you. I sat there in the delivery room and Emily rooted around and the milk started flowing and I thought, I am a mammal!'

'Sounds *gross*,' Momo says.

'It wasn't gross, it was comforting. We spend our whole life overruling what remains of our instincts and this one – how does that Carole King song go? – "Oh, you make me fee-eel like a nat-u-ral woman."'

Shouldn't have started singing. Pink Sweater overheard and clearly thinks I am being sarcastic about her doing the Earth Mother bit in public. I try to make amends by giving her a conspiratorial, Don't-worry-I've-been-there! smile. But I have forgotten that I'm in uniform. Seeing the suit and the laptop, she obviously mistakes me for the childless enemy and shoots me a twelve-bore glare.

I must try and get some sleep, but the thoughts are sparking in my brain like an electrical storm. When I think about Jack, I feel, what do I feel? I feel idiotic – who is he, anyway, and what does he want with me or I with him? But mainly I feel excited, I feel *ambushed*. There are forces gathering around my heart and shouting at me to come out with my hands up. Sometimes I want to surrender. And then I think about my children, waiting like those owl babies in Ben's book for their mummy to come home from hunting. I know the damn thing off by heart.

'And the baby owls closed their eyes and wished their Owl Mother would come. AND SHE CAME. Soft and silent, she swooped through the trees to Sarah and Percy and Bill. "Mummy!" they cried, and they flapped and they danced, and they bounced up and down on their branch.

'"WHAT'S ALL THE FUSS?" their Owl Mother asked. "You knew I'd come back."'

'Momo, d'you think we can get some more gin over here? I appear to still be in radio contact with my conscience.'

With the Atlantic below, I try to compose a message to Jack that will make things right again between us.

1.05 pm:
From: Kate Reddy
To: Jack Abelhammer
Unaccustomed as I am to being undressed by a strange man while drunk –

No. Too flippant. Delete. Try business-as-usual approach.

1.11 pm:
From: Kate Reddy
To: Jack Abelhammer
Further to our recent meeting, I have been thinking of

increasing the turnover of the fund temporarily. Should you have any further desire –

Should you need me –

I am most eager –

You know I would bend over backwards –

I have been considering some options which need to be put to bed –

Oh, hell.

1.22 pm:

From: Kate Reddy

To: Jack Abelhammer

Jack, I just want to say how entirely out of character my behaviour was last night and I hope that temporary aberration will in no way alter our professional relationship which I value so highly. My memory of events is a little vague, but I trust that I was not too great an embarrassment when you kindly returned me to my hotel room.

Obviously, I hope that this will in no way affect your future dealings with EMF for whom you remain a most esteemed client.

yours faithfully, Katharine

And that's the one I send, as soon as I get home.

From: Jack Abelhammer

To: Kate Reddy

In the United States, when a woman kisses you on the mouth and invites you to join her on a desert island of your choice this does tend to 'alter the professional relationship' somewhat, although maybe this is now part of standard client management techniques on your British MBA program?

The Sinatra Inn was a great evening. Please don't be embarrassed about the hotel room: I kept my eyes closed at all times, ma'am, except when you asked me to take out your contacts. The left eye is greener.

When I got back to the apartment, Butch Cassidy was on TV.
Kate, do you remember the end when Sundance and Butch are
holed up with the Mexican army waiting outside? They know
it's no good, but they run out all barrels blazing anyway.
For a moment there, I thought we were in trouble.
Jack

Must Remember
Children, bouncy castle, rabbit moulds for blancmange, husband.

Must Forget
You, You, You.

18

The Court of Motherhood

WHENEVER SHE APPEARED before the Court of Motherhood, the woman never seemed to do herself justice. It was hard to figure out exactly what went wrong. There she was, all the arguments on the tip of her tongue, the perfectly good reasons why she went out to work, the way it benefited both her and the children, the killer quote from Gloria Steinem about how no man has ever had to ask for advice on how to combine fatherhood and a career. And then, the minute she was standing in that dock, the justifications turned to ashes in her mouth.

She thought it was something to do with the way they always summoned her at night, when she was asleep, so obviously she wasn't at her brightest. The courtroom didn't help either. Airless, oak-panelled and lined with mournful wigged figures in black, it was like testifying in a giant coffin while the undertakers looked on, waiting for you to dig your own grave. And she loathed the judge. Must be at least sixty-five and very hard of hearing.

'Katharine Reddy,' he booms, 'you appear before the Court of Motherhood tonight charged with leaving a sick child in London while you flew on business to the United States of America. How do you plead?

Oh, God, not that. 'I left Emily in London with a temperature, that's true, Your Honour. But if I'd pulled out of the final at such short notice, Edwin Morgan Forster would never ever have let me do another big pitch.'

'What kind of a mother leaves her daughter when she's ill?' demands the judge, peering stonily down at her.

'Me, but—'

'Speak up!'

'Me, Your Honour. I did leave Emily, but I knew she was getting the proper treatment, she was on antibiotics and I did speak to her every day I was away and I am planning on organising a swimming party for her birthday and I do genuinely believe women should be role models for their daughters and . . . I do love her so much.'

'Mrs Shattock,' the prosecuting counsel is on his feet now and pointing at her. 'This court has heard how you confessed to your colleague, a Miss Candace Stratton, that you felt a surge of what you termed "almost orgasmic relief" at leaving your family after half-term and returning to the office. How do you answer that?'

The woman laughs. A dark, bitter laugh. 'That's incredibly unfair. Of course, it's nice to be in a place where you're not being followed around all the time by someone shouting, "Mummy, poo!" I don't deny that. At least people in the office can see that you're busy and don't ask you for toast or lollies or to pull their knickers up. If it's wrong to find that a relief, then I'm sorry: guilty as charged.'

'Did you say guilty?' The judge has perked up.

'In my defence,' she continues, 'I'd like to have it taken into account that I did build three sandcastles at St Davids and I did let Emily plait my hair with the bits of crab she said were mermaid's jewels. And I did all the songs and all the sandwiches. I made two kinds every day, even though they only ever eat the crisps –'

'Mrs Shattock, could you please confine yourself to the charges,' roars the judge. 'Guilty or not guilty? Seaside activities are not the business of the Court of Motherhood.'

The woman cocks her head to one side and you can see something mischievous, almost mutinous, enter her eyes. 'Is there a Court of Fatherhood, m'lud? Stupid question, really. Think how long it would take to process the backlog of cases. All those blokes who just popped into the pub on the way home and didn't make it back for the bedtime story for, what shall we say, two thousand years?'

'Silence! Silence, I say. If you continue in this manner, Mrs Shattock, I shall have you taken to the cells.'

'Sounds lovely. I could get some sleep.'

The judge pounds his gavel on the bench. He is getting larger by the minute and his old white face suffuses with scarlet like a syringe taking in blood. The defendant, meanwhile, is growing smaller and smaller. No bigger than a Barbie doll, she scrambles up on to the edge of the dock and balances there precariously in high heels. When she starts to shout at the judge, her voice is a gerbil squeak:

'All right, you really want to know the truth? Guilty. Unbelievably, neurotically, pathologically guilty. Look, I'm sorry, but I have to go now. For heaven's sake, just look at the time.'

19

Love, Lies, Bleeding

CAN YOU SMELL treachery on your lover? I am convinced Richard can. He's been all over me since I got back from New Jersey, perching on the edge of the bath while I tried to soak away the journey, insisting on washing my back, complimenting me on a hairstyle that hasn't changed in three years. And staring and staring, as though trying to place something he can't quite put his finger on, then looking quickly away when our eyes meet. For the first time, there is a shyness between us; as carefully polite as dinner-party guests, we will have been married seven years at the end of July.

While Rich is locking up downstairs, I jump into bed and simulate deep slumber to avoid reunion sex. Lying next to him with my eyes closed, a montage of guilt, work, desire and shopping flickers across my lids: bread, rice cakes, Jack's smile, canned tuna, check cash level of funds, apple juice, Alphabite potato thingies (ask Paula), spreadsheets, the word kiss spoken in an American accent, cucumbers, blancmange rabbit, green jelly for grass.

At first light, when Rich and I finally make love, as the children are starting to stir in their beds overhead, there is something driven and possessive about it, as though my husband were acting out some deep territorial impulse to plant his flag and reclaim me. And, in a way, I am grateful to be reclaimed; less scary than setting out for a foreign land with its curious habits, its unknown emblems.

Richard is still collapsed on top of me when the children come shrieking into the bedroom. Emily's first reaction on seeing that I'm back is of uncomplicated joy, complicated seconds later by a pout and an Othello-green stare. Ben is so delighted he bursts into tears and plumps down on to his nappy-cushioned bottom; that small body barely able to support the strength of his feelings. When the two of them climb on to the bed, Emily straddles Rich's chest and Ben lies in the damp cruciform his father has left on my naked body. Face level with mine, he starts to point at my features one by one: 'Ayze.'

'Eyes, good boy.'

'Nows.'

'Nose, that's right, Ben, clever boy. Have you been learning words while Mummy's been away?'

His index finger, slender as a pencil, comes to rest between my breasts.

'And that, young man,' says Richard leaning over and gently removing his son's hand, 'is the female bosom, of which your mother has a particularly lovely example.'

'Mummy looks like me, doesn't she?' demands Emily, climbing aboard and budging Ben down on to the belly whose soft dome still bears the memory of carrying them both. 'Me' chimes Ben happily. 'Me, Me, Me,' the children cry as the mother disappears under her own flesh and blood.

*

A NY WOMAN WITH a baby has already committed a kind of adultery, I think. The new love in the nest is so voracious that all the old one can do is to wait patiently, hoping for any crumbs the intruder does not consume in its cuckoo greed. A second child squeezes the adult love even harder. The miracle is that passion survives at all, and too often it dies in those early, early-rising years.

During the hours and days after I first get back from a trip, I always promise myself it's my last time away. The story I live by – that working is just one of a range of choices I could make that will not affect my children – is exposed for what it is: a wishful fiction. Emily and Ben need me, and it's me that they want. Oh, they adore Richard, of course they do, but he is their playmate, their companion in adventure, I'm the opposite.

Daddy is the ocean, Mummy is the port: the safe haven they nestle in to gain the courage to venture further and further out each time. But I know I'm no harbour; sometimes when things are really bad I lie here and think, I am a ship in the night and my children yell like gulls as I pass.

And so I get out my calculator and do the sums again. If I stop work, we could sell the house, clear the mortgage and the home-improvement loan that ran out of control when we first found rising damp and a bad case of descending house. ('You need underpinning, love,' said the builder. Damn right I did.) Move out of London, buy a place with a decent garden, hope Rich could pick up some more architectural work, see if I could work part-time. No foreign holidays; economy-size everything, bring the shoe habit to heel.

At times, I can almost be moved to tears by the picture of the thrifty, responsible homemaker I could and would become. But the idea of not having an income after all these years makes me so scared. I need my own money the way I need my own lungs. ('What your poor mum never had was Running Away Money,' Auntie Phyllis said, dabbing my face with her hankie.) And how would I be, left alone with the kids all day? The need of children is neverending. You can pour and pour all your love and patience into them and when is it all right to say when? Never. You could never say when. And to serve so selflessly, you have to subdue something in yourself. I admire the women who can do it, but the mere thought makes me sick with panic. I could never admit this to anyone, but I think giving up work is like becoming a missing person. One of the domestic Disappeared. The post offices of Britain should be full of Wanted posters for women who lost themselves in their children and were never seen again. So when my two bounce on the body they sprang from shouting, Me, a voice within me keeps repeating, Me, Me, Me.

*

7.42 am: Complete hell trying to get out of the house. Emily reports that all three changes of clothes I have offered her are unacceptable. Yellow is her new favourite colour, apparently.

'But all your clothes are pink.'

'Pink's silly.'

'Come on, darling, let Mummy pull your skirt up. Such a pretty skirt.'

She swats me away: 'I don't want pink. I *hate* pink.'

'Don't talk to me in that tone of voice, Emily Shattock. I thought you were going to be six next birthday, not two.'

'Mummy, that's not a very nice thing to say.'

How are you supposed to deal with a child who within twenty seconds can drop her impersonation of John McEnroe in favour of the ethical rigour of Dame Mary Warnock? On the way out, I shout up to an invisible Rich, asking if he can get a man to take a look at the dishwasher. I hand Paula a list of stuff we need plus all of my cash and make sure to say please four times. Then, just as I reach the door, Emily crumples into tears at the foot of the stairs. From this end of the hall, she looks less like a winged fury than a very small sad girl. Feel my anger deflate into remorse. Go back and cuddle her, removing jacket first to avoid snail-trail of snot.

'Mummy, did you go to the Egg Pie Snake Building?'

'What?'

'I want to go to the Egg Pie Snake Building with you. It's at America.'

'Oh, the Empire State Building. Yes, love, Mummy will take you one day, when you're a bigger girl.'

'When I'm seven?'

'Yes, when you're seven.' And her face clears as fast as the sky after a storm.

From: Jack Abelhammer
To: Kate Reddy
Big consultants pow-wow here in May. Stop.
Urgently require presence of amazing British fund mgr. Stop.
Great oyster bar Grand Central Station. Stop.
Can you swallow a dozen oysters? I can't. Stop.

2.30 pm: At King's Cross, I board the train to York for a conference. Am only allowing myself to think about Jack twice an hour, an act of incredible self-discipline slightly compromised by the fact that I have used up my allocation before we have even pulled out of the station. When I remember kissing him and him kissing me back at the Sinatra Inn, it has a molten effect on my core. I feel full of gold.

The train shudders and groans from its berth and I spread my stuff out on the table: for once I have a chance to sit down in peace and relax with the papers. Headline on page 2: WHY A SECOND BABY CAN KILL YOUR CAREER. Definitely not reading that. Since Emily was born, I swear to God that every month there's been some new research proving that my child wrecks my work prospects or, more painfully, my work wrecks my child's prospects. Every way you look, you stand condemned.

I turn to women's page instead and start to fill in something called a Stress Quiz.

Do you find you suffer from any of the following?
a/ Sleeplessness?
b/ Irritability?

For God's sake, what is it now? Damn mobile. It's Rod Task from the office.

'Katie, I hear the final with Moo Moo went great.'

'Momo.'

'Right. Think you girls should stick together; go after some more ethical accounts.'

Rod says he needs to access a Salinger file. But he can't get into my computer. Wants my password.

'Ben Pampers.'

'Pampas? Didn't know you had a thing for the Argies, Katie.'

'What?'

'Pampas. South American grasslands, right?'

'No, P. A. M. P. E. R. S. , it's a kind of, er, cosmetic.'

When did you last find time to read a book?
a/ Within the last month?
b/ Not since —

Mobile again. My mother. 'Is it a busy time, Kath love?'

'No, it's fine, Mum.'

I lie back on the headrest and prepare for a long conversation. I can hardly tell my mother that busy no longer means what busy meant in her day. Busy isn't a morning with the twin-tub and a cheese and pickle sandwich for lunch before collecting the kids from school. Busy has got busy since my childhood; busy has gone global.

My mother thinks that if I don't return a phone call from her within twenty-four hours then something bad has happened. It's hard to explain that the only chance to return the call will be when something bad *isn't* happening. Stormy being the prevailing climate with surprise outbreaks of calm.

Mum says she just rang to check how Emily's getting on at school since her friend Ella left.

Bad moment. I had no idea Ella had left. Haven't been into school since I started preparing for the final. 'Oh, fine. Really, she's been great about it. And she's doing brilliantly at ballet.' Enter a tunnel. Line cuts out.

The tightening knot in my stomach makes it hard to focus on the Stress Quiz. When did I start lying to my mother? I don't mean the obligatory daughter-mother falsehoods – 'Eleven at the latest, never tried it, three Cokes, but *everyone's* wearing them, he slept on the floor, yes, a friend of Deb's, no, not overdrawn, in the sale, yes, an absolute bargain, fine, couldn't be better.'

No, not those lies which are simply mutual protection. When you're young your mother shields you from the world because she thinks you're too young to understand and when she's old you shield her because she's too old to understand – or to have any more understanding inflicted on her. The curve of life goes: want to know, know, don't want to know.

What I'm talking about here is the lies to my mother about

being a mother. I tell her Emily has coped well with the departure of her best friend, even though I haven't heard about it. I'd rather Mum thought I was a failure at work than a stranger to my children. She thinks that I have it all and she's so pleased for me. I can't tell her, can I? It would be like finding out that after Cinderella got to the Palace, the Prince put her back on hearth-cleaning duty.

The Cloisters Hotel, York, 7.47 pm: I ring my mother back. She sounds breathless. With a little gentle prompting from me she admits that, yes, she has been feeling a bit under the weather lately which, translated from Mother Speak, means she has lost all feeling in her limbs and her vital organs are shutting down. Oh God.

I don't even bother to replace the handset before keying in the number of my sister Julie, who lives just round the corner from Mum. Steven, Julie's eldest, answers the phone. He reports that his mum's watching 'The Street', but he'll get her.

Julie's tone still takes me by surprise: the adoring lisp of my little sister has been supplanted in recent years by something tense and grudging; whenever we speak these days, she seems to be spoiling for a fight about a grievance that's too painful to have a name.

I got away and Julie didn't. Julie fell pregnant and got married when she was twenty-one and had three kids by the time she was twenty-eight and I didn't. Julie's husband is an electrician and mine is an architect. Julie lives a mile away from our mother and tries to look in every other day and I don't. Julie, who is good with her hands, brings a bit of extra cash in by making tiny curtains and bits of furniture for a local doll's house company and I, who am good with my head, don't. (In fact, I probably invest my clients' money indirectly in the Far Eastern sweatshops that are driving Julie's employer out of business.) Julie has been abroad once – Rimini, unlucky with the weather – whereas it is not unknown for me to go twice in a single week. And none of this is anybody's fault, but we exist now, my sister and I, in an atmosphere of guilt and blame.

I ask Julie if she thinks Mum should go and see a doctor, and her sigh blows across the Pennines, flattening trees in its path. 'Mum won't listen to me,' she says. 'If you're that bothered why don't you get up here and tell her yourself?'

I'm explaining what my schedule has been like when Julie jumps in: 'Anyroad, it's not physical. She's had some bother with men coming round to the flat. Said they were after money Dad owed them.'

'Why didn't you tell me?'

From my sister's living room floats the mournful theme tune of *Coronation Street*. Julie and I both loved the soap when we were kids: there was a period when we fought furiously over the affections of Ray Langton, a mechanic with dark wavy hair, until he got squashed under one of his own cars. I haven't seen it in twenty years.

'I've left a couple of messages on that machine, Kath,' says my sister, 'but you're never there, are you?'

8.16 pm: The conference is for dot.com entrepreneurs, or what's left of them. The guys who persuaded the City that they could read the future turned out to have been talking crystal balls. You wouldn't believe how much venture capital was thrown at firms who were going to sell designer clothes on the Net. But, guess what? People prefer to go to shops and try stuff on. (Women fund managers were a lot less badly burned in the meltdown. Better at evaluating risk-reward, we spent far less on untried stock than our male colleagues. People said we were lucky; I don't agree. I think it's innate: we must like to have some reliable staples in the cupboard, to keep those small mouths fed when the sabre-tooth tiger is blocking the entrance to the cave.)

Unpacking my suitcase before going down to dinner, I find a large envelope marked 'Do Not Open Till Sunday!' in Richard's handwriting. I open it. My Mother's Day cards. One is a print of Ben's hands in red paint. I half-smile, half-grimace at the thought of the mess that must have attended its making. Emily's has a drawing of me on the front. I am wearing a crown and holding a green cat and I am so tall that I dwarf my nearby palace. Inside, she has written: 'I love my Mummy. Love is speshal it makes my hart sparKle and tresha appea.'

I can't believe it. I've forgotten Mother's Day. Mum will never forgive me. Dial reception. 'Can you get me a number for Interflora?'

From: Jack Abelhammer
To: Kate Reddy
Will you come to NYC? Or should I. Stop.
Thinking about you. Stop.

From: Kate Reddy
To: Jack Abelhammer
Don't. Stop.

Must Remember

Get dishwasher fixed. Stair carpet? Fund transitions to be arranged – no fuck-ups! Call Jill Cooper-Clark. Application form for nursery for Ben? Emily schools find out NOW! Cheque for ballet. Remind Rich to get cash out for babysitter. MONEY FOR JUANITA! Change computer password. Paula's birthday – BMW? George Michael concert tickets? Spa treatment, aromatic relaxation pillow. Call Dad and tackle about his debts. Find time to visit Mum. Buy Sinatra CD. Ginseng for better memory or Gingko thingy?

20

The Way We Were

3.39 am: Woken by the doorbell. It's Rob, our neighbour from three doors down. Says he heard a noise and saw a group of lads by our car, but he shouted and they ran off. Richard goes out to inspect the damage. Side window completely smashed in, forked-lightning crack across the back one. Of course, the car alarm didn't go off. The car alarm, usually triggered by a cat's breath, is hopelessly mute when there's actual burglary taking place.

Rich goes out to tape up the windows while I get on the phone to Prontoglass 24-Hour Service.

'Sorry, your call is held in a queue. Due to demand. Please hold while we try to connect you.'

Demand? What demand? It's four o'clock in the bloody morning.

'If you know the extension you require, please press one. If you wish to speak to an operator, please press two.'

I press 2.

'Please hold while we try to connect you, your call will be answered shortly. Thank you for choosing Prontoglass! If you wish to speak to an operator, please press three.'

I press 3. 'Sorry, your call cannot be taken at the moment. Please try later!'

I think of all the time that must be wasted every day in those echoing antechambers where calls wait. Hell is not other people: hell is trying to get through to other people while listening to seven minutes of Vivaldi played on pan pipes. I decide to get dressed and crack in early to some work. This is a good time of day to talk to Tokyo. But as I'm fumbling with my blouse buttons in the still dark bedroom, there is a yell from above. When I go up, Ben is standing in his cot remonstrating with the monster who has dragged him from sleep. He jabs a debater's accusing forefinger at his invisible assailant.

'I know, sweetheart, I know, some bad men have woken us all up.'

Ben is so spooked he won't go back to sleep. I lift him on to the sofa bed which is just next to the cot and lie down beside him.

'Roo,' he moans, 'Roo.' So I get up and fetch the scruffy little kangaroo and tuck it under his arm.

Babies have this magic spot between their brows. If you stroke your finger down over it, and along the ridge of the nose, their eyes close automatically: the human roller-blind. My boy hates sleep; it separates him from the life he relishes, but he starts to drift off, the indigo eyes emptying of thought. I lie there contemplating the cracks on the ceiling around the light fitting where bits of plaster are starting to peel off. Even my ceiling has stress eczema. I imagine a finger stroking my own brow and, clothes wrinkling around me, I tumble into a crowded dream.

6.07 am: Richard comes into Ben's room to relieve me. The baby is splayed flat out on his tummy like a puppy. We talk in whispers.

'I did say buying the Volvo was a bad idea, Kate.'

'Some little bastards break into our car and it's my fault?'

'No, just that round here it's clearly a provocation, isn't it?'

'Come off it, Rich, even Tony Benn doesn't think property's theft any more.'

He laughs. 'And who was it who once said crime is the just punishment for an unjust society?'

'I never said that. When did I say that?'

'Shortly before taking possession of your first open-top Golf, Mrs Engels.'

My turn to laugh. Encouraged, Rich starts kissing my hair and puts an exploratory hand down the front of my nightie. Even when you're not in the mood, startling how quickly nipples stiffen to Iced Gems. Rich is just pulling me down on to the Winnie the Pooh rug when Ben sits bolt upright, gives his parents a how-could-you look and then points to himself. (Did I mention that babies are anti-sex too? You'd think they'd have some nostalgia for the act that made them; instead they appear to have an alarm to see off the threat of rivals, wailing on cue as though their cry was wired up to your bra-clasp.) Rich sweeps up his son and goes down to an early breakfast.

I try to doze off again, but I can't sleep for thinking how Richard and I have changed. First time we met was fifteen years ago at university; I was picketing Barclays Bank and he was opening an account there. I shouted something about South Africa – How dare you invest in brutality? – and Rich walked over to our righteous huddle and I handed him a leaflet, which he studied politely.

'My, that does sound bad,' he said before inviting me for coffee.

Richard Shattock was the poshest man I had ever met. When he spoke, he sounded as though Kenneth Branagh had swallowed Kenneth More. Forearmed with the knowledge that all public schoolboys were emotionally stunted berks, I didn't know what to do when it became clear that this one was capable of more affection than I had ever known. Rich didn't want to save the world like my idealistic friends; he just made it a better place simply by being in it.

We made love for the first time six days later in his college room under the eaves. The sun was falling in a dusty gold column through the skylight as he solemnly unpinned my Cyclists Against the Bomb badge and said, 'I'm sure the Russians will sleep more soundly, Kate, for knowing you have passed your cycling proficiency test.'

Had I ever laughed at myself before? Certainly the sound that came out that night was rusty with lack of use, a stopped-up spring gurgling into life. 'Your Bournville laugh,' that's what Richard called it, 'because it's dark and bitter and Northern and it makes me want to eat you.' It's the sound I still like best: the sound of when we were us.

I remember how much I loved his body, but even more I

loved the way my body felt in relation to his – for every straight edge a curve; the vertebrae down his back like rocky steps into a cave of pleasure. By day we cycled across the Fens and shouted 'Hill!' whenever we felt the slightest incline, but at night we explored another terrain.

When Rich and I first started sleeping together – I mean actually sleeping, not having sex – we would lie in the middle of the bed, face to face; close enough to feel the gusts of each other's warm, night-time breath. My breasts would be pushed against his chest and my legs, I still can't figure this out, disappeared over and under his like a mermaid's tail. When I think of us in bed back then, I think of the shape of a sea-horse.

Over time we began to face outwards. You could probably date that, our first separation, to the purchase of a king-size bed from Heal's in the late Eighties. And then, with the arrival of our first child, the battle for sleep began. Bed became a place you sank into rather than dived into. We who had slipped in and out of consciousness as easily as we slipped in and out of each other were now jealously guarding our place of rest. My body shocked me by bristling at anything that threatened to take away its remaining strength. A stray knee or elbow was enough to spark a boundary war. I remember starting to notice how loud Rich's sneezes were, how eccentrically articulated. Har-CHEW! he went. Har-CHEW!

When we were still students we had travelled round Europe by train and one night we wound up in a small hotel in Munich where we collapsed in hysterics on the bed. It looked like a double, but when you pulled the cover back it turned out to be two mattresses, divided and united by a thin wooden strip which made meeting in the middle an effort rather than an inevitability. It all felt so Teutonic. 'You be East Germany and I'll be West,' I remember saying to Rich as we lay there on our separate halves in the light of the street lamp. We laughed, but in time I came to wonder whether the Munich arrangement was the true marriage bed: practical, passionless, putting asunder what God had joined together.

*

7.41 am: After breakfast, Ben, wearing a bib like a Jackson Pollock, is terribly clingy. Paula peels him off me when Winston arrives to drive me to work. 'All right, sweetheart, it's all right,' I hear Paula say as I pull the door behind me.

Sitting in the back of Pegasus, I try to read the *FT* to bring myself up to speed for my presentation, but I can't concentrate. There is music playing, a jazz piano arrangement of something I can almost place – 'Someone To Watch Over Me'? It sounds as though the pianist has smashed the tune into a thousand pieces and keeps throwing them into the air to see which way they land. The riffs are like a man shuffling a pack of cards. Winston hums along, holding the main line of the tune and occasionally letting out a little whoop to salute the pianist for a particularly cunning resolution. This morning, my driver's ease and pleasure feels like an insult, a rebuke. I want him to stop.

'Do you think we could avoid the New North lights, Winston, and cut round the back? I'm not convinced this is the quickest way.'

He doesn't answer for a while, but allows the track to finish. Then, with the final chord still thrumming in the air, he says: 'You know, lady, where I come from it takes a long time to do things suddenly.'

'Kate, my name is Kate.'

'I know what your name is,' he says. 'Way I see it, rushing around just a waste of time. Fly too fast, lady, and you pass your nest.'

The laugh I laugh sounds darker than usual. 'Well, I'm afraid that is the more leisurely perspective afforded to the driver of the minicab . . .'

Winston doesn't bite back at my snottiness, he just gives it a long gaze in the mirror and says thoughtfully: 'You think I want to be you? *You* don't even want to be you.'

That's it. 'Look, I don't pay you for psychotherapy. I pay you to get me to Broadgate in the shortest time possible, a feat which seems increasingly beyond you. If you don't mind, I'll get out here, it's quicker to walk.'

As I hand over the twenty and Winston digs into his pocket

for change, he begins to sing: 'There's a somebody I'm longing to see/I hope that he/Turns out to be/Someone to watch over me.'

8.33 am: Shoot out of lift straight into Celia Harmsworth.

'Something on your jacket, dear?' smirks the Head of Human Relations.

'No. Just back from the cleaners, actually.' I glance down at my shoulder to see a smeary mess, an epaulette of Ben's banana porridge. No. God, how can You do this to me?

'I'm amazed how you manage this job, Katharine,' coos Celia, clearly delighted at further proof that I can't.

(Celia is one of those spinsters who adored being the only woman in a man's world: it was a licence to feel pretty before girlies like me showed up and ruined her monopoly.)

'Must be such a struggle with all those kiddies,' she offers helpfully. 'I was saying to Robin Cooper-Clark when you were away for – half-term, was it? – I don't know how she does it.'

'Two.'

'I beg your pardon?'

'Two. All those kiddies. I have two of them. That's one less than Robin has.'

Turn on my heel, walk over to desk, shrug off stained jacket, shove in bottom drawer. Incredible noise from the window. Out on the ledge, the pigeons have decided to move in together. The male is sitting there with a twig in his mouth looking faintly foolish. I recognise the expression. It's the look Rich gives when I bring home a flatpack of shelves for self-assembly. The female, meanwhile, is busy forming a heap of small sticks into a raft-like structure roughly the size of a dinner plate. Oh, this is great, now they're building a nest.

'Guy, did you get on to the Corporation about the hawk man? Damn pigeons are about to start a breeding programme out there.'

I check my neck in handbag mirror for any Ben bites – no, all clear – and then I stalk coolly into a meeting with Robin Cooper-

Clark and other senior managers to begin my presentation. It goes remarkably well. All eyes in the room are glued on me, especially those of the bastard Chris Bunce. Am obviously starting to command serious respect: the tactic of behaving like a man, never mentioning the children etc., is clearly paying off.

As I switch from slides to overheads, it suddenly occurs to me that I am the only person in the room without a penis. Not a good thought to have right now, Kate. Can we not think about dicks in a gathering of seventeen men? Talking of which, do they have to stare at me quite so intently? Look down. Am wearing red Agent Provocateur demitasse bra under white voile shirt, grabbed from chest of drawers in half-dark at 4.30. Oh Jesus, I look like Pamela Anderson at the Oscars.

11.37 am: I'm sitting in the ladies' loo, with my cheek pressed up against the cubicle wall to cool the furious blush. Tiled in black marble riddled with white stars, the wall is like a map of the universe: I feel as though I'm being sucked into deep space and more than happy to go there. How about disappearing into a black hole for a few millennia till the memory of public humiliation fades? I used to smoke in here when things got desperate; since I gave up, I sing under my breath. 'I am strong. I am invincible. I am Wo-man.'

It's a Helen Reddy song from when I was at school. I loved the fact that she had the same name as me and she sounded, well, just so full of it, so confident that women could deal with anything life threw at them. At college, when Debra and I were getting ready for a night out we used to play the record over and over to psych ourselves up. Dance round the room, playing catch with Deb's Action Man. (After his leg broke off, Deb said we'd have to call him Inaction Man 'after all our useless blokes'.)

'Oh, yes, I am wise,
But it's wisdom born of pain,
Yes, I've paid the price,
But look how much I've gained!
I am strong. I am in-vin-ci-ble.
I am Woman.'

Do I believe in equality of the sexes? I'm not sure. I did once, with all the passionate certainty of someone very young who knew absolutely everything and therefore nothing at all. It was a nice idea, equality; noble, indisputably fair. But how the hell was it supposed to work? They could give you good jobs and maternity leave, but until they programmed a man to notice you were out of toilet paper the project was doomed. Women carry the puzzle of family life in their heads, they just do. Every night on the way home from the City, I watch the women scurrying along in the Lucozade light of the street lamps, bags of shopping balancing briefcases, or twitching at bus stops like over-wound clockwork toys.

Not long ago, my friend Philippa told me that she and her husband had drawn up a will: Phil said she wanted a clause stipulating that in the event of her death, Mark would promise to cut the children's fingernails. He thought she was joking. She wasn't joking.

One Saturday late last year, I got back from a Boston trip to find Richard in the hall, all set to take our two out to a party. Emily, hair uncombed, appeared to have a duelling scar on one cheek – it was ketchup from lunch. Ben, meanwhile, was bent double, wearing something very small and dotted in apricot that I didn't recognise. On closer inspection, it turned out to be an outfit belonging to one of Emily's dolls.

When I suggested to my husband that our offspring looked as though they were going out to beg on the Underground, Rich said that if I was going to be critical I should do it myself.

I was going to be critical. I would do it myself.

*

From: Kate Reddy
To: Candy Stratton
Simply marvellous day so far. Have just shown breasts in error to head of investment & the troops. Chris Bunce came up to me afterwards and said:
'You were a total pro in there, Kate, with knobs on.' Laughed

like a drain and said something about putting me on his website. WHAT WEBSITE??

Plus Abelhammer has invited me for SX rendezvous in New York.

Why men all bull and cock?

From: Candy Stratton
To: Kate Reddy
Hon, don't worry, U hve trrifc tits. Penis Envy is So Yesterday. Hallo Boob Envy!
Bunce is piece of shit. His website will be Jerkoff Central.
Hope U R going to meet up with the Hammer Man in NYC, He sounds Gr8.
I H8 U when U act British.
Candida Thrush xxx

1.11 pm: Lunch with Robin Cooper-Clark and a new client, Jeremy Browning, at Tartuffe. Located in the penthouse of a building overlooking the Royal Exchange, the restaurant has the kind of hush that, outside a monastery, only money can buy. This must be the silence they call golden. The low seats are scooped out of toffee leather and the waiters arrive on castors. The menu is my least favourite kind: chops for chaps with no concessions to the female palate. When I ask our waiter if there's a salad I could have he says, '*Mais oui, Madame,*' and offers me something with *gésiers* in it.

I nod uncertainly and Robin gives a little cough and says, 'Roast throat, I believe.' How can anyone swallow a throat?

I say that I'd like the salad, but could they please hold the throats. On Robin's lips there is an Alec Guinness ghost-of-a-smile, but the waiter is not amused. Red blood is the currency of the neighbourhood.

'Any relation to the Worcestershire Reddys?' Jeremy asks as Robin consults the wine list. Our client must be in his early fifties, but he's in good shape and he knows it: ski-bronzed from the neck up, gym-bulked shoulders, succulent with success.

'No. I shouldn't think so. I'm from a bit further north.'

'The Borders?'

'No, more Derbyshire and Yorkshire. We moved about.'

'Ah, I see.'

Having established that I am no one worth knowing and no one who will know anyone worth knowing, our new client feels safe to blank me. Over the past decade, my country has become a classless society, but the news has been slow to reach the people who own it. For men like Jeremy, England still ends at Hyde Park, and then there is Scotland, where they go to kill things in August. The North, that great expanse of land between SW1 and Edinburgh which is best crossed by plane or at night in the sleeper car of a fast train, is a foreign country to them. Jeremy Browning's forebears may have conquered India, but you wouldn't get them going to anywhere as remote as Wigan.

Robin would never – could never – treat me as Jeremy does, but then Robin's spent the last twenty years with Jill, who knows in her bones that snobs are a joke and that, in every sense, women mean business. I get a real kick out of watching my boss on these occasions. Convivial, clubbable and effortlessly smarter than any of his clients, he nonetheless has a way of making them feel as though they're the captain of the winning team. Seeing me sidelined by the Browning version of events, he gently but firmly tries to draw me back into the conversation: 'Now, Kate will be the senior manager on your fund. She's the one to consult on the structure of your portfolios and so forth. She can even explain the mysterious workings of the Federal Reserve.'

And then, a few minutes later, when our guest has a mouth full of squab: 'Actually, Jeremy, Kate's funds delivered our best returns in the past six months, at what's been a pretty bumpy time for equities by any standards, wouldn't you say so, Kate?'

I love him for it, but it's no use. There are some men who will always prefer to deal with another man, any man, rather than a woman, and Jeremy Browning is one of them. I can see him struggling to place me: I'm not married to him, clearly I'm not his mother, I didn't go to school with his sister and I'm sure as hell not going to go to bed with him. So what, he must be asking himself as he chews on his pigeon, is this girl doing here? What is she *for*?

I've been observing this for more than ten years now and still I'm not sure I understand. Fear of the unknown? After all, Jeremy was packed off to a boys' school at the age of seven, he went to one of the last all-male colleges, his wife, Annabel, stays home with the sons and heirs and, privately, he thinks anything else is some kind of crime against the natural order of things.

'Sorry, could I possibly have my wine back?'

Jeremy is tapping me on the sleeve. I realise that I have been pushing my neighbour's glass towards the centre of the table to prevent accidental spillage: a reflex from mealtimes with Emily and Ben.

'Gosh, I'm terribly sorry, when you have children you always think people are going to knock things over.'

'Oh, you have children,' he says.

'Yes, two actually.'

'Not planning any more, I hope.'

This hangs in the air, this presumption that my fertility is part of his fiefdom, that he's paying me to be his alone, not to be carrying the young of a rival male. I feel like returning the compliment and kicking him so hard under the table that he's unable to have any more kids of his own. But the phrase 'Crushed balls' tends not to look good on the client report.

'Naturally,' I say, clearing a throat from my lettuce, 'you will be my top priority, Jeremy.'

From: Jack Abelhammer
To: Kate Reddy
Further to your communication on borrowing limits, I attach some thoughts on LOANS. Not my thoughts, I'm afraid, although they come pretty close to some of my own about the person who manages my fund.

It is no gift I tender,
A loan is all I can;
But do not scorn the lender;
Man gets no more from man.
Oh, mortal man may borrow
What mortal man can lend;
And 'twill not end tomorrow,
Though sure enough 'twill end.

If death and time are stronger,
A love may yet be strong;
The world will last for longer,
But this will last for long.

From: Kate Reddy
To: Jack Abelhammer
Thank you for your thoughts about the LOAN. As your fund
manager, I should point out that the value of your investment
can go up as well as down. The market is quite depressed at the
moment, but I will be in the US soon and may be available to
discuss raising levels of exposure.
It's a beautiful poem.
K xxxxx

3.44 am: Have left the children alone asleep in the house and
just popped into work. Stuff to do. It can't wait. I won't be
long. Twenty minutes, maybe forty tops. They won't even
notice I'm gone.

The office is silent except for the sighs and shunts of
machines making machine love to each other in the half-light.
With no distractions, I work with great efficiency; figures
swarming beneath my hands, an army of ants marshalled into
platoons. File quarterly fund report, put screen to sleep and steal
back out of the building. Outside, the City is in a post–nuclear
dawn – a warm gust of wind, some dancing litter, sky the
colour of saucepan. Spot a cab, fuzzy yellow light on the
horizon. I wave as it approaches. It does not stop. Another cab
sweeps past, blank as a hearse. Frantic now. Third cab nears.
Step out into the road to make it stop. He swerves to avoid me
and I see his big pocked mushroom face mouthing through the

glass, 'Yeww stew-pid cow,' he spits. 'Cancha fuckin' look where ya going?'

I'm sitting on the kerb, weeping with frustration and self-pity, when a fire engine streaks up the street with an inconsolable wail. The engine stops and the guys let me clamber aboard. I'm so grateful for the lift, I forget to tell them where I'm going, but we move swiftly through familiar roads till we reach my own. As we get close to our house, I can see a knot of people standing outside.

Smoke purls out of a bedroom window. Emily's window.

'Stand back, Miss, we'll handle it,' a man says.

I am slapping my hands against the door. I am calling the children's names, but I can't hear for the siren. Can't hear myself scream. Turn the siren off. Please could somebody please turn that fucking siren off—

'Kate! Kate, wake up. It's all right. It's all right.'

'What?'

'It's all right, darling. You've had a bad dream.'

I sit up. My nightie is a shroud of sweat. Inside my ribcage, there is a bird scrabbling to get out.

'I left the children, Rich. There was a fire.'

'It's OK. Really, it's OK.'

'No, I left them by themselves. I went into work. *I left them.*'

'No. No, you didn't leave them. Listen, that's Ben crying. Listen, Kate.'

It's true. From upstairs, comes the siren call – the inconsolable wail of a teething baby, a one-man fire brigade.

21

Sunday

THE DAY OF REST, otherwise known as day of ceaseless manual labour. I start by chucking out extinct ready-meals from fridge. (Or 'Reddy meals', as my sister-in-law likes to call them.) Swab down curious, algae-like residue from glass shelves. Discard knuckle of Parmesan which smells of old people's home. Get rid of disgusting Happy Chicken Shapes that Paula feeds the children and make sure to hide them right at the bottom of bin-bag. For my vulnerable young, only free-range. How many times must I tell her?

Fill and empty washing machine three times. Juanita, because of chronic back problem (three and a half years) cannot be expected to carry heavy laundry around the house. Adult washing is outside nanny's duties, although Paula does occasionally break strict demarcation to put in one of my hand-wash-only sweaters. (I always consider complaining about this, but file instead under Pending Paula Grievances: Volume 3.)

Today, I have invited Kirsty and Simon round for a 'relaxing' lunch. It's important to see friends, remember there is more to life than work, weaving the social fabric that strengthens sense of community, etc. It's also important for the children to see Mummy at ease in a domestic context, to build up glowing childhood memories, instead of a woman in black running out of the door yelling instructions.

Everything is totally under control. The recipe book is open like a bible under the clean plastic lectern, ingredients are in pleasing formation. There's a very dinky bottle of olive oil with Sienese silk ribbon. I'm wearing charming Cath Kidston apron with retro floral print which gives an ironic nod to the role of Fifties homemaker while signalling jokey distance from appalling domestic servitude of women like my mum. Possibly. Also have planned casual weekend hostess outfit to change into seconds before guests arrive: Earl jeans, pink cashmere Donna Karan. Try to follow instructions for salsify, leek and blue cheese filo tart, only Ben keeps rock-climbing up my legs, using his uncut nails as crampons. Every time I put him down, he gives his fire-engine wail.

There are those who make their own filo pastry, but they are like people who go in for bondage in the bedroom: you admire the effort and technique without necessarily wanting to do it yourself. I unwrap the pastry from its packet and brush one sheet with melted butter. Then I place another sheet on top. Very restful. Enter Emily with bulbous lower lip: 'Where's Paula?'

'It's Sunday. Paula doesn't come in today, sweetheart. Mummy and Emily are going to make some lovely cookies together.'

'Don't want to. I want Paula.' (The first time she said that I swear I could feel the skewer going into my heart, and there is still nothing to rival it, the pain of your firstborn's infidelity.)

'Well, I'd really like you to help me with the biscuits, darling. It'll be fun.'

Through her great grey eyes, Emily weighs up the sight of her mother playing at being her mother. 'Daddy said I could watch *Rugrats*.'

'All right, you can watch *Rugrats* if you put your blue dress on by the time Kirsty and Simon get here.'

11.47 am: Everything under control. Return to recipe. 'Stir lemon juice and blue cheese into cold béchamel sauce.' What béchamel sauce?

Turn page. 'For béchamel sauce recipe see page 74.' What? Now they tell me. Mobile rings: It's Rod Task. 'Bad time, Katie?'

'No, absolutely fine. *Ow!* Ben, don't do that. Sorry, Rod. Go on.'

'I'm faxing through details of tomorrow's meeting, Katie. We need you to be up to speed on performance, asset allocation, attribution and strategy outlook. Your kind of stuff. Young Guy was singing your praises Friday night, said how great you managed, considering.'

'Considering what?'

'Oh, you know how guys get talking over a curry.'

No, I do not know. Would love to go out with Rod and the team for the Friday-night Indian, if only to keep that creep Guy from stalking my job, but I had to get home to read *Harry Potter*.

There's a sudden, ominous smell from the oven. 'Don't worry, Rod. Everything's under control. See you tomorrow.'

'Take it easy, sweetie!'

I open the oven door to reveal disaster. The filo pastry case has become a petrified forest. Don't panic. Think, Kate, think. Run out of door yelling instructions. Can Richard please dress Ben and tidy the kitchen?

12.31 pm: Back from the supermarket. Ben is dressed, but the kitchen looks like a scene from Disney Goes to Dresden.

'Richard, I thought I asked you to tidy up?'

He looks up from the paper, amazed. 'I *have* been tidying up. I've already put the CDs in alphabetical order.'

Kick Brio train track under sofa, hurl rest of toys into utility room and jam the door shut with a drying rack. Substitute M&S spinach quiche for salsify and Gruyère catastrophe. Now to make the dressing. Dinky bottle of olive oil has immovable crimson wax stopper. Try to pull out stopper with bottle opener, but merely shreds flakes of red rind into baby leaf salad. Use teeth. No use. Bugger. Bugger. Attack stopper with sharp knife. Miss bottle and slash back of hand instead. Looks like drunken suicide attempt. Search first-aid drawer. Can only find one plaster: Mister Bump. Run upstairs to change into relaxed hostess attire. Wriggle into new jeans, but no sign of Donna Karan pink cashmere jumper. Why is Nothing Ever in the Right Place in This House?

12.58 pm: Find jumper. Paula has hidden it at the back of the airing cupboard, and no wonder. Plainly it has only just survived kids' wash. Now so shrunken would only fit Mrs Thomasina Tittlemouse or Ally McBeal. Go downstairs to discover Ben posting remaining blue cheese into the video. Emily screaming because *Rugrats* has jammed. No sign of Richard. Doorbell rings.

Kirsty and Simon Bing are architect friends of Richard. The same age as us, they have no children but one exquisite grey-blue cat that drifts like smoke through the Japanese porcelain in their Clerkenwell loft. When we go to visit the Bings, I spend a lot of time shouting as Ben crawls up the open-plan staircase without any banister and peers gleefully into the abyss. There is an unspoken strain between the childless and those of us bowed down with infants. Before Emily was born, we rented a villa outside Siena with Kirsty and Simon, and our cooling relationship is occasionally warmed by memories of that week in the sun. These days, Rich and I, if we socialise at all, tend to hang out with people with kids. Because they understand. The sudden need to produce pizza and tissues, often simultaneously; the unpredictable smells and naps. The moods that arrive like tanks.

Kirsty and Simon always seem glad to see us, but I think it's fair to say that their goodbyes are particularly effusive, a prelude I always imagine to their explosion of shared relief as the door shuts on us and they can adjourn to their snot-free sofa. But today they have come to our place, where every piece of furniture is essentially a large handkerchief. Compared to its usual state, the kitchen is immaculate, but I see Kirsty direct an understanding smile at the single toy left in the middle of the floor and, quite unreasonably, I want to slap her.

Lunch goes fine and I accept compliments for the M&S tart with surprisingly little shame – well, I did make a huge effort to get it. The Bings' conversation ranges widely. Was it really a good idea to have the Great Court of the British Museum open in the evening? 'A failed experiment,' according to Simon, who would be taken aback to learn that I have forgotten where the British Museum actually is.

Then we're on to the stagnant state of current cinema. Kirsty and Simon have seen some French film about two girls working in a factory and were totally blown away by it. Rich reveals that he has seen it too. When did he find the time to see that?

'Kate worked in a factory, didn't you, darling?'

'Oh, how fascinating,' says Simon.

'Not really. Plastic caps for aerosol cans. Very boring, very smelly and very badly paid.'

The mildly awkward silence that follows is broken by Kirsty. 'So, how about you, Kate?' she asks brightly. 'Seen any good movies?'

'Oh. I enjoyed Crouching Tiger.' I pause. 'And Crouching Dragon.'

'Hidden,' murmurs Rich.

'Hidden Tiger,' I say, 'I loved the, er, Chinese bits. Mike Leigh's very good, isn't he?'

'Ang,' murmurs Rich.

'I like *Mary Poppins*,' chimes in Emily, God bless her, running up from the other end of the kitchen, naked except for her Little Mermaid green silk tail. 'Jane and Michael go to work with their daddy at the bank. It's near where Mummy works and there's lot of pigeons.' She begins to sing loudly and tunelessly, with a child's open-faced fearlessness: ' "Feed the birds, tuppence a bag, tuppence, tuppence, tuppence a bag." Do you feed the birds, Mummy?'

No, I get men to come and kill them. 'Yes, of course, darling.'

'Can I come to your work?'

'Certainly not.'

Kirsty and Simon laugh politely. Kirsty picks at the sliver of orange Play-Doh stuck between the prongs of her dessert fork and wonders whether they shouldn't be starting to make a move.

Must Remember

Avoid social engagements which require clean clothes or clean furniture. Packing list for EuroDisney. Bread? Milk. Stair carpet. Call Dad. Application form for Ben nursery. Call Jill Cooper-Clark!! Thorntons chocolate ducklings!

22

How Much Does It Cost?

Wednesday, 10.35 pm: Debra calls me at home, which is weird because we scarcely talk these days, only e-mail. Hearing her voice, I know instantly that something's wrong. So I ask, How's things? And with one deep breath, she's off: Oh, just the usual; Jim will be away over Easter tying up some deal and she has to drive the kids to Suffolk to stay with her family and her father's had a stroke and her mum's pretending to cope but can't, and they don't like to bother Deb because she's so busy and important and, of course, she'd like to be bothered but she's too busy at work where they're still holding out against giving her a full partnership because that bastard Pilbutt says there's 'a question mark over my commitment' and she's bloody earned that partnership, she really has, and then Anka, the nanny she's had since Felix was one, has been stealing from her. Had she mentioned the stealing?

No, she hadn't.

Well, if she's honest, she's known about the stealing since last summer, but not allowed herself to know, not wanting to know. First, it was just small amounts of cash she thought she'd left around the house and couldn't put her hands on. After that, other stuff went missing – a Walkman, a silver picture frame, that dinky digital camera Jim brought back from Singapore. The whole family, well, they'd all joked about their pilfering poltergeist and Deb had some better locks put on the doors. Because you never know. And then, just before Christmas, she mislaid her leather jacket, the lovely, buttery one from Nicole Farhi she couldn't possibly justify buying, and she could swear she hadn't left it anywhere. Called all the restaurants she'd been to; emptied her wardrobe. Nothing. Joked bitterly to Anka that she probably had early-onset Alzheimer's and Anka made her a cup of tea with three sugars – no wonder Slovakians have no teeth – and said sweetly, 'You are a little tired only, I think. Not mad.'

So Debra would never have found out if she hadn't popped home one afternoon between client meetings. Fiddling with her keys at the front door, she turned and saw Anka walking down the street pushing Ruby in the buggy and wearing the leather jacket. Said she felt so weak she could hardly move, but managed to get behind the dustbins and hide so Anka didn't spot her.

Then, last Saturday, when Anka was away, Deb had gone into her room, like a burglar in her own home. And there in the cupboard, not even hidden at the back, was the jacket and a couple of Deb's better sweaters. In a drawer, she found the camera and her grandmother's watch, the one with the silver fish for the minute hand.

'So what did you say to her?'

'Nothing.'

'But, Deb, you have to say something.'

'Anka's been with us for four years. She brought Felix to the hospital the day Ruby was born. She's a member of the family.'

'Members of your family don't generally nick your stuff and then sympathise with you about it.'

I'm shocked at the flatness of my friend's voice: all the fight knocked out of it.

'I've thought about this, Kate. Felix is anxious enough already with me being away all the time. His eczema gets so bad . . . And he loves Anka, he really does.'

'Come off it, she's a thief and you're her boss. You wouldn't put up with it at work for a minute.'

'I can live with her stealing from me, Kate. I can't live with the children being unhappy. Anyway, that's enough of me. How are you?'

I take a deep breath and then I stop myself. 'I'm fine.'

Debra rings off, but not before we've made another lunch appointment we won't keep. I put her name in my diary, anyway, and around it I draw the dumb smiley face Deb always drew in the margin next to mentions of Josef Stalin in our mutual European history notes in 1983. (One of us had to go to the lecture; the other got the lie-in.)

What is the cost when you pay someone else to be a mother to your children? Has anyone calculated it? I'm not talking about money. The money's a lot, but how much is the other thing?

Thursday, 4.05 am: Emily wakes me to tell me she can't sleep. So now that makes two of us. I check her forehead, but the fever turns out to be excitement over Disneyland Paris, where we are heading later today, if I can get all my jobs done in time. My daughter has wanted to go to Disneyland ever since she figured out that the Sleeping Beauty castle at the end of her videos was a real place.

Now she climbs into bed beside me and whispers, 'Will Minnie Mouse know my name, Mummy?' I say, of course she will, and my daughter burrows marsupially into the small of my back and drifts off, while I lie, more awake by the second, trying to remember everything I need to remember: passports, tickets, money, raincoats (obviously, it will be raining, it's a holiday), jigsaws/crayons/paper in case we get stuck in Channel Tunnel, dried apricots for nourishing snack, Jelly Babies for bribes, chocolate buttons for total meltdowns.

Didn't Mrs Pankhurst say something about women needing to stop being a servant class for men? Well, we tried, Emmeline, boy did we try. Women do the same jobs now as men, and do them equally well. But all the time, women are carrying around the information that won't leave them alone. I reckon that inside a working mother's head, every day is Gatwick airport. MMR vaccinations (to jab or not to jab), reading schemes, shoe sizes, holiday packing, childcare cunningly assembled from wings and prayers – all circling and awaiting further instruction from air traffic control. If women didn't bring them safely in to land, well, the whole world would crash, wouldn't it?

12.27 pm: The pigeon has laid two eggs. Elliptical in profile, they are startlingly white with a faint blue tinge. The mother and father appear to be taking it in turns to sit on them. Watching them reminds me of the shifts Rich and I do with the kids when one of them is sick.

By the end of today, I need to have written four client reports, sold a vast number of shares (with the markets melting down, company policy is to have more cash) and bought a flock of chocolate ducklings from Thorntons. Plus Momo and I are working on another pitch for an ethical account in Italy. And I haven't even heard from Jack this morning and I long to see the little envelope appear in the top right-hand corner of the screen that tells me he's out there thinking of me as I am thinking of him.

(What did it feel like before? Before I was waiting for his messages. Waiting and waiting. Either waiting or reading his last message or composing my reply and then waiting again. No longer in a state of living, but in a constant state of waiting. The impatience like a hunger. Staring at the screen to summon the words into existence, willing him to speak.)

From: Kate Reddy
To: Jack Abelhammer
Jack, are you there?

From: Kate Reddy
To: Jack Abelhammer
WHAT ARE YOU THINKING? Speak dammit!!

From: Kate Reddy
To: Jack Abelhammer
Did I say something wrong?

From: Kate Reddy
To: Jack Abelhammer
hello?

From: Kate Reddy
To: Jack Abelhammer

What could you POSSIBLY be doing that's more important than talking to me?

xxxxxxxxxxxxxx

From: Jack Abelhammer
To: Kate Reddy

Being your slave, what should I do but tend
Upon the hours and times of your desire?
I have no precious time at all to spend,
Nor services to do, till you require.

From: Kate Reddy
To: Jack Abelhammer

OK, you're forgiven. That's lovely. Sonnet by Bill Gatespeare, right? But let's get one thing clear: any more silences that long and you're in Big Trouble. In fact, you're a dead man.

That's a promise xxxxx

From: Jack Abelhammer
To: Kate Reddy

Bill Gatespeare, I find, has the emotional software to fit any occasion . . . As far as you're concerned, Katharine, I'm already in Big Trouble. If killing me means I can look forward to a personal appearance from my fund manager then I'm prepared to die like a man.

I knew you were going to Disneyland with the kids, so I figured you'd be caught up in the preparations and not welcome any msgs. I try to think of you being happy without me, without letting it make me unhappy.

Nor dare I question with my jealous thought
Where you may be, or your affairs suppose,
But like a sad slave, stay and think of nought
Save, where you are, how happy you make those.

You write so well about the children – Emily's reading, the way Ben tries to talk to you – that I can tell you're a great Mom.

And you notice so much. My Mom stayed home and played bridge and drank vodka martinis with her friends. She was there all day and never really around for the three of us. Don't go romanticising the stay-home parent – you can screw up whether you're near or far.

Because you live in my head, you're very portable, you know. I find myself talking to you all the time. The worst thing is I'm starting to think you can hear me.

Jack xxxxxxx

From: Kate Reddy
To: Jack Abelhammer
I can hear you.

23

Easter

Saturday lunch, Toad Hall Restaurant, Disneyland Paris
Enthusiastic French kiss and passionate hug from a tall dark
stranger. Regrettably, his name is Goofy. Overcome with
shyness at meeting her favourite cartoon characters, Emily hides
behind her mother's legs and refuses to say hello.

Seconds later, Paula enters the restaurant like a struck gong,
reverberating with resentment. She 'agreed' to accompany us
to EuroDisney in much the same way the British 'agreed' to
give back India. I just know the short-term relief of having her
here to help out will not be worth it for the long-term tactical
disadvantage.

I feel I have to spend the entire time apologising profusely for
things I haven't done. Sorry Ben woke everyone up last night
with his snoring, sorry room service is so slow, sorry French
people don't speak English. Oh, and I forgot to apologise for
the rain. For that I am truly sorry.

Meanwhile, Paula sits back and observes my mothering skills
with the fat, contented air of a driving instructor guiding a
know-it-all pupil towards the inevitable prang.

After fifteen minutes of queuing for lunch in Toad Hall –
mock baronial, gargoyles made of grey polystyrene – we reach
the counter and Paula orders chicken nuggets for herself, Emily
and Ben. On the grounds that the chicken is more likely to be
antibiotics in breadcrumbs, I decide to take a stand. Suggest that
it might be nice for the children to have quiche instead, on the
off-chance it will be made of ingredients from a farm rather
than a test-tube. 'If you say so,' says Paula cheerfully.

At the table, when I present Ben with quiche, his tiny almost
prim mouth contorts into a gash of grief. He starts those

hiccupy sobs where he can barely take in air quick enough. French families sitting nearby, all with *enfants* in navy or grey linen sitting up straight eating *haricots verts*, turn and glare at barbarous Anglo-Saxons. After one mouthful, Emily announces that she doesn't want quiche because it tastes like egg. She wants chicken nuggets. Paula does not say, I told you so. Instead, she gives Ben one of those extra-reassuring, never-mind hugs and feeds him fries off her own plate.

(Sometimes when I'm with Paula and the kids, I get that feeling I had at school when three girls in my group got closer, apparently overnight. How had I missed it? I, who had always been allowed to link arms on the way home with the fabulous, popular Geraldine – Farrah Fawcett blonde, ankle bracelet, breasts – was bumped to the outside of the line, where I was expected to take the elbow of Helga – glasses, Alp-tall, Austrian. I was still a part of the group, but excluded from the inner core and its giggles, whose target I increasingly, achingly, took to be me.)

'Stop that, Emily, please.'

Em is decapitating paper batons of sugar and pouring them all over the table. We do a deal: she can make a sugar mountain for her Minnie Mouse key-ring to ski down, but only if she eats her quiche and three green beans. No make that *five* green beans. OK?

I wish I could relax more, but a buzzing in my brain tells me I've forgotten something. *What else? What else?*

7.16 *pm:*   At bedtime, an overexcited Emily wants to go over the Easter story one more time. She has been obsessed with it since she figured out last week that the Baby Jesus she sang carols about at Christmas grew up to be the man on the cross. It's one of those occasions when you wish you could press a button and the Fairy Godmother of Explanations would appear and wave her wisdom wand.

'Why did Jesus get killed?'

Oh, God. 'Because, well, because people didn't like the things he was saying and they wanted to make him stop.'

I can see Emily searching her mind for the worst crime she can imagine. At last, she says, 'They didn't want to do sharing?'

'In a way that's right, they didn't want to share.'

'After Jesus died he got better and went to Heaven.'

'That's right.'

'How old was he when they crossed him?'

'Crucified. He was thirty-three.'

'How old are you, Mummy?'

'I'm thirty-five, darling.'

'Some people can be a hundred years old, can't they, Mummy?'

'Yes, they can.'

'But then they die, anyway?'

'Yes.' (She wants me to tell her I won't die. I know that's what she wants. The one thing I can't say.)

'Dying is sad because you don't get to see your friends any more.'

'Yes, it is sad, Em, very sad, but there will always be people who love you . . .'

'Lots of people are in Heaven, aren't they, Mummy? Lots and lots.'

'Yes, sweetheart.'

As Sunday lie-in agnostics, Richard and I decided that when we had children of our own we would not give them the false consolation of a guaranteed afterlife. No angels or archangels, no harps, no Elysian Fields full of those people you couldn't stand at college in dodgy footwear. That resolve lasted, oh, approximately three seconds after my daughter first said the word 'die'. How could I, who wouldn't let her have Roald Dahl stories on the ground that they were too cruel, open a furnace door and invite her to contemplate the extinction of everyone she would ever know and love?

'And the Easter Bunny is in Heaven?'

'No, the Easter Bunny is not. Absolutely not.'

'Sleeping Beauty is, though.'

'No, Sleeping Beauty is in her castle and we're going to see her tomorrow.'

Emily's questions often shock me, but not as much as the fact that I'm allowed to give her any answer I like. I can tell her there is a God or that there is not a God, I can tell her that Oasis were better than Blur, although by the time she's old enough to buy albums there won't be albums anymore and Madonna will be as distant as Haydn. I can tell her that Cary Grant is in a dead-heat for the title of Greatest Englishman with William Shakespeare, I can encourage her to support a football team or I can tell her sport is incredibly boring, I can advise her to be careful who she gives her virginity to or I can give her brisk, early advice on contraception. I can suggest she starts paying a quarter of her annual income into an index-linked pension as soon as possible or I can tell her that love is the answer. I can tell her any damn thing I like and that freedom feels both amazing and appalling.

When they sent a baby girl home from the hospital with us almost six years ago, they forgot to hand out a Meaning of Life manual. I can remember Richard carrying her in from the car in her little seat with the big handle and setting her down with extreme tentativeness on the living-room floor. (At that stage, we still believed we might break her; not knowing it was more likely to be the other way round.) Rich and I looked at our daughter and then at each other and we thought: 'What now?'

You needed a licence to drive a car, but with a baby you were expected to pick it up as you went along. Becoming a parent was like trying to build a boat while you were at sea.

What the hospital did give us was a thin booklet in a blue plastic binder with several cartoons to the page, each starring two stick-figure parents. There were stick-figure parents tentatively dipping their angular elbows into baths or trying out the temperature of milk on the back of their stick hands. There was a feeding timetable, tips on the transfer from formula to solids and, or so I seem to recall, a list of common rashes. But there was definitely no word on how to prepare your child for the fact of your own death.

As I look down at Em's face, at once radiant and perplexed,

I get that breathless feeling you get every so often as a mother, the pressure of hundreds of millions of mothers before you, all fighting tears as the child poses the most ancient of questions.

'Are *you* going to die, Mummy?'
   'One day I will. But not for a very very long time.'
   'How long?'
   'Not for as long as you need a mummy.'
   'How long?'
   'Not until you're a mummy yourself. Quick now, Em. Eyes shut.'
   'Mu-um?'
   'Go to sleep, love. Sleep now. Exciting day tomorrow.'

Well, did I handle it right? Is that how you tell them? Is it?

*

Sunday, 3.14 pm: Emily and I together on the circus roller-coaster, our screams riding shotgun with our stomachs. I close my eyes and take a Polaroid for my memory: I am having fun with my wonderful child. Her hair in the wind, her hand tight in mine. But even here I can't escape: there's something about this ride that says *work*. Equity markets going up, up, up, then, whump; the trapdoor in your belly opens.
   Oh, Kate, you stupid, *stupid*, unbelievably brainless . . . woman . . . God, no . . . Forgot to place trades on Thursday. Needed to sell 5 per cent of fund – Edwin Morgan Forster house policy is to have more cash, less equities with the markets melting down. As we crest the hill, northern France and my entire career flash before my eyes. EMF already has a recruitment freeze. Redundancies next. And who will be prime candidate? Step forward the fund manager who forgot to sell her clients' shares because she was buying chocolate bloody Easter ducklings.
   'I'm sacked.'
   'What?' Richard is there to meet us as we clamber out of the little train.

'I'm fired. I forgot. I was trying to remember everything and I forgot.'

'Katie, slow down. Just tell me slowly.'

'Daddy, why is Mummy crying?'

'Mummy's not crying,' says Paula, who has appeared out of the crowd and picked Emily up. 'Mummy's having such a great time she laughed till the tears fell out by themselves. All right, who wants to get a crêpe? Do you want jam or lemon? I'm having jam.'

'OK if I take them, Kate?' Paula asks quickly. And I nod because, obviously, I can't speak. And with Ben in the buggy, and Emily skipping along beside her, Paula takes the children away. How would I manage without her?

4.40 pm: Calmer now. The calm of the condemned woman. Absolutely nothing to be done; it's a Bank Holiday. Can't sell anything till Tuesday. No use spoiling the rest of our trip. I am climbing out of one of the Mad Hatter's Dancing Teacups, when I notice a man in the queue trying to place me. It's Martin, an old boyfriend. You know that weird sensation seeing an ex can induce? I feel it now. The ghost of a passion, a silk handkerchief being pulled out of the heart. I turn away quickly and secure Ben's already tight buggy straps.

First Thoughts: Reasons Not To Be Recognised by Ex
a/ Am wearing yellow plastic rain poncho, purchased from Disney-land Universal Stores, which is decorated with Mickey Mouse logo and smells of lightly rolled condom.
b/ My hair, dried this morning with gnat's buzz of a hairdryer in the hotel bathroom, lies basted to my skull like threadbare helmet of old lady in retirement home.
c/ Am about to be fired, therefore poorly placed to show how sensationally well my life has gone without him.

Second Thought
a/ He doesn't recognise me. HE DOESN'T EVEN RECOG-NISE ME. Am hideously changed and shrivelled and no longer

desirable to man once sexually obsessed with me.

Across the pastel blur of spinning teacups, I meet the eyes of the man. He smiles at me. It's not Martin.

8.58 pm: We take the Eurostar home to London. Ben is lying on his back across me. His eyelashes are long, his hands still chubby baby hands, the dimples along the knuckle like air bubbles in batter. When he's big, I won't be able to tell him how much I loved his hands. Maybe I won't remember. I stretch to reach my laptop, but the baby turns and sighs as if to wake. I don't want to check my e-mail, anyway: there's probably a nuclear bollocking from Rod and gloating 'commiserations' from the ghastly Guy. I'll prepare for my fate as a penniless stay-at-home mother, purchase penitential Gap sweatshirts in khaki. And try to remember the words to 'Incy Wincy Spider'.

So, you see, that was why I didn't pick up the e-mail from Rod that evening. The one that told me everything was OK, the one that told me things were much much better than OK.

From: Rod Task
To: Kate Reddy
Kate, **WHERE THE FUCK ARE YOU?** Fed cut the rate again. Rest of team liquid up to their necks. You the only one who didn't sell. What's your secret, genius? Are you shagging Greenspan?
Push the old guy off you and come back. Buy you a beer.
Cheers Rod

24

Kate Triumphant

Tuesday, 9.27 am: Hallelujah! I am a guru. My superb market timing – otherwise known as forgetting to place several trades and being saved by a surprise rate cut – has granted me temporary office goddess status. I hang around at the coffee machine receiving tributes from grudgingly awed colleagues.

'You must be the only person to have anticipated the Fed cut *and* the market recovery, Kate,' marvels Dandruff Gavin. I compose my features into what I hope is an impersonation of humility and quiet pride.

'Shit, I was 6 per cent liquid. That cost us a few basis points,' groans pink-faced Ian. 'And Brian was 15 per cent liquid. That's another nail in his coffin, poor sod.' I nod in sympathetic condescension and say casually, 'I only had 1 per cent cash, actually.' Tasting success, enjoying its champagne tang on my tongue.

Chris Bunce walks past on the way to the Gents and can hardly bear to meet my eye. Momo comes up and gives me a dry little kiss which lands on my cheek around the same time that Guy's look harpoons into my shoulder blades. Across the office, I see Robin Cooper-Clark approaching with an amused smile as if he were a bishop and I were a jammy young curate.

'And on the third day she rose again,' says Robin. 'Well, well, Miss Reddy, who says Easter is drained of all meaning?'

He knows. He knows. Of course, he bloody knows. Brightest man in the solar system.

'I was extremely fortunate, Robin. Alan Greenspan rolled the rock from the tomb.'

'You were very fortunate, Kate, and you're very good. Good

people deserve their good fortune. By the way, did Rod tell you we need you to go to Frankfurt?'

When I sit down at my desk, I'm so buoyant I practically don't need a chair. Scan the currencies, check the markets, then call up my e-mails. Smile when I see that, at the top of the Inbox, are two from my dearest friends.

From: Debra Richardson
To: Kate Reddy, EMF

Desperately trying to recruit new nanny. Anka stormed out after I confronted her over the stolen property. Jim's mum has come up from Surrey to cover for a bit, but she has to go back Friday. Help!!!! Any ideas? Most candidates seem to require a car, all the rest are 37 w. severe personality disorder demanding salary equal to editor of Vogue.

Reason to Give up Work: Because I can't afford to go out to work any more!

When do we get to the fun bit of our lives? The bit where you say, 'Ah! so this is what the struggle and pain was all for!' Lunch Thurs?????

PS: Must try to put more positive spin on life. I do know there are people out there living in abject poverty w no shoes etc.

From: Kate Reddy
To: Debra Richardson

Well, I'm GLAD she's gone. Good for you confronting her. You'll find someone soon – don't panic! Aussie girls are very good, I hear. Will send numbers of agencies and ask Paula if she knows anyone looking for job. Today am top dog in office. Total fluke.

If you can meet with Triumph and Disaster
And sell the second as though it were the first
– THEN you can be a Woman, my girl!

And my reward? Trip to Germany on cut-price flight – airline called Go or Slo or No or something.

Auf Wiedersehen Pet. Can we rearrange lunch?

Sorry, all love K xxxxx

From: Candy Stratton
To: Kate Reddy
O fuck. Am pregnnt.

I immediately look across the office to where Candy sits. Sensing my glance she looks up from her work and gives a little wave. It's like a child's wave, funny and sad at the same time.

*

CANDY IS PREGNANT. Not just late, but pregnant. Four and a half months gone at least, according to the clinic in Wimpole Street where she went yesterday. Her cycle had been pretty irregular for a couple of years – the drugs, most probably – and she hadn't noticed anything unusual, except a little extra weight and a tenderness in her breasts which she put down to some ambitious sex with Darren, the black-run specialist from Treasury on her recent skiing trip.

'I'm gonna get rid of it.'

'Fine.'

We are in Corney and Barrow, perched on our usual stools overlooking the arena where the ice rink lives in winter. Candy has a flute of champagne, I have a bottle of Evian.

'Don't do that agreeing shit when you don't mean it, Kate.'

'I'm just saying I'll support whatever decision you take.'

'Decision? It's not a decision, honey, it's a fucking disaster.'

'I just think, well, a late abortion, it's not much fun.'

'And bringing up a kid by yourself for twenty years, that's fun?'

'It's not impossible and you're thirty-six.'

'Thirty-seven on Tuesday, actually.'

'Well, you're running out of time.'

'I'm getting rid of it.'

'Fine.'

'What?'

'Nothing.'

'I know your nothings, Kate.'

'It's just that I think you could really regret it, that's all.'

She grinds out her cigarette and lights up another. 'There's

216

this place in Hammersmith. Not cheap, but they do them real late, no questions asked.'

'Fine. I'll come with you.'

'No.'

'Well, I'm not letting you go by yourself.'

'It's not a baby shower, it's a fucking abortion.'

I study my friend's face. 'What if it cries?'

'What are you, Katie, some kind of pro-Life nut?'

'It has been known for a foetus to cry at that stage of development. I know you're tough, but that would kill me.'

'Can we get another glass over here?' she gestures to the barman. 'So, go on, explain it to me.'

'What?'

'Kids.'

'I can't. You have to feel it for yourself.'

'Come on, Kate, you can sell anything to anybody. Try.'

The look on her face. Such a Candy look, defiant and bruised at the same time; the look of a seven-year-old who has fallen out of a tree she's been told not to climb and doesn't want to cry even though it really hurts. I want to put my arms round her, but she'd bat a hug away rather than let on how much she needs it. The only way to get her to buy anything is to make it sound like an opportunity she'd be a fool to turn down.

'You know the two days when I gave birth to my babies?'

She nods.

'Well, if I could only keep two days from the whole of my life, those are the days I would keep.'

'Why?'

'Awe.'

'*Awe*?' Candy detonates one of her big bad laughs. 'You can't drink, you can't smoke, you can't go out nights, your tits look like two dead rodents, your pussy's stretched wider than the fucking Holland Tunnel and she offers me awe. Jeez, what are the other highlights, Mom?'

No deal. 'I have to go now, Cand. E-mail me the date and time and I'll meet you there.'

'I'm getting rid of it.'

'Fine.'

25

Back to School

8.01 am: 'OK, Emily, let's go. Quick now. Mummy's going to be late. Lunchbox? Good. Library books? No. No, you can't have plaits. Just no. Teeth? Oh, for heaven's sake. Quickly do teeth, please. Hurry up. And take the toast out of your mouth first. It's not toast? Well, I don't want you eating Easter egg . . . Well, Daddy shouldn't have said that. I am not horrible. OK, let's go.'

First day back after the school holidays and the children are as bolshy and febrile as ponies before a gymkhana. Emily is using that goo–goo baby talk she regresses to when I've been away or am about to go again. It drives me mad.

'Mamma, who's your best character in "Bear an da Big Blue House"?'

'I don't know. Er, Tutter.'

'But Ojo is my bestest.' Emily crumples in disbelief at my treachery.

'People don't have to like the same things, Em. It's good to like different things. For instance, Daddy likes silly Zoe on breakfast TV and Mummy really doesn't care for Zoe at all.'

'She's not called Zoe, she's Chloe,' says Rich, not bothering to look up from the TV. 'And for your information, Chloe has a degree in anthropology.'

'Is that why she feels the need to go naked from the waist up?'

'But why don't you like Ojo, Mamma?'

'I do like Ojo, Em, I think he's totally fantastic.'

'She's not naked, she just has remarkable self-supporting breasts.'

'She's not a boy. Ojo's a *girl*.'

8.32 am: I am bundling Em out of house when Rich, who is still in a T-shirt and boxers, mooches into the hall and wonders when it would be convenient for him to go on a five-day wine-tasting course in Burgundy.

Burgundy? Five days? Leaving me alone with the children and the markets bucking like the Disneyland rollercoaster?

'I can't believe you're asking me that now, Rich. Where on earth did you get such an idea?'

'You. You gave it to me for Christmas, Katie. My present, remember?'

Oh, God, it's all coming back to me now. A moment of intense guilt masquerading as generosity. Must learn to suppress those till the impulse passes. I tell Rich that I'll think about it, smile and file under: To Be Forgotten.

In the car, Em kicks the back of the passenger seat with absentminded fury. No point telling her off; she barely knows what she's doing. Sometimes a five-year-old's feelings are simply too big for their body.

'Mamma, I gotta idea.'

'What's that, sweetheart?'

'How about if da weekends were weeks and da weeks were weekends?'

As I wait for the lights to change, I have a scratchy sensation in my chest, as though a bird were in there trying to escape.

'Den all da mummies and daddies could be wid dare children more.'

'Emily, will you please talk properly. You are not a baby.'

In the rear-view mirror, I catch her eye and look away.

'Mummy, my tummy hurts. Mummy, will you put me to bed tonight? Are you putting me to bed tonight?'

'Yes, I promise.'

*

I CANNOT IMAGINE WHAT I was thinking of when I let Alexandra Law, Abbess among the Mother Superiors, sign me up for the Parent Teachers Association. No, that's not true, I know exactly what I was thinking of: I was thinking that just for one hour in some underlit, overheated classroom I could pretend that I'm like any other mother. When the chair makes a reference to Roy, the absentee caretaker, I want to give a knowing little smile. I want to groan when someone brings up the matter of the summer fête – that time of year again *already!* – and I want to breathe that fuggy companionable air. And afterwards, when we've voted on a computer levy and plans to improve the sports facilities, I want to clasp my fingers round a white plastic cup containing a boiling orange beverage and I want to refuse a HobNob, patting my waist significantly, and then I'll say, 'Oh, go on then!' as though succumbing to a chocolate biscuit was the most reckless, heady thing I'd done for a very long time.

But, realistically, what were the chances of my making the PTA meeting at 6.30 on a Wednesday night? Alexandra described 6.30 as 'after work', but what kind of work lets you go before 6.30 these days? Teaching, obviously, but even teachers have Himalayas of marking to do. When I was a child, there were fathers who still came home in time for the family's evening meal, dads who, in the summer months, would mow the lawn while it was still light and water the sweet peas in the dusk. But that age – the age of working to live instead of living to work – feels far away in a land where district nurses arrived by Morris Traveller and televisions glowed like embers. I don't know anyone at the office who eats with their kids in the week now.

No, it really wasn't realistic to sign up for the PTA, and three months after joining I have yet to attend a single meeting. So when I drop Emily off at school I try to avoid bumping into Alexandra Law. Easier said than done. Alexandra is harder to avoid than the NatWest Tower.

'Oh, Kate, there you are –' She barrels across the room. Her dress this morning is so densely floral it looks as though she has run into an armchair at speed. 'We were thinking of sending out a search party. Ha-ha-ha! Still working full-time? Gosh. I don't know how you do it. Oh Diane, I was just saying, we don't know how she does it, do we?'

Diane Percival, mother of Emily's classmate Oliver, extends a thin tanned hand with a sapphire the size of a sprout on the second finger. I immediately recognise the type. One of those wives, tensed like longbows, who have a full-time career keeping in shape for their husbands. They exercise, they get their hair done twice a week, they wear full make-up to play tennis and when that is no longer enough, they willingly submit to the surgeon's knife. 'Those rich stay-home mums are jogging for their lives,' Debra says, and she's right. These women are not in love, they are in fear: fear that the husband's love will slip away and land on some replica of their younger selves.

Like me, they are in asset management, but my assets are most of the world's resources and their asset is themselves – a lovely product, but threatened with diminishing returns. Don't get me wrong. When the time comes I'll probably have my neck lifted to the back of my ears and, like the Dianes of this world, I'll have it done to please someone; the difference is, that someone will be me. However much I sometimes don't want to be Kate, I really really don't want to be Diane.

I have never actually spoken to Diane Percival before, but this does not stop me going cold at the very thought of her. Diane is the mother who sends notes. Notes to invite your child to a play-date, notes to thank your child for coming to a play-date. (It was nothing, really.) Last week, in a spectacular burst of note one-upmanship, Diane actually sent a note from Oliver thanking Emily for an invitation to tea. In what kind of life is it possible to send a note acknowledging an event of almost no significance, which will feature fish fingers and peas and has yet to take place? Deprived of office hierarchies, many of the mothers at my daughter's school have set about inventing meaningless tests whose sole purpose is that other mothers with better things to do can be seen to fail them.

'Thank you for your thank-you note, I look forward to receiving your note acknowledging receipt of my note. Thank you and get lost.'

221

Novalis Hotel, Frankfurt, 8.19 pm: Shit. I won't be able to put Emily to bed tonight after all. The meeting with the German client was brought forward and I had to get on the next plane. It went as well as can be expected. I blagged and blagged and I think I bought us a couple more months by which time we may have been able to turn around the fund's performance.

Back at the hotel, I pour myself a large drink and have just got into the bath when the phone rings. Christ, what now? For the first time in my life, I pick up the bathroom extension: a cream phone in its cradle on the wall next to the towel rail. It's Richard. There is something different about his voice. 'Darling, I'm afraid I have some sad news. Robin just rang.'

26

Death of a Mother

JILL COOPER-CLARK DIED peacefully at home in the small hours of Monday morning. She was forty-seven. Diagnosed just after the children broke up from school last summer, the cancer swept through her like a forest fire. The surgeons went in first, and after them a SWAT team of pharmacologists and radiotherapists, all trying to contain the blaze. But the cancer was unquenchable – breasts, lungs, pancreas. It was as though Jill's energy – she was the most prodigiously energetic person I've ever met – was being used against her; as if the life force itself could be hijacked and redeployed in the fell purposes of death. The last time I saw her was at the Edwin Morgan Forster party, a zillion-dollar bash on an Arabian theme with real sand and an angry camel. Wearing a turban to hide her tufted baldness, Jill was, as usual, making me laugh.

'Slash and burn, Kate, you'd hardly believe how bloody primitive the treatment is. I feel like a medieval village they're razing to the ground. Only one would rather be pillaged by Vikings than an oncologist, don't you think?'

Before the treatment, Jill had dense, springy auburn hair and that Celtic top-of-the-milk skin with a sprinkling of cinnamon freckles. Three babies – all hefty boys – had not managed to weigh down the coltish body of the sometime netball Goal Attack. Robin said that to get the full measure of his wife you had to see her tennis backhand: just when you thought it was all over, when there was no possibility of the ball being returned, she would uncoil and whip it down the line. I watched her do it at the Cooper-Clark place in Sussex two summers ago, and when she struck the ball, Jill let out a defiant, joyous, 'Ha!' I think we were all waiting for her to pull that stroke on the cancer.

Jill is survived by her three sons and by her husband, who has just stepped out of the lift. I hear the smart rap of his black Lobbs across the central square of beech that might be used for tea-dancing if this was another, gentler kind of business. We are both in the office appallingly early: Robin to catch up, me to get ahead. He rustles around in his room; coughing, opening and closing a drawer.

I take him in a mug of tea and he starts. 'Oh, hello, Kate. Look, I'm so sorry, leaving you to manage alone. I know how much hassle it is and on top of the Salinger stuff. But after the funeral, I'll be all yours.'

'Don't worry. Everything's under control.' A lie. I want to ask how he is, but that early warning system of his, the one that sees off painful personal questions, is on red alert. So I ask something else. 'How are the boys?'

'Well, we're luckier than a lot of people,' says Robin, switching smoothly into Head of Investment mode. 'You know Tim's at Bristol now, Sam's doing GCSEs and Alex is nearly nine. It's not as though they're little boys any more who really, um, need a mother in the way that younger boys do actually need their mothers.' And then he makes a noise that no one has ever heard in the offices of Edwin Morgan Forster before. Halfway between a bark and a moan, it is barely human, or maybe all too human and I never want to hear it again.

He pinches the bridge of his nose for a few furious seconds and then turns back to me. 'Jill left this,' he says, handing over a sheaf of paper. Twenty pages of neat, handwritten script, it bears the title 'Your Family: How It Works!'

'Everything's in there,' he says, shaking his head in wonder. 'She even tells me where to find the bloody Christmas decorations. You'd be amazed how much there is to remember, Kate.'

No, I wouldn't.

Friday, 12.33 pm: If I leave the office now, I will make it to Jill's funeral in Sussex at three o'clock with plenty of time to pick up a sandwich on the way to the station. Momo and I are going through some stuff for another final. Momo asks if I knew Mr Cooper-Clark's wife and I tell her Jill was an amazing person.

Momo looks doubtful. 'But she didn't work, did she?'

I look at Momo's face. What is she – twenty-four, twenty-five? Young enough not to know what women put up with before her; young enough to take her own freedom for granted. Calmly I say, 'Jill was fast-track Civil Service until Sam, her second, was two years old. She'd have been running the Home Office by now, but she decided to run her own home instead. She just didn't think that she and Robin could both have ball-breaking jobs without the children being affected. She said she tried to believe it was possible, but her heart wouldn't let her.'

Momo bends down to put something in the bin, and out of the window I can see the pigeon, her feathers puffed out like a crinoline over the eggs. Daddy pigeon is nowhere to be seen. Where is he?

'Oh, how sad,' says Momo. 'I mean, what a waste to end up doing nothing with your life.'

1.11 pm: If I leave the office right this minute, I should make it to the train.

1.27 pm: Am running out of the office when Robin's secretary hands me Jill's family memo: he's forgotten it. I sprint to Cannon Street. By the time I reach the river, lungs are hoarse, beads of sweat cascading over my breasts like a broken necklace. Stumble on steps to the station and gash left knee of tights. Damn. Damn. Dash across station concourse, skid into Knickerbox and grab first pair of black tights I see. Tell startled girl to keep the change. At the barrier, the guard grins and says, 'Too late, love.' Swerve round the barrier, board accelerating train pursued by guard. Through the window, London recedes with surprising speed, its grey circuitry soon blurring into deep country. I can hardly bear to look at the spring; so ear-splittingly green, so childishly hopeful.

I buy a cup of coffee from a passing trolley and open my briefcase to take out some work. On the top of the pile is Jill's family memo. I shouldn't read it, but I really want to read it. I want to hear my friend again, even if it's only her words written down. Maybe if I just look at one page?

When you supervise Alex's bath, don't forget to do in between his fingers, there's usually a load of black fluff in there and the odd raisin! MUST put Oilatum (turquoise bottle, white writing) in the water for his eczema. Please pretend it's bubble bath, he hates being reminded about his skin.

Alex will tell you he doesn't like pasta. He does like pasta. So persist. Persist gently. Yes, he can have a Cheese Whirl — hideous, Day-Glo, no cheese — but only if he eats a real piece of cheese as well. No, he can't live on sweetcorn. Suggest family switch to Red Bush tea (cancer prevention, apparently).

I promised Sam he could have contact lenses for his 15th birthday. Whenever you're about to shout at him, count silently to ten and think 'testosterone'. He won't be revolting for long, I promise. Remember all the grief we had with Tim and how well he worked out? Timmy's current girlfriend is Sharmila — lovely, v. bright from Bradford. Her parents disapprove of slacker white boy — ours — so could you invite them to the house and do your charm thing? (Father, Deepak, is keen golfer: both parents vegetarian.) Tim will pretend to hate it when you ask him, but be chuffed when it happens.

BIRTHDAYS: Your mother's favourite perfume is Diorissima. Tapes are always a good bet. Anything by Bryn Terfel, except Oklahoma! *which we gave last year. Also Alan Bennett books and Turkish Delight. My mother likes anything by Margaret Forster or Antonia Fraser. You might like to give Mummy my rings, or maybe you should hold on to them as one of the boys might want for an engagement ring in due course?*

GODCHILDREN: Your godchildren are Harry (Paxton), Lucy (Goodridge) and Alice (Benson). Their birthdays are marked on the calendar next to the fridge. In the present drawer, bottom of study filing cabinet, are gifts marked with their initials which should take you through to the Christmas after next. Simon and Clare's marriage is a bit shaky, so you might take Harry out and let him know you're there if he needs you. Don't forget Lucy's confirmation in September.

ANY OTHER PROBLEMS

1 / How to work washing machine. In emergencies, you may need to know this. See Brown Book. NB: temperature for your wool socks.

2 / Bin-bag sizes. Ditto.

3 / Cleaner – Mondays and Thursdays. £7 an hour plus we help Jean out with bigger bills and holidays. Single mother. Daughter is Aileen. Wants to be a nurse.

4 / Babysitters – numbers in Green Book. NOT Jodie who had sex with boyfriend in our bed while we were at Glyndebourne.

5 / Arnica for bruises (bathroom cabinet).

6 / Ignatia for grief (yellow bottle, my bedside table).

7 / Postman called Pat (really); paperboy is girl (Holly). Dustmen come Tuesday morning; won't take garden stuff. Xmas tips in Brown Book – be generous!

8 / After the funeral, the boys could see Maggie, counsellor at the hospice. A bit alternative for your taste, but I think the boys would really like her and they may say things to her that they wouldn't to you for fear of upsetting you, my darling. Kiss them for me and don't stop just because they get taller than you, will you?

It's all there. For page after page. The minutiae of the children's lives, the rhythm of their days. I wince when I think how badly qualified I would be to write such a memo for Richard. On the Birthdays Page, there is a stain the size of a cup. Something oily with a scab of flour. Jill must have been baking as she wrote.

I want to read on, but am prevented by a blur of tears. I pick up the *Daily Telegraph* instead and flick to the obituaries page. Today, there is an eminent biologist, a man who ran IBM in the Sixties and a platinum showgirl, name of Dizzy, who 'romanced' Douglas Fairbanks and the Aga Khan. No Cooper-Clark to be seen. Jill's kind of life doesn't get recorded for posterity. What was it Momo called it: 'a waste'? How can all that love be a waste?

2.57 pm: In doll-size train loo, I remove my laddered tights and execute a Houdini wriggle into new black pair. Back in the corridor, I'm surprised to attract a whistle of approval from the steward. Looking down I see that the black tights have Playboy rabbits picked out in diamanté up back of my legs. I swear I can hear Jill laughing.

St Botolph's, Greengate, 3.17 pm: I arrive in time to hear the vicar invite the congregation to thank God for the life of Jillian Cordelia Cooper-Clark. I didn't know she was a Cordelia. It suits her, principled and defined by love.

I can see Robin and the boys in the front pew. Robin has to stoop right down when he bends to kiss his youngest son's auburn head. Alex is trembling slightly in his new suit, his first suit. Jill told me they'd come up to London together to pick it out: she must have known when he'd wear it for the first time.

We sing 'Lord of All Hopefulness', her favourite hymn. The tune has a Scottish melancholy to it I hadn't noticed before. As it fades away, there is an outbreak of suppressed coughing and the vicar, a birdlike man with a crest of fair hair, asks the congregation to spend a few moments in silence remembering Jill.

I close my eyes and rest my hands on the back of the pew in front and instantly I'm back in a wood outside Northampton. August. Two months after Emily was born and James Entwhistle, who was my boss before Rod, had organised a shoot on some country estate for clients. He insisted that I attend, even though I can't shoot and I was barely capable of remembering where Germany was, let alone schmoozing a bunch of Frankfurt bankers. By lunchtime, I felt as though I had burning rocks strapped to my chest. Breasts screaming to be emptied. There was only one loo, a portable thing hidden in the trees. I locked myself in the cubicle, undid my blouse and started to squirt the milk into the toilet. Breast milk is different from cows' milk, finer, less creamy, it has the bluish aristocratic pallor of porcelain; when mine hit the green chemical in the steel bowl it made an opaque soup.

But at first the milk was reluctant to come. To keep it going I had to visualise Emily, her smell, her huge eyes, the touch of her skin. Hot and panicky, I became aware of coughing on the other side of the door. A queue was building up and I hadn't even emptied the left side and the right still to do. Then I heard a woman's voice speaking quite briskly, a voice which derived authority from its warmth: 'Well, gentlemen, why don't you all run along and avail yourselves of the bushes outside? That's one of the natural advantages you enjoy over us ladies. I suspect that Miss Reddy's need of the lavatory is greater than yours. Thank you so much.'

When I got outside about ten minutes later, Jill Cooper-Clark was sitting on a log in the clearing. Seeing me, she waved and from a coolbag produced a bag of ice which she held aloft in triumph. 'I seem to remember this is the best thing for sore boobs.'

I had noticed her before at corporate events – Henley Regatta, some rain-soaked beano at the Cheltenham Gold Cup – but I had taken her for just another golfing wife. The sort who buttonholes you about tennis-court maintenance or how hard it is to get a little man round to deal with the swimming pool.

Jill asked about my baby – the only person connected with work to have done so – and then confessed that Alex, who had just celebrated his fourth birthday, had been her present to herself. Everyone said it was crazy to go back for a third when you were finally clear of all the nappies and broken nights, but she felt she'd missed out on Tim and Sam's babyhoods by being in work. 'Oh, I don't know, I felt that time had been stolen from me and I wanted it back.'

Because we were in confessional mood, I told her that I was

afraid of letting myself feel too much. I didn't know how I could go back to the job without hardening my heart.

'The thing is, Kate,' Jill said, 'they treat us as though they're doing us a great favour by letting us· go back to work after we've had a child. And the price we pay for that favour is not making a fuss, not letting on how life can never be the same for us again. But always remember it's we who are doing them the favour. We're perpetuating the human race and there's nothing more important than that. Where are they going to get their bloody clients from if we stop breeding?'

There was a sound of gunshots and Jill laughed. She had this wonderful liberating laugh: it seemed to blow away all the stupidity and mean-mindedness of the world. And you know something else? She was the only person who never said: I don't know how you do it. She knew how you did it, and she knew what it cost.

'Dearly beloved, let us say together the words which Jesus taught us: Our Father, who art in Heaven.'

*

JILL'S GRAVE IS at the bottom of a hill that falls away sharply from the back of the church. At the top are the towering Victorian headstones – plinths and tombs and catafalques heavy with attendant angels; the farther you crunch down the gravel path and the nearer to the present you get, the smaller and more modest the memorials become. Our forefathers knew they had a reserved seat, even a box, for the afterlife: we put in a tentative request for any returns.

Jill's spot looks out across a valley. The hills opposite have mascara smudges of fir trees along their ridges, and in the green bowl beneath hangs a dense silver vapour. As the vicar intones the liturgy, and Robin steps foward to drop a handful of earth on his wife's coffin, I look away quickly and with washed eyes focus on the headstones all around us. Devoted son. Father and grandfather. Precious only child of. Beloved wife and mother. Sister. Wife. Mother. Mother. In death, we are not defined by what we did or who we were, but by what we meant to others.

How well we loved and were loved in return.

Must Remember
All things must pass, mankind is grass.
Kissing a child's cold cheeks.
Return phone calls.

27

A Change of Heart

Courtship takes place during the spring and summer, and in Europe breeding continues from April to late autumn. During courtship, the males coo loudly, display before the females, and indulge in display fights. Pigeons can live to 30 years of age. They are monogamous and tend to mate for life, a feature remarkable in birds so strongly gregarious.

A pair of courting pigeons may be silent for hours on end, while one of the pair, usually the male but sometimes the female, gently runs its beak through the feathers of its mate.

For about five or six months, before it is fully adult, the cooings of the male have a dull and melancholy sound, these having replaced the feeble and rather nasal calls of the adolescent. The cooings eventually take on a richer quality when the bird is mated.

From *The Habits of the Pigeon*

It's quiet out here on the ledge. You can hear the hoots and the snarls of the City below, but they are muffled by height, smothered in a duvet of air.

I am very near the pigeon now. I can see her and she can see me. She is making a low chirruking sound and there is a fierce shuddering in her neck. Every instinct is telling her to fly away; every one except the one that tells her to stay with her chick. One of the eggs hatched while I was in Sussex. It was hard to see the baby from inside the office, but this close I get a good view. You simply can't believe that this creature will ever be capable of flight. It doesn't look like a bird, more like an anguished sketch towards a bird. Shrivelled and bald, like all newborn things it seems ancient, a thousand years old.

I did try to open the window and reach out, but there's so

much triple-glazing you can't budge any of the panels near the nest: there was nothing for it, I would have to climb out through the next window. So now, on hands and knees, I edge my collection of big books along the ledge. The volumes have been carefully chosen for size and durability:

The Square Meal: a Guide to the City's Restaurants
Brokers' Predictions for 2000
CFBC's Global Directions for 1997, 98 and 99
A Review of the Pharmaceutical Industry
A Linguarama book for the Italian course I started and
   never finished
The Warren Buffet Way
The Ten Natural Laws of Successful Time and Life Management:
   Proven Strategies for Increased Productivity and Inner Peace.

The birds can definitely have that last one. Just in case these are not up to the task, I have included *A Handbook of Financial Futures*, a manual with all the depth and interest of a breeze block. The idea is to build a protective wall around the pigeon and her nest. On the way back from Jill's funeral, I got a call from Guy. Good news, he said, a man from the Corporation had returned his call and told him that the falconer would be along tomorrow. I was the one who insisted that the hawk show up and now I very urgently want him to stay away.

Down in the piazza, thirteen floors below, I'm attracting a bit of a crowd, the first commuters pointing up at the woman on the ledge. Probably wondering if I'm a casualty of the recession or of the heart. A broker threw himself under a train at Moorgate the other morning and he missed: fell into that pit under the rails instead and got pulled out by an emergency team. Everyone kept saying what a miracle it was, but I wondered what it would be like to feel so bad you try to end it all and then to fail at that too. Would it feel like a rebirth or a living death?

Behind me, from inside the office, floats the voice of Candy, droll as ever but streaked with anxiety.

233

'Kate, get back in here.'

'I can't.'

'Honey, these things are often a cry for help. We all love you.'

'I am not crying for help, I am trying to hide the pigeon.'

'Kate?'

'I've got to help her.'

'Why?'

'There's a hawk coming.'

I actually hear Candy's snort. 'There's always a fucking hawk coming. I can't believe we're having this conversation about some stupid bird. Get in here this minute, Kate Reddy, or I'm gonna call security.'

Through the glass, a group of EMF colleagues are monitoring my progress, giving an ironic little cheer as another volume is shunted into position. As I pick up Warren Buffet, I catch sight of my hand, its wedding ring glinting, the ridge of eczema across the knuckle, and I think of what would happen to it if I fell – tendons, skin, blood. No, don't think about it, let's just finish the fortification with *The Ten Natural Laws of Successful Time and Life Management.* Edging back along the ledge, ahead I can see Candy leaning out of the window and Guy hovering behind her. My assistant's face is touched not by fear, but something that looks like hope.

From: Debra Richardson

To: Kate Reddy

Jim is away for second weekend in a row. Not sure if I'll murder the kids before they murder me. Has left me to organise his 40th birthday party – told me to invite 'the usual suspects'. How come he can clear his head of everything to do with home when he has a big deal on and I can't?

As I think you will have gathered am just a teensy bit fucking pissed off with him. Know any gorgeous single men? . . .

NO DON'T ANSWER THAT QUESTION

From: Kate Reddy
To: Debra Richardson
Q: What should you do if you see your ex-husband rolling
   around on the ground in pain?
A: Shoot him again just to make sure.
You have got to take Tough Line with Jim – tell him your job is
not a hobby. Must do his share etc. Mind you, Richard is very
helpful, but I end up having to do everything again after he's
done it . . . so maybe better to do it yourself in first place???
Am worried about you. Am worried about Candy too. Did I tell
you she's pregnant? Won't even talk about it. Pretends it's
not happening to her. Been feeling pretty crazy myself since
Jill's funeral. Have just consolidated reputation as office
madwoman by climbing out on window ledge to save baby
pigeon.
What is Meaning of Life? Please advise soonest xxxxxxxxxxx

12.17 pm: So Momo and I did it. Rod got the news late last
night. We won the New Jersey final. Momo is so excited that
her feet leave the ground. Like Emily, she literally jumps for joy.

'You did it, Kate, you did it!'

'No, we did it. We. You and me together.'

Rod takes the whole team out to lunch to celebrate at a place
in Leadenhall Market. It's changed a lot since I was here before.
Limestone was clearly last year's material; now it's all opaque
glass forming faux Japanese bridges over streams full of gaping
carp, who can't decide whether they're art or lunch.

Rod hauls himself on to the stool next to me; Chris Bunce
is opposite Momo. I don't like the look he gives her, avid, sly,
lip-moistening, but she seems to be enjoying herself flirting
with him, trying out the power that her new confidence brings.
I find myself mentioning the Salinger Foundation several times,
just for the pleasure of saying Jack's name aloud. I love hearing
and seeing his name – on the side of vans, over the front of
shops. Jack Nicholson, Jack and the Beanstalk, Jack of Hearts.
Even the Foreign Secretary has become a more attractive man
since he was called Jack.

'Katie, what's with the fucking pigeon?' demands Rod as the lobster arrives. 'You gonna race it or roast it?'

'Oh, it's a kind of ethical fund action. Part of my new brief to be friendlier to the environment.'

'Jeeez,' my boss says tearing a granary roll in half, 'taking things a bit far, aren't you?'

By the way, Rod says, he has some business he wants Momo and me to pitch for. Stone something. 'One Stone with two birds, geddit?'

I say fine, but I will need more resources.

'Can't increase the head count, Katie,' says Rod. 'You just gotta get out there and kick the fucking tyres, kid.'

28

What the Mother Saw

SO I RUSH HOME from work and when I get through the door I call out, but there's no reply. There are squeals coming from the sitting room and my first thought is pain – they're in pain – and my heart flubs over and I go in and there's Paula on the sofa with Emily and Ben. All snuggled up together with *Toy Story* on the TV and giggling uncontrollably.

'What's so funny?' I say, but they're laughing too much to answer. Emily's laughing so much she's crying. And seeing the way they are, so snug and happy there, I suddenly think, You're paying for this, Kate. You're literally paying for this. For another woman to sit on your sofa and cuddle your children.

So I ask Paula if she hasn't got something better to be getting on with, and I hate the sound of my voice: priggish, pious, lady of the bloody manor. And they all look at me, eyes widening in amazement, and then they start giggling again. Can't help it. Giggling at the silly lady who's come in and tried to stop the fun. As though you could turn fun off just like that.

Sometimes I think Paula's too close to them, it's not healthy. Mostly, I'd do anything for her to stay. Paula told me she's known mothers who sack the childminder every six months. So they don't get too attached. I mean, how selfish can you get? Denying them a familiar loving presence just because you want it to be you and it can't be you.

Of course, I sometimes find myself worrying that she doesn't talk to the children as I would talk to them. When I was a kid, I used to say dinner for lunch and tea for dinner, but now I've joined the professional classes I teach my kids lunch and dinner, and then Paula comes along and teaches them dinner and tea. I can't complain, can I? Richard corrects them. 'Loo,' he says firmly as Emily demands once again to go to the toilet; but to be honest I feel more comfortable with the words I learnt myself. I know Paula lets them watch quite a bit of TV, but in other ways I can see she's much better than I would be – consistent, more patience. After a weekend with them, I'm screaming to be let out the house, but with Paula, it's steady as she goes. Never raises her voice. A lot that's good in their characters comes from her.

When I went into school for a meeting with the teacher the other night, the headmistress took me aside and she said that if Emily was going to have any hope of getting into Piper Place she would need – how to put this? – more of the right kind of stimulation at home. Children with mothers who didn't go out to work were being taking on regular visits to museums, they had a broader perspective. Even if they ate Alphabetti Spaghetti, it was always in sodding Latin. Whereas homes with both parents out at work. 'Well, there can be a tendency to rely on the te-le-vis-i-on,' said Miss Acland, getting five syllables out of the dreaded word.

'Emily,' she said, 'seems to have a quite remarkable knowledge of the cartoon films of Walt Disney.'

This was her way of telling me Paula wasn't good enough. 'Emily,' continued Miss Acland, 'will need to show a wide range of interests to secure a place at a good secondary school. Competition in London is very fierce as you know, Mrs Shattock. I suggest an instrument – not the violin, too common now; perhaps the clarinet, which has plenty of personality – and you could consider one of the more unusual sports.' Rugby for girls, she believed, was gaining in popularity.

'Emily needs a CV at the age of six?'

Maybe I should have tried to keep the incredulity out of my voice.

'Well, Mrs Shattock, in certain home situations where neither parent is present these kinds of things can, shall we say, slip. Did you learn an instrument yourself as a child?'

'No, but my father sang a lot to us.'

'Oh,' she said, the kind of 'Oh' that kind of woman holds in a pooper-scooper.

238

Hideous money-grubbing education witch.

In her last job, the one before us, Paula worked for a family in Hampstead. Julia, the mother, said the kids weren't allowed to watch TV.

'And Julia worked in telly making all this crap for Channel 5,' Paula told me one day, laughing loudly at the memory. 'And it's like her kids weren't allowed telly because it's evil!' At the weekends, Julia and her husband Mike stayed in bed while the kids were downstairs watching videos all morning. Paula found this out because Adam, the youngest, told her one Monday when she was trying to switch the TV off. When I think of that story, I can feel myself redden. Aren't I guilty of the same double standard? I tell Paula that Ben must have water not juice and then, at the weekend, if he asks me for apple juice I give in quickly to buy myself some peace and quiet. I want my nanny to be a better mother than I would ever be: I expect her to love my two like they're her own, and then, when I come home and find her loving them like they're her own, they're suddenly My Children and to be loved by nobody except me.

As I unload the dishwasher and start to wash by hand all the plates that aren't properly clean, I can see Paula looking at me from the other end of the kitchen. She's brushing Emily's hair and really looking at me. I wish I knew what she thought. She said to me once that she would never have a nanny if she had kids; she knew too much about what went on – the girls who suck up to the mums and then, as soon as they're out the door, it's on the mobile.

Emily lets out a cry as the brush encounters a tangle. 'Hush now,' Paula chides, 'princesses have to have their hair brushed a hundred times every night, don't they, Mummy?' She looks across the room, seeking an act of conciliation and consent.

No. I don't want to know. If I knew what she really thought it would probably kill me. Still, a part of me wishes I knew what she thought.

Part Four

29

The Supermarket Shop

EMILY'S BIRTHDAY ALWAYS means the start of summer for me. When my waters broke six years ago and I took a cab to the hospital, there were people sitting at café tables on the pavements and spilling into the street and it felt as though the whole city was in carnival for the arrival of my child.

The day before her party, I do the supermarket shop with Ben. The supermarket shop. Who could imagine that such a small phrase could contain so much pain; an *Oresteia* of suffering. First off, I try to liberate one of the extra-wide trolleys which is in coitus with another trolley outside the store: I pull and pull and push with one hand, holding on to a runaway toddler with the other.

An aviary on wheels, the extra-wide trolley is roughly as manoeuvrable as the Isle of Wight. I try to persuade Ben to sit in the baby seat. He declines, preferring to ride in the cargo hold where he can eject any purchase he disapproves of. In desperation, I crack open a box of Mini Milks and give him two: while both his hands are full of lolly, I slip him into the seat and snap the clips. (Bad, bad, bribing mother.) Now, all that remains is to track down the thirty-seven items on my list. After I threw the radio at him this morning, Richard said he thought the whole birthday thing was perhaps stressing me out a little. Why didn't I take a break and he'd do the supermarket shop? Impossible, I said, he would buy all the wrong things.

'But there's a list, Kate,' he reasoned in his man-in-a-white-coat voice, 'how could I possibly go wrong?'

What every woman knows and no man can ever grasp is that even if he brings home everything on the list, he will still not have got the right things. Why? Because the woman truly believes that if she had gone to the supermarket she would have made better choices: a plumper chicken from a more luxuriantly pastured region of France, a yummier yoghurt, the exact salad leaf she had yearned for and whose precise name had, until the epiphany in front of the Healthy Eating cabinet, eluded her. Men make lists to order the world, to tie it down; for women, lists are the start of something, the co-ordinates by which we plot our journey to freedom. (Don't get me wrong here: I'm not claiming that any of this is fair. When a woman buys an item not on the list which turns out to be inedible, this is called 'an experiment'; when a man does the same thing it is 'a waste of money'.)

3.31 pm: Join the checkout queue. Am sure I have forgotten something vital. What?

3.39 pm: Oh great, Ben has a dirty nappy. Just wondering how long I can hang in here and defy the astounded nostrils of nearby customers when my son puts his hand, the one holding what's left of the second Mini Milk, down his shorts. When he withdraws the hand it is marbled with ice-cream and excrement. I want to faint with misery. Instead, holding the boy aloft like a grenade with the pin out, I sprint the length of the store to the baby-changing facility.

4.01 pm: Rejoin queue. Sixteen minutes. Estimate Ben has now eaten at least one-twelfth of the party food. As he munches contentedly, I grab a magazine from the rack by the till and try to lower my blood pressure by reading my horoscope.

Jupiter is now transiting your 9th house, which is truly one of the most beneficial things it can do for you. Your consciousness is lifted and your perspective grows. You find yourself imbued with loving feelings towards everyone – even children who have been impossible to control. The most positive effect of this moment is that your rage level sinks to an all-time low. The trick will be to hold on to this feeling of serenity once the euphoria wears off.

'Excuse me, madam?'

I look up, expecting that it's my turn to put items on the conveyor belt. Instead, the checkout girl informs me that I have been queuing in a regular aisle through which the Isle of Wight cannot pass. 'Sorry, madam, if you could just move to one of the designated wider aisles.'

'*Sorry? Sorry doesn't exactly cover it, does it?*' For five seconds I go very quiet, then drive my fist into a twelve-pack of Hula Hoops. The bang brings a security guard vaulting over the barrier. Ben bursts into tears, as does every other child in the immediate area. I am imbued with loving feelings towards everyone.

4.39 pm: The checkout person is so slow she may as well be underwater. Even worse, she is helpful and friendly.

'You know if you buy another one of those you get one free?'

'Sorry?'

'Fromage frais, doncha want one free?'

'No, I don't.'

'Having a party, are ya?'

No, I am buying eighty mini sausages, twenty-four Barbie chocolate rolls and a bumper bag of Iced Gems for my own consumption because I am a deranged bulimic.

'My daughter. She's six tomorrow.'

'Ah, lovely. Gotta Reward Card?'

'No, I—'

'You want one with this lot, doncha? Save yourself a bit, love.'

'Actually, I haven't got time to—'

'Cashback?'

No, really, I just have to go—'

'Inshee lovely?'

'Sorry?'

'Your little gel. Inshee lovely!'

'He. He's a boy.'

'Oh, wouldn't know it with all them curls. You wanna tell your mum to getcha 'air cut, little man.'

Why can't supermarkets designate a Working Mother Aisle where you can be served by surly, super-efficient androids? Or French people. The French would be perfect.

9.43 pm: Everything is under control. Both children are in bed. Pass the Parcel took a mere one hour and forty-five minutes to assemble. Debra warned me that you're not allowed to have just one gift in the middle like we used to have when we were little. These days, there has to be a present in each layer in an attempt to convince kids that life is fair. Why? Life is not fair; life is layers of wrapping with one broken squeaker in the middle.

Next door, Richard is filling party bags in front of the TV. (In theory, of course, I disapprove of the escalation of gifts that kids expect to take home: like the arms race, it can only lead to mutually assured ruination. In practice, I am too cowardly to hand over the balloon and piece of cake I feel would be more than sufficient. The Muffia would take out a contract on me.)

Unfortunately, the supermarket was unable to swap the pink-iced birthday cake I had ordered for a yellow one at short notice. Pink used to be Emily's favourite colour, then it became yellow. When I ordered the cake, pink was once more in the ascendant, but yellow made an overnight comeback while I was away last week. Never mind, I have bought a Victoria sponge and will now ice it myself in a wobbly but loving manner: the mother's touch that means so much. Oh shit, where is the icing sugar?

11.12 pm: Find the box wedged at the back of a cupboard under a weeping bottle of soy sauce. A year past its sell-by date, the icing sugar comes out of the packet in one piece. It looks a lot like one of those Apollo moon rocks my dad cooked up thirty years ago. Or £50K of crack cocaine. Luckily it is not the latter, otherwise would consume entire piece by myself and lie down on kitchen floor awaiting merciful instant death.

It should be just enough to cover the cake, anyway. It takes eight minutes to pound the icing rock to dust. I'm careful not to add too much warm water, then eke in the teeniest drop of yellow colouring. This produces a shade of pale lemon: a bit mimsy, a bit – how can I put this? – a bit head boy's mother's dress at prep-school speech day. Need something cheerier for a birthday: egg-yolk yellow, Van Gogh yellow. Emboldened, I add a couple of drops more. The colour is now both watery and intense like a rank urine specimen. I add a further two drops and stir furiously.

I am tearfully contemplating the contents of the basin, when Rich comes into the kitchen talking about some documentary on child development. 'Do you know that babies identify their gender roles from three months? Probably why Ben spends all day sitting on the potty reading the sports pages. Like father like— Christ, Kate, what's that?'

Rich has spotted the icing. The icing is now a colour which, if you were being kind, could be described as Safari Yellow. It is disturbingly reminiscent of one of Ben's more challenging nappies.

Richard laughs. That unforgivable, liberated laugh that escapes when you're just so fantastically grateful someone else screwed up, not you. 'Don't worry, honey,' he says, 'let's work the problem. We have icing the colour of dung, so we will make – a cow cake! Got any white chocolate buttons?'

*

Sunday, 7.19 pm: The party went pretty well, if you discount Joshua Mayhew throwing up in the hall and the moment when I brought in the cake and started the singing: 'Happy birthday dear Emily, happy birthday to you!'

'But, Mummy, I don't want brown icing,' she wailed.

'It's not brown, darling, it's yellow.'

'I don't want yellow. I want *pink*.'

When all eighteen guests have departed, I set about clearing up the debris – juice cartons like collapsed lungs, Barbie paper plates, thirty-six untouched egg sandwiches (there to make the parents feel better; no self-respecting child would even nibble anything so free of additives). Earlier today, I sent an e-mail to

Jack Abelhammer suggesting that, under the circumstances, it might be better if I handed over his fund to a colleague. My feelings for him – it started as a minor crush and now I feel as though I'm lying under a steamroller – have made our professional relationship hard to handle. The tone of my message was friendly but firm. For a couple of hours afterwards, I felt the steady glow of having acted responsibly, the brightest bulb in the maternal firmament. Since then, though, the bulb has blown. Either that, or I have tripped over the lead and unplugged myself from the mains: no juice, no flow of energy, certainly no current affairs. I've already checked my Inbox five times for his reply. Come on, Kate, grow up; stop acting like a lovesick teenager.

In my self-denial, have so far eaten two chocolate Barbie rolls, a bowl of Twiglets and poured a half-bottle of gin into the home-made lemonade I bought at Marks & Spencer then decanted into a pink jug to pass off as my own.

It's a hot night: viscous, thirsty for rain. The fan I dug out from under the stairs is no use: it sits on the kitchen table, sluggishly stirring the soupy air. There was an attempt at thunder earlier, just as we were leaving the swimming baths around four, but it was more like a ripping of brown paper than the full-throated roar we need to scare off the heat. Christ, the heat. And the smell. I am out in the garden scraping the rug over which Joshua Mayhew threw up. The oatmeal vomit is studded with the pastel minarets of Iced Gems.

I did notice Josh looking pale and clammy during Pass the Parcel and managed to get him out into the hall, but as I was struggling with the front door he deposited his birthday tea on the runner. When his mother turned up, she shrieked, 'What has happened to poor little Joshie?'

I managed to suppress the obvious reply: what has happened is that little Joshie has carpet-bombed £500 worth of Uzbekistan kelim. If it had been the contents of my child's stomach, I would have been down on my knees proferring a chequebook. But Imogen Mayhew, a person so wholesome her entire being seems to have been woven from camomile, just demanded to know if Joshua had been allowed to have 'excess sugar'.

I laughed a tinkly hostess laugh and said that sugar was a traditional staple of birthday parties, but Imogen did not join in the laughter. She left with a look which suggested I can expect imminent litigation against my Nigella fairy cakes. Then, as soon as she was out of the door, I had another encounter with Angela Brunt who was kneeling by the coats and scraping strawberry Frube off Davina's green velvet. 'Have you got Emily in anywhere yet, Kate?'

'Ygno.'

'Well, Davina has a guaranteed place at Holbrook House, but her second interview at Piper Place is on Thursday and that's the one we're holding out for because it opens the door to so many other things, doesn't it?'

'Yes, doesn't it.'

After washing my hands to try and remove the smell of vomit, I go into the sitting room where Richard has crashed out on the sofa, a Sunday review section tented over his face. Every time he breathes out, he inflates the breasts of Madonna, whose picture is on the cover above a feature entitled: 'From Virgin to Blessed Mother.' Perhaps I should call Madonna for a mum-to-mum chat about how to sponge vomit from a kelim? Presumably at her daughter's parties she has a designated sick wrangler. How much do I hate the celebrity Having It All Mother who boasts about how fulfilled she is when you just know she has a fleet of substitute mothers doing it all for her?

'Rich?'

'Hmmmmm?' The paper slides down on to the bridge of his nose.

'We have to get Emily down for Piper Place.'

'Why?'

'Because it opens so many doors.'

'You've been talking to Angela Brunt again.'

'Ygno.'

'Katie, that woman's poor kid is so pressurised she's going to end up as the neighbourhood crack dealer.'

'But she can play the oboe.'

'All right, the neighbourhood's oboe-playing crack dealer. Your daughter knows all of *Mary Poppins* by heart, so give her a break, OK?'

Richard spent most of Emily's swimming party in the deep end with Mathilde, the mother of Laurent who is in Em's class at school. I was in the shallows, pulling ten screaming children round on a snake made of orange tubing. On the way home in the car, Rich said, 'French women do keep themselves in good nick, don't they?'

He sounded exactly like his mother.

'Mathilde doesn't work,' I said crossly.

'What's that got to do with it?'

'After the age of thirty, body maintenance is a full-time job. And I already have one of those in case you haven't noticed.'

For a second, he rested his head on the steering wheel. 'It wasn't a criticism of you, Kate. Not everything's a criticism of you, you know.'

When the kitchen is clean and I've crawled the length of the hall pinching up orange Wotsit dust with my thumb and forefinger – if I use the Hoover it'll wake them – I sit down for five minutes to watch TV. An hour later I'm woken by the phone. It's Barbara, my mother-in-law. 'I hope you don't think I'm talking out of turn, Katharine, but Richard did sound awfully fed up when I spoke to him earlier. It's not for me to say anything, of course, but let things go in a certain department and before you know where you are, well, the whole shop closes down.'

'Yes, Barbara, but it's been Emily's party and—'

'Anyway, Richard's father and I are coming down on Saturday to take in that marvellous show at the Royal Academy.'

I realise that the pause indicates I should say something. 'Oh, that's nice, Barbara, where will you be staying?'

'Now don't go to too much trouble, will you? You know Donald and I, hot water and a clean bed and we'll be right as rain.'

9.40 pm: Upstairs, Emily is still awake but wild-eyed with tiredness after her big day. So hot she has shucked off both duvet and nightie and lies there on the sheet, her body casting a mother-of-pearl sheen in the darkened room. Over the past year – can it really be a whole twelve months since she was five? – her distended baby's pot belly has disappeared; her tummy dips now and rises towards the contours of the woman she will become. More beautiful for not knowing she is beautiful. I want to love and protect and never ever hurt her. I make a silent vow to be a better mother.

'Mummy?'

'Yes, Em.'

'Next birthday, I will be seven! Then I will be eight, nine, ten, 'leven, twelve, fourteen, twenty!'

'That's right, but you don't want to grow up too soon, sweetheart.'

'I do.' She juts out that chin of hers. 'When you're a adult you can go to Morantic.'

'What's Morantic?'

She rolls her eyes in incredulity, my world-weary sophisticate of six: 'You know, *Morantic*. It's a country where adults go out to dinner and kiss.'

'Oh, *Romantic*.'

She nods, pleased I've heard of it: 'Yes, Morantic!'

'Who told you about Morantic?'

'Hannah. And anyway you have to go with boys, only sometimes they're too naughty.'

I stand here in the thick hot dark thinking of all the conversations we will have on this subject in the years ahead and of the ones we won't have, because she will need to have secrets in order to grow away from me and I will need to have secrets to keep her close. As I bend to kiss her, I say, 'Morantic is a fantastic country.'

Perhaps seeing something sorrowful in my expression, my daughter reaches out and takes my hand in her small one; it triggers a flicker, no more, of holding my own mother's hand, its coolness, the meshing of its bones.

'You can come to Morantic too, Mummy,' she says. 'It's not very far.'

'No, love,' I say leaning down to extinguish the Cinderella light, 'Mummy's too old.'

From: Jack Abelhammer
To: Kate Reddy
Dearest Katharine,
Perfectly understand your reservations about our meeting again in this life and appreciate the suggestion that your esteemed colleague Brian Somebody might take over the handling of my business. Weirdly, I find myself unwilling to do without you, Kate. Reddiness is all.
Good news, however. Found this great restaurant in a parallel universe. No veal and they can do us a corner table. How are you fixed?
love Jack

From: Kate Reddy
To: Jack Abelhammer
The twelfth of Never looks good for me. Can we sit by the window?
K xxxxx

Out in the garden, through a night as dense and soft as cloth, I swear I can hear Jack calling to me. When I was young I left men as I left clothes, in heaps on the floor. It seemed better that way. I had figured out that it was hard for someone to leave you when you'd gone already. Emotionally, I always had my suitcase packed – a therapist, if I ever had time to consult one, would probably say it was something to do with my dad walking out on us. Besides, I took the Groucho Marx line: why would I want to be in a relationship with anyone dumb enough to want a relationship with me? It took Richard to show me that love could be an investment, something which could silently accrue and promised long-term returns instead of a gamble that would leave you broken and broke.

252

Before Richard, and before children, leaving was easy. Leaving now would be nothing but grief. To the kids, Richard and I are an all-purpose love hybrid called mum'n'dad. To split that unit in half, to teach them there are two people they must learn to love separately. I just don't feel I can ask my children to do that. Men leave their children because they can; women, in general, don't leave because they can't.

To be with Jack, I would have to go into exile from my homeland. To find the courage to do it, I would need to be so unhappy that staying was harder than jumping. And I'm not there yet.

Must Remember

Debt you owe to your children. Debt you owe to yourself. Figure out how to reconcile the two. Minutes of meeting to be written up (Secretary Lorraine says she's off sick, but Lorraine always off sick in heatwave). Self-tan must: look like Morticia Addams's younger sister. Grovel to clients over completely disastrously hideous performance for May (-9% versus index of -6%). May has wiped out all hard work for previous four months: great results now drowned in sea of red. Suggest to clients that performance is only temporary and am taking measures to address it. Think of measures to address this. Deflate bouncy castle, confront Rod over shameful sexist/racist treatment of Momo. Stair carpet??? Book stress-busting spa day, including protein facial as recommended by ace Vogue *beauty woman. Wedding anniversary. When is wedding anniversary?*

30

The Patter of Tiny Feet

11.29 pm: Impending visit from the parents-in-law fills the air with apprehension like the thunder of distant wildebeest. 'Don't go to any trouble, darling,' says my husband. 'What have you got planned for Sunday lunch?'

'Don't go to any trouble, Katharine,' says Barbara, calling for the third time. So then you don't go to any trouble and she takes one look in the fridge when they arrive, tugs on her string of pearls as though it was a rosary and drags Donald out to the car. They return with the entire contents of Sainsbury's, 'so we have something in for emergencies'.

Everything is under control this time, however. I will not be found wanting: there are clean sheets on the guest bed and clean white towels snatched up in M&S at lunchtime. I have even put a nodding sprig of lily of the valley in a bedside vase for that graceful, womanly touch of the sort practised by Cheryl, my Muffia sister-in-law. Also I must remember to dig out all Donald and Barbara's presents from down the years and display them in prominent positions:

Watercolour of sunset over Coniston by 'the celebrated
local artist Pamela Anderson' (no relation, alas)
Royal Worcester egg coddlers (x4)
Electric wok
Dick Francis novel in *hardback*.
Beatrix Potter commemorative cake-stand.

Also, there was definitely another also.

I swab down the kitchen worktop, then check Em's bookbag ready for the morning. Inside, slotted among the pages of *Lily, the Lost Dog*, is a note from school. Could parents please contribute an example of food typical of their child's cultural background and bring it in for World Feast Day?

No. Parents could not. Parents are very busy earning a living thank you and happy for school to do the job for which it is paid. I read down to the bottom of note. Great Feast is tomorrow. ALL WELCOME! Next to this threatening injunction, Emily has inscribed in her fiercest, pressed-down writing: 'My Mummy Is a verray gud kuk much betaa than Sofeez mum.' Oh, hell.

I start to search the cupboards. What qualifies as English ethnic, for heaven's sake? Roast beef? Spotted dick? There's a jar of English mustard, but it has a disgusting rubbery collar of ancient gunge, like Mick Jagger lips, pouting around the lid. Fish and chips? Good, but no fish and never made chips in my life. I could take in McDonald's large fries wrapped in newspaper, but just imagine the faces of the wholefood Nazis led by Mother Superior Alexandra Law. At the back of the cereal shelf I discover two jars of Bonne Maman jam. Strawberry preserve is an excellent example of the indigenous culinary arts, except this stuff is made in France.

Brilliant idea. Boil the kettle. Picking up one jar and then the other, I hold them over the steam till the label wilts and slips off. In the freezer-bag drawer, I find some new labels and on them I write in rounded, bucolic lettering: *Shattock Strawberry Jam*. Overconfident now, I attempt to draw a luscious strawberry in the corner of the label. It looks like an inflamed pancreas. Glue labels on to jars. *Et voilà! Je suis une bonne maman!*

'Kate, what are you doing? It's past midnight.' Rich has come into the kitchen in boxers and T-shirt carrying a Furby. I detest the Furby. The Furby is a hideous cross between a chinchilla and Bette Davis in *Whatever Happened to Baby Jane?* Both Furby and husband squint dubiously at me through the half-light.

'I'm making jam. Actually, I'm remaking jam, if you must know. Emily's school are having this ethnic feast and she has to take in something English.'

'Couldn't you just buy something in the morning?'

'No, Rich, I couldn't.'

His sigh is almost a groan. 'God, how many times do we have to go through this? I've told you, you have to learn to let go. If women are working as hard as you are, Kate, other people are just going to have to accept that you can't do all the stuff your mothers did.'

I want to tell him that, even if other people accept it, I'm not sure I ever will. But the Furby gets there before me, breaking the silence with a crooning chirrup, and Rich disappears upstairs.

12.39 am: Too tired for sleep. I put the Furby in a black bin bag and tie a knot in the neck. In the dark kitchen, I open my laptop and sit bathed in its milky, metallic light. I call up the Salinger file. The figures on screen comfort me – the way they do my bidding so readily, the fact that I cannot lie to them. Whereas at home, I'm a forger, a faker. I'm not ashamed of it; I don't see any alternative. A good mum makes her own jam, doesn't she? Secretly, we all know that. When they start naming preserves Jetlag Maman or Quality Time Maman, when bread comes in wrappers marked Father's Pride, it will be safe for us bad, exhausted mothers to come out with our hands up.

Friday, 7.10 am: Richard raised his voice. I've never known him to raise his voice before, only ask me to lower mine. But there we were sitting in the kitchen at breakfast with the kids jabbering away and you should have heard him bite Emily's head off.

'Mummy, can I have a baby sister?'

'No, darling.'

'But I want one. Daddy, can we have a baby sister?'

'NO, YOU CANNOT!'

'Why?'

'Because to make a baby sister mummies and daddies have to have time together in the same room.' Rich is watching the TV with the volume turned down, his eyes glued to the crescent pout of Chloe-Zoe.

'Don't, Richard.'

'And your Mummy and Daddy never have time, Emily. Mummy is just about to go to New York again, so under those circumstances it will be particularly hard to make a baby sister. Or maybe Mummy would like me to get a man in for her. Isn't that what Mummy always asks Daddy to do when the dishwasher's broken? Get a man in.'

'I said don't.'

'Why not, Kate? Never lie to her, isn't that what you said?'

'Mu-um, Daisy's got a baby sister.'

'And you've got a baby brother, Em.'

'But he's A BOY.'

8.52 am: For once, I drop Emily off at school myself. (I called work and told them I had to see the doctor: in the hierarchy of excuses, poor health is better than a needy small girl.) Em is thrilled to have me there with the other mummies: she parades me before her friends like a show horse, patting my rump and pointing out my good features.

'My Mummy's so lovely and tall, isn't she?'

I was hoping to slip in my World Feast contribution unnoticed, but there is a table bang in the middle of the school hall groaning with ethnic offerings. One mother appears to have brought an entire curried goat along. Kirstie's mum has done haggis clad in genuine stomach. Christ. Quickly hide my strawberry jam behind a crenellated fortress of soda bread.

'Kate, hello! Have you gone part-time, yet?' booms Alexandra Law, unveiling a trifle the size of an inverted Albert Hall.

'No. I'm afraid where I work they don't really do part-time. To be honest, they think full-time is skiving.'

The other mothers laugh, all except Claire Dalton, senior partner at Sheridan and Farquhar. Claire, I notice, is trying to sneak a small bowl of green jelly on to the World Feast altar.

She is holding the jelly very still so as not to give away the fact that it is unset.

12.46 *pm:*   Candy is keeping the baby. She refuses to talk about it, but her belly has made her intentions increasingly clear. The Stratton wardrobe, always on the challenging side of slinky, is now straining to contain her. So today I have brought in a bag of maternity clothes: one or two nice pieces she can wear for work and a couple of useful sacks for later on. I hand the bag to her without comment over lunch in Pizza Navona. She lifts out a taupe shift dress and holds it up incredulously.

'Hey, brown paper packages tied up with string. These are a few of my favourite things!'

'I thought they might come in useful, that's all.'

'What for?'

'For your pregnancy.'

'Jesus Christ, what's this?' Candy takes out a white broderie anglaise nightie and flaps it like a flag to the amusement of the group of guys at the next table. 'I surrender, I surrender,' she pleads.

'Look, it has easy opening for feeding.'

'Why would I want to eat anything wearing a— oh, God, you mean someone feeding off me. That's *sooo* disgusting.'

'Yes, well, it's been pretty common practice for the past hundred and fifty thousand years.'

'Not in New Jersey, it hasn't. Kate?'

'Yes.'

'The baby. It's not gonna be needy, is it?'

I study Candy's face closely. She's not joking. 'No, it won't be needy. I promise.' Not after the first eighteen years, I should add, but for my friend's sake I hold my tongue. She isn't ready yet.

3.19 pm: A State of Emergency. Roo is missing. Paula calls and says she knows for definite that he was in the buggy when she took Ben to Little Stars music group this morning and she's pretty sure Roo came back with them. But then, when she went to put Ben down for his afternoon nap, they couldn't find him. Ben was devastated. Screamed and screamed while Paula searched the house. High and low, but there was no kangaroo to be seen. I can hear Ben hiccuping with grief in the background.

What was she doing taking Roo out of the house in the first place? I can't believe Paula could be so stupid when she knows how awful it would be if he got lost. I voice this thought out loud and, instead of snapping back, she just sounds culpable and sad.

'Do you think we can find another one, Kate?'

'I've no idea what the market in used kangaroos is like, Paula.'

3.29 pm: Call Woolworths where Roo came from originally. Assistant says sorry, but she believes they are out of kangaroos. Would I like to speak to the manager? Yes.

Manager says that kangaroos have been discontinued. 'There's been a big trend away from the softer animals towards plastic novelty creatures, Mrs Reddy. Would you perhaps be interested in a Mr Potato Head?'

No, I already work with a dozen of those.

3.51 pm: Try Harrods. Surely, they must have a Roo. They have everything, don't they? A woman in the toy department says she may have something, she'll just go and check in the next room if I can hang on. When she gets back, she describes something, but it sounds all wrong.

'No, I can't have one with a baby. It's an emergency. Australian, yes. I need one about eight inches long for tonight.'

'Kate, I didn't know you cared.' I look up to see Rod Task leering down at me. Oh God. 'Sorry, Rod, I'm just looking for a kangaroo.'

'Great. I never thought you'd ask.'

There is a nasty snicker from Guy two desks away. When Rod is out of earshot, I tell him to get on to the Internet and start researching toy marsupials right away.

9.43 pm: It takes two hours and forty-three minutes to persuade my son to go to sleep. All the substitute comforters I offer – lamb, polar bear, purple dinosaur, each of the Teletubbies in rotation – are hurled in a fury out of the cot.

'Roo,' he wails, 'Roo.'

To get him to settle, I have to let him hold my electric toothbrush and then we sit in the blue chair with him sprawled over me, clutching my shirt like a baby monkey. At the bottom of each boy breath there is a sticky catch, like a tiny gate being opened in his lungs. Please God, let me find another Roo.

*

EVERYTHING WAS GOING well during Barbara and Donald's visit; suspiciously well, I see that now. To the best of her ability, Barbara had complimented me on the kitchen. 'I'm sure it will be lovely when it's finished,' she said. But I smiled graciously throughout, even during tea with the children when Barbara turned to Donald and said: 'Isn't it funny, Emily looks like Richard when she smiles and Kate when she frowns!'

For dinner that night, we were having Italian. I had washed and dried a pile of rocket, the red peppers had been charred and then peeled with the same lavish care I used to devote to a scab on the knee in infants school. At the top of the oven there was a leg of lamb, and down the bottom the potatoes, suffused with rosemary from my very own garden, were hunkering down nicely. I had even squeezed in a bath after the kids' bedtime and put on a clean blouse and velvet skirt over which I wore the wipeable Liberty print apron the in-laws gave me for Christmas.

Yes, I thought, surveying the scene at dinner, this is one of those rare times when life approaches the condition of colour magazine. The domestic goddess entertaining her admiring parents-in-law in her lovely stylish home. Barbara had just asked me for the peppers recipe and then I saw it. Moving across the oak floor, the plump suede rear of a rat.

Etiquette books are unnaturally silent on the subject of rats at dinner parties. Do you:

a/ Laugh gaily and pretend the rat is a treasured pet?
b/ Exclaim, Ah, there's the main course! Nigel Slater says rodent's the coming thing. Very good done the Vietnamese way, apparently?
c/ Invite your guests to adjourn upstairs, ply them with as much drink as possible and put on a Burt Bacharach CD to drown out the sound from the kitchen where your husband is pursuing the rodent with your daughter's Mary Poppins umbrella?

Richard and I went for c.

Downstairs, the rat holed up in the playpen, perhaps hoping to pass for a soft toy. Before long, though, it was doing frisky circuits of the kitchen. Barbara said that, come to think of it, she remembered feeling something running across her feet: she would need to take some aspirin immediately and go and lie down. Nobody was in the mood for my amaretto peaches in raspberry coulis. I suddenly had a very bad feeling about the clumps of raisins that had been appearing on the kitchen floor.

'Don't get hysterical,' said Richard after he had got the rat out of the patio door and into the garden. 'Remember they're more afraid of you than you are of them.'

This seemed unlikely. The rat triggered what I can only call rat dread, that back-flip of the stomach every time you open a cupboard, not knowing whether you will come face to face with a face. That night, whiskers and paws scurried through my dreams.

Monday, 9.38 am: I have been fired by my own cleaner. In the annals of domestic humiliation, how high does that rate? When I came down this morning, I found Barbara and Juanita in an accusing huddle. My mother-in-law was tutting audibly as my cleaner mimed a rat scurrying along the worktop and pointed to parts of the kitchen made impassable by newspapers and toys. 'It's no wonder,' said Barbara. Although my mother-in-law is not a Spanish speaker, she was able to communicate with Juanita in the international female language of Disapproval.

'The rat man is on his way,' I announced loudly to alert them to my presence, and to stop them exchanging further examples of my sluttishness.

At the sound of the pest's name, Juanita unleashed a machine-gun-burst of woe.

'If you leave food out, it will attract vermin,' volunteered Barbara.

'I do not leave food out,' I said, but she was already out in the hallway where Donald was assembling the luggage. He gave me a rueful little wave.

When they had gone, Juanita told me she was very sorry, but she couldn't take it any more. All of this communicated via operatic arm gestures and sobs. Here at long last was my chance to point out that one of the reasons the house was in such a mess was because my cleaner had been unable to clean it for the past two years, owing to a succession of ailments which I had reacted to with enormous sympathy because – oh, probably because I am from a background where you don't expect to have anyone else tidying up after you and some sneaking shame is attached to the fact that you're a woman who can't keep her own house clean. ('Kate may be a whiz with figures,' my sister-in-law once said, 'but you should see the state of her skirting boards!')

So did I give Juanita a piece of my mind there and then? Not exactly. I gave her all the cash I had in my purse, promised to send more in the post and said I would recommend her to some friends in Highgate who were looking for a cleaner.

Must Remember

Chase RAT MAN! Hire new cleaner! Replacement Roo MUST. Proxy voting policy to be agreed with clients. Complete quarterly performance questionnaire. Meeting minutes do myself (Lorraine still off sick). Prospect for gaining client in final just done with Momo blown

by bloody awful June performance. Check competitors' performance –
perhaps theirs even worse? Conference call with Japanese office to
discuss stocks. Sandals for Emily – or will be questioned by NSPCC
over foot cruelty. Sugar Puffs, Panadol. Cancel spa day.

31

Nanny Crisis

6.27 am: It's still very early, but out here in the garden I can tell it's going to be a hot day. The air is glassy with the promise of heat. When I was away in the States, no one took care of the plants, so the snails have hoovered up my hosta and the pansies in the terracotta pots are all dried up. If you touch one it turns to purple ash. I planted that kind especially too because I loved the name: it's called heart's-ease. One day, when I have time, the garden will be beautiful. I am going to grow lobelias and camellias and a bay tree and sweet swags of jasmine, and there will be carved stone troughs overflowing with heart's-ease.

I hear a yelp escape from a window high up the house. Like me, the children are finding it hard to sleep these warm nights. Ben woke screaming around five when I was in the middle of some awful dream. You even dream differently in summer: fever dreams that sweat out thoughts you'd rather stayed buried. Anyway, when I went into his room, he was slithery with sweat, poor baby; slid through my arms like a seal pup. I took him into the bathroom, sponged him down – he's suddenly afraid of his Piglet flannel for some reason – then changed him. When I offered him a beaker of water, he was furious. 'App-ul,' he demanded, 'app-ul!'

How many times have I told Paula that he's not allowed juice? In my mind, I composed a major nanny bollocking, but Paula has been complaining of 'women's trouble' lately so could easily pull a sickie and the holidays are the worst possible time to find cover. Damn. Damn.

7.43 am: I could tell right away from Paula's voice that she wasn't coming in. And me chairing the Global Asset Allocation

Committee today because Robin Cooper-Clark's away with his boys and Emily and Ben with no school or nursery to occupy them and the nanny's not coming in. Great.

Traditionally a period of pleasure and relaxation, the summer holidays are the very worst time of the year for a working mother. Warm weather and careless days act as a constant rebuke. There are outings you wish you could join, cool paddling pools you would like to slip off your shoes and step into; ice-cream cones whose vanilla tributaries you would be more than happy to lick.

Paula exhales a long, complicated sigh. Says that she's not been feeling that well for a while and the rat thing, of course, has been very upsetting. But she didn't want to worry me because I Know You're Busy, Kate. A classic nanny tactic this, landing a pre-emptive strike before your own more powerful grievance has a chance to leave the ground. Even as I murmur mmm's of sympathy, I am riffling through my mental Rolodex searching for someone who can take the children just for today (Richard is away presenting plans for a Sunderland crafts yurt).

First thought: Angela Brunt, my neighbour and leader of local Muffia. I start dialling her number, but suddenly picture Angela's Ford Anglia face, headlamps on full gleam, when it becomes clear that the 'high-flyer' across the road is emerging from the burning fuselage of her own selfishness begging for help. No. Can't possibly give her the satisfaction. Instead, I call Alice, my TV producer friend and ask if I can beg a favour. Could her nanny Jo possibly have Emily and Ben? I wouldn't ask only I have this big meeting and, anyway, taking time off from EMF is practically illegal and—

Alice cuts me off with a raucous, I've-been-there yelp. Says it's fine so long as I have no objections to Jo taking the kids swimming with her boys. At this point, I have no objection to Ben and Emily going parascending in Borneo so long as I can get into the City and start preparing for my meeting.

7.32 am: I call Pegasus Cars. Winston answers the phone again. Why? Doesn't Pegasus have any other drivers? I'm starting to wonder what kind of racket he's running.

Winston says he'll be fifteen minutes; I tell him I need him in four.

'See what I can do,' he says coolly.

I have a sudden and impossible longing to climb on to the lap of a large, comforting person and be held there for – oh, twenty-five years should probably do the trick.

'Mummy?'

'What is it, Em?'

'Heaven's a nice place, isn't it?'

'Yes. Heaven's a very nice place.'

'Is there a McDonald's?'

'Where?'

'In Heaven.'

'God, no. Now, I need to pack Ben's wings.'

'For Heaven?'

'What? No. Water wings. You're going swimming. You remember Nat and Jacob, don't you?'

'Why doesn't Heaven have McDonald's, Mum?'

'Because. I've no idea. Because dead people don't need to eat anything.'

'Why don't dead people eat anything?'

'Ben, no. No, Benjamin. SIT DOWN. Mummy will fetch you that juice in a— Not on my dress.'

'Mummy. Can I have my next birthday party in Heaven?'

'Emily, WILL YOU PLEASE BE QUIET.'

7.44 am: Pegasus has pulled up outside the house in a new chariot, new to him anyway. The Nissan Primera is hidden behind a cloud of its own dirt, but at least when you open the door it doesn't rain rust on your clothes. I load the children into the back, clasp Ben on my knee and with the free hand call a nanny agency on the mobile. A Sloaney girl, her voice designed to carry across stag-rich moors, says she would really like to help, but it's a particularly bad time for temps.

'It's the school holidays, you know.'

Yes, I know.

Everyone's been snapped up ages ago, only she does have this new girl on the books. Croatian. Eighteen. English not her best thing, but really keen. Likes children.

Well, that's a start. I rack my brain trying to remember which side Croatia was on in Balkan massacres. I think they sided with the Nazis in the war and are the good guys now, or maybe it's the other way round? I say, OK, I'll interview her tonight. What's her name?

'Ratka.'

Of course it is. Must remember to call rat man. Why didn't he show up? Emily pats my leg urgently. She has been deep in conversation with our driver.

'Mummy, Winston says the nice thing about being in Heaven is if you're hungry, you can lean over and bite off a bit of cloud. Like candyfloss. The angels make it.' She looks far happier with this explanation than any I have managed to come up with.

Alice lives in a gentrified house on the edge of Queen's Park: she bought in the area before a four-bedroom terraced cost more than Colorado. Once inside, my daughter wanders off happily to play with Nat and Jake, but Ben takes one look at the unfamiliar Brio set and clings to my right leg like a sailor lashing himself to the mast in a Force 10. I need to get out of here fast, but I have to spend a few minutes humbling myself before Jo the nanny. I can see her eyeing the hysterical toddler and wondering what she's got herself into. End up having to shake him off me and run out of the room with his screams at my back.

Sitting in the back of Pegasus, I try to read the *FT* to get up to speed for the meeting, but I can't concentrate. Shake my head fiercely to dislodge memory of Ben's tears. I can see Winston studying me in the rear-view mirror. We are at the Old Street roundabout before he finally speaks:

'How much they paying you, lady?'

'None of your business.'

'Fifty? A hundred?'

'Depends on my bonus. But this year there isn't going to be

any bonus. After June's performance I'll be lucky to keep my job, frankly.'

Winston bangs the sheepskin steering wheel with both hands. 'You gotta be kidding. They got you every second of every minute of every day. You their slave, girl.'

'I can't do very much about it, Winston. I'm what's technically known as the main breadwinner.'

'Whoaa.' He stamps on the brake to avoid a nun on a zebra crossing. 'How your man feel about that? Kind of thing tend to make the guys feel a little small in the Johnson department.'

'Are you seriously suggesting that the size of my salary is shrinking my husband's penis?'

'Well, it would account for why no one out there can't make no babies no more, wouldn't it? Fertility rate was doing just fine till women went out to work.'

'I think you'll find that's down to oestrogen in the water.'

'I think you'll find that's down to oestrogen in the office.'

Even from the back seat, I can tell he is grinning broadly because his cheeks are stretched so taut they have rumpled up the skin under his ears.

'For God's sake, Winston, this is the end of the twentieth century.'

He shakes his head and a sprinkling of gold dust fills the cab. Like a fairy godmother, Emily said when she saw it. 'Don't matter what century it is,' he growls, 'the clock in men's head always set to the same time. Pussy Time.'

'I thought we'd all grown up and got over that caveman nonsense.'

'That's where people like you got it all wrong, lady. The women they outgrew it and the guys they just went along with it so they could keep getting the women to have sex with them. The guy, he just ask himself, what tune she want me to play now and he play it. Here, try one of these.'

Winston chucks a tin at me. I recognise the round bronze container from childhood: travel sweets. Julie and I preferred the frosted pears, the ones that tasted the way bells would taste if you licked bells, but we always got given these – barley sugars. Mum swore that barley sugars kept motion sickness at bay. So for me the taste of barley sugar is now the taste of being sick – the paper bag with its grim cargo, the lurch on to the roadside, the wiping your hands on the dead brown grass.

We have entered the City proper now, sweeping through the glass canyons where the heat hangs in a lilac haze. I open the sweet tin. Inside are six neatly rolled joints. Clearing my throat, I adopt the tone of a Radio 4 announcer: 'Company policy is quite clear that the consumption of any illegal drugs on the premises of Edwin Morgan Forster is specifically for-bidden. And . . . we're nearly there, so I'd better hurry up. Have you got a light, Winston?'

11.31 am: Research for my meeting is hampered because the typeface of the *Wall Street Journal* refuses to keep still. All squirmy black lines, the Market Returns Page looks like the Ugly Bugs' Ball.

Completely pathetic. Feel as woozy as a maiden aunt after a schooner of vicarage sherry. Motherhood – or abstinence brought on by motherhood – has wrecked my capacity to enjoy drugs of any kind except the occasional desperate slug of Calpol. I manage to walk into the meeting room OK, but once inside the walls keep receding into infinite reflections of themselves, like an Escher print. Every time I stand up to change a slide, I have to grab the edge of the table and tip my head slightly to one side to steady the horizon. Feel like a human spirit level.

When I open my mouth to address the twelve fund managers around the table, the voice that comes out sounds confident enough. But then I discover I have only a vague idea who's talking and none at all about what she's going to say next. It's like being a ventriloquist of myself. Nonetheless, a profound feeling of relaxation enables me to disregard the opinions of my colleagues and make the investment choices that will become policy for the entire company from tomorrow.

Bonds or equities? No problem. UK or Japan? Hell, only a fool would hesitate over that one.

Halfway through the meeting, Andrew McManus – Scots,

rugger bugger, shoulders like a Chesterfield sofa – gives a self-important little cough and announces that he hopes all present will forgive him, but he has to slip away early because Catriona, his daughter, has this swimming gala and he promised her that Daddy would be there. Everyone around the table reacts as though this is the most normal thing in world. The younger guys who think they may one day get around to having kids, but only when the Porsche Boxster comes complete with a nappy-changing shelf, don't flinch. The other fathers bask in conspiratorial, new-dad smugness. I see Momo, who knows no better, mouth, '*Sweeeet*.' Even Celia Harmsworth composes her Wicked Queen features into an approximation of a smile and says, 'Oh, how marvellous, Andrew! You're so hands on,' as though McManus had singlehandedly driven the Dow up 150 points.

Observing that I am the only colleague not to join in the cooing approbation, Andrew shrugs helplessly and says, 'You know how it is, Kate.' Slips into his jacket and out of the room.

Indeed, I do know how it is. Man announces he has to leave the office to be with his child for short recreational burst and is hailed as selfless, doting paternal role model. Woman announces she has to leave the office to be with child who is on sickbed and is damned as disorganised, irresponsible and Showing Insufficient Commitment. For father to parade himself as a Father is a sign of strength; for mother to out herself as a Mother is a sign of appalling vulnerability. Don't you just love equal opportunities?

From: Kate Reddy
To: Debra Richardson

Just chaired meeting where fellow manager announced he had to leave to attend daughter's swimming gala. Practically knighted on the spot for services to parenthood. If I tried that Rod would have me executed and my dripping bloody head stuck on the ramparts of Bank of England as a warning to other women slackers.

It's sooooo unfair. Am coming to conclusion that career-girl bollocks is one-generation-only trick. We are living proof that it can't work, aren't we?

Forget higher education. Think we should send our girls to catering college where they can learn to make decorative floral centrepieces and a delicious supper for two, then they can marry a man who will pay for them to stay at home and have pedicures.

URGENT: Pls remind me what was drawback to that way of life again???

From: Debra Richardson
To: Kate Reddy
Once upon a time, in a land far away,
a beautiful, independent, self-assured princess
happened upon a frog as she sat contemplating
ecological issues
on the shores of an unpolluted pond
in a verdant meadow near her castle.
The frog hopped into the Princess's lap and said:
Sweet Lady, I was once a handsome Prince,
until an evil witch cast a spell on me.
One kiss from you, however,
and I will turn back into the dapper young Prince that I am.
Then, my sweet, we can marry
and set up house in yon castle
where you can prepare my meals,
clean my clothes, bear my children,
and forever feel grateful and happy doing so.
That night, dining on a repast of lightly sauteed frogs' legs,
The Princess chuckled to herself and thought:
I don't fucking think so.

*

MEN TODAY CAN only be better fathers than their fathers. Simply by knowing how to change a nappy or figuring out which hole you stick the bottle in: these things mark them out as more capable parents than any previous generation. But

271

women can only be worse mothers than our mothers and this rankles because we are working so very very hard and we are doomed to fail.

At Edwin Morgan Forster, the desks of men with children are dense with photographs of their offspring. Before you get to the computer and the blotter, you have to negotiate a three-day-event course of family portraits – leather frames, mottled crocodile frames, double steel frames with a copper hinge, witty Perspex cubes. A missing tooth here, a soccer goal there; that skiing trip in February where Sophie wrapped her red scarf around Dad's neck and they both turned to face the camera with Steinway smiles. A man is allowed to advertise the fact that he is a father. It's a sign of strength, a sign he is a good provider. The women in the offices of EMF don't tend to display pictures of their kids: the higher they go up the ladder, the fewer the photographs. If a man has pictures of kids on his desk, it enhances his humanity; if a woman has them, it decreases hers. Why? Because he's not supposed to be home with the children: she is.

I used to have a photo of Ben and Emily on my desk. Rich took it just after the baby had learnt to sit up. Em was at the back, clutching Ben round the middle with fierce pride. He was bubbling up as though life was one big joke and he'd just heard the punchline for the first time. I kept the photo on my desk for a few weeks, but each time I caught the children looking at me I had the same thought: you are providing for them, but you are not bringing them up. So the picture's in the drawer now.

Last year, I went to a lecture by an American chief executive at the London Business School. She said she was going to train her daughters up as geishas: the real future for women was as nurturers and men-pleasers. There was nervous laughter in the room: she was joking, wasn't she? She was beautiful and she was incredibly smart and I don't think she was joking.

All I knew was that I didn't want my mother's life: I didn't need a role model to teach me that being dependent on some man was debilitating, maybe even dangerous. But will Emily want my life? When she looks at her Mummy, who does she see? If she ever sees her Mummy. Back in the Seventies, when they were fighting for women's rights, what did they think equal opportunities meant: that women would be entitled to spend as little time with their kids as men do?

*

12.46 pm: Chowzat! is the hi-tech cafeteria installed by EMF last year in the basement as part of its attempt to look less like a bank and more like a nightclub. The café is meant to have a funky, post-industrial ambience, but the effect is a lot like an airport coffee lounge. I am still lightly stoned after Winston's joint this morning. What could I have been thinking of? As I was getting out of the car, Winston invited me to join him at a concert a fortnight on Sunday. Might find it not totally my scene, he said, the music was a bit overwhelming, but he thinks it would do me good. As the proud-fortress fund manager composed her polite but frosty refusal, I opened my mouth and out fell the word yes. Presumably, I now have a date at a rave with my new drug dealer. What the hell am I going to tell Richard?

As the weed wears off, I feel both nauseous and ravenous. I weigh up the rival merits of the jumbo blueberry muffin and its dainty, lo-cal sister, lemon and sesame seed. Buy both. I'm stuffing alternate fistfuls into my mouth when I look up and see familar brick-red features glowering down at me.

'Jesus, Katie. You're not eating for two, are you? Got enough trouble in that department with Candy.'

Rod Task.

'Ygno,' I splutter, shooting blueberry bullets across the table.

Rod tells me he needs me to go to New York on Wednesday to do a pitch to some brokers. Wants me to give them 'a little TLC'. This information followed by a grotesque wink.

'Wednesday?'

'Sure. As in tomorrow.'

'Actually, Rod, my nanny is off sick and I have to find a temporary to—'

He cuts me off with a karate slice of the hand. 'Are you telling me you can't make it, Kate? If you can't, I'm sure Guy can handle it.'

'Nyes. Ygno. Of course, I can, it's just that—'

'Great. And can you take a look at this for me, sweetie? Thanks.'

I study the photocopy in the lift on the way back to the thirteenth floor. It's an article from *Investment Manager International* under the headline: THE GENDER EQUALITY PENNY IS FINALLY DROPPING!

> *Investment management firms are increasingly jumping on the bandwagon of gender equality as they realise that a more welcoming attitude towards women employees makes good business sense. Herbert George and Berryman Lowell have recently won laurels for their efforts in this area. Julia Salmon, a vice-president at Herbert George, says: 'The City offers fabulous opportunities for women. More are being promoted every year. Most firms have now appointed diversity co-ordinators.'*
>
> *Many institutions lament, however, that while they offer great careers for women, preconceptions of anti-social working hours and macho culture are still deterrents to female applicants.*
>
> *'Puncturing the stereotype of old-boy cronyism associated with the Square Mile is not easy,' admits Celia Harmsworth, Head of Human Relations at Edwin Morgan Forster.*

Well, she should know. Seeing Celia's name in an article on gender equality is like finding Heinrich Himmler conducting a guided tour of a synagogue. '*Harmsworth announced that EMF, formerly considered to be one of the City's more old-fashioned outfits, has recently appointed a Diversity Co-ordinator, Katharine Reddy.*'

WHAT?

'*Thirty-five-year-old Reddy, the youngest senior director at EMF, has been tasked with identifying gender issue obstacles in the business culture.*'

I notice that Rod has circled the phrase 'gender issue obstacles'. Next to it he has scrawled: 'What the fuck is this?'

From: Kate Reddy

To: Debra Richardson

hello hello from yr borderline psychotic friend. Do you think post-natal depression can last up to 18 months after the birth? If so, when does it go away?

Did I mention we have RATS. One ran across the floor when the inlaws were staying. OH, AND MY CLEANER HAS FIRED ME. Came into work to discover 61 e-mails, nanny 'sick', only available temp is close relative of Slobodan Milosevic. Plus I am EMF's new 'Diversity Co-ordinator'. Have to take urgent steps to redress the firm's gender imbalance. Any idea where I can purchase some kind of automatic weapon?

Can we PLS do that lunch? name a day xxxx

From: Debra Richardson

To: Kate Reddy

Believe that post-natal depression can last up to 18 years after the birth and then we have a hysterectomy and start watching old episodes of Friends from red rubber old-lady chairs in gated retirement community.

Don't worry. rats now v. middle class. No stylish home dare be seen without one. Felix has been diagnosed with Attention Deficit Disorder. Think that's what his Dad suffers from too, but that could be because he's having an affair???

Too knackered to care. Read in Good Housekeeping that half of all working mothers are worried relationship with their husband is suffering because of a terrible 'time famine'. What are the other half doing: 30-second blow-jobs?

What news of the gorgeous unsuitable Abelhammer? You do realise that, as my oldest friend, your sole role is to give me reasons to envy and disapprove of you.

Lunch nxt Tues or Thurs? xxxxx

6.35 pm: I collect Emily and Ben from Alice's house. They fall on me like famished things. Alice's nanny, Jo, is incredibly nice, and says what great kids they are. How thoughtful and imaginative Emily is. I feel a burst of pride and pang of shame simultaneously as I realise how often I see them as a problem to be dealt with rather than something to be enjoyed.

Must appoint a temporary nanny tonight. Unless I can persuade Richard to work from home or Paula makes miracle recovery. I have a total horror of asking favours on my own or my children's behalf – reminds me of when Dad pushed me towards a woman at the bus station in Leeds one Christmas and told me to ask if she could let us have a fiver to get home because we'd run out of petrol. We didn't even have a car. But the lady was so nice about it; she gave me the money and a packet of Jelly Tots for myself. The sweets stuck inside my hot cheeks like ulcers.

Jo says that Ben has been clingy all day and she thinks he has some kind of rash on his chest. Has he had chickenpox? No, he hasn't. But he can't have it now. Am booked on 8.30 am flight to New York.

10.43 pm: I can't believe it. I stand on the landing outside the bathroom draped in a tiny towel screaming for Richard.

'There's no hot water.'

'What?' He stands halfway up the stairs from the hall, his face in shadow. 'Oh, they turned the water off today when the rat guy was checking the pipes. Must have flicked the switch.'

'I have to have my bath.'

'Darling, be reasonable.' His voice is parched with weariness. 'I'll put it on now and it'll be hot in twenty minutes.'

'Now. *I need a bath now.*'

'Kate –' He stops, looks as if he's about to say something. But then just tightens his lips and stares at me, shaking his head.

'What? What is it?' I snap.

'Kate. We . . . can't go on like this.'

'Too right we can't. I have no hot water. I have rats. I have a house that is a complete tip and no one to clean it. I needed to be asleep an hour ago and I really really really would like there to be some hot water, Richard. I work all the hours God sends and I live in conditions of medieval squalor. Is A BATH too much to ask for?'

Rich reaches out an arm, but I bat it away. My tears are alarmingly hot – the temperature of the bath I'm not going to have. Must try to calm down. My husband looks wild-eyed. Why hasn't he shaved?

Just now, from over our heads, comes a voice. 'Roo,' it whimpers, 'Roo.'

32

I Went Back Too Soon

1.05 am: Have you ever thought how much time you waste falling asleep? Falling sounds satisfactorily fast, but you don't fall, do you? I find I have to sort of sidle up on sleep and ask if it could please let me in, like someone in the queue for a club trying to catch the eye of a doorman who is always looking the other way. Seven minutes of pillow-plumping and hollowing, the obligatory tussle with the duvet (Richard likes one leg hooked outside, which pins it down like a groundsheet and leaves me barely covered). I take a herbal sleeping tablet to summon instant shut-eye.

3.01 am: Can't sleep for worrying that the sleeping tablet is so strong I will sleep through my alarm and miss the flight. I switch on the bedside light and read the paper. Next to me, Rich grunts and turns over. The foreign pages have more on the story of the American chief executive who went back to work four days after her twins were born. She chaired a meeting via speakerphone from her hospital bed. Her name is Elizabeth Quick. No, seriously. Sister to Hannah Haste and Isabel Imperative, presumably. 'Liz Quick has become a poster woman for working mothers,' the article says, 'but opponents say motherhood will distract her from her job.'

I can feel my whole body crumple. Do people like Ms Quick have any idea how their valiant effort to act as though nothing has changed can be used as a stick to beat other women?

God knows, I can't talk. I went back to work too soon after Emily. I didn't know. How can you? That this new life will be almost as strange to you as it is to them. Mother and baby: newborns both. Before Children – my life is divided into BC and AC – when I still had time to go to the National Gallery on Sunday afternoons, I used to like to sit in front of that Bellini Madonna, the one where she's in the foreground of some kind of farm, baked by the sun, gazing down at the lovely infant in her lap. I'd always thought it was serenity in her eyes. Now, I see only exhaustion and mild puzzlement. 'Christ, what have I done?' Mary asks the son of God. But he's sleeping, full of milk, one plump arm flung in abandon over his mother's blue dress.

I was the first woman on the investment floor at Edwin Morgan Forster to get pregnant. Six months gone when James Entwhistle, Rod Task's predecessor, called me into his office and said he couldn't guarantee there would be a job for me when I got back from maternity leave. 'You know how fast things move on with clients, Kate. It's nothing personal.'

Civilised, erudite James. I suppose I could have quoted the legislation at him, but there's nothing they hate more than being reminded of their family-friendly policy. (EMF's family-friendly policy exists so they can say they have a policy, not so people with families can invoke it. No man would ever use it, anyway, so neither can any woman who wants to be taken seriously.) 'Of course, the baby won't make any difference, James,' I heard myself saying and he made a note on the jotter with his gold Cartier pen. 'Commitment?' he wrote and underlined it twice.

Would I be wanting to scale back my foreign clients? Of course not.

I didn't know.

At thirty-two weeks, I went to see the consultant at University College Hospital. Routine appointment. I'd missed the last one. (Geneva, conference, fog.) The consultant steepled his long white fingers like a cardinal, and told me he was signing me off work because I was under too much pressure during the crucial weeks of foetal brain development. I said that was out of the question: I planned to work up to my due date so I could have some time at home with the baby afterwards.

'I'm not really worried about you, Mrs Shattock,' he said coolly, 'I worry about the child you're carrying and the damage you could cause it.' I was crying so much when I stepped out on to Gower Street that I was nearly run over by a milk float.

So, I took it easy. I took it easier. Technically, I had to stop flying at seven months, but a taupe shift dress saw me through till eight. The bump got so damned big by the end I had to do a three-point turn to get out of the lift. Jokes were made in meetings about needing to reinforce the office floor to support Kate's weight and I laughed louder than anyone. Every time I walked past the dealing desk, Chris Bunce used to whistle the Elephant March from *Jungle Book*: 'Hup two, three, four, Keep it up two, three, four!' Bastard.

Sitting at the computer one afternoon, stomach so taut my skin felt it was crawling with ants, I had a few Braxton Hicks, those practice contractions that sound like a retired colonel living in Nether Wallop. By the end, I used to dream of Colonel Hicks coming to my aid. He would carry my briefcase and, when I was standing at the bus stop on City Road nearly keeling over with exhaustion, he would hold out a hand and say, 'Will you step aboard, madam?'

I did enrol in an ante-natal class, but never could make it there for the 7.30 start. I ended up going to a birthing weekend in Stoke Newington run by Beth: oat biccies, whale music, a pelvis made out of a coat-hanger and a baby from a stocking pulled over a tennis ball. Beth invited us to have a conversation with our vaginas. I said I wasn't on speaking terms with mine and she thought I was joking. She had a laugh like a moose down a well.

Richard loathed the class. He couldn't believe he had to take his shoes off, but he liked the bit with the stopwatch. You could swear he was going to be officiating at the Monaco Grand Prix.

'Knowing you, Kate,' he said, 'you'll have the fastest contractions in history.'

Beth said if you did those panting little breaths she taught us it was a way of mastering the pain. So I practised them religiously. I practised them secularly – at checkouts, in the bath, before bed. I didn't know.

My waters broke on the escalator at Bank, splashing the Burberry of a Japanese futures analyst who apologised profusely. I cancelled my client lunch on the mobile and took a cab straight to the hospital. They offered me an epidural, but I didn't take it. I was the bitch who had endangered her baby's brain development: not having drugs was my way of showing how sorry I was, showing the baby there was something its mother would bear for it. There was an ocean of pain and I dived into it again and again. The water was as hard as wood. It smacked you like a wave hitting a deck and each time you got to your feet it smacked you again.

After twenty-five hours of labour, Rich put the stopwatch down and asked the midwife if we could see a consultant. Now. Down in the operating theatre, during my emergency Caesarean, I heard the surgeon say, 'Nothing to worry about, this will feel a bit like I'm doing the washing-up in your tummy.' It didn't. It felt like the baby was an oak being pulled up by the roots from claggy, November earth. Tug and wrench and tug again. Finally, one of the junior doctors climbed on to the operating table, straddled me and yanked her out by the heels. Held her up like a catch, a thing from the sea, a mermaid marbled with blood. A girl.

Over the next few days a number of bouquets arrived, but the biggest came from Edwin Morgan Forster. It was the kind of baroque arrangement that can only be commanded by war memorials or a City expense account. There were priapic thistles, five foot high, and giant lilies that filled the air with their pepper and made the baby sneeze. A card was attached with a message written by a florist who couldn't spell: 'One down, free to go!'

God, I hated those flowers; the way they stole our air, hers and mine. I gave them to the day midwife who slung them over her shoulder and took them home to Harlesden on her scooter.

After thirty-six hours, the night midwife – Irish, softer, more musical than her daylight counterpart – asked if she could take baby from me so I could get some rest. When I protested, she said: 'Part of being a good mum, Katharine, is having enough energy to cope.' And she wheeled away my daughter, who furled and unfurled those frondlike hands in her little Perspex aquarium.

Headlong, I fell down a mineshaft of exhaustion. It could have been hours later – it felt like seconds – that I heard her crying. Up till that moment, I didn't know that I knew my baby's cry, but when I heard it I knew that I would always know it, would be able to pick it out from any other cry in the world. From somewhere down a brown corridor, she summoned me. Hitching the catheter over one arm and guarding my stitches with the other, I started to hobble towards her, guided by that sonar which had come as a free gift with motherhood. By the time I got to the nursery, she had stopped yelling and was staring, enthralled, at a paper ceiling lantern. I had never experienced joy and fear in such a combination before: impossible to tell where the pain stopped and the love began.

'You'll have to name her,' the smiling midwife chided. 'We can't keep calling her baby, it's not right.'

I'd thought about Genevieve, but it seemed too big for the intended owner. 'Emily was my grandmother's name, she always made me feel safe.'

'Oh, Emily's lovely, let's try it.'

So we tried it and she turned her head towards her name, and it was settled.

Three weeks later, James Entwhistle rang and offered me a job in strategy. A nothing job going nowhere. I accepted it gratefully and put down the phone. I would kill him later. Later, I would kill all of them. But first I had to bath my daughter.

Nine weeks to the day of the Caesarean, I was back in the office. That first morning my mind was so disconnected that I actually dialled a number and asked if I could speak to Kate Reddy. A man said he didn't think Kate was back yet. And he was right. I reckon she wasn't really back for a year and the old Kate, the one Before Children, never returned. But she did a great impersonation of being back and maybe only a mother could have seen through her disguise.

I was still breastfeeding – taking a cab home in my lunch hour to feed her. But five days later, they told me I had to fly to Milan. All weekend, I tried to get Emily to accept a bottle. Coaxed and pleaded and finally paid a woman from Fulham a hundred quid to come and wean my daughter off me. I can remember the baby yodelling, lungs raw with fury, and Richard standing out in the garden smoking.

'She'll take the bottle when she's really starving,' the woman explained and, yes, she herself would prefer cash. Sometimes I think Emily has never really forgiven me.

On the drive to the airport, the cab radio started playing that Stevie Wonder song. 'Isn't she lovely . . .' The one where you hear the baby crying at the start. And my blouse was soaked suddenly with milk.

I didn't know.

33

The Note

Sherbourne Hotel, New York, 11.59 pm: Unbelievable. Plane got in on time and I took a cab to the Herriot off Wall Street. The plan was to swot up for tomorrow's presentation and get a decent night's rest before strolling across the road to the Wall Street Center. I should have known. The reception clerk – hopelessly young, trying to give himself a little authority in a cheap, shiny blazer – was having trouble meeting my eye. Finally he said, 'I'm afraid we have a problem, Ms Reddy.' A conference. Overbooking. 'I am happy to offer you free accommodation at the Sherbourne, mid-town, great location opposite our world-renowned Museum of Modern Art.'

'Sounds delightful, but I'm here to do business, not get a headache staring at early Cubists.'

I ended up yelling at him, of course. Totally unacceptable, frequent customer, blah blah blah . . . I could see his eyes darting around for a superior to save him from the crazy Brit. As though I were mad, and I'm not mad, am I? It's these people driving you crazy with their inefficiency, wasting my precious time.

The manager was incredibly apologetic, but there was absolutely nothing he could do. So, by the time I got to the new hotel, it was nearly midnight. Called Richard, who was ready with a list of queries. Thank God, Paula's better, so we don't have to get a temp. It's Emily's first day back at school tomorrow.

Had I done the name-tapes?

Yes.

Had I got new gym shoes?

Yes. (In her navy gym bag on the peg under the stairs.)

Where would he find her reading books?

(Red library folder, third shelf of bookcase.)

Had I bought a new coat, the old one now comes up to her waist? (Not yet, she will have to make do with Gap raincoat till I get back.)

Then I dictated the contents of her lunchbox – pitta bread, tuna and corn, no cheese, she's decided she hates cheese – and told him to remember the cheque for ballet, the amount's written in the diary. And he needs to give Paula money to get Ben some new trousers, he's just had a growth spurt. Richard tells me that Em was upset going to bed: she said she wanted Mummy to take her to school because it's a new teacher.

Why does he feel he needs to share that with me when there's absolutely nothing I can do about it? Says he's had an exhausting day.

'Tell me about it,' I say back and ching down the phone.

No time to go through notes for my presentation, so I'll have to wing it. Tomorrow's shaping up to be a total nightmare.

From: Debra Richardson
To: Kate Reddy
Just got yrs to say you're cancelling lunch. AGAIN. The first 49 times it was funny. I realise you have the most disgustingly demanding job on the planet, but if we don't make time for friendship what hope is there?
Are we next going to meet after our deaths? How is the afterlife looking for you, Kate?

Oh, hell. No time to reply.

Wednesday, 8.33 am: Been standing outside the hotel for at least fifteen minutes now. It's impossible to get a cab and the journey downtown will take at least twenty-five. Am going to be late. Still, my senses quicken at the prospect of seeing Jack tonight; it's months since I last saw him and I'm having trouble calling his face to mind. When I think of him all I get is a broad smile and a general impression of ease and happiness.

It's a fabulous morning, one of those glittering New York days that hurt your heart. Incredible rain last night has given everything a remarkable windscreen-wiped clarity. As we reach the bottom of Fifth, I see the buildings of the financial district quiver with the slight watery shimmer that comes from the play of humidity and light and glass.

8.59 am: Brokers Dickinson Bishop are on the 21st floor. My stomach does an Olga Korbut flick-flack in the elevator on the way up. Gerry, a beaming fellow with a broad Irish face and straggly red sideburns, meets me at the landing. I tell him I need forty-five minutes and a place to show slides.

'Sorry, you got five, lady. Things are pretty crazy in there.'

He heaves open a thick wooden door and unleashes the sounds of an average day at the Colosseum, plus phones. Men bawling into receivers, fighting to make themselves heard, or shouting instructions across the room. Just as I'm wondering whether to make a run for it, a message comes over the PA: 'OK, listen up, you guys, in two minutes Miss Kate Reddy of London, England, will be talking to you about international investing.'

About seventy brokers gather round, mastiff-necked New Yorkers in those terrible shirts with the white collars and the marquee stripes. They lean back against the desks, arms crossed, legs apart. The way that kind of man stands. Some carry on trading, but pull down their headpieces to lend me half an ear. There is no way I'm going to be seen or heard down here, so I take a split-second decision to stand on a desk and shout my wares.

'Good morning, gentlemen, I'm here to tell you why you MUST BUY MY FUND!'

Cheers, whistles. The closest I'll ever get to being a pole-dancer, I guess.

'Hey, Miss, anyone ever tell you you look like Princess Di?'

'Is your stock as good as your legs?'

What strikes me about these Masters of the Universe is how hopelessly, helplessly boyish they are. Fifty years ago, they would have been landing on the beaches of Normandy, and here they are gathered round me as if I was their company commander.

I give them my big speech about the Money – the way it's awake when I'm asleep, the way it moves around the world, its amazing power.

Then, they fire questions at me. 'Whaddya think about Russia, ma'am? Isn't Russian money the pits?'

'Did you see a Euro yet?'

It's gone well. Unbelievably well. At the lift, a grinning Gerry tells me the guys normally only get that fired up for a Knicks game. Now I should really go back to the hotel and pick up my messages, but I walk for a while along Wall Street, feeling charged up, plugged into the power supply. On the corner of Third and Broadway, I hail a cab and take it uptown to Barney's for some post-traumatic shopping.

The store has an immediate consoling effect. I take the little lift to the top floor where I spot an evening dress. I don't need an evening dress. I try it on. Black and floaty with a fragile braid of diamanté fixed down each side and in a plunging V under the bust, it's the kind of dress they once danced the Charleston in. I just about have the figure for it: I just don't have the life. My life is the wrong size; there's no room in it for a dress this beautiful. But isn't that part of the thrill? Buying a dress and hoping the life to go with it will follow soon like a must-have accessory? When the girl at the till hands me the chit to sign, I don't even check the amount.

3 pm: The hotel room is like a hundred I've stayed in before. The wallpaper is beige embossed on beige; the curtains, in bold contrast, look like an explosion in a herbaceous border. I check the minibar for emergency chocolate and then the drawer of the bedside table: there is the Gideons' Bible and – a more contemporary touch – a collection of sayings from the World's Great Religions.

I check my watch. If I call home now, it should be around the kids' bedtime. I'm expecting to hear Richard's voice, but it's Paula at the other end. She says Rich has asked her to stay over a couple of nights until I get back and left a note for me that he made her promise to deliver in person.

I ask Paula to open the note and read it to me. Just look at the time. Where the hell is he? I think of all the things my husband could be doing to help out while I'm not there as our nanny starts to speak his words aloud.

'"I've been trying to talk to you for a while now, but I find it increasingly hard to get your attention."'

'Yes, but does it say what time he'll be back?'

'"Kate, can you hear me. Are you listening?"'

'Of course I can hear you, Paula.'

'No, that's Richard. In the note. He says, "Kate, can you hear me. Are you listening?"'

'Oh, right, sorry. Go on.'

'"I am so sorry, my darling, that we have reached this terrible imp—"'

'What imp?'

'—ass.'

Oh, for heaven's sake. 'How do you spell it?'

Paula announces each letter carefully. 'I. M. P. A. S. S. E.'

'Oh, *impasse*. I see. It's, you know, French . . . well, anyway, what else?'

Paula sounds dubious. 'I'm not sure I should be doing this, Kate.'

'No, please carry on. I have to know what his plans are.'

'He says, "If you need to get hold of me I will be staying at David and Maria's for a few nights until I find a place of my own." He says, "Don't worry, I'll still go and pick Emily up from school."'

So it really can happen. In real life. A thing you've seen in bad TV drama and turned over because it's so implausible. Only this time there is no turning over. And maybe no turning back. One moment, the world is pretty much as it should be – rocky and a little barren, perhaps, but still the world as you know it – and then suddenly you have the sensation of the ground giving way beneath your feet. My husband, Richard the rational, Richard the reliable, Richard the rock has left me. Rich, who in the letter he gave me the day before our wedding wrote, 'I'm Ever and You're Reddy – here's to longlife, my darling', has walked out. And I have been paying so little attention that our nanny has had to break the news.

During the long pause, Paula's breathing has got heavier; there is a wheeze of anxiety coming down the line. 'Kate,' she asks, 'are you OK?'

'Yes, I'm fine. Paula, you can sleep in the spare room – or in our bed' – as I say the words it occurs to me that it may be my bed now, not ours – 'the sheets are clean. I know this is asking an awful lot, Paula, but if you could just hold the fort. And if you can please tell Emily and Ben that Mummy will be back as soon as she can tomorrow.'

Paula doesn't reply at once and I think if she lets me down now I don't know what I'll do. 'Is that all right, Paula?'

'Oh, sorry, Kate, I've just seen there's a PS on the other side. Richard says, "I know I can never stop loving you because, believe me, I've tried."'

There is no possible reply to that and into my silence, Paula murmurs: 'Don't worry, I'll take care of everything here. Ben and Em will be fine. It's going to be all right, Kate, really it is.'

After I've put the phone down, I forget how to breathe for a few seconds. Suddenly the mechanics of taking in air seem complicated and strenuous; I have to heave my diaphragm up and then pump my chest out, heave and pump again.

When I'm a little steadier, I call Jack and leave a message on his mobile cancelling dinner. Then I get undressed and take a shower. The towels are that hopeless Italian kind; thin and frugal as an altar-cloth, they pat the water round your skin rather than absorbing it. I need a towel that can hug me.

Catching sight of myself in the bathroom mirror, I am startled to see that I look much as I did the last time I looked. Why isn't my hair falling out? Why aren't my eyes weeping blood? I think of my children asleep in their beds and of how far I am from them, how unbelievably far. From this distance, I see my little family as an encampment on a hillside and the winds are lashing round them and I have to be there to tie everything down. I have to be there.

> *The water is wide, I cannot get o'er*
> *And neither have I wings to fly.*

I climb into bed, between the stiff white sheets, and I move my hand over my body. My body and for so long Richard's body. With this body I thee worship. I try to think of the last time I saw him. Saw him properly, I mean, not just the way you see the blur of a person in the rear-view mirror. In the past few months, I go out and he takes over or he leaves and I take over. We swap instructions in the hall. We say Emily has eaten a good lunch, so don't worry too much about her tea. We say Ben needs an early night because he wouldn't take a nap this afternoon. We say bowel movements have been successful or are still pending and perhaps some prunes would help. Or else we leave a note. Sometimes we barely meet each other's eyes. Kate and Richard, like a relay team where each runner suspects the other of being the weaker link, but the main thing is to keep running round the track so the baton can be exchanged and the race can go on and on.

> *O, Love is handsome and love is kind,*
> *And love's a jewel when it is new.*
> *But when it is old, it groweth cold;*
> *And fades away like morning dew.*

'Mummy, I know why you get cross with Daddy,' Emily said to me the other morning.

'Why?'

'Because he does wrong things.'

I knelt down beside her, so I could look straight into her eyes. It felt important to set the record straight. 'No, sweetheart, Daddy doesn't do wrong things. Mummy just sometimes gets very tired and that makes her not patient with Daddy, that's all.'

'Patient means wait a minute,' she said.

I pick up *Sayings of the World's Great Religions* from the bedside table and flick through it. There are sections on Belief, Justice and Education. I pause at the one on Marriage.

'I have never called my wife "wife", but "home".'

The Talmud

Home. I look at the word for a long time. Home. Hear its rounded centre. Picture what it means. I am married but am not a wife, have children but am not a mother. What am I?

I know a woman who is so afraid of her children's need for her that rather than go home after work, she sits in the wine bar to wait until they're asleep.

I know a woman who wakes her baby at 5.30 every morning so she can have some time with him.

I know a woman who went on a TV discussion programme and talked about doing the school run. Her nanny told me she barely knew where her kids' school was.

I know a woman who heard that her baby boy took his first steps from a babysitter down the phone.

And I know a woman who found out her husband left her from a note that was read out to her by a nanny.

I lie there for a long time in the bed, maybe hours, waiting until I start to feel something. And finally it comes. A feeling both intensely familiar and shockingly strange. It takes me a few seconds to know what it is: I want my mother.

34

Home to Mum

HOWEVER HARD I SEARCH, I can't come up with a memory of my mother sitting down. Always standing. Standing at the sink holding a pan under running water, standing by the ironing board, standing at the school gate in her good navy coat; bringing in plates of hot food from the kitchen and then clearing them away again. Common sense suggests there must have been an interval between bringing the plates in and taking them out when she sat down and ate with us, but I don't remember it. Dishes, once they were let out of cupboards, became a mess to my mother, and a mess needed clearing up. You could still be in mid-forkful, but if the plate looked empty Mum would whisk it away.

My mother's generation was born for service; it was their vocation and their destiny. The gap between school – routine, things you do because you must, bad smells – and motherhood – routine, things you do because you must, bad smells – was a matter of a few years. Those Fifties girls had a window of freedom, but the window was seldom wide enough to climb through and, anyway, what would become of them if they got out? Women like my mum didn't expect much of life and, in general, life did not disappoint them. Even when the men they served ran out on them or died too early from strokes and disorders of the stomach, they often stayed at their posts, pre-paring meals, hoovering, grabbing any ironing that was going from their children or grandchildren and never sitting down if they could possibly help it. It was as though they defined themselves in doing for others, and the loss of that definition left them blurred, confused; like those pit ponies who kept their tunnel vision long after they had been let loose in a field.

For my generation, coming to it later and sometimes too late, motherhood was a shock. Sacrifice wasn't written into our contract. After fifteen years as an independent adult, the sudden lack of liberty could be as stunning as being parted from a limb; entwined with the intense feeling of love for your baby was a thin thread of loss, and maybe we will always ache like an amputee.

What my mum still calls Women's Liberation had just about taken off by the time I was born, but it never reached the parts where my parents lived and, to a remarkable extent, still hasn't. One summer, my mother grew her perm out and had her hair cut short in a feathery style that flattered her elfin features. Julie and I loved it, she looked so pretty and cheeky, but when my dad came in that night he said: 'It's a bit Women's Lib, Jean,' and the style was grown out without fuss, without any more needing to be said.

As I entered my teens, it occurred to me that things were not what they seemed: although the men round our way took all the leading roles, it was the women who were running the show, but were never allowed to be on stage. It was a matriarchy pretending to be a patriarchy to keep the lads happy. I always thought that was because where I came from people didn't get much of an education. Now I think that's what the whole world's like, only some places hide it better than others.

*

IN THE PLAYGROUND, the children's cries fill the air like starlings. The school is a red-brick building, with tall churchy windows, dating from an era when people had faith in both God and education. Over in the far corner, next to the climbing frame, there is a woman in a navy three-quarter coat bending down. When she straightens up, I can see she is holding a handkerchief which is attached to the bloody nose of a small girl.

My mother is a nursery school assistant. She's been here for years and, basically, she runs the place, but they still call her an assistant. Because they can get away with it – Mum doesn't like to make a fuss – and because it means they can pay her less. The money's terrible. When she told me how much, I shouted with dismay. I could blow it on cab fares in three days. But if you use words like exploitation, my mother just laughs. Says she likes the job, it gets her out the house. Besides, she has a way with children. If your three-year-old had a bleeding nose, believe me, you'd want my mother to be the one holding her hand. Jean Reddy is one of those souls who exude comfort like a human hot-water bottle.

When she looks across the yard, she knows it's me instantly, but it takes another second before the pleasure floods into her face. 'Oh, Kathy, love,' she says coming over with the wounded tot in tow, 'what a lovely surprise. I thought you were in America.'

'I was. Got back a couple of days ago.'

When I kiss her cheek, it's apple cold. 'Now, Lauren,' my mother says, addressing the sniffing child, 'this is *my* little girl. Say hello!'

The ringing bell signals the end of Mum's shift and we go indoors to fetch her bag from the staffroom. In the corridor, she introduces me to Val, the headmistress. 'Oh, yes, Katharine, we've heard so much about you. Jean showed me the cutting in the paper. You've done so well for yourself, haven't you?'

I'm eager to get out of here, but my mother enjoys showing me off. The hand she puts on my arm as she steers me between colleagues reminds me of Emily at World Feast Day parading Mummy in front of her friends.

Parked in front of the school, the Volvo is filled with kids' stuff. 'How are they?' Mum asks as we climb in. I tell her they're fine and with Paula. On the drive to the flat, we pass my old school and she sighs. 'Did you hear about Mr Dowling? Terrible.'

'He took early retirement, didn't he?'

'Yes. A lass. Can you imagine a young lass doing something like that, Kath?'

Mr Dowling was my head of history twenty years ago, a blinky soft-spoken man with a vast enthusiasm for Elizabethan

England and the poetry of the First World War. A few months ago, some little cow in the fifth form punched his glasses into his face and he took early retirement soon after. Mr Dowling, an archetypal grammar school boy, had become one of the casualties of the comprehensive system – a doctrine of equality which means that all the kids round here who want to learn something are in classes with kids who don't.

'They'll expect you to have read widely, Katharine, but we've very little time,' Mr Dowling said to me when he was preparing me for Cambridge entrance. I was the only one in my year, the only one for as long as anyone could remember except Michael Brain, who got to Oxford to read law and was now at the Bar, which we were told had nothing to do with pubs. It was after school, in Mr Dowling's room off the library with the electric fire on. I loved being in there with him, reading and hearing the click of the filaments. We did the Chartists in a day, the First World War over a weekend. 'You won't know everything, but I think we can give an impression of you knowing the ground,' my teacher said. But I had the famous Reddy memory: England under the Tudors and Stuarts, the Ottoman Empire, witchcraft. I had the dates of battles down pat, the way my father memorised the pools. Corunna, Bosworth, Ypres. Raith Rovers, Brechin City, Swindon Town. We could wing anything, Dad and I, if we thought it would pay. Walking up the steps to take my seat alone in the exam room I knew I could do it, if I could only hold the knowledge in there for long enough. *Must remember.*

'Nice cup of tea. And I'll do some sandwiches, shall I? Ham all right?' Mum is busying herself with the kettle in the kitchen of the flat. More an alcove than a kitchen; there's only room for one person in there.

I never want to eat the sandwiches, but a couple of years ago I had one of those maturity leaps when I realised that eating wasn't the point of my mother's sandwiches. They were there to give her something she could do for me, when there is so much she can't do any more. Overnight her need to be needed seemed more important than my need to get away. I sit down at the Formica table with the fold-down flaps, the table that sat in all the kitchens of my childhood: it has a black scab gouged out of the side by a furious Julie after a row with Dad over finishing her swede. As I eat, Mum puts up the ironing board and starts to work her way through the basket of clothes at her feet. Soon the room is filled with the drowsy, comforting smell of baked water. The iron makes little exasperated puffs as it travels the length of a blouse, or gets its snout into a tricky cuff.

My mother is a champion ironer. It's a pleasure to watch her hand move an inch or so ahead of the small steam train, smoothing its path. She smooths and smooths and then she snaps the cloth taut like a conjurer and finally she folds. Arms of a shirt folded behind, like a man under arrest. As I watch her, my eyes go swimmy: I think that after she's gone there'll be no one who will ever do that for me again – no one who will iron my clothes taking such infinite pains.

'What's that over your eye, love?'

'Nothing.'

She comes over and lifts my fringe to get a better view of the eczema and I blink back the tears. 'I know your nothings, Katharine Reddy,' she laughs. 'Have you got some cream off the doctor for it?'

'Yes.' No.

'Have you got it anywhere else?' 'No.' Yes, in a flaming itching belt around my middle, behind my ears, behind my knees.

In my pocket, the mobile begins to thrum. I take it out and check the number. Rod Task. I switch the phone off.

'What have I told you about looking after yourself? I don't know how you manage with work on at you the whole time' – Mum jabs her finger in the direction of the mobile – 'and the kiddies as well. It's no life.'

Back behind the ironing board, she says, 'Anyway, how's our Richard keeping?'

I give a crumby mumble. I've come all the way up here to tell her that Rich has gone. I hated the idea of leaving the kids with Paula so soon after getting back from the States, but if I put my foot down I can do the journey here and back in a day. And I didn't want Mum to find out that Richard and I were separated, as I did, down the phone. But now I'm here I can't quite find the words. 'Oh, by the way my husband left me because I haven't paid attention to him since 1994.' She'd think I was joking.

'Richard's a good man,' she says, trapping a pillowcase on the curved end of the board. 'You want to hang on to him, love. They don't come much better than Richard.'

In the past, I have taken my mother's enthusiasm for my man as a sign of its opposite for me. Her exclaiming over another of his supposedly miraculous virtues (his ability to make a simple meal, his willingness to spend time with his children) always seemed to draw attention to my matching vices (my reliance on cook-chill food, my working weekends in Milan). Now, sitting here in my mother's home, I hear her praise for what it is: the truth about someone who has Mum's gift for putting others before themselves.

We had tea in this room the first time I brought Rich back to meet her. I was so determined not to be ashamed of where I came from that by the time we got here, after a hot and clogged drive from London, I had stoked myself up into a defiant, take-us-as-you-find-us mood. So, what if we don't have matching cutlery? What if my mother says settee instead of sofa? Are you going to make something of it, are you, are you?

Rich made nothing of it. A natural diplomat, he soon had my mother eating out of his hand merely by tucking into heroic quantities of bread and butter. I remember how big he looked in our house – the furniture was suddenly doll's furniture – and how gently he negotiated all the no-go areas of my family's past. (Dad had walked out by then, but his absence was almost as domineering as his presence had been.) Panicked by the idea of Kath's posh boyfriend, my mum, who always goes to too much trouble, had, on that occasion, gone to too little. But Rich volunteered to go to the shop on the corner for extra milk and came back with two kinds of biscuit and an enthusiasm for the hills whose sooty shoulders you could glimpse from the end of the street.

'Julie said that some men have been round here asking for money that Dad owes them.'

With one hand my mother pats her helmet of grey curls: 'It's nothing. She'd no need to go bothering you with that. All sorted now. Don't go fretting yourself.'

I must have pulled a face because she adds: 'You shouldn't be too hard on your father, love.'

'Why not? He was hard on us.'

Chuuuussh. Chuuuuussh. The iron and my mother chide me simultaneously with their soft sighs.

'It's not easy for him, you know. He's that bright but he's not had the outlets, not like you. In your dad's family, there was no question of going on to college. Always liked the sound of medicine, but it was years of studying and there just wasn't the money.'

'If he's that clever why does he keep getting himself into trouble?'

My mother always ends conversations she isn't keen on with a non-sequitur. 'Well, he was very proud of you, Kathy. I had to stop him showing your GCSE certificates to everyone.'

She folds the sleeves behind the last blouse and adds it to the basket. There is no sign of the two I bought her last year in Liberty's for her birthday, nor of other gifts. 'Have you worn that red cardigan I got you, Mum?'

'But it's cashmere, love.'

Since I've been working, I've bought my mother lovely clothes. I wanted her to have them, I needed her to have them. I wanted to make things all right for her. But she always puts everything I bring her away for best. Best being some indeterminate date in the future when life will at long last live up to its promise.

'Can I get you some cake?'

No. 'Yes, lovely.'

On the sideboard, next to the carriage clock purchased a

quarter of a century ago with Green Shield stamps, there is a photograph of my parents taken in the late Fifties. A seaside place, they're laughing, and behind them the sky is flecked with gulls. They look like film stars. Dad doing his Tyrone Power thing, Mum with her inky Audrey Hepburn eyes and those matador pants that end at the calf and a pair of little black pumps. When I was a child that photograph used to taunt me with its happiness: I wanted the mother in the picture to come back. I knew that if I waited long enough she would come back. She was just saving herself for best. Next to the picture is a silver frame containing one of Emily on her second birthday. She has just seen the cake and is lit up with glee. Mum follows my glance.

'Gorgeous, isn't she?'

I nod happily. No matter how battered family relations, a baby can make them new. When Emily was born and Mum came to see us in hospital and laid her hand, speckled with age, on the newborn's, I understood how having a daughter could help you to bear the thought of your own mother's death. I wondered then, but never dared ask, whether it helped Mum to bear the idea of leaving Julie and me.

There is a clatter of pans from the kitchen. 'Mum, please come and sit down.'

'You just put your feet up, love.'

'But I want you to sit down.'

'In a minute.'

I can't tell her about Richard. How can I tell her?

*

JULIE LIVES FIVE minutes' drive from my mum. Streets in this type of estate were always named after plants and trees, as though that might in some way make amends to the natural environment that had been torn up to build them. But Orchard Way and Elm Drive and Cherry Walk look like cruel taunts now, pastoral notes in a symphony of cement and reinforced glass. My sister's house is in Birch Close, a horseshoe of Sixties semis hemmed in by properties from the succeeding decades, all full of good ideas from town planners for restoring a sense of community so carefully destroyed by town planners.

As I pull up in the Volvo, a group of kids who are kicking around on the pavement let out a noise between a cheer and a jeer, but as soon as I climb out and glare at them they scarper; even the thugs lack all conviction up here. The front garden of Number 9 has a circle of earth carved out in the centre of the lawn with one skinny rhododendron surrounded by clumps of that tiny white flower I always think of as being England's answer to Edelweiss. Parked with one wheel on the ribbed concrete drive is a trike that must have been abandoned when Julie's kids were small: in its rusty yellow seat, there is a dark compote of leaves and rain.

The woman who answers the door is already into middle age, with a listless pageboy haircut, although she is three years and one month younger than me, a fact I will never forget because my very first memory is of being carried into my parents' bedroom to see her the night she was born. The wallpaper was green and the baby was red and wrapped in a white shawl I had watched my mother knit in front of the Rayburn. She made funny snuffling sounds and when you gave her your finger she wouldn't let go. She was called a sister. I told Mum that her name should be Valerie after the *Blue Peter* presenter. So, thinking they might be spared some jealousy if I had an investment in the new arrival, my parents christened her Julie Valerie Reddy and she has never let me forget it.

'You'd best come in, then,' my sister says. Spotting the car over my shoulder, she tuts and says: 'They'll have the tyres off that. Do you want to bring it up the drive? I can clear this stuff.'

'No, it'll be fine really.'

We squeeze through the narrow hall with its white wrought-iron stand overflowing with spider plants.

'Plants are doing well, Julie,' I say.

'Can't kill them if you try,' she shrugs. 'There's tea in the pot, do you want a cup? Steven, get your feet off the settee, your Auntie Kath's here from London.'

A good-looking small boy trapped in the body of a lunk,

300

Steven lollops through to greet me while his mum fetches the cups.

I am bringing the news that my husband has left me as a gift to my sister, as a peace offering. Julie grew up wearing my clothes, overheard teachers comparing her with the other Reddy girl, the one who got to Cambridge, and has never ever had anything nicer than I have in her whole life. Well, now her big sister has failed to keep her man and in this, the oldest contest of all, I can concede defeat.

'Place is a tip,' Julie says by way of description, not apology, before she clears some magazines off the settee and kicks Steven's soccer kit towards the door.

She sits me down in the armchair next to the gas fire. 'Come on, then, what's up with you?'

'Richard's left me,' I say, and it's the first time I've cried since Paula told me on the phone. There were no tears when I explained to Emily that Daddy would be living in a different house for a while, because there was no way I wanted to share my distress with a six-year-old whose idea of men is founded on the prince in *Sleeping Beauty*, and no tears either when, last night, Richard and I had a civilised exchange on the doorstep about arrangements for the children. We are always discussing arrangements for the children, only the conversation usually ends with me running out the door and saying I have to go; this time it was Richard who walked down the steps and away, yanking over his shoulder the grey sweater I bought him to match his eyes two birthdays ago.

'Well, a right useless bugger he turned out to be,' Julie says. 'All that you've got on your plate, and he hops it.' Without my noticing, she has knelt down in front of me and has an arm around my neck.

'It's my fault.'

'Like hell it is.'

'No it is, it is, he left a note for me.'

'A note? Oh, that's great that is. Bloody men. Either they're too clever to feel owt or they're like our Neil and they're too thick to say owt.'

'Neil's not thick.'

When Julie laughs, the little girl I once knew is there in the room, full of fun and not afraid. 'No, but you'd have more clue how the hamster's doing than Neil, quite frankly. Has he got another woman, then, your Richard?'

It hadn't even occurred to me. 'No, I don't think so, I think it's me that's another woman. The one he married isn't there any more. He said he couldn't get through to me, that I don't listen to him.'

Julie smooths my hair. 'Well, you're working too hard to keep him in pencils.'

'He's a very good architect.'

'It's you who keeps the show on the road, though, paying all the bills and whatnot.'

'I think that's hard for him, Jules.'

'Aye, well, if the world was run according to what men found hard to take we'd still be walking round in chastity belts, wouldn't we? Are you having sugar?'

No. 'Yes.'

A little later, Julie and I go for a walk up to the recreation ground at the top of the estate. The path is choked with ferns and there is a burnt-out Fiesta threaded with foxgloves. When we get to the swings, we find a couple of schoolgirl mothers sitting there on the bench. Teenage pregnancy ranks as a hobby round here. These two are pretty typical: waxy with tiredness and caked in make-up, they look like cadavers with their young jumping up and down on them, full of rude life.

Julie tells me that the breathlessness and the pains in our mother's chest date from a few months back, when a couple of Dad's creditors turned up at the door. Mum explained that Joseph Reddy didn't live there any more, had not in fact lived there for many years, but the men came in anyway and looked over the furniture, the carriage clock, the silver frames I'd given her for the children's photographs.

Not cursed with the elder child's desperate need for approval, Julie managed to stay outside the immediate blast-area of Dad's charm and for most of our lives has observed him coldly and without fear of side-effects. I tell her about the day he came to see me at the office and she explodes with indignation.

'Bloody typical, that is. Not worried about embarrassing you in front of your boss. What does he think he's playing at?'

'He's designed a biodegradable nappy.'

'*Him?* He's never seen a baby's bum in his life.'

And we both start to laugh, my sister and I, great snorts of laughter escaping through our mouths and our noses and finally running in tears down our cheeks. From a corner of my coat pocket, I produce a hanky crusty with use; Julie volunteers one in a similar condition but spotted with blood.

'Emily's carol concert.'

'Steven's rugby match.'

We turn and look out across the town. Its ugliness is draped in a ludicrous Vivienne Westwood sunset, all knicker-pink tulle and scandalous purples. The skyline is dominated by giant chimneys, only a few still active: they let out quick, small puffs like furtive smokers. 'You didn't give Dad owt, I hope,' Julie says, and when I don't reply, 'Oh, bloody hell, Kath, you're a soft touch.'

'City Ice Maiden,' I announce in my Radio 4 voice.

'Ice Maiden that melts pretty easily,' snaps my sister. 'You've got to get over Dad, you know. He's not worth it. There's millions of crap dads out there, we're nothing special. Remember the way he used to send you to the door when they came round asking for the rent money. You remember that, don't you?'

'No.'

'You do remember. I know you do. That's no way to treat a kid, Kathy. Getting them to lie for you. And he thumped Mum when things weren't going his way.'

'No.'

'No? Who was it that went downstairs to distract him when they were beating the shit out of each other? Little girl name of Katharine. Ring any bells?'

'Jules, what were those ice lollies with the hundreds and thousands on them called?'

'Don't change the bloody subject.'

'Do you remember?'

'Course I do. Fabs. But you never had them. Always saved your pocket money and bought the Cornish Mivvi. Mum said you always had to have the best of everything from when you could stand up. "Champagne tastes on beer money, that's our Kath." So you went and made the money for champagne, didn't you?'

'It's not that great,' I say studying my wedding band.

'Bubbly?' Julie looks at me as though she really wants to know.

How can I tell my sister that money has improved my life, but it hasn't deepened it or eased it? 'Oh, you spend most of your money trying to buy yourself time to make money to pay for all the things you think you need because you've got money.'

'Yes, but it's better than that.' Julie gestures across the recreation ground to the child mothers. She speaks angrily, but when she says it again it sounds like a blessing: 'It's got to be better than that, love.'

*

THERE WAS A Mr Whippy van that used to go round our estate playing a hectic version of 'Greensleeves'. One day during the summer holidays, Annette and Colin Jones were buying an ice-cream from the van when their kitten ran out and got caught in the back wheel. We yelled out, but the driver didn't hear us and the van started pulling away. I remember it was boiling hot, the tarmac was rearing up in the road and it stuck in clumps on the bottom of our sandals like rabbit droppings. And I remember the way Annette screamed and I remember the music and the sense of something infinitely gentle being broken as the wheel spun round.

The Joneses lived two doors down from us. Carol Jones was the only mother we knew who went out to work. She started off doing some bar work for pin money and soon after she got a full-time job in the accounts office of a metals factory.

Dissecting their neighbours over elevenses, my mother and Mrs Frieda Davies decided that Carol spent her wages on going to the hairdresser and other things that came under the category of 'enjoying herself'. They couldn't have been more delighted when Annette failed her Eleven-plus. Well, what can you expect with no one at home to get the poor child a cooked tea?

Me, I remember Carol wearing lipstick and laughing a lot and seeming younger than my mother, whose birthday she shared.

The day of the accident, Mum heard our screams and ran out and took us all inside while the Mr Whippy man tried to clear up the mess. I had dropped my strawberry Cornish Mivvi on the road. Mum calmed Annette down, made orange squash for everyone and found Colin a plaster (he had no graze or cut, but he needed a plaster). And then she gave the Joneses their tea while we all waited for their mum to get home from work.

Carol arrived late and flustered with shopping bags. She had got Mum's phone message, but she had been unable to get away any quicker. When I think back to how it was when Carol came into the kitchen, and us all sitting at the Formica table, I can remember the heat hanging there like wet towels and Colin spilling his squash and how Annette wouldn't look at her mum, but I can't remember if it went unsaid, the thing everyone was thinking.

Did anyone say it? 'But if you'd been here, the kitten wouldn't be dead.'

35

No Answers

6.35 pm: 'And, furthermore, there is a good deal of evidence that mixed-gender teams are critical to effective team functioning.'

'Jesus, Katie, I never thought I'd hear you say anything like that.' Rod Task is unimpressed, and he's not the only one; the place is full of people who'd rather be in the wine bar than being addressed by me in my new capacity as Diversity Co-ordinator. I feel like a vegan at an abattoir.

Chris Bunce lies back in his chair with his feet up on the conference table. 'I'm all for mixing genders,' he says, picking his teeth.

'Can we get the hell out of here now?' asks Rod.

'No,' says Celia Harmsworth, 'we need to produce a mission statement.'

As the room groans, there is an answering thrum from the phone in my pocket. A text message from Paula.

Ben ill
come now.

'I've got to go,' I say. 'Urgent call coming in from the States. Don't wait for me.'

I call Paula from the cab on the way home. She fills me in. Ben fell downstairs. 'You know that dodgy bit of carpet near the top of the stairs by his room, Kate?'

Please God, no. 'Yes, I do.'

'Well, he caught his foot somehow and he fell and bumped his head this morning. It came up a bit, but he seemed fine. Then he was sick a bit ago and he went all limp.'

I tell Paula to keep him warm. Or should she be keeping him cool? Numb, my fingers feel like stumps as I dial Richard's mobile number. I pray for it to be him, but it's the voice of that damned announcer saying, please leave a message.

'Hello. I don't want to leave a message. I want you to be here. It's me. Kate. Ben's had a fall and I'm going to take him to the hospital. I'll have my phone with me.'

Next, I call Pegasus Cars and ask Winston to be waiting when I get home. Need to get Ben to hospital.

8.23 pm: How long is too long to wait for your child to be seen? Ben and I are told to take a seat in the rows of grey plastic chairs in Casualty. Next to us are a couple of public school boys who are off their heads on something. Ecstasy, probably. 'I've got no feelin' in my fingers,' wails one over and over, pretending he has no idea why. I don't care: I want to tell him to get back to whatever swamp he came from and expire quietly. I want to slap him for wasting hospital time.

Winston, who has gone to park Pegasus, returns and approaches the reception desk. Seeing my expression, he stands in and becomes the pushy one. 'Excuse me, Miss, we got a baby here needs some attention. Thank you kindly.'

After an eternity – maybe five minutes – Ben and I are ushered in to see the doctor. Half-slept and unshaven since last Thursday, the young houseman is seated in a cubicle cut off from the busy corridor by a thin apricot curtain. I start to explain Ben's symptoms, but he silences me with a hand while he studies the notes on the desk in front of him.

'Hmmm, I see, I see. And how long has the little boy had a temperature, Mrs Shattock?'

'Well, I'm not entirely sure. He was very hot up till an hour ago.'

'And earlier today?'

'I don't know.'

The doctor moves to put his hand on Ben's forehead. The baby mews as I relax my grip on him. 'Sickness, vomiting in the past twenty-four hours?'

'I think he was sick yesterday afternoon, but Paula thought, she's my nanny – we thought that it was just a bad tummy.'

'Bowel movement since then?'

'I'm afraid I don't know.'

'So you didn't see him at all yesterday?'

'Yes. No. I mean, I try to get home in time to put him to bed, but not last night no.'

'And not the night before.'

'No, I had to go to Frankfurt. You see, Ben fell down the stairs this morning and he seemed to be fine but then Paula got really worried and he became limp so—'

'Yes, I see.' I don't think he sees. I must try to talk calmly and slowly so he sees.

'Can you undress baby for me?'

I slip him out of his Thomas the Tank Engine sleepsuit, undo the poppers at the crotch of his vest and pull it over his head. Ben's skin is so fair it's almost translucent and through the rack of ribs you can see the tiny bellows of his lungs.

'And the baby's weight. What does he weigh now, Mrs Shattock?'

'I'm not entirely sure. He must be about 28, 30 pounds, I think.'

'When did you last have him weighed?'

'Well, he had his eighteen-month check, but you know he's my second and you're not as worried about things like weight with the second so long as they're –'

'And at the eighteen-month check, his weight was?'

'As I said, I'm not sure, but Paula said he was absolutely fine.'

'And Benjamin's date of birth – you are familiar with that, I presume?'

The insult is so biting that the tears jump to my eyes as if I had walked out into snow. I do really well in tests. I know the answers, but I don't know these answers and I should know. I know I should know.

Ben was born on the 25th January. He is very strong and very happy and he never cries. Only if he is tired or if his teeth hurt. And his favourite book is *Owl Babies* and his favourite song is

'The Wheels on the Bus' and he is my dearest sweetest only son and if anything happens to him I will kill you and then I will burn down your hospital and then I will kill myself. 'The 25th of January.'

'Thank you, Mrs Shattock. Now, little man, let's take a look at that chest.'

12.17 am: I don't know how I would have managed without Winston. He stayed all the time with us at the hospital, fetching sweet tea for me from the machine, holding Ben when I had to go to the loo and only showing any sign of distress when I offered to pay him for his time. As he helps me and the sleeping baby out of the cab, I can just make out a figure standing on the steps of our house. I think that if it's a mugger I won't be responsible for my actions, but a few steps nearer and I realise that it's Momo. Can't bear to see anyone from work. Not now.

'Whatever it is, surely it could have waited till the morning?' I say, stabbing the key in the lock.

'I'm sorry, Kate.'

'Sorry doesn't really cover it, I'm afraid. I've just got back with Ben from the hospital. He's been under observation. It's been a long night. If the Hang Seng fell 10 per cent I don't give a shit frankly and you can tell Rod that in those precise words. Oh, God, what is it?'

In the blade of light that the opening door casts into the street, I suddenly see that Momo has been crying. It's a shock to find that perfect face puffed up with misery.

'I'm sorry,' she says, and can say nothing else because speaking has triggered a fresh bout of crying. I get her inside and sit her in the kitchen while I take Ben up to his cot. A viral rash, the doctor called it. Unconnected to his fall, and definitely not meningitis either; we just have to be sure to keep baby's fluids up for the next twenty-four hours and keep an eye on his temperature. Turning the corner to the flight of stairs that leads up to the kids' rooms, I see the patch of worn carpet where Ben tripped. I hate that bloody carpet, I hate the fact I didn't get a quote for a new one, I hate the fact that finding the time to call someone out to measure my stairs seemed like an impossible luxury when it was a necessity all along. Triage. The order of urgency. I got it wrong: things that could harm the children come first, everything else can wait. Looking in on Emily, I find her curled around Paula, who has fallen asleep on the bed. I go in and switch off the Cinderella light and cover them both with the duvet.

Back downstairs in the kitchen, I make a pot of mint tea and try to get some sense out of Momo. Ten minutes later, I understand why she is having trouble explaining the problem: she simply doesn't have a vocabulary crude enough to describe what she has seen.

After work tonight, Momo went to 171, a bar opposite Liverpool Street with a bunch of people from the US Desk. Later, she dropped by the office to collect some files for our forthcoming final. Chris Bunce was there with a group of guys all gathered round his screen, laughing and making raucous comments. They included her friend Julian, who joined EMF the same day Momo did last year. The men didn't hear her come in and they didn't notice until too late that she had come over to look at what they were looking at.

'Pictures of a woman, you know, Kate, wearing nothing, I mean worse than nothing.'

'But they download that stuff all the time, Momo.'

'You don't understand, Kate, they were pictures of *me*.'

2.10 am: I have helped Momo upstairs, found her some nightclothes and tucked her up in the guest bed. Floundering in my Gap XXXL T-shirt with the dachsund motif, she looks about eight years old. Calmer now, she manages to tell me the whole story. Apparently, she screamed at the top of her voice when she saw the pictures on the screen, demanding to know who had done this.

Bunce, naturally, toughed it out. Turned to Momo and said: 'Well, now the real thing is here, perhaps she'd like to show us what she can do, guys?'

They all laughed at that, but when she started crying they left

310

the office pretty quickly. Only Julian hung around and tried to calm her down. She yelled at him until eventually he told her Bunce had taken headshots of Momo from the EMF website – the ones the firm was using in its brochure to illustrate its commitment to diversity – and digitally spliced them on to other women's bodies that are freely available on the Net. 'Bodies with no clothes on,' Momo repeats, and her primness makes it doubly painful.

Momo says she stopped looking when she saw her own head giving head. There were captions to go with the pictures, but she found it hard to make them out because she dropped her glasses and they cracked on the dealing floor.

'There was something about Asian Babes, I think.'

'There would be.'

'What are we going to do?' she asks, and the *we* feels both presumptuous and entirely right.

Nothing is what we're going to do. 'We'll think of something.'

I put the main light out and leave the bedside lamp on. Next to it in a vase is a desiccated sprig of lily of the valley, left over from Donald and Barbara's visit.

'I don't understand, Kate,' Momo says. 'Why would Bunce do that? Why would anyone want to do that?'

'Oh, because you're beautiful and you're female and because he can. It's not very complicated.'

For a second, she ignites with anger. 'Are you saying what Chris Bunce did to me was nothing personal?'

'No. Yes.' I feel exorbitantly tired, as though my veins were filled with lead. The terror of there being something wrong with Ben, and now this. Why do I always have to explain things to Momo, important things, when I'm at my most stupid? I lay my hand on her cool brown one and will the words to come. 'I'm saying that there was all history and now there's us. There's never been anything like us before, Momo. Century after century of women knowing their place and suddenly it's twenty years of women who don't know their place and it's scary for men. It's happened so fast. Chris Bunce looks at you and he sees someone who's supposed to be an equal. We know what he wants to do to you, but he's not allowed to touch any more, so he fakes pictures of you that he can do what he likes with.'

Under the duvet, she shakes; the shudder of a still fresh shame, and tightens her grip on my fingers.

'Momo, do you know how long they reckon it took for early man to stand upright?'

'How long?'

'Between two and five million years. If you give Chris Bunce five million years he may realise that it's possible to work alongside women without needing to take their clothes off.'

I can see the opal precipitate of tears in her eyes. 'You're telling me we can't do anything, Kate, aren't you? About Bunce. I just have to put up with it because that's what they're like and there's no use trying to change anything.'

That's exactly what I'm saying. 'No, I wouldn't put it quite like that.'

As Momo sighs and winces her way to sleep, I go downstairs to switch off the lights and lock up. I miss Richard all the time, but this is the time that I miss him most. Locking up is his job and the bolt feels less safe when I draw it across, the creaking in the window frames more ghostly. As I close the shutters, I keep thinking of what will happen over the next few days. In the morning, Momo Gumeratne will make a formal complaint about the behaviour of Christopher Bunce to her line manager, Rod Task. Task will refer the complaint to Human Resources. Momo will then be suspended on full pay pending an internal inquiry. At the first meeting of the inquiry, which I will be invited to attend, it will be publicly noted that Momo Gumeratne is of previously impeccable character. It will be silently noted that Chris Bunce is our leading performer, who last year made £10 million for the company. Quite soon, the offence against Momo will be referred to as 'a bad business' or simply 'that Bunce business'.

After three months at home – enough time for her to start

feeling anxious and depressed – Momo will be called into the office. A financial settlement will be offered. The Cheltenham Lady in her will stand up straight and say she cannot be bought off; all she wants is to see justice done. The inquiry panel will be shocked: they too want justice to be done, it's just that the nature of the evidence is – how shall we say? – problematic. Casually, imperceptibly, it will be implied that Momo's career in the City could be over. She is a young woman of exceptional promise, but these things have a way of being misinterpreted. No smoke without fire, all tremendously unfortunate. If news of the pornographic computer images, say, were to get out to the media . . .

Two days later, Momo Gumeratne will settle out of court for an undisclosed sum. When she walks down the steps of Edwin Morgan Forster for the last time, a woman reporter from the TV news will poke a microphone in her face and ask her to give details of what happened. Is it true that they called her an Asian Babe and ran porno pictures of her? Lowering her lovely head, Momo will decline to comment. Next day, four newspapers will run a story on page 3. One headline reads: ASIAN BABE IN CITY PORN PICS STORM. Momo's denial will appear in the second-to-last paragraph. Soon after, she will take a job abroad and pray to be forgotten. Bunce will hold on to his job and the black mark against his character will be erased by a steady tide of profits. And nothing will change. That much is certain.

As I'm reaching for the light switch, I notice a new picture stuck to the fridge under the Tinky Winky magnet. It's a drawing of a woman with yellow hair; she is wearing a stripy brown suit and her heels are as high as stilts. The glare from the light means it's hard to make out the writing in pencil underneath. I go up close. The artist is Emily and, with the help of a teacher, she has written: 'My Mummy goes out to work, but she thinks about me all day long.'

Did I really say that to her? Must have. Can't remember when, but Em remembers absolutely everything. I heave open the freezer and force my face into its arctic air. The impulse to get in and keep walking is immense. I'm going in now; I may be some time.

Back upstairs, I look in on Momo. Her lids are closed, but the eyes beneath them flutter like moths. Dreaming, poor baby. I'm turning the lamp off when the eyes open and she whispers, 'What are you thinking, Kate?'

'Oh, I was just thinking about what I said to you the day we first met.'

'You said that I had to stop saying sorry.'

'Too damn right you do. And what else?'

She stares up at me with that trusting spaniel look I saw at the final all those aeons ago. 'You said that compassion, although expensive, is not necessarily a waste of money.'

'I didn't say that.'

'You did.'

'God, how appalling. I'm such a cow. What else did I say?'

'You said that money can't tell what sex you are.'

'Exactly.'

'Exactly?' she echoes uncertainly.

'Where does it hurt them most, Momo? Where can we hurt them most?'

All that night, I couldn't sleep. I kept creeping into Ben's room, checking his breathing as I used to check Emily's when I first brought her home from the hospital and I worried she would never wake. Ben slept on and on, but there was nothing to be afraid of. He was sleeping like a baby.

Richard rang about two. He was in Brussels pitching for a Euro grant for a Northern arts centre, and had only just got my message. He asked me if I was OK and I said no. He said we needed to talk and I said yes.

At 5.30, I rang Candy, who I knew was being woken early these days by the baby kicking her in the ribs. Told her about the pictures of Momo on the system. I had no idea what we could do about it, but I thought that she might, with her technical know-how and her background in Internet companies. Between 5.50 and 6.30, she wrote a program that would seek and destroy all files containing references to Momo Gumeratne.

'It'll be hard tracking down any stuff that's gone out of the building,' she said, 'but I can nix anything still held in the EMF system.' We agreed that she should keep one copy of the pictures for evidence.

At six, Momo came into the kitchen and held something up. 'I found this in my bed. Does it belong to anybody?'

I went across and hugged her. 'That's Roo. He's a member of the family.'

I gave her a cup of tea to take back to bed, then I walked up with her and went into Ben's room. Still fast asleep. I tucked Roo next to his cheek. In a very short time one little boy was going to be happier than Christmas.

Going into my own bedroom, I opened the wardrobe and ran my hand along the rail until I got to my finest Armani armour. A crow-black suit. From the rack beneath I chose a pair of patent heels with snakeskin toes – heels it was impossible to walk in, but walking wasn't really the point of them today. As I got dressed, I went though all the resources I could draw on, the forces I could muster. I wanted Richard to come home and I knew now that I would do whatever it took to make that happen, but first Mummy had to finish her work.

Must Remember
Destroy Bunce.

36

The Sting

IT WAS GENERALLY agreed that the business plan for Power's Biodegradable Nappy was an exceptional document. Over thirty handsome pages of A4, it featured details of the target market for the miracle new nappy and the projected growth rate. There was an impressive rundown on the competition, a review of the environmental advantages and a detailed implementation plan. The figures were excellent without being unduly optimistic. The CVs of the management team were first-rate, particularly that of the inventor himself, Joseph R. Power, who, it was noted, had enjoyed connections with the Apollo space programme and subsequent lucrative spin-offs. The patent for the biodegradable nappy was still pending, but the patent application which described the product in such crystalline detail left you in no doubt of its success. It seemed a pity that only one person would get to see the document. The target market for Power's Biodegradable Nappy was not a billion leaky babies, but a Mr Christopher Bunce.

Bunce had just been made head of EMF's Venture Capital unit. This was good news in two ways. First, it made it easier to get him to take a huge punt on my dad's crappy nappy: gambling on exciting new products before anyone else got to them was part of the job. Second, Veronica Pick, the number two on Venture Capital who had been expecting to get the top job herself and was furious at having to make way for a novice in the area, could be relied upon not to steer her new boss clear of any minefields – might, indeed, be persuaded to guide him towards one with a friendly smile.

'OK, so let's go through this one more time.'

Candy is not even attempting to hide her scorn. 'Your dad, a guy who can't remember the name of his own kids and has never, to anyone's knowledge, seen their tushes, has invented a diaper that's gonna change the face of world diaperdom, except that we know the diaper doesn't work because you have tried the prototype on your son Benjamin and when Benjamin took a—'

'Candy, please.'

'All right, when Ben needed to go to the bathroom, the diaper fell apart. So what we're gonna do is we're gonna sell the diaper project to the new chief of our own Venture Capital unit who, being an arrogant cocksucker and knowing even less than your dad about the asses of little kids, will invest thousands of dollars in the Great Diaper Adventure and will then lose all that money because . . . Remind me of the because, Kate.'

'Because my father's company is heavily in debt and the money EMF invests will be claimed by his creditors and the nappy company will immediately go into liquidation and Bunce will lose his shirt, his socks and his poxy boxers and be exposed for the appalling chancer he is. Do you have any problem with the plan, Candy?'

'No, it sounds great.' She sniffs the air as though testing a new perfume. 'I just need to hear from you how we are gonna keep our jobs when I'm about to become a single mom and, until Slow Richard returns to the Reddy ranch, you are a *de facto* single mom.'

'Candy, there's a principle at stake here.'

She looks momentarily alarmed. 'Oh, I get it. It's our old friend Oates.'

'Who?'

'The snow man. The one you told Rod about? Pardon me, gentlemen, I'm goin' out now, I may be some fucking time. That's not a plot, Katie, that's a noble act of meaningless self-sacrifice. Very British, but you know in the States we have this really weird thing where we like the good guys to be alive at the end of the movie.'

'Not all self-sacrifice is meaningless, Candy.'

My friend detonates her big laugh and everyone in the club turns to stare at the crazy pregnant woman. 'Whoa,' she says. 'You're beautiful when you're ethical.'

'Look, there will be nothing to link you to the nappy deal, I promise.'

'So all roads will lead to Reddy? You know that after this no one's gonna employ you ever again, Kate. Nobody. You're not gonna get hired to change the fucking fax paper.'

With this dire warning, Candy reaches across, takes my hand and guides it on to the swell of her bump. Through the drum-taut skin, I feel the unmistakable jab of a heel. This is the first time she has acknowledged the baby as something permanent, not disposable, and I know better than to say anything mushy.

'Is it kicking a lot?'

'Uhuh. When I'm taking a bath, you can see her going crazy in there. It's like some goddam dolphin show.'

'It's not necessarily a girl, Cand.'

'Hey, I'm a girl, she's a girl, OK?' Candy clocks my smile and quickly adds: 'Course, I can still get her adopted.'

'Of course.'

I seem to recall it was Candy's idea that seven women meeting in secret in the City would look less conspicuous in a lap-dancing club than in, say, a restaurant where people were wearing clothes. Sitting here, I wish I had a Polaroid camera to capture the expressions on the faces of my friends as they enter the venue. In the case of Momo, good breeding immediately conquers shock and she sweetly enquires of the blonde at the desk, 'Oh, how long have you been open?'

We are not the only women in the Suckling Club, a gentle-men's entertainment emporium located within easy reach of the world's premier financial district, but we are the only ones with unexposed breasts. Everyone who has turned up this lunchtime has important work to do. I already knew that Chris

Bunce was greedy and ambitious enough to plough some money into a project without running it by anyone on his team: why would he want to share the credit if he could take it all himself?

But I also knew that we would have to do a highly professional job on the biodegradable nappy to get him to buy it. Dad's drawing of a winged pig had to be upgraded: there needed to be a brochure, knowledge of the market and production, plus input from a top commercial lawyer. When I called Debra, I was scared she would say no – our string of cancelled lunches over the past year had stretched our friendship to twanging point – but she didn't need to be asked twice. Without ever having met or heard of Chris Bunce, Deb knew instantly what manner of man he was and what we had to do to him.

So, our merry band consists of Candy, me, Debra and Momo, and Judith and Caroline from my old Mother and Baby group. We're still waiting for Alice. (It was vital for Alice, who's a TV producer, to help us, but I didn't hear back from her, so I assumed she wanted no part in it. Luckily, she phoned this morning. Said she'd been away filming, and she'd be delighted to join us, although she'd be late.)

A patent agent before becoming a full-time mum, Judith has written the patent application for the nappy and made it so convincing I want to order a truckload for Ben immediately. In her cool marshalling of language and science, I see a side to Judith I have never known. Caroline, the graphic designer, has come up with a brochure which stresses the nappy's eco-friendliness and features an irresistible picture of her own baby, Otto, sitting on a potty made of lettuce leaves.

Debra tells me that EMF will have no comeback against my father. 'Look, this isn't fraud. It's naughty, but it's not illegal. It's a clear case of *caveat emptor* – if the buyer doesn't take care over what he's buying, then that's his lookout.'

Deb will be acting as my dad's lawyer during the meeting he will need to have with Chris Bunce; we have arranged for it to be held in a suite at the Savoy.

'You have no idea how brilliant I am at this,' Deb exclaims as she takes me through the documentation. 'What are we going to call ourselves: the Seven Deadly Sisters?'

'Deb, this is serious.'

'I know, but I haven't had so much fun since Enid Blyton. God, Kate, I've missed fun, haven't you?'

Momo has been given the task of researching the global nappy market. In a few short days she has become an incredible bore on urine dispersal and olfactory containment. 'I'm sorry, Kate, but are you aware of how many insults the average nappy can sustain?'

'I can get that stuff at home, thank you.'

My assistant looks anxious: 'It won't work, will it?'

'The plan?'

'No, the nappy.'

'Of course it won't.'

'How can you be sure, Kate? If Bunce made a killing, I couldn't bear it.'

'Well, my dad designed it, so it's an odds-on catastrophe. Plus, I took a prototype home and put it on Ben.'

'And?'

'It's so biodegradable it falls apart at the first poo.'

Alice arrives late at the club from a meeting with the BBC at White City. Over the throbbing music, she points at the girls on stage and mouths: '*Are we auditioning?*'

Alice's role begins after Bunce has invested in the nappy. It's a pincer movement of the kind deployed by generals in all those battles I used to know the names of: attack him on one flank and then cut off his route of escape. Evidence that Bunce has recklessly thrown away money on a duff product won't be enough on its own to get Edwin Morgan Forster to sack him; if he can say embarrassing things in an interview which Alice records and gets into print, then he'll become a liability with the clients and after that he's hanging from a meat hook in Smithfield.

Shouting over the bass track, Alice tells us she has already called Bunce and invited him to appear in a major BBC2 series called 'MoneyMakers' – the City made sexy for the person on the sofa.

'How did he take it?' asks Momo, who is more nervous than anyone.

Alice grins. 'He practically came down the phone. I don't think I'll have any trouble persuading him to talk.'

I try to call the meeting to order, but I am competing with 'Mamma Mia' on the speakers. Instead, I hand round a photocopy of what everyone needs to know, plus a picture of Chris Bunce which Candy has lifted from the EMF website. I excuse myself and head for the ladies' room.

In the corner booth at the back, next to the exit, is a dark-haired figure I vaguely recognise. A little closer and I know exactly who it is.

'Jeremy! Jeremy Browning!' I greet my client with a warmth and volume that will sing in his soul for ever.

'Well, Jeremy, fancy seeing you here,' I enthuse. 'And this must be . . . it's Annabel, isn't it?'

The girl sitting on my client's left thigh gives a look that is smirk, sneer and smile combined. It says that unfortunately she is not Mrs Browning, but wouldn't say no if offered the chance.

I extend a friendly hand towards the girl, but it is Jeremy who grasps it eagerly. 'Gosh, Kate,' he says, 'I didn't expect to see you here.'

'Well, I'm doing some research into expanding my leisure portfolio. Maybe you can give me some pointers? This sector is new to me. Fascinating, isn't it? Well, must go, lovely to meet you . . .?'

'Cherelle.'

'Lovely to meet you, Cherelle. Look after him for me.'

I walk away, confident that I have at least one man in my power for all eternity. When I get back to the table, Candy is busy pointing out which of the girls on stage she believes to have had a boob job, and how successful it has been.

'Christ, look at the poor kid with the red hair. I thought they were gonna remove all nuclear weapons from British soil.'

'You should have seen the state of my boobs when I had twins,' says Judith, who is on her third Mai Tai.

I watch in horror as the dancer in question leaves the stage and advances upon us, cupping her breasts in the way a dog breeder holds up puppies for inspection.

'Now, that's what I call juggling,' shouts Alice. 'The work-life balance – what d'you reckon, Kate?'

'Her pelvic floor must be in good shape,' says Caroline, pointing to another dancer, who is making Mr Whippy motions as though trying to give birth to an ice cream.

'What's the pelvic floor?' ask Candy and Momo together.

When I explain, Candy, who thinks ante-natal classes are all run by Communists, doesn't hide her disgust. 'But the pelvic thingy goes back into place after the birth, right?'

And the dance floor shudders, and the mothers around the table laugh and laugh and the men in the club look uncomfortable in the way that only women's laughter can make them uncomfortable.

I raise my glass. 'Screw our courage to the sticking place and we'll not fail!'

'*Die Hard 2?*' asks Momo.

'No, Lady Macbeth.' What are they teaching them these days?

37

Lunch with Robin

WHEN ROBIN COOPER-CLARK is ill at ease, he looks like a man trying to arrest himself, one arm clasped tight around his own chest, the other hooked around his neck. This is how uncomfortable he looks on our walk to Sweetings, three days after the meeting in the Suckling Club. The restaurant is quite a distance from the office, but Robin is absolutely insistent that we eat there so, as he marches out with his seven-league stride, I scurry along, taking three paces to his one.

Sweetings is a City institution. A fish place that wants to look like a fishmongers, lots of cheery shouting, bustle, marble slabs – a Billingsgate for the moneyed classes. There are counters at the front where people can sit on high stools and pick at crab. and at the back there is a room with long tables like a school canteen. If privilege is another country, then Sweetings is its corner café.

Robin and I are seated at the far end of one of the long communal tables.

'Bad business, this Bunce thing,' he mutters, studying the menu.

'Mmm.'

'Momo Gumeratne seems a good thing.'

'She's terrific.'

'And Bunce?'

'Toxic.'

'I see. Now, what are we going to have?' The waiter stands there, pen at the ready, and for the first time I notice what a mess Robin is: the right wing of his shirt collar is furrowed like a brow and there are commas of shaving foam in his ears. Jill would never have let him out of the house looking like that.

'Ah, yes. I think something ferocious with teeth for the lady and an endangered species for me. Turtle soup, perhaps, or is it cod that's been fished to death by the bloody Spaniards? What d'you reckon, Kate?'

I'm still laughing when Robin says, 'Kate, I'm getting married again,' and it's as though the noise in the room is turned off at the tap. The diners around me mouth mutely like the fish they're about to consume.

And suddenly I know why he's brought me here, to this restaurant, to this room. It's a place where you can't shout in anger or cry out in pain: a place indeed for Sweeting, for *bonhomie*, for a mild bollocking at worst, a man's kind of place. How many souls have been grilled at these tables with a smile, how many politely encouraged to step down or step aside over a surprisingly decent glass of Chablis? Now I feel as though it's Jill Cooper-Clark who's been let go and I who have to do the decent thing. Look interested, pleased even, instead of upending the table and leaving the men gaping with their napkins and their bones. Only six months dead.

I become aware that Robin has started to tell me about someone called Sally. Lovely, incredibly kind, used to boys – got two of her own. Not quite Jill's speed, but then who is? Helpless shrug. And she has so many qualities, this Sally, and the boys need – well, Alex he's just ten – he still needs a mother.

'And you,' I say, finding some words in the dry vault of my mouth, 'you need her?'

'Mmmh. I need a woman, yes, Kate. We're not much good on our own, you know. I can see how you might find that' – he waves away the proffered tartare sauce –

'What?'

'Feeble, I suppose.' He lowers his glass and pinches the bridge of his nose. 'No one can ever replace her, if that's what you're thinking.'

Then why replace her, if she's irreplaceable? That's what I'm thinking. I feel caved in with sadness, as I did that day at Jill's funeral. I always knew where to find Robin, he always seemed so rooted and so reliable; looking at him now across the table, it's a shock to see a lost boy. Men without wives might as well be men without mothers; they are more orphans than widowers. Men without wives, they lose their spines, their ability to walk tall in the world, even to wipe the shaving foam from their ears. Men need women more than women need men; isn't that the untold secret of the world?

'I'm so glad for you,' I say. 'Jill would be really pleased. I know she couldn't bear the idea of you not managing.'

Robin nods, grateful to get the news out of the way, glad to pull up the drawbridge once more. With the plates cleared away, we turn to the menu again and study it like an exam paper. 'How about a treacle tart with two spoons?' says Robin. 'Have you heard they're looking for a new name for spotted dick, Kate?'

'Chris Bunce.'

'Sorry?'

'Spotted dick. Bunce is the venereal disease champion of the office. Ask any of the secretaries.'

Robin dabs his mouth with his napkin. 'It makes you very angry, doesn't it?'

'Yes, it does.'

For a moment, I consider telling him about the plan. But as my superior he would be obliged to veto it and as my friend and mentor he would probably do the same. Instead I say, 'I don't think someone should be allowed to go on being a shit because it's not convenient to stop him.'

Robin semaphores to the waiter for the bill. 'Jill always said that you can get a man to do anything so long as he doesn't notice he's being made to do it.'

'Did she do that to you?'

'I never noticed.'

3.13 pm: I leave Robin at the corner of Cheapside. Next, I call Guy on the mobile and tell him I won't be back this afternoon: I have an urgent appointment with conkers.

'Conquers?'

'It's a leisure group I'm thinking of investing heavily in. Need to check out the consumer angle.'

When I get home, the kids are so startled to see me they don't react at first. I tell Paula to take the rest of the day off and I get Emily and Ben into their coats and we walk to the park. Or at least Em and I do: Ben refuses to walk anywhere, preferring to run until he falls over. It's been an Indian summer and the leaves, still green in many cases and stippled with apricot, look mildly surprised to find themselves on the ground. We spend – I honestly don't know how long we spend – kicking around in them.

Ben likes rushing into the leaves just for the rustle, for the pleasure of the noise. Emily loves to tell him off while clearly finding him adorable. The deal between my girl and boy is that he can be naughty so she can enjoy being good. Watching them screech after each other, I wonder if that isn't a variation on the game that boys and girls have always played.

Further along the path, we find the conkers. Some of the spiky cases have split on impact and we prise the glowing nuts from their pithy hollow.

'You can make the conkers harder,' I say to Em.

'How?'

'I don't know exactly, we'll have to ask Daddy.' Damn, didn't mean to mention him.

Emily looks up in bright expectation. 'Mummy, when will Daddy come back to live in our house?'

'Daddy,' chirps Ben, 'Daddy.'

Back at the house, I put Ben down for his nap and let Em choose a video while I start to prepare a bolognese sauce for dinner. I can't find the garlic press, and where is the grater? I suggest watching *Sleeping Beauty*, which was always the great sedative when Em was little, but I am way out of date. My daughter is talking about something with a warrior princess I have never heard of.

'What's warrior, Mum?'

'A warrior is a brave fighter.'

'Do you know what *Harry Potter*'s about?'

'No, I don't.'

'*Harry Potter*'s about braveness and witches.'

'That sounds good. Have you decided what we're watching?'

'*Mary Poppins*.'

'Again?'

'Oh please, Mu-um.'

When I was Emily's age, we saw a film or two a year, one at Christmas, one in the long summer holiday. For my children, the moving image will be the main vehicle of their memories.

'She's a suffer jet.'

'Who?'

'Jane and Michael's mummy is a suffer jet.'

I'd forgotten that Mrs Banks was a suffragette. It's not the bit of the film you remember. I put the sauce on low, then go over and curl up on the sofa with Em. And there she is on screen, the lovely daffy Glynis Johns, back from a rally and marching up and down the great white house singing: 'Our daughters' daughters will adore us, And they'll sing in grateful chorus, Well done! Well done, Sister Suffragette!'

'What's a suffer jet?' I knew that was coming.

'Suffragettes were women, Em, who a hundred years ago went out and marched in London and protested and tied themselves to railings so that they could persuade people that women should be allowed to vote.'

She sinks back on to me, nestling her head in under my breasts. It's only when Mary and Bert and the kids have jumped into the chalk picture on the pavement that she says: 'Why didn't women be allowed to vote, Mum?'

Oh, where is that Fairy Godmother of explanations when you need her? 'Because back then, in the olden days, women and men were – well, girls stayed at home and people thought they were less important than boys.'

My daughter gives me a look of furious astonishment. 'That's silly.'

We lie back together. Em knows every song; she even

breathes when the actors breathe. Watching it as an adult, *Mary Poppins* looks so different. I had forgotten that Mrs Banks, who wants to make the world a better place for women, is dizzily oblivious to her own children. That Jane and Michael are sad and rebellious until the nanny shows up and brings consistency and excitement into their lives. Mr Banks, meanwhile, works too hard – his name alone tells you that this man *is* his job – and is a stranger to his children and his wife, until he gets sacked and is confronted in his own drawing room by Bert the chimney sweep, who warns him in song:

> *You've got to grind grind grind at that grindstone,*
> *Though childhood slips like sand through a sieve,*
> *And all too soon they've up and grown,*
> *And then they've flown,*
> *And it's too late for you to give . . . Just a . . .*

'. . . spoonful of sugar to help the medicine go down.'

Emily and I join in, our voices twining round each other in a silvery helix. Suddenly, I have the most disturbing feeling that the film is talking to me and it's then that Emily announces: 'When I have babies, Mummy, I'm going to look after them myself till they're a adult. No nannies.'

Has she made me watch *Mary Poppins* so that she can say that? Is it her way of telling me? I search her face, but there is no sign of calculation; she doesn't appear to be watching for a reaction.

'Maaa-aaaa.' The baby monitor crackles into life. Ben must be waking up. Before I go upstairs, I sit Em on my knee.

'I thought you and I could go on a special outing together one day, would you like that?'

She wrinkles her nose the way Momo does when she's excited. 'Where?'

'The Egg Pie Snake Building.'

'Where?'

'The Egg Pie Snake Building. Do you remember that's what you called the Empire State Building?'

'I didn't.'

'Yes you did, love.'

'Mu-mmy,' says Emily, dragging out my title with maximum scorn, 'that's a baby way of talking. I'm not a baby any more.'

'No, darling, you're not.'

It goes so quickly, doesn't it? One day they're saying all those funny little things you promise yourself you'll write down and never do, and then they're talking like some streetwise kid or, even worse, they're talking just like you. I will my children to grow up more quickly and I mourn every minute I have missed of their infancy.

After I have fed them and bathed them and dried their hair and read *Owl Babies* and gone to fetch her a glass of water, I finally come downstairs and sit by myself in the dark and think of all the irretrievable time.

From: Kate Reddy
To: Debra Richardson
This afternoon was spent in Illicit Mummy Time. The most profitable few hours of the financial year to date. How much per hour do you think I can bill clients for kicking leaves and watching Mary Poppins?
Sneaking time with the kids feels like what an affair must feel like: the same lies to get away for the tryst, the same burst of fulfilment and, of course, the guilt.
Think I have forgotten how to waste time and I need the kids to remind me how to do it.
Don't hate me if I stop work, will you? I know we said how we all need to keep going to prove it can be done. It's just that I used to think that maybe my job was killing me and now I'm scared I died and I didn't notice.
Our daughters' daughters will adore us and they'll sing in grateful chorus, well done, well done, well done, sister suffragette!
all my love K xxxxxxxxxxxxx

38

The Waterfall

7.54 am: As I wait for the knock at the door, I realise how much I have been looking forward to telling Winston about the plan. Finally, here is something I can impress Pegasus with; proof that I am not just some blinkered lackey of the capitalist system. But after I've blurted out all the stuff about Dad's nappy and Alice's interview with Bunce, Winston doesn't say anything except a curt, 'You gotta remember you got two babies to feed.'

Five minutes later, though, when we're stuck in our usual jam, he asks me if I know the story of Scipio. I shake my head.

'OK, so there's this Roman general Scipio he had a dream. And in the dream he found a village which was built right next to this big waterfall. The noise from the waterfall, it was so bad you had to shout to make yourself heard. "How do you live with that sound all day?" Scipio asked the head of the village over the roaring of this water. "What sound?" the old guy said.'

Pegasus shudders forward a couple of inches and when Winston hits the brake there is a moan like a cow dying. 'And the moral of the story, please, sir?'

In the mirror, I see his grin, sly and full of relish. 'Well, it's like I think we all of us have this background noise and we're so used to it we can't hear it. But if you move far enough away you can hear again and you think, Jesus, that waterfall was making one helluva racket. How did I live with that noise?'

'Are you saying I have a waterfall, Winston?'

He lets out that deep grainy laugh that I love. 'Kate, you got Niagara fucking Falls.'

'Do you mind if I ask you a personal question, Winston?'

As he shakes his head, the cab is filled with that gold dust once more. 'Am I your main client?'

'You the *only* one.'

'I see. And how many drivers does Pegasus Cars have? Let me guess. You the only one?'

'Yah. Gonna finish cabbing soon, though. Got my exams to do.'

'Mechanical engineering?'

'Philosophy.'

'So, you're by way of being my chauffeur, my very own winged horse?'

He honks the horn in joyous acknowledgement that this is so.

'Did you know that chauffeurs are tax deductible and childcare isn't, Winston?'

Another honk on the horn startles a group of suits on the pavement; they scatter like pigeons. 'It's a crazy fucking world out there, man.'

'No, it's a crazy fucking *man's* world out there. Have you got change?'

As I'm walking away from the cab, I'm just thinking how much I'm going to miss him when I hear a voice shout after me. 'Hey, you need a getaway car, lady?'

10.08 am: A call from Reception. They says there's a man called Abelhammer waiting for me and my heart actually tries to punch a hole through my chest wall. When I get downstairs, he is standing there with a large grin and two pairs of skates.

I'm shaking my head as I move across the floor towards him. 'No. I can't skate.'

'Yeah, but I can. Enough for the both of us.'

'Absolutely not.'

Later, when we are making our fourth circuit of the rink, Jack says, 'All you have to do is lean on me, Kate, is that so hard?'

'Yes. It's hard.'

'Jesus, woman. If you just lean on me here: remember your

John Donne, think of us as a pair of compasses. I'm holding still and you're sweeping round me, OK? You're not gonna fall, I've got you. Just let go.'

So I just let go. We skated for an hour and I'm not sure what we wrote on the ice. You'd have to be a bird – one of my pigeons – or sitting high up in my boss's office to see what we wrote that day. Love or Goodbye or both.

He wanted to buy me a hot chocolate, but I said I had to go. The smile never faltered. 'Must be an important date?'

'Very. A man I used to know.'

*

IT'S SURPRISING HOW quickly you can forget how to hold someone, even your husband. Maybe especially your husband. It takes a certain absence from touching to make you fully appreciate the geometry of the hug: the precise angle of your head in relation to his. Should it be roosted in under the neck, as pigeons do, or nose pressed to his chest? And your hands – cupped in the small of his back or palms laid flat along the flanges of his thighs? When Richard and I met that lunchtime outside Starbucks, we both meant to deliver a peck on the cheek, but it felt too silly, the kind of kiss you could only give to an aunt, so we splayed awkwardly into the hug. I felt as gauche, as painfully observed, as when my dad first took me shuffling round the floor at a dinner-dance. Richard's body shocked me by being a body: his hair and its smell, the bulk of shoulder under his jumper. The hug wasn't that dry click of bones you get holding someone when the passion has drained away. It was more like a shadow-dance: I still wanted him and I think he wanted me, but we hadn't touched in a very long time.

'Hey, you're glowing,' Rich says.

'I've been skating.'

'Ice skating? On a work morning?'

'Sort of client liaison. A new approach.'

Rich and I have arranged a meeting to talk things over. We

have seen each other almost every day since he left. As he promised, he has collected Em from school and then often stayed to have tea with both children. Starbucks feels like the right sort of place to negotiate a peace, a modern No Man's Land, one of those businesses which dresses itself up to look like the home that we're all too busy to go to. It's surprisingly quiet in here, but the meeting has all the anxieties of a first date – will he, won't he? – only now they're attached to divorce. Won't he, will he?

We find a couple of big squashy velvet chairs in a corner and Rich goes to get the drinks. I have requested a skinny latte; he comes back with the hot chocolate I want and need.

The small talk feels unbearably small: I am impatient to get on to the big talk, so it can be over, one way or another.

'How's work, Kate?'

'Oh fine. Actually, I may soon be leaving my job. Or rather my job may soon be leaving me.'

Rich shakes his head and smiles. 'They'd never fire you.'

'Oh, under certain circumstances they might.'

He gives me that man-in-the-white-coat look. 'We're not talking about meaningless self-sacrifice, Mrs Shattock, are we by any chance?'

'Why do you ask that?'

'Just that I'm old enough to remember your Cyclists Against the Bomb phase.'

'I've given the firm everything, Rich. Time that belonged to you and the children.'

'And to you, Kate.'

Once I could read his face like a book, now the book has been translated into another language. 'I thought you'd approve, Rich. Breaking away from the system.' He looks younger since he left me. 'Your mother thinks I've let myself go.'

'My mother thinks Grace Kelly let herself go.' We both laugh and for a moment Starbucks is filled with the sound of Us.

I start to tell Rich about the story Winston told me.

333

'Who's Winston?'

'He's the one from Pegasus Cars, but it turns out he's a philosopher.'

'A philosopher driving a minicab, that sounds safe.'

'No, he's fantastic, really he is. Anyway, Winston told me the story about this general who found a tribe by a waterfall and the head of the tribe—'

'Cicero.'

'No . . .'

'Cicero, it's by Cicero.' My husband breaks a cookie in half and hands one piece to me.

'Let me guess. Someone dead for a long time that I've never heard of because I went to a crap comprehensive, but who forms a vital part of every civilised person's education?'

'I love you.'

'So, you see, I was thinking of moving away from the waterfall to see if I could hear better.'

'Kate?'

He pushes his right hand across the table so it's near mine. The hands lie next to each other as if waiting for a child to draw round them. 'There's nothing left to love, Rich, I'm all hollowed out. Kate doesn't live here any more.'

The hand is on mine now. 'You were saying about moving away from the waterfall?'

'I thought if I, if *we* moved away from the waterfall we could hear again and then we could decide if—'

'If it was the noise that stopped us hearing or the fact that we didn't have anything to say to each other any more?'

Do you know those moments – the sheer merciful relief of there being someone in the world who knows what you're thinking as you think it? I nod my grateful acknowledgement. 'My name is Kate Reddy and I am a workaholic. Isn't that what they have to say at those meetings?'

'I didn't say you were a workaholic.'

'Why not? It's true, isn't it? I can't "give up" work. That makes me an addict, doesn't it?'

'We need to buy ourselves some time, that's all.'

'Rich, do you remember when Em tried to save Sleeping Beauty? I keep thinking about it.'

He grins. One of the best things about having children is that it enables you to have the same loving memories as another person: you can summon the same past. Two flashbacks with but a single image: is that as good as two hearts that beat as one?

'Daft kid. She was so upset that she couldn't reach that stupid princess, wasn't she?' Rich says, with that exasperated pride Em provokes in us.

'She'd really like you to come home.'

'And you, how about you, Kate?'

The option to say something proud and defiant hangs there waiting to be picked like a ripe fruit. I leave it hanging and say, 'I'd like to come home too.'

Sleeping Beauty was always Emily's favourite, the first video she really noticed. When she was two years old she became obsessed with it, standing in front of the TV and shouting, 'Wind it, wind it!'

She always shouted at that part where Aurora, with her stupefied doll face, makes her way up the long staircase to the attic pursued by a raven's shadow and a bad fairy cackle. For a long time, Richard and I couldn't work out what was making Emily so furious, then it clicked. She wanted us to rewind the tape so that the Princess wouldn't make it to the attic, so she never would prick her finger on the old woman's spindle.

One day, Emily actually tried to climb inside the TV set: I found her standing on a chair attempting to insert her red-shoed foot through the screen. I believe she had plans to grab the hapless Princess and stop her meeting her fate. We had a long talk – well, I talked and she listened – about how you had to let things like that happen, because even when you got to a scary bit the story knew where it was heading, and it couldn't be stopped no matter how much you wanted it to be. And the good thing was you knew it would turn out happily in the end.

But she shook her head sadly and said, 'No. Wind it, Mummy, wind it!' Soon after, my daughter transferred her allegiance to *Barney the Dinosaur*, which featured no deeds of darkness that required her personal intervention.

Adults want to rewind life, too. It's just that along the way we lose the capacity to shout it out loud. Wind it, wind it.

39

Endgame

A<small>N ARTICLE FROM</small> the November issue of *Inside Finance*:

Edwin Morgan Forster, one of the City's oldest financial institutions, triumphed at the fifth annual Equality Now awards on Tuesday night, winning the category for Most Improved Company for its commitment to diversity.

The firm scored highly in an annual benchmarking survey conducted by Equality Yes!, an organisation committed to gender parity whose members include 81% of the FTSE 100 companies.

The judges were particularly impressed by the volume of business generated by Katharine Reddy, EMF's youngest female manager, and Momo Gumeratne, a 24-year-old Sri Lankan graduate of the London School of Economics. Unfortunately, the two women were unable to attend the ceremony, but the award was collected by Rod Task, EMF Head of Marketing. In his acceptance speech, Task said: 'There is a good deal of evidence that mixed-gender teams are critical to effective team functioning. EMF is at the forefront of bringing women into major roles in the financial community.'

Striking a less positive note on the evening, was Catherine Mulroyd, chair of Women Mean Business. 'These awards are not telling the whole story,' said Mulroyd. 'It's hard enough to reach a position of real influence as a woman in the Square Mile without wrecking your career by opening your mouth to criticise the culture. Equality for women remains a marginal issue for most City firms. It seems pointless for banks to spend vast sums on training female recruits, only to lose them because they do not have flexitime or any of the things that could keep mothers on board.'

Asked if the old boy culture was a thing of the past, Task pointed

*out that he was from Australia and was therefore very much part of
the new boy network: 'The girls have done just great this year and
I'm proud of them.'*

*

M Y FATHER GAVE the performance of his life during the
presentation to Chris Bunce of the biodegradable nappy.
Debra, who was present throughout in her capacity as legal
adviser, told me that Dad was not only sober but clearly relished
the part of maverick inventor. His master-stroke, Deb said,
came when Bunce offered to write a cheque there and then and
Joe, who had spent a lifetime trying to wheedle cheques out of
people, said that he and his lawyer would be meeting a number
of interested parties over the coming days, but, naturally, they
would keep EMF informed.

I had explained to Dad that I thought I had found some
venture capital for his invention, but it would require him to
pretend to be someone else and to be rather creative with the
truth. In almost any other father–daughter relationship, this
would have been a bizarre exchange, but for us it felt like the
natural culmination of years of pretence, an admission that
forgery is woven into the Reddy DNA along with blue eyes
and a facility with numbers.

'He's a brilliant guy, your dad,' said Winston, who acted as
chauffeur for the nappy entrepreneur, in a black BMW with
tinted windows that he had borrowed from a man he described
as his uncle. 'Joe's a really great tipper.'

'Yes, with my money.'

Three days later, Bunce signed over the cash. Swaggering in
from lunch that afternoon, he told his deputy, Veronica Pick,
that she should pay attention to his amazing coup: this was
where men scored over women, acting decisively, scenting a
great opportunity and not getting bogged down in the fine
print.

'Oh, you did your due diligence, did you?' asked Veronica
sweetly.

'What d'you mean?' said Bunce.

'Due diligence,' said Veronica. 'You know, checking the directors' credentials, sussing out plant and production viability, veracity of bank references . . . But I'm sure I don't need to tell you about any of that.'

'If I need your advice I'll ask for it,' said Bunce.

Nor could he resist gloating to me the next morning as we gathered in the conference room, one hand massaging his manhood as though it were Aladdin's lamp. 'Found this brilliant new nappy product, Kate. Gonna make us a shitload of money – geddit? Shitload! Just your kind of thing, Mum, pity I got there first.'

I bestowed upon him my most understanding maternal smile.

The money Bunce invested was enough to cover the business's debts and therefore to pay off my father's creditors. No sooner had it landed in JR Powers's account than it was gone. As I had predicted, neither that nor Momo's formal complaint of sexual harassment was quite sufficient to sink Bunce for good at EMF.

That was taken care of a few days later when an interview that Edwin Morgan Forster's Head of Venture Capital had given to the investigative TV journalist Alice Lloyd appeared in a tabloid newspaper under the headline: PORN AGAIN! (HOW CITY'S MR BIG KEEPS IT UP).

Alice had taken Bunce to a favourite media haunt in Soho. After ingesting quantities of drugs legal and illegal, he became very forthcoming and the sighting of a young soap star across the room sent him over the edge. 'I'd like to have her on my website,' he told Alice. 'Actually, I'd like to have her anywhere she likes it.'

Boasting about his ability to pick winners, Bunce cited a recent investment in a certain biodegradable nappy which he reckoned was 'gonna be bigger than fucking Viagra'.

The City can always act to neutralise bad smells within the Square Mile, but when the stench reaches beyond, to the sensitive nostrils of clients and opinion-formers, then retribution is swift and merciless.

The morning after the article appeared, Candy and I stood and watched as Chris Bunce was called into Robin Cooper-Clark's office, escorted by two security guards to his desk, which he was given three minutes to clear, and then finally marched out of the building.

'Anybody got that falconer's number?' shouted Candy. 'There's a rat in the street.'

In the ladies' washroom a few minutes later, I found Momo Gumeratne crying, her face buried in the roller-towel. 'Happy crying,' she insisted between hiccups.

And me? I was glad he was gone, of course. But without noticing it, I had started to find Bunce more sad than bad.

At lunchtime, Momo and I took a cab to Bond Street. I told her it was important, work-related business, which it was.

My assistant was puzzled. 'What are we doing in a shoe shop, Kate?'

'Well, we're looking for a glass slipper that can take the highest possible pressure per square millimetre and doesn't fall off at midnight. Failing that, we'll take these, and these, oh, and those brown boots are great. Excuse me, do you have these in a four?'

'Are your feet size 4?' asks Momo dubiously.

'No, yours are.'

'But I can't possibly.'

Twenty minutes later, we were standing at the cash desk with four boxes. Faced with the choice between the tan kitten heels and the navy slingbacks, we chose both. And then we took the black stilettos because they were too beautiful not to own and the toffee boots, which were a total bargain.

'I love the black ones,' she says, 'but I can't actually walk in them.'

'Walking isn't really the point, Momo. Walking tall is the point. And if the worst comes to the worst you can always use one of the heels to puncture Guy's carotid artery.'

The smile vanishes: 'Where will you be?'

'I'm going away for a while.'

'No,' she says, 'I don't want a goodbye present.'

'You're going to be fine.'

'How do you know?'

'Hey, who trained you? . . . Anyway, you've stopped saying sorry, so I know you're ready.'

'No,' says Momo. And she looks at me sideways. 'Only one of us can ever be Reddy, Kate.' Then she puts a hand on my shoulder and kisses me quickly on the cheek.

On the way back in the taxi, a mountain range of shoes at our feet, she asked me why I was leaving and I lied. Told her I needed to move to be nearer my mother, who was ill. Some things you can't say even to the women you love. Even to yourself.

Reasons to Give up Work

1/ Because I have got two lives and I don't have time to enjoy either of them.

2/ Because 24 hours are not enough.

3/ Because my children will be young for only a short time.

4/ Because one day I caught my husband looking at me the way my mother used to look at my father.

5/ Because becoming a man is a waste of a woman.

6/ Because I am too tired to think of another because.

*

THE NEXT MORNING, before I resigned, I had a bit of tidying up to do. The pigeon family was long gone – the two chicks finally flew the nest when spring was easing into summer – but the books that had hidden mother and babies from the City hawk were still in place. This time, I didn't risk the ledge. I called Gerald up from security to give me a hand forcing open the window. The books had all survived quite well, except *The Ten Natural Laws of Successful Time and Life Management: Proven Strategies for Increased Productivity and Inner Peace*. It looked like the floor of a cave, with little stalagmites of pigeon shit obscuring its uplifting cover slogans.

When I went into Rod's office, I found him sitting at his

desk behind the Equality Now! trophy: a set of scales with a tiny bronze female figure in one of the pans. In the other, Rod had put a handful of jelly beans.

He took the news of my leaving pretty badly. So badly, in fact, that the noise travelled through the wall to Robin Cooper-Clark next door.

'Katie's doing a fucking runner,' Rod announced as the Head of Investment put his head round the door to establish the source of the roar.

Robin called me into his office, as I knew he would.

'Is there anything I can do to persuade you to change your mind, Kate?'

Only changing your world, I thought. 'No, really.'

'Maybe part-time?' he ventures with that ghost of a smile.

'I've seen what happens when a woman tries to go part-time, Robin. They say she's having her days off. And then they cut her out of the loop. And then they take her funds away from her, one by one, because everyone knows that managing money's a full-time job.'

'It is hard to manage money less than five days a week.'

I don't say anything. He tries another tack. 'If it's a question of money?'

'No, it's time.'

'Ah. S*ed fugit interea, fugit inreparabile tempus.*'

'If that means you shouldn't waste fourteen hours a day staring at a screen, then yes.'

Robin comes round to my side of the desk and stands there with that awkwardness they call dignity. 'I'm going to miss you, Kate.'

By way of reply, I give him a hug; perhaps the first ever administered in the offices of Edwin Morgan Forster.

Then I go home, taking care to run across the grass.

40

The Court of Motherhood

SHE WAS NOT AFRAID of the court any more. They had nothing left to throw at her. Nothing they could charge her with that she hadn't accused herself of a thousand times. So there she was, feeling quietly confident, and then they said the name of the next witness and, suddenly, she knew it was all over. Her time was up. As she swayed forward, feeling slightly sick, her hands clutched the oak rim of the dock. Here was the one person in the world who knew her best.

'The court calls Mrs Jean Reddy.'

The defendant was upset at the sight of her mother entering the witness box to give evidence against her, but there was something about the older woman's appearance that she found oddly cheering. It took her a few seconds to place it: Mum was wearing red cashmere, the cardigan Kate had given her for Christmas, over the Liberty's floral blouse she had bought her for the birthday before last. The things kept for best were getting their first outing.

'State your full name, please.'

'Jean Katharine Reddy.'

'And your relation to the defendant?'

'Kath – Katharine's my daughter. I'm her mother.'

The prosecuting counsel is not just on his feet, he is standing on tiptoes with excitement. 'Mrs Reddy, your daughter is accused of putting her job before the welfare of her children. Is that an accurate description of the situation you have observed at first hand?'

'No.'

'Speak up, please,' bellows the judge.

Mum tries again. Clearly nervous, she is tugging on her

343

charm bracelet. 'No, Katharine is devoted to her children and she is very hard-working, always has been. Keen to get on and better herself.'

'Yes, yes,' snaps the prosecution, 'but I understand she is not presently living with her husband, Richard Shattock, who left her after he said that she had "ceased to notice he was there"?'

The woman in the dock makes a low moaning sound. Kate's mother doesn't know that Richard has left her.

But Jean Reddy takes the news like a boxer taking a blow and fires magnificently back: 'No one's saying it's easy. Men want looking after and it's hard for a woman when she's got her work as well. Kath's got that many calls on her time, I've seen her make herself ill with it sometimes.'

'Mrs Reddy, are you familiar with the name Jack Abelhammer?' says the prosecution with a quick, tight smile.

'No. No!' The accused has climbed over the side of the dock and is standing in front of the judge in an XXXL Gap T-shirt with a dachsund motif. 'All right, what do you want me to say? Guilty? Is that what you want me to say? There really are no lengths you won't go to in order to prove I can't live my life, are there?'

'Silence!' booms the judge. 'Mrs Shattock, one more inter-ruption and I will find you in contempt of court.'

'Well, that's fine, because I am in utter contempt of this court and every man in it.' And then she starts to cry, cursing herself as she does so for her weakness.

'Jean Reddy,' resumes the prosecution, but the witness is not listening to him. She too has left her box. She moves towards the weeping woman, whom she gathers into her arms. And then the mother turns on the judge: 'And how about you, Your Honour? Who'll be getting your tea tonight. It's not you, is it?'

'For God's sake,' splutters the judge.

'People like you don't understand anything about women like Katharine. And you think you can sit in judgment on her. Shame on you,' says Jean Reddy quietly, but with the force that generations of children had heard in her voice when she was rebuking a playground bully.

41

Baby, It's You

O<small>N THE DAY</small> that Seymour Troy Stratton entered the world, a coup in Qatar sent oil prices spiralling and equities plunged around the globe, helped by an unprecedented rate hike from the mighty Federal Reserve. In the UK alone, £20 billion was wiped off the value of the FTSE 100. A minor earthquake outside Kyoto caused further shock waves in an already shaken global environment. None of this had an adverse effect on mother and baby, who dozed peacefully in their curtained cubicle on the third floor of the maternity wing off Gower Street.

As I walk down the corridor towards them, I am returned powerfully to my memories of this place – the midwives in their blue pyjamas, the grey doors behind which the great first act of life is performed over and over by small women and tall women and a woman whose waters broke one lunchtime on the escalator at Bank. Place of pain and elation. Flesh and blood. The cries of the babies raw and astounded; their mothers' faces salty with joy. When you are in here you think that you know what's important. And you are right. It's not the pethidine talking, it's God's own truth. Before long, you have to go out into the world again and pretend you have forgotten, pretend there are better things to do. But there are no better things. Every mother knows what it felt like when that chamber of the heart opened and love flooded in. Everything else is just noise and men.

'I just want to look at him,' Candy says. Propped up on pillows, my colleague has undone every button on my white broderie anglaise nightdress to give her son access to her breasts. The nipples are like dark fruit. She uses the palm of her right hand to cup his head while his mouth sucks hungrily. 'I don't want to do anything except look at him, Kate. That's normal, right?'

'Perfectly normal.'

I have brought a Paddington Bear rattle for the baby, the one with the red hat that Emily always loved, and a basket of American muffins for his mom. Candy says that she needs to get the weight off right away and then, because her hands are full, I feed morsel after morsel into her unprotesting mouth.

'The baby will suck all the fat out of your saddlebags, Cand.'

'Hey, that's terrific. How long can I keep nursing? Twenty years?'

'Unfortunately, after a while they come round and arrest you. I sometimes think they'd send the social services in if they knew how passionately I feel about Ben.'

'You didn't tell me,' she rebukes me with a tired smile.

'I did try. That day in Corney and Barrow. But you can't know until you know.'

Candy lowers her face and smells the head of her son. 'A boy, Kate. I made one. How cool is that?'

Like all newborn things, Seymour Stratton seems ancient, a thousand years old. His brow is corrugated with either wisdom or perplexity. It is not yet possible to speculate on what manner of man he will grow up to be, but for now he is perfectly happy as he is, in the encircling arms of a woman.

Epilogue: What Kate Did Next

I THINK AN ENDING may be out of the question. The wheels on the bus go round and round, all day long.

A lot happened, though, and some things stayed the same. Three months after Seymour's birth Candy went back to work at EMF and put the baby into a daycare place near Liverpool Street that charged more than the Dorchester. Candy reckoned each diaper change cost her $20. 'That's a helluva lot for a dump, right?'

On the phone, she sounded like the same old Candy, but I knew that that Candy, the Candy Before Children, had gone. Sure enough, the long, brutal hours she had worked uncomplainingly all her adult life soon seemed to her stupid and unnecessary. She minded that when she tried to leave at 5.30, Rod Task called it 'lunchtime'. She minded not seeing her son in daylight. When Seymour was seven months old, Candy walked into Rod's office and told her boss she was very sorry, but she was going to have to let him go. She was having some problems with his level of commitment: it was too high.

Back in New Jersey, she stayed for a while with her mom until she found a place of her own: Candy said Seymour had made her understand what her mother was for. Soon after, she spotted a hole in the booming mail-order market and established a business which in a short time saw her tipped as one of *Fortune* magazine's Faces To Watch. All Work and No Play was a range of sex toys for the female executive who has everything except time for pleasure. A box of samples was shipped to me in England, and it was opened on our breakfast table during a visit from Barbara and Donald. Richard, in what many consider to be the finest half-hour of our marriage, pretended the vibrators were a range of kitchen utensils.

My beloved Momo stayed on at EMF where she flew up the ladder, barely touching the rungs. That touch of steel in her nature I had noticed at our first meeting proved invaluable, as did her ability to listen and absorb what clients wanted. Occasionally, she would call me for advice in the middle of the day from the ladies' washroom, her whispers half drowned by flushing. In the summer, she snatched a couple of days off and came up to stay with us. For the first time in her life, Emily was impressed with me: at long last, her mother had produced a real princess. 'Are you Princess Jasmine from *Aladdin*?' Em asked and Momo said, 'Actually, more Sleeping Beauty. I was sort of asleep and then your mummy woke me up.'

Debra discovered that Jim was having an affair with a woman in Hong Kong. They got divorced and Deb arranged to work a four-day week at her law firm. Soon, she found some of her biggest clients were taken away from her, but she let it pass. The time for fighting back, she told herself, would come when Felix and Ruby were older. Deb and I are planning a weekend break together at a spa and so far we have only cancelled four times.

Winston went on to take his degree in philosophy at the University of East London and his ethics dissertation, 'How Do We Know What Is Right?' achieved the highest mark in the year. To pay his final-year fees, he sold Pegasus, which seamlessly entered a new career in stock-car racing.

Flourishing a guilty, and therefore glowing, reference from me, Paula landed a job as nanny to the B-movie action star Adolf Brock and his wife, a former Miss Bulgaria. The family lived for a while at The Plaza in New York, until Paula, whose room overlooked Central Park, announced that she was feeling cramped, whereupon the Brocks moved obediently to Maine.

After that morning on the ice rink, I never saw Jack Abelhammer again. I changed my e-mail address because I knew that my willpower was not strong enough to stop me returning a message from him. I also knew that my marriage would have a fighting chance only if I let go of my fantasy lover: if Jack was the place I went to play, what did that make Richard? Even so, every time I log on part of me still expects to see his name in the Inbox. People say that time is a great healer. Which people? What are they talking about? I think some feelings you experience in your life are written in indelible ink and the best you can hope for is that they fade a little over the years.

I never went to bed with Jack – a regret the size of a continent – but the bad food and the great songs in the Sinatra Inn were the best sex I never had. When you've felt that much about a man and he disappears from your life, after a while you start to think it was just some foolish illusion on your part and that the other person walked clean away, no scar tissue. But maybe the other person felt the same. I still have the last message he sent me.

From: Jack Abelhammer
To: Kate Reddy
Kate,
I didn't hear from you in quite a while, so I'm working on the theory that you took up conkers and motherhood full time. But I know you'll be back. Hail the conkering heroine . . .
Rod at EMF said you left London. Remember what your Dad called Sinatra? The Patron Saint of Unrequited Love.
The great thing about unrequited love is it's the only kind that lasts.
yours forever Jack

Richard and I sold the Hackney heap, moved up to Derbyshire, near my family, and bought a place on the edge of a market town with a view and a paddock. (I'd always wanted a paddock, and now I had one I had no idea what to do with it.) The house needs loads of work, but there are a couple of good rooms and the rest can wait. The kids love having the space to run around in and Richard is in his element. When he's not working on the new arts centre, he's building a dry-stone wall, and every five minutes he asks me to come and look at it.

Not long after I resigned, I got a call from Robin Cooper-Clark asking if I'd come in with him on a hedge fund. Part-time work, minimal foreign travel, all promises that I knew would be scorched away in the heat of the chase. It was tempting: with the money he was offering I could have bought half the village and things are pretty tight for us with just Richard's income, but when Emily heard me say Robin's name, she stiffened and said, 'Please don't talk to him.' Cooper-Clark was a name she associated with the enemy.

I know my daughter a little better these days. A couple of months after leaving work, I realised that all those carefully timetabled bedtime chats had told me nothing about what was really going on in Em's head. That stuff comes out spontaneously, you can't force it. You just have to be around when it happens. As for her brother, his sweetness grows in direct proportion to his capacity for mischief. Recently, he discovered Lego, with which he builds a wall, and every five minutes he asks me to come and look at it.

Richard and I took both kids down to meet Sally Cooper-Clark. She was as kind and warm as Robin had described and I could see how she gave him back his ease and elasticity, not to mention his immaculate shirts. On the drive back, I left Rich and the kids in a pub garden for ten minutes and I walked across to the church and down the hill to Jill Cooper-Clark's grave.

Weird, isn't it, how you want to seek out the physical place where someone is buried? If Jill is anywhere now she's everywhere. But I stood there anyway, in front of the neat white headstone with the soft grey lettering. At the bottom it says: She was well loved.

I didn't actually speak aloud – this was Sussex, for heaven's sake – but I thought all the things that I wanted Jill to know about. They say that women need role models and I suppose we do, but high achievement is not confined to high-flyers. There is a currency that we were never called upon to trade in at EMF, and in that Jill was the richest person I've ever met.

And me? Whatever happened to me? Well, I spent some time with myself, a pretty unsatisfactory companion. I loved walking Emily to the local school and standing at the gate to collect her; the puddles are iced over this time of year and we like to stand on them and wait for the creak before the crack. During schooltime, Ben and I pottered around the house and hung out at coffee mornings with other mums with small kids. I was bored to the point of manslaughter. My eczema cleared up, but my cheeks ached from trying to keep my face looking friendly and interested. Queuing in the local bank, I would find myself sneaking looks at the foreign exchange rates. I have a feeling they thought I was planning a robbery.

Then a couple of days ago, I got a call from Julie. It was a crackly mobile, but I could tell she was in tears. For a second I thought, Mum, and my stomach went down a mineshaft, but it wasn't that; the factory where Jules does piecework had gone bust. Manager done a bunk; receivers called in. They were putting padlocks on the doors. All the women who had still been at their machines were now shivering out in the yard. Could I come down?

No, I said. Ben needed his lunch and, besides, I really didn't know what use I could be. When Julie answered, it was in a voice I recognised from childhood, the one my little sister used when she asked if she could get into bed with me as the raging voices of our mother and father came through the floorboards. 'But I've told everyone you're a businesswoman, Kath, and you'll be able to tell us what's what.'

Combed my hair, put some lipstick on and dug out Armani jacket from the wardrobe in the spare room. I wanted to look like the woman Julie had described to her colleagues. When I slipped the jacket on, it was like being back in uniform: the grey wool impregnated with the smell of power, of money being made and things getting done. I wrestled Ben into the baby seat – seat's getting too small, must get a new one – and drove down to the industrial estate. It wasn't hard to find Julie's place. The notice on the fence said Traditional English Doll's Houses and over that was a sticker: Liquidation Sale: Everything Must Go! In the yard, there were about forty women: seamstresses, many wearing the most amazing saris. They parted as I arrived and it was like walking through a flock of tropical birds. I waved my old Platinum Amex at the guy standing by a side door, told him I'd come up from London and was looking to buy some stuff. Inside, the doll's houses were abandoned in mid-decoration: tiny sofas, footstools, velvet pelmets, porcelain toilets awaiting their wooden seats, grand pianos the size of a powder compact.

'What can we do, Kath?' asked Julie when I came out.

Absolutely nothing. 'I'll try and find out what's happened.'

The next day, I dropped Em at school, left a delighted Ben with his equally delighted grandmother and got the train down to London. Cab across town to Companies House: it didn't take long to get the doll's house people's accounts for the last five years. You should have seen them. The business was a wreck – disappearing margins, no investment, piles of debt, a complete financial basket case.

On the train back up North, I tried to read the paper, but the type wouldn't stay still. There were plenty of ethical funds out there under instruction to invest in women-only companies, I knew that better than anyone. Money for the taking, really. But when the train shuddered to a halt at Chesterfield, it shook some sense into me.

Kate Reddy, I can't believe you are even having this thought. Take on something like that? You'd have to be out of your mind, woman. Out of your bloody mind.

*

7.37 pm: Bedtime. Brush teeth, 2 readings of *The Cat in the Hat*, 4 recitations of *Goodnight Moon*, 3 *Owl Babies*, visits to the bathroom (4), attempts on potty (2), time taken till lights out: 48 minutes. Must improve.

8.37 pm: Call to Candy Stratton in New Jersey to discuss mail order market and distribution with view to global doll's house business.

'I knew it,' she hollers.

'I'm making enquiries for a friend.'

'Yeah, right. Tell her to wear that red bra of hers when she goes to get the financing.'

9.11 pm: Call to Gerry at Dickinson Bishop in New York. Sussing out funds specifically designated to invest in women-only companies. Gerry says it's a steal: 'Ethical's the new Viagra, Katie.'

10.27 pm: Ben has accident in bed. Change sheet. Try to find pull-up nappy. Where are nappies?

11.48 pm: Wake Momo Gumeratne at home to talk about possibility of wooden doll's house frames being made by workers employed by Sri Lankan aid agency she's been advising.

'Kate,' she says. 'Can I do it with you?'

'I'm not doing anything. Go back to sleep.'

Midnight: Take glass of water up to Emily. The great grey eyes stare up at me in the dark.

'Mummy, you're thinking,' she says accusingly.

'Yes, love, it's allowed, you know. How would you like to help Mummy build a palace?'

'Yes, but it's got to have a tower where Beauty sleeps.'

'It absolutely does.'

1.01 am: Still time to go over the figures from the factory. What is required is a proper marketing plan and some diversification. How about a range of buildings instead of the traditional Georgian townhouse? A New York brownstone, maybe? A cottage, offices, castles, ships, Emily's palace. Richard could design them.

1.37 am: 'Kate, what do you think you're doing? It's two o'clock in the morning.'

My husband Richard is standing in the doorway of the

kitchen. Rich with his acres of English reasonableness and his invincible kindness.

'Darling,' he says, 'it's so late.'

'I'm just coming.'

'What is it?'

'Nothing.'

He squints curiously at me in the light. 'What kind of nothing?'

'Oh, I was just thinking about, you know, homemaking.'

He raises an eyebrow.

'Don't worry. Warm my side of the bed, I'm just coming.'

The kiss he plants on my forehead is a question as much as a gift.

Seeing my husband go upstairs, I long to follow him, but I can't leave the kitchen in this state. I just can't.

The room bears signs of heavy fighting; a small defensive wall is under construction and there is Lego shrapnel over a wide area. In my absence, three apples and three satsumas have been added to the big glass bowl, but no one has thought to discard the old fruit beneath and the pears at the bottom have started weeping a sticky amber resin. As I throw each pear in the bin, I worry about the cost. After washing and drying the bowl, I carefully wipe any stray amber goo off the other fruit and put it back. All I need to do now is get Emily's lunchbox ready for the morning, check the time for Ben's appointment at the surgery, see if I can get from there to the bank to talk to my manager, convene a meeting of workers at the factory, call the Receivers and still get back in time for school pick-up. Chicken out of freezer. Chicken out of PTA meeting. Emily wants horse. Over my dead body. Who will end up cleaning out the stable? Rich's birthday – surprise dinner? Bread. Milk. Honey. And there was something else. I know there was something else.

What else?

Author's Note

Ten Years On

IT HAS BEEN ten years since this book was published, yet I vividly recall the struggle to write it. I was a working mother with two small children – much the same age as Emily and Ben – and I would start writing after the kids had gone to sleep. At midnight, I would save what I had done, then set the alarm and get up five hours later to revise the paragraphs of the night before. Often my baby boy would join me at the computer and he would hold his own milk bottle to his lips while his mother cradled him and typed at the same time. And so the story of a sleep-deprived, crazy working mum was penned one-handed by a woman who had no time to write the story of a crazy working mum. Well, at least I was tired enough to make it authentic!

I remember one morning, when my job was taking me away for four days, I handed my husband some sheets of paper with a list of the stuff that would need taking care of in my absence. He studied the notes for quite some time until, finally, he said in a plaintive voice, 'But it looks like a plan for invading a small country.' And so, in a way, it was. As a mother, my other job was to run the small country called Home.

I was not doing Kate Reddy's high-wire, high-finance job, nor was I in her income bracket, but I knew that I desperately wanted to tell her story because Kate was a magnified version of almost every woman I knew and loved. In the latter part of the twentieth century, women had been given the opportunity to do our fathers' jobs, but we had retained our mothers' responsibilities. The result was a frantic double-shift, which teetered constantly between comedy and disaster. Take my friend Anne, a political reporter. Anne went to interview the then Chancellor of the Exchequer in Downing Street when her son was just a few months old. The interview was delayed and delayed, and Anne felt her boulder-like boobs grow harder and more painful. Eventually, she had to take emergency action: Anne undid her blouse and expressed the thwarted milk into the Chancellor's wastepaper basket. My, how I would love to have been there when Gordon Brown found it.

Meanwhile, in New York, my dear friend Sharon was working as a TV anchor. Occasionally, when the babysitter didn't show up, Sharon would take her daughter, Samantha, into work and place her in a little baby-seat on the desk, just off-camera. One afternoon, while Sharon was solemnly reading the news, a tiny foot began appearing and then disappearing in the bottom right-hand corner of the TV screen. Samantha was awake and kicking!

Such were the tales we told each other. I guess they were our war stories. We laughed when we probably felt like crying. Our unspoken fear was that, as mothers, we were not good enough. I tried hard to get those feelings into the pages of this book – the dedication you feel to your job and the overwhelming passion you feel for your children. The best thing about being the author of *I Don't Know How She Does It* was that the novel inspired so many thousands of readers across the world to write to me and share their own experiences. The stories were hilarious, moving and sometimes almost too painful to write down. I plan to publish those stories in due course, but meanwhile you can find some of them – and me – at www.allisonpearson.co.uk. Please drop in. We need each other's wisdom, perspective and laughter.

Now, *I Don't Know How She Does It* is finding a second life as a wonderful movie, starring Sarah Jessica Parker as Kate. When I met SJP on the set of the film back in January, she said she hoped that the movie would be one for all the mums out there who do such a terrific job. I hope so too. For every mother has to run that small country called Home, and it's a lot, what with all the other things the world asks of us these days.

Among all the emails and letters, I remember one from a man in his fifties who told me that his bright, funny mother used to start drinking martinis in the early afternoon. 'She was like a caged tigress, pacing our kitchen,' he wrote, 'I wish she'd had a job to fulfil herself'. Whatever choices you make for you and your family, remember the caged tigresses of the past and rejoice that our daughters are free to decide.

Ten years after my novel was published, if I have any one insight to offer it would be this: You are the best mother your kids will ever have. However you handle it, however many mistakes you think you make, however many mince pies you fake, they're going to think you're great anyway so don't let guilt consume you. Guilt is to motherhood what rain is to South Wales. It's just the prevailing climate. Get used to it and buy yourself a bloody good umbrella.

Allison Pearson,
Cambridge, summer 2011

Acknowledgements

THIS BOOK COULD not have been written without my beloved friend Miranda Richards, who taught me not to be afraid of the Dow Jones and so much else.

I want to thank Hilary Rosen for her heroic research into the subject of this novel and for the emails which made me laugh out loud whenever life got too Kate-like. There are many Kate Reddys out there who offered up their disasters with incredible good humor. I salute them.

Caroline Michel believed in this book from the very beginning, first as a publisher and now as my agent. Her gale-force nurturing got me through Triumph and Disaster, and treated those two imposters just the same. No author could ask for more.

Two other remarkable women were responsible for bringing *I Don't Know How She Does It* to the big screen. Donna Gigliotti, President of Production for the Weinstein Company, is the living embodiment of Margaret Thatcher's maxim: 'If you want something said, ask a man. If you want something done, ask a woman.' The gifted screenwriter Aline Brosh McKenna was the perfect person to adapt this novel. Aline has a rare wit and an even rarer passion to show women in movies doing a job that they love, instead of waiting for someone to love them.

Episodes from *I Don't Know How She Does It* first appeared in the *Daily Telegraph*. I am indebted to Sarah Sands for giving Kate her big break and to Charles Moore for his forbearance and kindness.

Nicola Jeal, a terrific editor and mentor, was a constant support, and now that she has a baby herself, she can find out if I'm telling the truth.

As a first-time author, I was very fortunate in my agents, the late Pat Kavanagh in London and Joy Harris in New York. It takes a great team effort to make an international bestseller. My editors – Jordan Pavlin at Knopf and Alison Samuel at Chatto – delivered the baby into the world with loving care. Rachel Cugnoni did a superb job with the paperback. A first-class publicity campaign was orchestrated by Tasja Dorkofikis in the UK and in the US by Jill Morrison and Katie Barrett at Knopf. Faye Brewster and her sales team in London were indefatigable. Subsequently, I have been blessed to have support from Beth Coates at Vintage and from my fantastic publicist Emma Draude.

Others offered moral support and practical criticism: Nicola Jeal, Adam Gopnik, Martha Parker, Anne McElvoy, Kathryn Lloyd, Claerwen James, Philippa Lowthorpe, Prue Shaw, Tamsyn Salter, Justine Jarrett, Naomi Benson, Richard Preston, Quentin Curtis and Niamh O'Brien.

A book about mothers naturally owes a great deal to the writer's own. I want to thank my mother for her precious time, the value of which I am only just starting to appreciate.

The character of Ben would not have been created without the lovely hindrance of Thomas Lane. Emily's observations were inspired by the wit and wisdom of Eveline Lane, Isabelle and Madeleine Urban and Polly, Amelia and Theodora Richards.

Finally, I send all my love and gratitude to Anthony Lane, who can take credit for most of the commas in this book and for all of the semi-colons. While the fictional life of a harassed working mother was being created in our house, he loaded the washing machine, cooked dinner, read *Owl Babies* three hundred times and even found time to write the odd movie review. I don't know how he does it.

Allison Pearson
Cambridge, July 2011

Credits

Now read the first chapter of Allison Pearson's
latest bestselling novel

I THINK I LOVE YOU

Also published by Vintage

1

His favourite colour was brown. Brown was such a sophisticated colour, a quiet and modest sort of colour. Not like purple, which was Donny's favourite. I wouldn't be seen dead in purple. Or in a Donny cap. How much would you have to like a boy before you went out wearing a stupid purple peaked cap?

Honest, it's amazing the things you can know about someone you don't know. I knew the date of his birth – 12 April 1950. He was a typical Aries, but without the Arian's stubbornness. I knew his height and his weight and his favourite drink, 7-Up. I knew the names of his parents and his stepmother, the Broadway musical star. I knew all about his love of horses, which made perfect sense to me because when you're that famous it must be comforting to be around someone who doesn't know or care what famous is. I knew the instrument he learned to play when he was lonely. Drums. I knew the name of the dog he left behind when he had to move away from New Jersey. I knew that when he was a boy he was small for his age and he had a squint and had to wear an eyepatch and corrective glasses, which must have been hard. Harder than for a girl even. I didn't wear my glasses if I could help it. Only in class for the blackboard, though I couldn't see well without them and it got me into trouble a few times when I smiled in the street at total strangers who I mistook for members of my family. A few years later, when I got contact lenses, I was stunned by the trees. They had leaves, millions of leaves, with edges so sharp and defined they looked like God had made each one with a pastry cutter. Basically, before I was sixteen, the world was one big Impressionist painting, unless I screwed up my eyes really tight to bring it into focus. Some things, as I would discover, were best left a blur.

Back then, I wasn't interested in the real world. Not really. I answered my parents' questions, I gave the appearance of doing homework, I lugged my cello into school on my back, I went down the town on Saturday afternoons with girls who sometimes felt like friends and sometimes didn't, but I was living for Him. Each night, I spread my long dark hair out on the pillow and made sure to sleep on my back so my face was ready to receive a kiss in case he came in the night. It wasn't that likely, obviously, because I lived in South Wales and he lived in California, which was five thousand miles away, and he didn't even have my address, although I had once sent a poem for him to a magazine. Choosing the right colour paper took longer than writing the actual poem. I settled on yellow because it seemed more mature than pink. I thought all the other girls would choose pink and part of loving him was finding better ways to please him so he would know how much more I cared. They didn't sell brown writing paper or I would have used brown because that was his favourite colour. Some time later – three weeks and four days if you're counting, and I definitely was – a reply came in the post. It was seventeen words long including my name. It didn't matter that the letter said they were sorry they couldn't publish my poem. In some crucial way, I felt as though I had made contact with him at long last. Someone important in London, someone who had been in the same room as him, had touched the yellow paper I had touched and then typed my name on an envelope and licked the stamp. No rejection slip has ever been more treasured. It took pride of place in my scrapbook.

I knew exactly where he lived in California. In a canyon. A canyon was like one of our valleys, only much bigger. We said much bigger. David said way. Way bigger. Way was American for much. America was so big that Americans would drive one hundred miles just to have dinner with someone and they didn't think that was a long way to go. In America, way to go means you've done something well. Way to go, baby! And they have gas instead of petrol.

Other words I had learned were cool, mad and bathroom. You have to be careful because a bathroom is not a bathroom in America, it's a toilet.

'The Americans are a most polite people who are not standing for vulgarity,' said my mother, who was German and beautiful and disapproved of many things. You might say that my mother's whole life was a battle to keep the vulgar and the ugly at bay. In our town, she had found the perfect enemy. I just liked knowing American words because they brought me closer to Him. When we met, it would be important to retain my individuality, which was one of the top things David looked for in a girl.

In every interview I had read, David said that he preferred a girl to just be herself. But to be honest I was unsure of who myself was, or even if I had one, although I still maintained a touching faith that this unknown and as yet undiscovered me would be deeply appealing to David when we eventually met. How could I be sure? The understanding in his eyes told me so. (Oh, those eyes. They were deep green pools you could pour all your longing into.) Still, I reckoned that meeting David would be awkward enough without any unnecessary confusion, so I did my best to pick up American. It would be tricky to go to a bathroom in his house in Los Angeles, for example, and find there was no bath, wouldn't it? Or imagine saying someone was mad. David would think that I meant they were angry. Crazy means mad in America. Back then, I couldn't imagine David ever being angry, he was so gentle and sensitive. Sorry, do I sound mad?

'Donny Osmond's a moron,' Sharon said firmly. She was kneeling on the floor, picking at the staples in a centrefold with her thumbnail trying to free a male torso. The slender, headless body was naked to the waist and practically hairless, except for a fine golden down just above the belt, which boasted a heavy bronze buckle. It looked like the door knocker to an Aztec temple. Sharon eased the poster off the frail metal pins until it rested on her hands, trembling a little in the hot air blowing from the small heater beside her. Sharon's bedroom was small, painted in a sickly shade of ointment pink and reeked of burnt hair, a bad candyfloss smell that got in your nostrils and stayed there. Sharon had dried her hair in front of the heater and a few strands got sucked into the back, but we didn't really notice the smell, so absorbed were we in our work.

'I don't think Donny's a moron, to be honest with you,' I said carefully.

'All the Osmonds are morons. I read it in a mag,' she insisted without looking up from the poster. Sharon was an expert restorer. The best artist in our class. When she grew up she could probably get a job in a museum or an art gallery. I loved to watch her work. The way she rolled her tongue into a little tunnel when she was concentrating and applied her attention to the tiny puncture holes in David's stomach, soothing the torn paper with her fingertips until the flesh appeared to seal up.

'There you go, lovely boy,' she said, and placed a noisy smacking kiss on his belly button before adding the poster to the pile.

There was a prickle in my throat like a piece of trapped wool. I badly wanted to correct Sharon about the Osmonds being morons, but our friendship was still too new to risk disagreement. We liked each other because we agreed. We agreed because we both thought David Cassidy was the most wonderful boy currently alive and maybe in all of human history. At thirteen years of age, I couldn't imagine the luxury of having a friend you could disagree with. If you disagreed with her you could fall out. Then, before you knew it, you'd be back out there in the playground by yourself, sighing and checking your watch every couple of seconds to indicate that you did have an arrangement to meet someone and were not, in fact, the kind of sad, friendless person who had to pretend they were waiting for friends who did not exist.

Even worse, you could find yourself entering into anxious negotiations with some other borderline outcast to be your partner in PE so you didn't have to be in a pair with Susan Davies. Susan Smell, who had a disease of the skin no one could spell. Her face, her arms and her legs were all cratered like the surface of the moon, only some days the holes were filled in with the chalky dust of calamine lotion. We knew exactly what it was because our mothers dabbed the lotion on us when we got chickenpox. The angry, itchy spots were like tiny volcanoes around which the soothing pink liquid hardened into a tempting lava crust. Mustn't pick it, mind, or it would leave a scar. The worst thing about Susan Davies, apart from the way you felt really sorry for her but still didn't do anything to help her, was the pong. Honest to God, Susan smelt so bad it made you retch in the corridor when she went past, even though she always walked on the side with the windows.

'Donny's a *Mormon*. I think it's a religion they founded in Utah,' I said cautiously, trying the sounds in my mouth.

Ooh. Ta.

I knew exactly what Mormons were. Donny Studies were part of my deep background research on David. I knew everything about the other Osmonds too, just in case, even Wayne. At a pinch, I could have given you the star sign of every member of the Jackson Five, and details of their difficult upbringing, which was in such contrast to their carefree, joyful music. Twiddly diddly dee, twiddly diddly dee. Twiddly diddly dee. Dee dee!

You know, I can never hear the opening chorus of 'Rockin' Robin' without a spasm of regret for what became of that remarkable little boy and all his sweetness.

Even as a child, I had this overdeveloped taste for tragic biographical information, a sort of twitching inner radar for distress. I may have been the only one not to be in the least bit surprised when Michael Jackson began to take leave of his adorable black face in painful cosmetic stages.

372

You see, I understood all about hating the way you looked and wanting to magic away the child who made a parent feel angry or disappointed. When you grow up, they call this empathy. When you're thirteen it just makes you feel like you're not so horribly alone.

'D'you reckon Mormons all have to wear purple because it's Donny's favourite colour?' I asked.

Sharon giggled. 'Get away with you, Petra, you're a case, you are!'

We thought we were hysterically funny. We laughed at anything, but lately boys had become a particular target for our witticisms. We laughed at them before they could laugh at us, or ignore us, which curiously felt even more wounding than being teased or insulted. You know, I always liked Sharon's laugh better than mine. My laugh sounded like a nervous cough that only starts to let itself go too late, when the joke has passed. Sharon made that happy, hiccupy sound you hear when you pull a cord in a doll's back. She looked a bit like a doll, did my new maybe friend. She was round and dimpled and her eyes were an astonishing bluebell blue beneath the palest barely there lashes. Her hair was that bone-dry flaxen kind that bursts out of a person's head like a dandelion clock. When we sat next to each other in Chemistry, her hair would float sideways on an invisible current of hot air from the Bunsen burner and stick to my jumper. If I tried to sweep it off the static gave me a shock that made my arm swarm.

Sharon was pretty in a way everyone in our group could agree was pretty without feeling bad about it. It was a mystery. Her weight seemed to act as a sort of protective jacket against jealousy. When she lost her puppy fat I think we all sensed it might be a different story. In the meantime, Sharon posed no threat to Gillian, who had got the two of us together in the first place and who was the star of our group. No, that's not right. Gillian was our Sun. We all revolved around her and you would do anything, anything at all really, really humiliating and shameful things, just in the hope she might shine on you for a few minutes because the warmth of Gillian's attention made you instantly prettier and more fascinating.

As for me, the jury was still out on my looks. I was so skinny that next to Sharon I looked like a Victorian matchgirl. And don't go thinking, 'Oh, get her, she's proud of her figure.' Skinny is not the same as slim, no way. Skinny is the last-girl-but-one-to-get-a-training-bra because you've got nothing up top. God, I hate that expression. Up top. 'Hasn't got much up top, has she?'

Where we lived, girls had Up Top and Down There. You don't want to let a boy go Down There, but sometimes he was allowed Up Top, if you'd got anything there, like.

Skinny is always being late for hockey and being made to run five times round the games field because you keep your blouse on until the others have left the changing room so they don't see your sad little girl's vest. A vest with a single shaming rosebud on the front.

The magazines told us to identify our good points. Mine was eyes. Large and grey-blue, but sometimes green-blue flecked with amber, like a rock pool when the sun is shining on it. But my eyes also had these liver-coloured smudges under them which no cucumber slices or beauty sleep could ever cure. I never stopped trying though.

'Petra's dark circles are so bad she could go to a masked ball and she wouldn't need a mask,' Gillian said and everyone laughed, even me. Especially me. Be careful not to show her what really hurts or she'll know exactly where to put the knife in next time.

My worst feature was everything else really. I hated my knees, my nose and my ears, basically anything that stuck out. And I had pale skin that seemed even paler because of my dark hair. On a good day, I looked like Snow White in her glass coffin.

Expertly, my mother took my face in one hand, chin pinched between thumb and forefinger and tilted it sharply towards the bathroom light. She squeezed so tight my jaw ached. 'You are not unattractive, Petra,' my mother said coolly. 'Bones really quite good. If you pluck the brows when you are older, here and here, like szo, revealing the eyes more. You know, you are really not szo bad.'

'It's *too* bad, Mum, not so bad. I don't look *too* bad.'

'That is exactly what I am saying to you, Petra. Relax, please. You are not szo bad for a girl at her age.'

My mother believed she spoke perfect English and my dad always said now was not the time to tell her. Did I mention my mother was beautiful? She had a perfect heart-shaped face and eyes that were wide open yet sleepy at the same time. I'd never seen anyone who looked like my mother until one Saturday night I was round Sharon's house and there was a show on TV. This woman was sitting on a high stool in a dress made of something that shone like foil with a white fur cape draped around the shoulders. She looked glamorous and hard, but her voice was like a soft purr.

'That's all woman, that is,' Sharon's dad said, which made me wonder what the rest of women were. Were they halves or quarters? Marlene Dietrich didn't look like she had kids, but then neither did my mum. Put my blonde mother in a gathering of my father's dark, stocky Welsh relatives and she looked like a palomino among a herd of pit ponies. Guess which side of the family I took after.

'Got it! Knew it was here somewhere.' Sharon was grinning in triumph. She had found the legs to match the torso. *Jackie* was giving away a free life-size David poster, but it came in parts over three weeks. Last week was jeans and cowboy boots, this time it was the body. They always saved the head till last.

'So you got to keep buying the mag, isn't it? Do they think we're blimmin' stupid or something?'

I couldn't see Sharon's face, but I knew she was frowning and funnelling her tongue as she lined up David's belly with his jeans. This was the hard part. Once she'd got them in position she flipped the shiny pages over and I handed her the strip of Sellotape, ever the dutiful nurse to her surgeon. We both stood up to get a better view of our handiwork. It wasn't a typical David pose. Among the thirty or so posters on Sha's walls there wasn't another quite like it. His thumbs were tucked into his waistband, the top button of his flies was undone and the jeans wrenched apart so you glimpsed that inverted V of hair that the zip normally hid. I tried to think of something funny to say, but my mouth felt dry and oatmealy. The absence of his head was definitely a problem. We urgently needed David's smiling face to reassure us about what was going on down below. I felt a flicker as a tiny pilot light ignited in my insides and a warmth like liquid spread across my stomach and trickled down into my thighs.

Sharon had seen a penis, but it was her brother's so it didn't count. Carol was the only girl in our group who had touched a real one. Chris Morgan's in the tree house down the Rec where the boys went to look at dirty mags. Carol said the penis felt like eyelid skin. Could that be right? For weeks after she told us, I would brush a finger over the skin above my eye and I would marvel that something which was made of boy could be so silky and fine like tissue paper.

When we went through the mags, Sharon and I always flicked past the bad boys. Mick Jagger and that David Bowie, he was a strange one. We sensed instinctively that those stars were not for us. They might want to come down off the posters on the wall and do something. Exactly what they would do we didn't know, but our mothers would not have it.

'It's really weird,' Sharon said contemplating the headless, semi-naked David.

'Weird,' I agreed.

It was our new favourite word, and we used it as often as we could, but it really bothered me that we weren't saying it right. When David said it on *The Partridge Family* it had one syllable. Whirred. Our accent put the stress in the wrong place somehow. However hard I tried it still came out as 'whee yad'. On the cello, I could play any note I liked. I knew if it was wrong the same way I knew if I was cold or hungry, but controlling the sound that came from my own mouth was different. Funny thing is I didn't even realise I had a Welsh accent. Not until our year went on a school trip to Bristol Zoo and some English girls in the motorway services mimicked the way I asked for food.

'Veg-e-tab-ils.'

I pronounced the 'e' in the middle, but English people didn't.

They said 'vedge-tibuls'.

Why did they bother putting an 'e' in there, then, if you weren't supposed to say it? So people like me could sound *twp* and they could have a laugh.

Sharon and me were doing our top rainy Sunday-afternoon thing to do, listening to David's *Cherish* album and flicking through magazines for any mention of him. After Sunday school, which lasted for two long hours, there wasn't much else to do in our town on the Sabbath, to be honest with you. Everyone abided by some unwritten law that people should stay indoors and keep quiet. Even if you didn't go to chapel, which we always did because my father was the organist, it felt as though chapel had come to you. My Auntie Mair never used scissors on a Sunday, because God could see everything, even the wax in your ears and the dirt under your nails. You could grow potatoes under there. *Achafi!* Disgusting. And you didn't hang your washing out on the line because of what the neighbours would think. The judgement of the neighbours might not be as bad as that of the Lord Thy God, Dad said, but you knew about it sooner.

Sundays lowered the temperature in the rows of grey-stone terraced houses clinging to the mountain which rose steeply above our bay, and even the sea became a bit subdued. It always made me think it was a good day for Jesus to walk on the water. People shivered on the Sabbath and went upstairs to put a cardigan on and came down to watch the wrestling on TV, but always with the sound down, out of respect. It was really 'whee yad' looking in through the windows as you ran down the hill towards the seafront, using your back shoe as a brake till you smelt the rubber, and seeing the big men in their leotards throwing each other about, silently bellowing and stamping their boots on the floor of the ring.

Going round Sharon's house was like a holiday for me. She had an older brother called Michael who teased us, but in a funny way, you know, and a younger sister, called Bethan, who had a crush on little Jimmy Osmond, if you can believe it. (We called him Jimmy Spacehopper because he had these little bunny features stuck in the middle of a round face like a balloon.) Sha also had a baby brother called Jonathan who sucked Farley's Rusks in his highchair till he got a crusty orange moustache which you could peel off in one piece when it got hard and there were visitors who dropped in for a chat and stayed because they were too busy talking to notice the time. As for Sharon's mum, well, she was lovely, you couldn't ask for a nicer person. She knocked on the bedroom door, really respectful, and came in and offered us squash and Club biscuits. Always remembered that I preferred the currant ones in the purple wrapper, not the orange. Mrs Lewis said she liked our David posters and she told us she still had a book of matches and a cocktail stick from the night Paul McCartney dropped into a club in Cardiff. 1964 it was. Sharon's mum was absolutely crazy about Paul. Said she had hated Linda for marrying him.

'He was mine, you see.'

Yes, we saw.

My favourite thing was the David shrine on the back of Sharon's door. She got it in a *Tiger Beat* her Auntie Doreen brought back all the way from Cincinnati, America. Four pictures fixed at mouth height so Sha could snog him on the way out to school in the morning. Like she was saying goodbye to a real lover boy. In the first picture, David had that shaggy haircut and a naughty smile. The second was this look – you know. In the third, his lips were puckered up, and in the fourth, well, he just looked really happy and pleased with himself, didn't he?

Over time, the four Davids became smeared and blurry with the Vaseline that Sharon used to soften her lips, a trick we copied from Gillian. Sometimes, Sharon let me have a go at kissing David Number 3. I wasn't allowed posters on my wall at home because my mother believed that popular music could make you deaf and was really common and therefore appealing only to people like my dad, who worked down the steelworks and was a big Dean Martin man on the quiet, though that's another story and I'm meant to be telling you this one.

Well, at the start of that year, several things happened. Gillian – she was never just Gill – lent Sharon to me as my special friend. I was really happy, you know, but I sensed the loan could be called in any minute if Gillian's infatuation with Angela, the new girl from England, ever cooled. The uncertainty gave me this feeling in my stomach like I was on a ferry or something and couldn't get my balance. Most nights, I woke with a fright because my legs were kicking out under the sheets as if I had to save myself from falling, falling. Another thing was the headmaster told me after assembly one morning that I was going to play the cello for Princess Margaret when she came to open our new school hall. She was the Queen's sister and the Lord Mayor and some people called dignitrees were coming. But the really big news

380

was that David Cassidy had postponed his tour of Britain after having his gall bladder removed. Two girls in Manchester were so upset they set themselves on fire, according to the mag.

On fire! My God, the thought of the passion and the sacrifice of those girls, it burned in our heads for weeks. We hadn't done anything that big for him. Not yet anyway.

Another couple of fans wrote to David asking if they could have a gallstone each as a souvenir. Sharon and I pretended to be shocked and disgusted by the gallstones story. *Achafi!* Secretly, we could not have been more delighted. The blimmin' cheek of it! Honest to God, where were their manners? It was in bad taste and unladylike. David, as any true fan knew, liked girls to act really feminine. We shook our heads and crossed our arms indignantly, as we had seen our mothers do, resting them on the invisible shelf where soon our breasts would be. Asking for David's gallstones!

Feeling superior to your rivals was one of the sweetest pleasures of being a fan, and maybe of being female in general.

We found out all about the tour cancellation and the gallstones from *The Essential David Cassidy Magazine*. It was brilliant, our Bible really. God's own truth. At 18p, it was way more expensive than any other mag.

'Dead classy, mind,' Sharon said, and so it was with its thick, glossy paper, gorgeous recent pix and a monthly personal letter written by David himself actually from the set of *The Partridge Family* in Hollywood, America. You couldn't put a price on something like that, could you?

From David's letters, we collected facts like eager

381

squirrels, putting them by for some vital future use. If you'd asked us what that use was we couldn't have told you. All we knew was that one day it would become magically clear and we would be ready.

'David writes lovely, mun,' Sharon sighed.

'David writes *well*.' I heard my mother's voice correcting Sharon's speech inside my head. She looked down on people with bad grammar, which was everybody except the lady who did the tickets at the library and the announcers on the BBC.

'Don't talk tidy, please talking the Queen's English, Petra,' rebuked my mother whenever she caught me speaking the way everyone else in town spoke.

But there in Sharon's room, with the little heater filling the place with sleepy warmth and David on the turntable singing 'Daydreamer' I could tune out the voice of my mother and start learning how to be a woman all by myself.

> 'Nothing in the world could bother me
> Cos I was living in a world of make believe . . .'

The cancellation of the Cassidy tour at the start of 1974 was a bitter blow, but it also came as a relief. It gave me more time to perfect my plan for meeting David when he came later in the year. Maybe autumn. He would call it 'the fall', which seemed perfect to me. I knew that somehow I would have to travel to London or Manchester because Wales was so small it had no concert venue big enough to hold all the fans. I wasn't sure how I would get there – no money, no transport, a mother who thought any singer who wasn't Dietrich Fisher Dishcloth shouldn't be allowed – but once I got there and was safely outside the concert hall I knew that everything would be fine.

I would be hit by a car. Not a serious injury, obviously, just bad enough to be taken to hospital by ambulance. David would be told about my accident and he would rush to my bedside. Things would be awkward at first, but we would soon get talking and he would be amazed by my in-depth knowledge of his records, particularly the B-sides. I would ask him how he was enjoying the fall and if he needed to use the bathroom. It would not be at all weird, it would be cool. David would be impressed by my command of American. Jeez. He would smile and invite me to his house in Hawaii where I would meet his seven horses and there would be garlands round our necks and we would kiss and get married on the beach. I was already worried about my flip-flops.

Yes, it was a kind of madness. It didn't last all that long, not in the great scheme of a life, but while I loved Him he was the world entire.

The next day was school. I hated Sunday nights, hated the melancholy hour after getting home from Sharon's warm funny house, hated having to revise for the Monday morning French test.

I love, I will love, I was loving, I have loved, I will have loved. *J'aurai aimé*. Future perfect.

The only thing that made it bearable was reading the David mags I kept under a floorboard by my bed and listening to the Top 40 in a cave beneath the sheets.

My mother's voice drifted up the stairs: 'Petra, finishing your homework, at once, and then cello practice.'

'I'm *doing* my homework.'

And so I was. Lying on the brown candlewick bedspread, reading by the light of the bedside lamp, I studied that week's words and committed them to heart.

Dear Luvs,

I guess I'm like everyone else. I just dig getting letters! I like to know who you guys are. That's why I'm totally thrilled when I get a letter and YOU tell me something about yourself – your favourite colour or where you live. Pretty soon, I feel like we're old friends. That's so nice.

I reckon I should return the favour. Well, you probably all know what I look like by now . . . But the thing is I'm sitting in my trailer in between takes of *The Partridge Family*. It's a real home from home, with family photographs and all my favourite sodas.

Hey! I've just caught sight of the amount I've written – and this was supposed to be just a short letter! I guess I must have had so much to say to YOU that I got carried away.

See the effect this has had on me? I never used to like writing letters and I used to have to stretch my literary efforts to get them to seven or eight lines. Now I can't wait to make contact again next month. Till then.

Luv,
David

www.vintage-books.co.uk